*Acclaim for*

# WARSAFE

"Smyth's pixelated YA sci-fi thriller *Warsafe* levels up as a story, combining gaming, political intrigue, and virtual reality with bigger questions of life where we ask ourselves if we're players or being played—and what exactly we're going to do about it. A wonderful fast-paced adventure."
    —Parker J. Cole, *USA Today* best-selling author

"Lauren Smyth issues her readers a bespoke passport to a chilling dystopian vision of the future in *Warsafe*. This thrilling sci-fi adventure blurs the lines between reality and virtuality as richly developed characters navigate a high-stakes game for survival. With fast-paced action and expertly crafted storytelling, all the twists and turns keep the reader on the edge of her seat. A must-read for sci-fi enthusiasts, *Warsafe* offers a captivating exploration of identity and humanity in the digital age."
    —Reece Smyth, Senior Foreign Service Officer and Professor

"Lauren Smyth's *Warsafe* is an exciting novel told from the puzzling, poignant perspectives of her characters. It begins as a collection of seemingly disconnected events that intertwine in an engaging singular storyline. Through reactionary vantage points and perfectly painted drama, Smyth lures us into a seamless combination of complex and competing worlds with the ease of a seasoned storyteller."
    —Lori Owen, Professor of English

"Lauren is a modern Isaac Asimov. Her blending of video gaming, futuristic totalitarianism, and virtual reality created a captivating story that holds the reader hostage and never lets go."
 —DAPHNE SELF, author of award-winning *When Legends Rise* and *What Legends Become*

"An enjoyable thrill ride through a near-future techno landscape. With strong characters and an enigmatic plot, Smyth gives us a well-crafted page-turner. A compelling story where the plot unfolds with the reader, keeping us glued to the page and cheering for the flawed but brave heroes."
 —ERIC LANDFRIED, author of *Solitary Man*

# WARSAFE

# WARSAFE

## LAUREN SMYTH

*Warsafe*
Copyright © 2025 by Lauren Smyth

Published by Enclave Publishing, an imprint of Oasis Family Media, LLC

Carol Stream, Illinois, USA.
www.enclavepublishing.com

All rights reserved. No part of this publication may be reproduced, digitally stored, or transmitted in any form without written permission from Oasis Family Media, LLC.

This is a work of fiction. Names, characters, places, and incidents are products of the author's imagination or are used fictitiously. Any similarity to actual people, organizations, and/or events is purely coincidental.

ISBN:  979-8-88605-198-8 (printed hardcover)
ISBN:  979-8-88605-199-5 (printed softcover)
ISBN:  979-8-88605-201-5 (ebook)

Cover design by Emilie Haney, www.EAHCreative.com
Typesetting by Jamie Foley, www.JamieFoley.com

Printed in the United States of America.

*To all the reluctant adventurers.*

*You're not in this alone.*

# 01

## HALLEY

**I'D SEEN HER NAME AT THE BOTTOM** of the list that morning. I remembered thinking it was a miracle she hadn't been killed yet. But I was more interested in the names at the top of the list—those who still had a fighting chance to win the game—and I soon forgot about her. It's hard to worry about mortality when you're scrubbing burnt egg off a saucepan.

A flurry of noise invaded our kitchen, interrupting the piano music streaming from the living room. Faraway voices, or possibly the wind. I let the pan I was washing clatter into the sink and peeked out the window, but it was too dark to see much besides the glowing orbs of the streetlights. Maybe somebody's clothesline had blown away. Maybe the wind had knocked over a streetlight and started an electrical fire, which would raze the village from one beach to the other and kill all its inhabitants. Or maybe I was hallucinating. A hypochondriac streak comes with the territory of being a doctor's daughter. Probably that was it.

My curiosity expired quickly, and I returned to my fight with the saucepan. That stubborn egg wasn't going anywhere no matter how hard I scrubbed. I'd already shredded two sponges, and I was well on my way to ruining a third. Mother was going to have my hide if I didn't figure out a way to rescue both pan and sponge.

Fortunately for my aching arms, the noise started up again

before I had time to hunt for a new scrubber. This time I could tell what it was. Echoing shouts and yells, half-drowned by a violent gust of wind.

And then a single, high-pitched scream.

Surely that was serious enough to justify procrastinating on the pan. I draped my towel over the edge of the sink and darted into the living room. Pausing in front of the automatic dresser, I selected the first outfit that appeared as an option and waited impatiently while the machine replaced my ratty pajamas with daytime clothing, a brown jumper over a rough-knit sweater. That old dresser always took its time when I was in a hurry. I poked at it to make it go faster and hit the wrong button. It stopped with a grunt, and no amount of coaxing would get it running again.

Well, who cared if the grandmas saw me halfway in my pajamas? It wasn't like they never went outside in bathrobes themselves. Without waiting for the dresser to reboot, I slipped on a pair of Mother's work boots. They fit like buckets, and my bare skin peeked through holes in the toes, but I reminded myself that I had the whole evening to dry myself by the fire and maybe get started on that new book I'd "borrowed," too. I draped a scarf over my shoulders and let myself outside.

A sheet of rain struck my face, ice cold and needle sharp. It soaked through the thin clothes I'd chosen haphazardly and chilled me until my eyes watered. The wind whipped my braids across my cheeks, ripping them free of the knot I had secured at the base of my neck. So thickly was the village covered in mist that I could barely make out the houses across the street from ours. Darkness wrapped the sky in an ugly blanket, stifling despite the chill.

I was expecting to walk up to a fight—perhaps one of the Mercs gone insane, running around with a weapon—but there was only one person to be seen in the street. A dark shadow, barely visible in the gloom, she stumbled over the cobbles with her face turned to the sky. Water poured down her pale cheeks, the glaring streetlights crowning her hair in a dim halo. Her skirt was in tatters around her knees, and her coat was hanging off one shoulder. It slipped free and made a soggy landing into a puddle, but the girl didn't stop to pick it up.

For one startled moment, I thought she was an angel. Something unnatural, otherworldly. But when she finally turned to look at me, I realized it was *her*. Petra. The girl whose name was at the bottom of the list.

The girl I'd assumed would be dead by now.

Her lips moved like she was calling to me, but all I could hear was the rain crashing down and the wind shrieking between the houses and the neighbors screaming from their invisible doorsteps.

"Don't touch her!"

"Get away!"

"It's too late to help her!"

"Go back inside!"

"Halley!"

I reached for the doorknob behind me, never taking my eyes off Petra.

She limped toward our house. She was twenty steps away, then ten. Five. I could have reached out and touched her. My fingers slipped on the wet metal handle behind me. I couldn't get the door open unless I turned my back to her, and what then? The Mercs rarely hurt the villagers—not never, but rarely—and I thought I remembered Mother telling me they always carried knives . . .

Just before Petra reached the doorstep, her legs gave out, and she sank into a heap on the ground. Her neck twisted sideways, her eyes squeezed shut, and her mouth pinched into a thin line. Something dark crisscrossed her cheek—her hair, it had to be—and it was growing longer, and longer, and longer, until it became a snake crawling along the ground and her whole right side was a mass of expanding darkness.

The light above me flicked on, triggered by my movement.

I screamed.

The doctor came running. Old though he was, he was at the door faster than a blink. Not that I could have closed my eyes. They were fixed on the miserable girl sprawled over the doorstep, on the bloody red mess that was, or had once been, her right shoulder.

The snake had turned into a puddle, and it was spreading faster now, lapping at my shoes.

"Go find Maria," the doctor ordered, kneeling over the girl's body. He had never raised his voice, not in my memory, but he came close to it now. "Go! We'll save her if you hurry!"

I darted through the kitchen to the back of the house, chased by the piano soundtrack playing in living room, and pounded my fist against the bedroom door.

"Mother!" The words emerged as a muddle of mispronounced syllables, a sleepwalker's attempt at forming a sentence. "There's a patient!"

Slippers scuffed the floor, and Mother appeared with her face a mess of annoyance and disordered wrinkles—the kind you get from sleeping too hard. She had probably been out for hours, morning sparrow that she was, and she didn't take kindly to unexpected awakenings.

"What's happening?" she grumbled, about to launch into a speech about how the doctor could manage on his own, didn't need her help, never had needed her help before. But I didn't let her get that far. There was no time to explain.

"You have to come with me," I urged, pinching her sleeve and tugging her into the kitchen. "There's a patient. A Merc."

"At this time of night? They're not on duty."

"Maria," the doctor's voice called from the living room. "Hurry."

We found him silhouetted against the ugly white light seeping in from the front door, with Petra draped across his arms. Her head was angled sharply back, exposing three short gashes on her neck, and her hair, loose and damp, dripped and mixed water with the blood on the floor. Her left arm was pressed against his chest. The right was invisible, lost among the shredded remains of her jacket and her matted hair.

In a moment, Mother had disappeared, bustling off to the dispensary to find the surgical tools.

I helped the doctor unfold the emergency cot we kept behind the sofa. It was an easy task to roll Petra onto it—she weighed less than Mother's washing tub, and I could have picked her up myself without the doctor's help. The back of my hand brushed up against her neck, and I felt no warmth, only a chill unnatural for human skin. I pulled my hand away and shoved it in my pocket, trying to rid myself of that clammy wetness.

Mother returned with the doctor's bag, and I scuttled out of her way. Doctor's daughter notwithstanding, I was no surgeon, and I had the iron constitution of a mouse. But I couldn't bring myself to abandon her altogether. I had found her, so she was my charge. I huddled behind the sofa and peeked over the back, half-blocking my view with the fringe of a pillow, ready to cover my eyes the moment the black fuzz gathered around my vision and I thought I'd be sick.

From my hiding place, I saw little that made sense except a few bright flashes of light as the doctor applied his tools to Petra's right side. The scent of something burning wafted into the air, and the *drip, drip* of blood slowed to a stop. I hadn't realized how much the sound grated on me until it vanished. Like Spanish water torture, it was off-rhythm with the music that no one had bothered to turn off, a dissonant and disturbing beat.

Mother placed a bag of blood on a stand next to the bed and produced a needle from the metal tray. Cold, silver, metallic. I buried my face in the pillow, fighting nausea.

When I dared to look again, there was a thin red tube connected to Petra's other arm and a clear mask over her nose. It fogged over in spurts as she breathed, obscuring her face.

"We can't sedate her," the doctor said. "I haven't gotten anesthesia in months."

"She'll never sleep through this."

"We don't have a choice." He looked at me. Of course he knew I hadn't left the room, even though I'd hidden myself. He always knew when I wasn't where I was supposed to be. "Come here, Halley."

"No," Mother snapped. "I'll do it."

I clenched the pillow so tightly that the fabric tore. A pinch of stuffing wedged itself between my fingers.

The smoky smell was joined by a taste. Coppery like a coin and saccharine like spoiled honey. I plugged my nose, but there was no escaping it. It poured itself down my throat, filled my lungs, made my stomach clench and burn. Something in the air, it had to be, but I couldn't see anything besides a little hissing steam from the doctor's electric knife.

The doctor brushed the edge of the knife against a black object Mother had placed on the cot. It sizzled when it made contact, and the smell—taste, whatever it was—grew stronger until my mouth watered.

"Are you ready?" He poised the knife over the girl's shoulder.

I shut my eyes and clung to the pillow.

*Hiss.*

Steam wafted over the back of the sofa. I felt it soak through my hair, moistening my scalp.

*Fwish.*

That knife was so hot it seemed to singe the air.

Her cry shattered my ears.

I cupped my hands over my face and squeezed my eyes, but nothing could block out that hideous sound. It beat me to the floor until my forehead brushed the wood, and I might have been screaming, too, only I couldn't hear my own voice over hers.

Then the shrieks were replaced by whimpers. I wasn't screaming after all, only huddled with my mouth open and every muscle surrounding it tight.

Then silence.

I peeked around the sofa. The doctor and Mother were shining with sweat, and they both had the same pasty color of old piano keys. Tears trickled down Petra's cheeks. Her chest rose and fell, so I knew she was alive—but her breathing was too fast. Her left fist clenched around the bed frame, and she trembled all over.

There was a faint indigo glow on the table that hadn't been there before. I couldn't see where it was coming from until the doctor put his hand on Petra's forehead. As he did so, he raised something black and faintly metallic, crisscrossed with glowing indigo lines.

"It's alright," he assured Petra, brushing sticky black hair from her face. The music swelled, as though it, too, wanted to comfort her. "Rest now."

The tip of the black metal twitched.

Fingers.

A prosthetic.

Her new arm looked so real, yet so alien. Proportional, yet unnatural. It was sleek and shining, solid black except for the indigo lights, clearly a mechanical device that did not belong with living human flesh. And yet—perhaps it was Petra's tattered sleeve that covered it—but the place where it joined to the skin was so evenly blended that it seemed to be a perfect part of her already.

Funny how blurry that light had gotten, and how much it looked like shimmering snow rather than a lamp. The bustling around me faded, and the pitch of the music became too high, distorted. Someone yelled my name, but I couldn't be bothered to respond.

I gave in to the dizziness and let my eyes fall shut, sinking between the sofa and the wall into a cold, heavy sleep.

# 02

## ROSCOE

## "YOU'RE THE WORST!"

Roscoe flashed her colleague an embarrassed grin. "I'm a designer, not a gamer," she reminded him, dropping her black-and-red controller on the desk. "Don't lord it over me like that. You can't even draw a respectable stick figure."

"Besides, you're hardly one to talk," said another voice from a few cubicles over. "You didn't survive your first round. She lost a lot of HP and her character's a little beat up, but she's still kicking."

"Kazumi's right," Roscoe affirmed, satisfied. "I could be worse."

The playful banter of her coworkers never failed to take the edge off Roscoe's exhaustion. Of course there were perks to having a job that allowed her to sit in front of a computer all day. For one thing, it was easy to watch cat videos while she was supposed to be working, which was enough to keep her from complaining. But she got lonely. She'd look up from her drawing pad only to realize that everyone had gone home and there was nobody to make small talk with as she tidied up her desk, stacked her papers, and threw away her empty energy drink cans.

Roscoe kept careful account of her strengths and weaknesses, and playing games was a weakness. She'd cursed her luck when she was assigned to work on a controller-only game. What was wrong with a good, old-fashioned keyboard and mouse, the kind she'd enjoyed since she was a child? Still, she couldn't just sit back and watch while her coworkers played. She'd poured so many hours into the game's design that she longed to see it in action, even if that meant dying repeatedly and subsequently defending herself against her coworkers' good-humored mockery. Today she agreed to play "a round or two" and had just finished her seventh.

"The graphics are fantastic," she remarked, gathering her pencils into a bundle. "It doesn't get much more realistic than that."

Kazumi stood near the opening of her cubicle. "You did a great job."

"Oh, that was just the menus. I'm talking about the characters, the landscapes, the—"

"Even so." He had a perfectly crooked smile. "I saw the character concept sketches you did. Your designs are just as good as the real in-game models. Better, actually."

She wondered if he could see the heat in her cheeks. Probably not. If he could, he would have fled long ago. Besides, she had applied enough blush to cover up any real pink.

"I was going to ask," he continued, "if you wanted to leave early and get coffee. You haven't taken a break in forever. I'm sure nobody would mind if you bailed just this once."

Roscoe cast an uncertain glance at her drawing tablet. She wasn't finished with her menu layout sketches, and they were due at the next morning's meeting. But she had all night to get the details worked out, so what could a few hours hurt?

"All right." She stuffed the pencils into her drawer and dusted off her hands, flashing Kazumi a pearly grin. "Let's go."

If she hadn't agreed to go with Kazumi that day, Roscoe reflected bitterly, she wouldn't be stuck in her home office with a controller glued to her hand.

"We need a broad group of players." That's what they'd told her, but it was a thin excuse. What they meant was: "We need you because you're terrible, so if you can figure it out, everybody else can too." Strongly implied: "We don't trust you to finish your projects on time after you failed to present the menu plan to the creative director." So much for being a graphic designer at the country's top game studio. Roscoe had been demoted to a lowly debugging position, paid by the number of hours she wasted struggling to beta-test the game.

She hated these "permadeath" games—if you could call it a game when it wasn't fun—where you had to restart at the beginning when your character was killed. She hated controllers; she hated violence. She hated, in short, everything about the game she'd worked on. Except the menus. Those had turned out quite well, if a day or two late.

For the sake of keeping her pantry stocked, she had designed a new character, a girl with fierce indigo eyes, stark black hair, and sickly pale skin. The xXRoscoeVersion13Xx was as striking and coldly beautiful as a Greek goddess. But her HP was near zero, and Roscoe knew she wouldn't last much longer. Roscoe didn't have enough credits to purchase any of the upgrades that might have extended her run, but she was content to play until her character was eliminated. Then she'd go to bed and restart tomorrow with Version 14.

The screen glitched, and her character reappeared in the safe area. A notification pinged.

*Congratulations! Physical upgrade obtained.*

Roscoe squinted at the icon and yelped. It was the upgrade Kazumi was always talking about, one of the rarest in the game, which none of the beta testers had found yet. She scrabbled among the stack of papers on her coffee table until she found the guide. There on page 450, near the end. There was no picture, but the important information was highlighted in bold.

*Shooting stabilizer: This upgrade negates recoil during shooting, allowing the user to fire faster and more accurately. Effect varies by character. Most useful on the upper floors, where characters have a greater percentage chance of finding rifles, pistols, etc.*

It didn't say how the upgrade was obtained, but Roscoe hadn't done anything noteworthy. There was probably just a glitch somewhere. A lucky glitch, but still a glitch, and therefore a thorn in her side. Her enthusiasm fading fast, she scribbled down the details on her notepad so that another lowly debugger could reproduce whatever she'd done. Then she hit save and powered off her console. Nothing to get excited about.

For a split second, Roscoe could have sworn she saw her character move. Lift her clenched fists to her eyes and rub them. Then the screen went black, and Roscoe sighed. The developers really had thought of every detail that could keep their future audience hooked.

The realistic graphics were supposed to be immersive, thrilling, real-stakes-high-heart-rates. Whatever new term marketing had coined to be printed in large type on the box. But Roscoe found the digital avatars repulsively lifelike. Sort of like the uncanny valley effect she'd read about online, but she couldn't fathom why she was scared of characters onscreen.

She pushed back her desk chair and stretched, tilting her head toward the ceiling. It was a relief, after the violence of the game, to admire that familiar pink paint. Pink desk. Pink chair. Pink controller. Pink coverlet. Pink everything. Pink was Roscoe's comfort color. Whenever she was in her apartment, she was surrounded by the charm of cherry blossoms.

She wandered into her kitchen, pondering whether it was too late in the evening to drink caffeinated tea. Probably not. And tea happened to go well with spicy ramen, which she was craving, as she did every night. Still thinking about the glitch and what she was going to do with the upgrade, she absentmindedly turned on her stove.

Her gaze landed on the poster taped to her fridge, the one she'd put up because Kazumi had made a big deal about getting her a copy. It was predominantly red and black, and it didn't match the rest of her décor. "WARSAFE GAMES" was stenciled in military type across the middle. At the bottom, in black marker, the company president had handwritten the game's slogan: *Safety requires the many to sacrifice the one.*

Oh, the money some teenager would pay to own that poster!

And oh, what Roscoe would give to sell it to them. If it weren't for Kazumi . . .

Just looking at it made her feel ill. A little *Call of Duty* now and then was one thing, but she hated being chained to her console, forced to play for pay and not for fun.

She tore the poster down, ripping the corner. It didn't matter. She would have felt guilty about selling it anyway.

Her phone vibrated. A message from Kazumi.

"All hands on deck. New character glitch, and they want it fixed tonight."

Roscoe wondered how they'd known. It was after seven o'clock, which was far too late for work to demand her attention, and she'd had no intention of reporting the glitch until business hours the next day. But if she had to choose between showing up to the office and getting fired . . .

"You've always wanted to work for Warsafe," she chided herself, slipping a cardigan over the T-shirt she'd been wearing all day. "Teenage you would've been proud."

Fine, but adult Roscoe wasn't.

"It shouldn't take more than a few hours." She slipped her credit card into her pocket. "You can get a donut from the gas station afterward."

Whatever it took to convince herself this was fine, that's what she'd do.

# 03

## HALLEY

**WHEN I WAS SHAKEN AWAKE FROM MY** faint and had recovered some color, according to the bathroom mirror, the doctor was quick to task me with taking Petra back to the House. I protested that neither of us was ready to walk that far, especially not in the pouring rain, but he ignored my complaints.

"Give me credit for a job well done." He was busy rinsing blood from his scalpel into the kitchen sink, staining the sponges I had used to scrub the saucepan. "With the prosthetic to give her some strength, and with time to heal her nerves, she might end up better off than she was before her accident."

This seemed unlikely, but I was under no delusions that my opinion would be appreciated.

"You can't send Halley up there alone, not with a Merc," Mother objected. "The enforcement chip will shock her, and then what will you do? Do you have anti-electrocution medications too?"

"Yes." He glanced at Petra, whose vacant eyes were half-closed. "But it's not against the rules for a villager to visit the House. Just not customary. She'll be fine if she's back by curfew."

"A custom's as good as a rule in this town."

"I told Halley to go," he said mildly. "So she's going."

It seemed like I should have gotten a say in all this, especially since I was the one risking electrocution. But I had neither the energy nor the social standing to argue.

A funny aftertaste lingered in my mouth, and I tried not to think about what the doctor had forced down my throat while I was unconscious. Deliberately, I stretched my arms. Those seemed alright. Then I tried wiggling my toes. Those worked too. I stood on one foot, then the other. I didn't feel even a trace of lightheadedness. He'd made a perfect cure of me.

Satisfied with my own limbs, I glanced at Petra. Surely she wouldn't be able to walk yet, not after how I'd seen her only a few minutes before. But the doctor was right. I'd underestimated him. Her movements were sluggish, but the way she wiggled her new fingers suggested curiosity rather than discomfort. There was a reason the doctor was the only doctor on the island. His medicine bordered on the miraculous. Although I suspected the pain would hit later once the medications wore off, Petra seemed to be in good shape for the moment.

I waved at her, pasting on a smile. She slid off the table, eyes darting around the room like she thought something might jump out at her. Then, with heavy steps, she dragged herself toward the door.

So much for introductions. I pulled my hood over my ears and tucked my hands into my pockets—this time I knew enough to wait for the dresser to reboot—and trailed her out into the cold.

The rain had nearly stopped, which meant I'd been unconscious for longer than I thought. What else had I missed?

Silver moonlight sliced through the already dissipating clouds, so bright that I could pick out every hole and weed and crack in the cobblestones. The air hung still, and I could hear nothing except our boots clattering on the road.

A stab of guilt ached in my chest. That morning I hadn't even acknowledged Petra's existence beyond noting that her name would soon disappear. It was different now that she was more than a number on a list. I'd seen her bleed, which meant she was human—so frighteningly, terribly human. The way the toes of her shoes dragged the ground as if they were made of lead. And the way her shoulders drooped, though she tried to pull them back when she remembered. Embodied in her every movement was a fierce desire to survive and to do it proudly.

I knew something about that pride, but only by hearsay. We villagers called the Mercenaries' mysterious work a "game" because that was what we had always done, and old habits were hard to change. Deep down, everyone knew that to the Mercenaries, this was no friendly competition, and there were no prizes to be won, only lives to be lost. What a beautiful, miserable existence Petra had—somewhere far removed from me, though I saw her almost every day.

By the time I thought of something worth saying aloud, we were already halfway up the hill, and we were making a snail's pace look good. Petra's feet continued to drag, scraping the cobbles.

"Lean on my shoulder." I took her arm, careful to catch her healthy one, and tried to drape it over myself. But the moment my fingers touched her skin, Petra jerked away so quickly that I was knocked off balance. I collapsed into a puddle, splashing ice-cold rain into my face. My foot folded under me with a stabbing *pop*.

Petra's lips puckered. She reached out her hand, wrapping thin fingers around my wrist, and helped me to my feet.

I hopped for a moment on one leg, then tenderly placed my injured foot on the ground. It held weight, barely, with creaks and stabs and electric tingling. But there was no way I'd be spending the night at the top of this hill. Even if it hadn't been for the enforcement chips, which would shock me to oblivion if I wasn't indoors at curfew, I could only stand so much darkness and shadow in a single day. One way or another, I'd have to make it back to the village.

"Are you alright?"

I started and almost slipped again.

"I said, are you alright?" Petra's voice was unexpectedly gravelly. Not unpleasant. Just strange, and not in keeping with her angular, childish frame.

She was the last person to whom I could complain about a sprained ankle. "I'm fine," I lied. "But what about you? Doesn't it hurt?"

"Not badly."

She was lying too. She had to be. The doctor was a doctor, not a magician. Her stubbornness inspired me, however, and I tried not to show my limp.

Between the empty tree branches, I could begin to see the outline of the House's roof. The building itself was eight stories tall, its roof an enormous, flat balcony. It was squashed into the side of a hill that was far too steep to climb, surrounded by vegetation that never died. Even now that fall had come and the trees in the village had shed their leaves, the undergrowth here was thriving and plentiful. In a set perimeter around the house, the greenery was immortal. Like the House itself, this was just another peculiarity we accepted without question. Things had always been like this.

The cobbles trickled off into a rugged dirt road, and the incline became steeper. I was never one to exercise, and I was getting wildly out of breath. Petra, who should have long ago dissolved into a puddle of blood, titanium, and tears, plodded along at the same pace she'd kept since we left the village.

The rumors that the villagers had been passing around since I was little, which were whispered between the children during the day and the adults at night, didn't seem so unlikely when I was faced with the cold reality of the House. Anything, any kind of "game" with any rules, could be lurking behind those black windows. Someone could be watching me, laughing at my limp. Cruelty belonged here, in this place of unholy darkness and silence.

Ghosts, probably. Surely a place this dark and terrific was haunted by something. But if I acknowledged its presence, the House might drag me inside through its windows that looked like holes, a sacrifice to its secrets.

Petra stopped abruptly and turned her head to me. Blue-tinted lips pursed, and disdain was written all over her face. She thought I was privileged to afford the luxury of being afraid to go to the place where she slept every night and dined every morning. And she was right.

"Go home."

I hesitated, chewing my fingernails and glancing back down the road to see if I could still make out the comforting light of the village below. Why had I come this far if I was only going to leave before I saw she was safe?

Muttering, I darted up the hill after her. Whatever she might think of me, I was no coward.

The quicker I walked, the dimmer her drooping figure appeared in the haze floating over the road. I had no intention of getting left in the dark, so I sprinted after her until my chest hurt and the gravel slipped under my feet and my ankle felt like it had been set on fire. Still, she reached the House before I caught up with her.

A dreary spotlight flicked on when it detected her motion on the porch, exposing her and throwing a harsh shadow on the old, sagging boards. She waved her hand over a sensor mounted on the wall, and the front door scraped open, creaking on rusty bearings.

Her foot caught the lintel, and she slipped. I lunged forward to catch her—but that was a ridiculous impulse. I was too far away. And I wasn't needed. Someone from inside reached out, and Petra collapsed into a pair of strong arms that pulled her inside.

"Are you stupid?" cried a man's voice. "I was going insane looking for you!"

The chastisement continued at a frantic pitch, but I couldn't catch the rest. The porch light flickered, then died, and the door scraped shut. The voice cut off. Petra was gone. I was alone. Alone with those windows like eyes to watch over me. To watch me.

I crept out of the bushes, my own eyes flicking in every direction. One glance back at the House, looming far above my head, blocking the moonlight and the stars. The tallest building I had ever seen. The most windows on one wall. The blackest windows.

Mother had told me when I was a child that they were blacked out for secret reasons. The doctor scolded her for spreading fairy stories, but I knew Mother wasn't the fanciful type. When I became old enough to understand that the world is only a little rose and mostly thorns, I began to formulate a guess, just as every child did. That was our little village's rite of passage to adulthood. After that, the curtains didn't seem sufficient to keep out what was inside. The shadowy terror of whatever lurked there crept out into the village and poisoned everything we did, everything we touched, everything we felt. Our words dripped poison and insincerity, and our homes sheltered murder. How could we be happy when we let this place exist, when we were content never to know the truth?

I imagined someone tearing the curtains away and seeing me gawping. They might think I could help them escape and try to reach out to me, ending by dragging me inside. Why would they? But fear could be irrational. Maybe they'd wish they were me. Maybe they'd recognize me. Maybe they'd come looking for me. Tell someone they saw me at the House and decide that my place was here instead of down in the village. Maybe I'd be conscripted. Become a Merc. Maybe . . . maybe . . .

I turned away, tripping over my own shoes, and fled.

# 04

## ANDY

*— THERE'S NOTHING YOU CAN'T SEE IF you look at the stars. Lions, queens, dragons, hunters. The world of the stars is the world in which everything is possible.*
   *- Well, that's all very nice, and it may even be true. But the stars are forever out of your reach.*
   *- You could change that.*
   He tapped his fingers against his desk, chewing his lip.
   *Those are the only lines I remember from a TV program that aired when I was eleven years old. Those are the only lines I needed. From there, I was inspired to study astrophysics in college . . .*
   And he was back to the mundane details of everyday life. Back on Earth. The stars were only a good metaphor because they were unattainable. If all challenges had been overcome, though the world would certainly be a better place, he wouldn't be writing this paper. He'd be useless, which was all he had ever wanted to be.
   He leaned back in his chair, twined his fingers together, and stretched luxuriously. Fifty words of creative writing was too much for a professional like him, someone who valued numbers and statistics and charts over alliterations and rhythms and rhymes. His fingers itched for the stack of computer equipment piled near the window. If he could just shift his twitching hands from his keyboard to those wires, he'd be one step closer to solving the problem of the stars.

He was never going to find anything. He never had. Nobody had. Nobody would. There was nothing to be found.

With a burst of energy, he pushed himself up from his chair and entered the kitchen. One by one, he opened each cabinet and was met by a burst of dust that fizzled into film on the counter. When he rubbed his finger over it, mildly disgusted, it left a clean streak. The cabinets were otherwise empty.

He tried the pantry next. Alone in a corner stood a can of soup. Chicken noodle soup. The taste always reminded him of being sick. But there was nothing else edible, not unless he counted the aloe plant wilting in the windowsill. So he opened the can and absent-mindedly put it in the microwave.

Half a second before he hit "start," he realized his mistake and yanked it out again.

Grumbling as though it was the microwave's fault, he slopped his soup into a paper bowl and slammed the microwave door behind it. Mistakes like this just went to show that writing drained his superior scientific energy.

He caught a glimpse of his reflection in the glass as he punched in the time. Twenty-three years old, young, strong, healthy. That's what he should have seen. But he hadn't been sleeping well lately, and by some fantastic illusion, he saw eighty years instead. Those tired brown eyes were too dark and shaded to belong to a young man. What did that make him, then? A geezer? Was it possible to be a geezer at two decades? His unwashed hair puffed around his face like Einstein's, except it failed to make him look intriguing, let alone any variety of smart. His shirt collar was misaligned, his buttons uneven.

*A mess. That's what you are. A miscompiled collection of bouncing atoms.*

Anyone unlucky enough to read the essay he'd been writing would be disillusioned when they saw him like this, no matter how flowery his prose. Not that looks mattered for a job like his, but really, what chance did he have of impressing others if he couldn't even stand to look at himself? Maybe he'd find a job in a laser laboratory. He didn't know a thing about lasers, but he'd pick it up quickly, and then nobody would have to look at his face unless they were wearing safety goggles.

From the corners of his eyes, he noticed his diploma dangling crookedly on the wall over the sofa. He'd had a clear goal four years ago—something he wanted to be—and now he had chicken noodle soup, a pile of radio parts, and an essay that wouldn't convince anyone. That diploma should have been a stepping stone, only it remained the greatest thing he'd ever done.

He straightened it anyway and returned to the kitchen as the microwave bell chimed.

Settling in front of his computer with the hot soup, he pulled up a job listing website. *Engineers. Astronomers.* No subcategory for radio astronomy. He wasn't sure that was considered a viable field of study these days. Modern technology was better than radio, and it had the added benefit of being legal. Nobody used radios anymore.

Nobody except him, of course, because he was always doing strange things that no one thought were useful.

He glanced at the pile of equipment. With his little hand-built radio, he was probably the only person on earth listening to the static his antenna picked up. There was no music these days, no talk shows, no misguided rants about the state of long-run aggregate supply and the unbridled degeneration of Congress and the economic sanctions on countries that failed to pay their membership dues. But the gentle hiss of emptiness was enough. It lulled him to sleep at night and woke him in the morning, a constant companion that replaced the betta fish his landlord hadn't let him buy.

One day, he hoped he'd hear something substantial. An alien with green skin and round ears would be ideal, but he'd take anything. Trial messages from a fellow nerd who dared to break the radio laws, a disturbance in the atmosphere. Something—anything—to make the unemployment pass a little faster.

There was just one problem with Andy's idealistic dream: Radios weren't SAFE.

As a radio enthusiast, Andy figured he knew more about that

acronym than most politicians did. SAFE stood for Strategic Alliance for Freedom and Engagement—meaningless government-speak if he'd ever heard it—and membership was voluntary, just like drinking water and eating food were "voluntary." SAFE mediated disputes between member countries, and radio usage was one of the conflicts the organization had stepped in to resolve. Which meant that SAFE was the reason, six months after he'd earned his degree, Andy found himself out of a job.

Studies had proven that radio operation was detrimental to human health, as every good thing, like sugar and alcohol and bungee jumping, eventually was. And since radio waves could theoretically travel with almost unlimited range, if one country used them, all countries would be at risk. Enter SAFE. Enter a mountain of legislation prohibiting radio use, which Andy had spent two weeks perusing, searching desperately for a nonexistent loophole. Almost before he could finish the six-hundred-page legal guide, the police came knocking at his door to demand he turn over the radio that he had once been operating under a permit. Andy figured he'd look even worse in an orange jumpsuit, so he handed over his supplies, manufactured some new transistors with spare parts, and kept quiet.

He liked to imagine the static represented a pleasant back-and-forth between the naturally produced radio waves bouncing off the ionosphere.

*Say, 700 kHz, what do you see up there?*

*Nothing, 1000 kHz, just a few blobs of light and some dust and maybe an asteroid on its way to crash in chunks somewhere in Siberia. No humans up here. It's peaceful.*

And then—

"Sending test signal to address one-four-zero-seven. Status: Operational. No authorization found."

Andy's spoon paused halfway to his mouth. He peered around his apartment. There was nobody there. Of course there wasn't. He lived alone because his landlord wouldn't let him have a betta—

"Permission to send abort signal?"

Louder now. Unmistakable.

Never, not once, not in all the years he'd been listening, had he heard a voice through his radio.

*Aliens?*

But the voice was speaking plain, if somewhat robotic, English. Surely the long history of British colonization hadn't extended into interstellar space.

Had someone else figured out how to build an old-fashioned radio? He'd thought his was the only one. Not that it was difficult, but it was useless since nothing was broadcast these days.

Nothing except this. Whatever this was.

The robotic voice continued: "Procedure authorization revoked."

He darted to his computer and started typing an email. *No, that's too slow.* It wasn't the time to think about how much he hated phone calls. Who knew if he'd ever hear a sound from his radio again? He snatched his phone from the kitchen counter. Who could he tell? Who would listen? Who would believe him?

He scrolled through his contacts until he found his friend from college, nowadays an underappreciated teacher's assistant at their local university. Rilo. Rilo would listen. They had studied radios together in school, and they occasionally still talked about them as a sort of ongoing joke, preferably over drinks when they were both tipsy enough to feel illogical.

He tapped the call button.

"Andy?" a groggy voice muttered after the first ring. "Aren't you usually asleep by now?"

"I've picked up a transmission on my radio."

There was a long pause. "What kind?"

"Voices."

Andy knew exactly what his colleague was thinking. *How long has it been since you slept? Are you experimenting with drugs? You know what they told us about drugs, Andy. Drugs are bad.*

"Can I come over?"

"You believe me?"

"We'll make a night of it. I'll bring the booze."

"Alcohol . . ." Andy sighed. "I have work tomorrow. I'm writing an essay."

"What are you, a high schooler?"

"A broke adult looking for a job." He couldn't hold back an unhappy laugh. "You'd think those recruiters would want a research paper. But no. It's endless short-answer questions. They know nothing about scientists, do they?"

"I'll be there in fifteen minutes. Tell the aliens to stay online until then."

# 05

## HALLEY

"WHY DIDN'T YOU WAIT FOR authorization before you applied that prosthetic?" Mother scolded. She was always in an argumentative mood when she was cooking. "You were reckless. You could have gotten us killed. I've told you a thousand times—"

"The girl was dying," the doctor answered between bites of cheese.

I considered cutting in with an imaginary scenario: *Oh, sorry, I see your arm just almost got lopped off. I need to send a quick message to HQ before I can do anything about it, though . . .* But Mother looked fierce, so I buried my thoughts in a spoonful of soup.

"You could have stopped the bleeding and ended the operation there." Mother slapped the ladle into the pot with such force that a few brown drops splashed over the side and sizzled on the stove. "She would have lived, and she could have come back for a second operation to attach the prosthetic once you'd filed the paperwork."

"The prosthetic is most effective if applied immediately," the doctor explained, eyes fixed on the trail of steam rising from my bowl. "If I'd waited until morning, I might not have been able to save her arm. As it is, between her natural limb and the prosthetic, she'll get almost all her movement back. Quite a medical miracle. Frankly, my professional pride was at stake."

"You put *her* at risk."

My ears perked up. I had cultivated the instinct of knowing when my guardians were talking about me, even when they didn't use my name.

"I was unconscious, mostly. It's not like I made the decision." Just in case anyone was listening, I wanted to make it clear that I had been a useless blob. Just in case. Not that anyone would be. "So how could I get in trouble?"

My question was met with chilly silence. The soup bubbled in the pot, the rain pattered on the roof, my spoon clinked against my bowl.

"Of course," I added hastily, "as a doctor, you don't have much choice about helping your patients."

"He has a choice." Mother's fiery temper reanimated. "He should have saved her life and made her leave. She would have been retired and that would have been best. It's not as if . . ." Her voice trailed off, but I could imagine what the rest of her sentence was going to be. *It's not as if she'll survive for long.*

"Well, I think you did the right thing."

The doctor and Mother both stared at me.

"It's only fair to give her a chance," I continued. "If she's retired as a Merc, she'll lose her sense of purpose. She'll—"

"Stop talking." Mother's face had gone red, but I couldn't tell whether it was because she was angry or because she had been staring down at the steam from the soup. "You have no idea what you're talking about. Purpose! That girl's dangerous." She glared at me. "And if you see her again, I want you to pass right on by as if you two had never spoken a word. I wish I hadn't let you walk her home tonight, but I thought it would be better than letting you clean up the bloody operating table." She gave a loud sigh. "I don't know what to do with children these days. There's no place for them in this town."

The doctor, always our peacemaker, removed his glasses and rubbed the lenses on his shirt. "Now, now," he consoled. "Halley, I agree with Maria. It's best for you not to associate with the Mercs, especially Petra. It's possible that I'll have to answer some questions from the Alliance about her prosthetic, and I don't want to get you involved." He pushed his chair back from the table and patted his beard with a napkin. "Maria, this was wonderful. I always appreciate your cooking."

"Don't start with the flattery." The smile on her lips was unmistakable. "The automated cooker does a better job."

"Would you like to go for a walk, Halley?"

From the doctor's tone, I guessed he meant a walk-and-talk.

"It's fifteen minutes until curfew," Mother pointed out.

"Well, we'll walk for fifteen minutes." The doctor got up from the table and went to the door, pausing in front of the wardrobe, which dressed him in a coat. Almost before I could gulp the last of my tea, he had disappeared outside. I had no choice but to assure Mother we'd hurry, then follow him.

We walked in silence at first, side by side, our shoes plopping in the puddles. We were headed nowhere slowly, but I knew he wouldn't risk being outside after curfew.

"I want you to take this seriously." He halted in the middle of the road and faced me. "I won't forbid you from talking to the Mercs or going to the House. But I will say, with your interest in mind, that you should be careful. Think about what could happen." He tapped the bare scar behind his ear, which was the same as mine, Mother's, everyone's. "These are waiting for you to break a rule."

We'd never talked about the House before. He had never even directly acknowledged its existence. I must have shown some reaction—raised an eyebrow, maybe—because his face creased.

"I know you'll do what you want. But this is for your own safety."

Safety. The one thing we had plenty of in the village. Nothing ever happened to us. It was always them.

"Is Petra going to die?"

"My prosthetic might have saved her," he answered, his voice so low I could barely hear it over the remnants of stormy wind. "I thought she deserved a chance, so I gave her one."

"A chance to keep fighting?"

"A chance to escape." He shook the rain off his hair and glanced at his watch. "We should head back."

If we hurried, I could get a glass of water before bed.

The doctor held the front door open for me, and I tiptoed into the kitchen, presuming Mother had already fallen asleep. There was nobody in the kitchen, and the lights had already dimmed themselves, as they did every night. The electric candles on the table emitted a glow faint enough to kindle a little fear of the dark and remind me that I was pushing my luck. I had fallen asleep on the floor a few times before, and it was a good recipe to awaken stiff and miserable.

I grabbed a glass and filled it with water in the sink, then trotted back down the hallway to my bedroom. Just enough time remained for me to take a sip and snuggle under the covers.

Then it hit me—a wave of blackness and fatigue, too strong to resist. I hated the feeling. Had hated it ever since I could remember. It felt like passing out, like falling into a warm, suffocating blanket of darkness.

I couldn't stop it. Nobody could. At eleven-forty-five, if you weren't inside behind closed and locked doors, you were likely to never be seen again. At midnight exactly, like clockwork, the whole village fell asleep. That was the way things had always been.

That night, for the first time in recent memory, I had a dream.

I saw Petra walking up the hill in front of me, just like I had a few hours ago. Except now we were walking up a grassy slope covered with delightfully fuzzy yellow flowers. I tried to pick one, but it dissolved into a blur before my eyes, and my fingers closed through the stem. The whole horizon, liminal and strangely claustrophobic, was cloudless sky and pseudo-dandelions and Petra's silhouette.

"Where are we going?" I shouted at Petra's receding back. I expected my voice to stick in my throat. This was a dream, and that was what voices always did in dreams. But I was so loud that I startled myself.

She turned to answer. Her dress was the same color as the flowers, instead of the drab-gray skirt and top I'd seen her wearing that night. There were drops of rain on her cheeks, wiped away by her loose hair, which billowed around her face, though I could feel no wind.

"To the Mercenaries' House."

My feet seemed frozen to the ground. I looked around to see what was holding me, and it was Mother. The doctor. The whole village. They were screaming for me to stop, and though their voices were distant, I sensed their urgency. Everyone was against me—against *us*, for Petra was holding out her hand, inviting me to follow.

There was something in her palm. I craned my neck to see it, but she tilted her hand. She seemed to be telling me that I would know if only I broke free and came a little closer, if I gave into the yawning curiosity eating my soul.

I ran forward, throwing off Mother and the doctor and everyone else. Selfish and youthful, that was the kind of freedom I wanted. To run and jump and swim and scream and make friends and talk to anyone and go everywhere and—

Soft like a tap and sharp like a knife came the pain in my chest. Petra's expression dissolved into terror, and she screamed. Her hands tilted, and something red and thick spilled out of them. *Blood.*

I could feel myself falling to my knees. Landing in the grass didn't hurt a bit. My face was among the flowers. They were just as blurry as they had been before, and I wondered if they were real. Surely not. They were too beautiful and wholesome and pure, and they were so far away, getting farther.

It was like falling asleep, but warmer. Like fainting, but less frightening. My fingers dug into the grass, then into the warm earth beneath. I had never felt so safe. But my eyes were closing, and the sounds were getting quieter, and I couldn't see the flowers anymore.

I woke with wet cheeks as my alarm shrilled in my ear.

By then, I was halfway up the hill. Not literally, of course. But I knew as though the idea had been inked into my brain that I had to go back to the House. I never had a second's doubt. It's funny how dreams leave such strong impressions, especially when you're not used to dreaming at all. Going was a requirement. A nonnegotiable necessity. I had to see her. I couldn't stop myself. I didn't even pause to ask myself why I was going or what I wanted to know. I just obeyed.

I slipped out of bed, stood in front of the automatic dresser, selected the same drab-brown dress and stockings I wore every day, and let myself outside. The front door clicked shut with an echo that seemed extraordinarily loud, and I crossed my fingers in hopes that neither Mother nor the doctor would investigate. Fortunately, they often slept through their own blaring alarms these days. Why not, when there was only an hour of free time each morning? It was too little to be valuable, too much to waste on eating and dressing. "You're young and flighty," Mother used to tell me, and I figured it was meant as a compliment, "but when you're our age, you'll prefer to stay in bed rather than go gallivanting with your friends or whatever it is you do in your free time."

If she'd known exactly what that "whatever" encompassed, she'd—well, there was no need to think about the bristly end of her broom.

The ankle I had sprained the night before ached, but I interpreted the pain as a reminder rather than a warning. This was a mistake. The first ten steps were bearable. The eleventh step was outright painful, and by the time I was halfway up the hill, I had an awkward limp.

On, on, and on I went. Up, up, and up some more. Up the hill I went, until the village faded into the mist behind me and I could no longer hear the faint sounds of the early birds bustling to life. My feet on the cobbles and the raindrops falling into the grass from the trees—cozy against a background of rattling branches and sweet-scented wind—dominated my senses and lulled me further into quiet acceptance. Nature was healing itself from the storm, shedding the excess water into the ground so that it could be drunk and turned into new growth. Only I did not belong. It was sacrilegious for me to be here so early, trying to slip through the forest when the trees hadn't yet clothed themselves in preparation for the day. They were looking at me, I imagined, wondering why I had come and what was driving me on.

It was romantic to think that the trees cared about my tiny human existence, but those bare branches were threatening too, sharp and prickly, like they might stab you if they fell. One got caught in a sudden gust of wind, and I flinched before I realized it was attached to the tree. The rattle increased in volume, as though the trees were laughing at me.

*What are you doing here?* they asked each other, giggling like schoolgirls caught in gossip. *Who are you, outsider?*

I reminded myself that they were only trees and couldn't do anything.

I thought of the village legends, the ones that had been whispered to me as a child. People said there were ghosts here, ghosts of everyone who had died in the House. I never understood why they'd come back to haunt a place they hated. Maybe they'd learned to see this house as both a haven and a prison. Friendly captivity. There had to be something here that they missed.

*Ghosts aren't real.* It was easier to believe that in the daytime.

My steps slowed as I approached the House. This was the part where I had no choice but to wake myself out of my doze and do something. But what, exactly? *Hello, Petra. I dreamed about you last night. Care to tell me what goes on in this place?* Of course that wouldn't be perceived as deranged and bizarre, and I'd definitely be invited back.

Besides, Petra was a means to an end. I wanted to see her face and confirm that my dream hadn't been prophetic. Because I had always thought that sometimes the subconscious could make predictions we wouldn't have thought of in broad daylight, when there were distractions all around and everything was illuminated in practicality.

It turns out that anyone could be brave if they were sufficiently scared of the alternative. I marched up and knocked sharply on the front door.

Nobody ever seemed to answer before the waiting got awkward. I could hear people moving inside. Whispers, footsteps, and rustles got closer for a few seconds, then faded, leaving me to wonder if it was really that easy to ignore me. I was torn between knocking again or sprinting off down the hill, satisfied that I had done my best to see Petra and that I'd try again another day.

But before I could make up my mind, the door opened a crack. A pair of glittering brown eyes stared out at me.

"Who are you?"

I dropped a curtsy. If I was ever going to use the wheedling skills that had been drilled into me by old-fashioned Mother, now was the time. Nobody but a Merc, or perhaps the doctor, should have been up this early in the morning. Since I lacked an explanation, I had to fall back on politeness.

"My name's Halley," I told the man. His eyes, all I could see of him, showed no recognition. Confused, I rushed ahead: "I'm looking for Petra."

"Why?"

"I wanted to see how she's doing," I stammered. "I . . . the doctor operated on her yesterday, and she seemed pretty out of it, and . . ." My voice trailed off. If he lived in the House, he knew what had happened. Explaining was a waste of breath.

The crack widened, and I peeked past the man's shoulder. I had never seen the House's interior before. All I could make out now was a dingy, half-lit room veiled by a swirling sheet of gray dust. It seemed stuck in a state of half-existence, quiet and untouched, utterly lacking homey charm. If I hadn't known better, I would have assumed the place was uninhabited.

He stepped out onto the porch and closed the door, cutting off my view. Now I could see that those eyes were good-humored, permanently crinkled in a laugh, surrounded by a mess of curly blond hair. He was so tall that the top of my head didn't pass his shoulders, although that might have been a psychological impression. He was dressed like he hadn't put much thought into what he was wearing. The top couple of buttons of his shirt were undone, and his neck was covered by a loosely tied red bandanna that provided a glimpse of a silver cross necklace.

But he was one of those rare people who could look untidy with remarkable success.

He put his hands in his pockets and looked me up and down, from my shoes to the top of my head, until I felt my cheeks redden. I wished I'd stopped in front of the mirror before I left the house.

"Did the doctor tell you to come?" he asked.

"No."

"Then you shouldn't have." For a moment I thought he was going to slam the door on me, but his face broke into a grin.

"Come on in," he said. "I suppose you can talk to Petra if you get back to the village by the time you're supposed to start your duties. Wouldn't want to get you in trouble."

I wasn't sure what to say to that. "What's your name?"

"Calhoun. But nobody remembers that, so you can call me Cal." He propped the door open with his boot. "No need to take your shoes off. A little more dust won't hurt. Hope you're not allergic. Can you imagine being allergic to dust?"

I could. My mouth was dry, and when I opened it to take a reassuring breath, I inhaled a wad of congealed dirt and mold and spat it out, coughing. The House didn't want me inside. It was doing everything it could to keep me out.

But Cal was waiting. Watching to see what I would do. Running away now would be cruel. *Er, yes, no, I don't think I'll be going in there. Absolutely not. Invitation rejected!* After that, I'd never be allowed back, no matter how much I begged.

I swallowed my fear and took one step, then another. And then I was in the House, really inside, all the way inside, swallowed by stone walls and thick, heavy air.

The door clanged shut behind me, and Cal locked us in.

# 06

## ROSCOE

**"YOU RECEIVED AN UNAUTHORIZED** upgrade, allowing you to bypass several chronological levels and circumvent normal methods of play."

Roscoe blinked the sleep out of her eyes and held back a yawn. Nod. Grin and bear it. Glitches weren't her territory. Why was this random programmer, someone she'd never seen before, lecturing her about something she couldn't control? If there was a glitch, there was a glitch. So what?

She hoped they wouldn't remove the upgrade before she had the chance to try it. Each night, servers were down for maintenance between 9:00 p.m. and 9:00 a.m., so she couldn't play again until the morning. She'd been happy about that at first, assuming it guaranteed her at least eight hours of sleep. But here she was, languishing in her office at the unholy hour of 12:38 a.m.

She'd been so sleepy when she left her apartment that she'd grabbed the wrong badge, forgetting that she needed her SAFE-approved ID to enter the building's inner sanctum, where the real programmers lived. The guard had recognized her, but he wouldn't budge on protocol. Back to her apartment she went, and back up the stairs, back down, and back on the road, until she was so frustrated she could have cried—if she hadn't been so dehydrated. So much for the ramen she'd been drooling over when Kazumi's text had interrupted her evening. He really did have a knack for ruining things.

Speaking of Kazumi, where was he? Why would he have been the one to call her if he wasn't at the office? Maybe he had already come and gone. She shouldn't have bothered adding that extra spray to her hair before she left home. Now she'd have to shower before she could crawl in bed. Not that bed would solve anything. The cycle was bound to restart in the morning. Games, games, play, play. Nothing but endless screen time and violence and pauses to note down glitches. *Character animation, skipped. Lag. No, really, it wasn't just my lousy reaction time.*

She blinked and discovered that the programmer was staring at her, waiting for a response. What was the last thing he'd said?

She smiled weakly. "What do you want me to do about it?"

"Nothing. We're going to allow you to keep the upgrade for as long as your character survives."

"You're not going to fix the glitch?"

"We are," he answered. "But there's no point in rescinding the upgrade."

"Why?"

That question seemed to irritate him. "You'd have to make a new character."

"Why—"

"Upgrades are—well, upgradeable, not removable. There would be too many Mercs online for the doctor to handle if they could go see him for every little change."

Yet another design flaw. Why have only one doctor for the whole server? Roscoe caught herself yawning again. What did it matter if Warsafe sabotaged itself by releasing a buggy game? At least then she'd have a valid reason to quit her job. Nobody could nag her about how much she was getting paid and how she shouldn't even think about quitting and how wonderful the benefits were and how lovely it would be to retire with a pension.

Interrogation complete, the programmer turned back to his computer. His slumped back indicated that his social meter was as drained as Roscoe's, and she didn't waste time trying to say goodbye.

She was ready to drag herself back to her car, drive home, and surround herself with her cherry-pink bed and cherry-pink blankets and cherry-pink pillows. Coziness and warmth and a paltry seven-hour snooze were all she wanted now. Forget the gas station donuts.

But on her way out the door, she caught a glimpse of her reflection in somebody's computer screen. Leaving without seeing Kazumi would be a shameful waste. That hair spray was expensive.

Chiding herself for her vanity, Roscoe trotted across the hallway to the debugging room. This was where she'd be working if she didn't prefer to linger at home. During work hours, it was filled with fluffy beanbags, soft carpet, relentless competition. But the atmosphere of the Warsafe Games Headquarters, jovial though it was, didn't suit her. It was all red and black, like her poster. The opposite of cozy.

She spotted Kazumi's outline through the frosted-glass door. Instead of the peppy, arcade-style music that usually wafted out into the hallway, all she heard was his voice, so low and muffled she could barely recognize it. The lights in the room were dimmed, too, and instead of the usual colorful lighting, someone had switched on the pale fluorescents. They hummed aggravatingly.

Pressed against the wall, Roscoe tapped her boots on the floor, just loud enough that Kazumi might hear it and just quiet enough that she could listen to him.

"Why her?" he was saying. There was no response, and Roscoe guessed he was talking on the phone. "We've never had any issues with the upgrade rules. There's no reason to think things would be different now."

She sighed. No matter where she went, she couldn't get away from glitches. Bugs, glitches, bugs, glitches everywhere. At least they weren't literal bugs.

"Was there some reason that character was chosen? The upgrade is one of the best in the game. It could change the rankings." He raised his voice. "I don't care what you have to do. Make sure this doesn't happen again. This is not a question of 'do no harm.' No harm would have been done had she not received the upgrade. You make that clear to him."

Suddenly Roscoe wondered what she was going to say when

he came out of the room and realized that she had been listening. Unintentionally, of course, but that wouldn't mollify him if he'd wanted to have a private conversation. *"Sorry, I was just passing by,"* or *"Fancy seeing you here!"* or *"Oh, Kazumi, you're still at the office? Imagine that."* She wasn't a habitual overthinker, but she was self-aware enough to know when she was in the wrong place at the wrong time.

The door swung open beside her, and she barely had time to jump away from the wall and into the middle of the hallway. *Casual. I'm just, you know, passing by.*

"Oh, hello, Kazumi." She smiled brilliantly. "Just passing by. Didn't expect to see you here." Impressive: every cliché she could think of fit into one short phrase.

He stared at her for a moment, and Roscoe's thoughts went wild. Had she offended him? Annoyed him? What was he thinking?

Then his face relaxed into its usual smile, and she inwardly sighed with relief. There was something about a Kazumi who didn't smile that unsettled her. She hesitated, then started down the hallway.

"Did you talk with the programming department?" He fell into step with her, and Roscoe tightened her lips so her elation wouldn't show. "I don't think anyone has been playing long enough to win an upgrade like that. You're seriously lucky."

Roscoe could hear opportunity oozing from his words. She took a breath. "Do you want to play with my avatar?" And the critical maneuver: "You could come to my house. I've got a nice setup, and I don't mind watching as you play."

"Sounds great."

And Roscoe, theatrical as always, pinched herself in case this was a dream.

"How about tomorrow?" Kazumi suggested. "I'm sure you'll want to mess around with the upgrade first. I could come over in the afternoon once you've had a chance to try it out."

"Lunchtime would be perfect. I'll make—uh, sandwiches."

"Terrific." Kazumi held the door open for her, and Roscoe felt like a queen. "I'll see you then."

*Words I never thought I'd hear.*

Her pink controller was gripped tightly in his hands—nice hands, too, not too small or large or sweaty or dry. Her TV screen reflected brightly from his focused eyes. Half a sandwich lay on a pink plate in front of him, and he had already told her it was delicious.

Kazumi was in Roscoe's house.

She wished she could relax and enjoy the moment she'd been hoping for since that first coffee date, the one that turned her career upside-down, but she was tightly wired. There was one inevitable fact she hadn't thought of the night before: Kazumi would see her play. He probably assumed she'd gotten better by now, but she hadn't. He never made fun of her, but what would happen when his patience ran out?

She settled into a chair beside Kazumi and hugged her flower-shaped pillow, trying to quell her anxiety. He had just turned on her console and was warming up her avatar. Maybe Kazumi could take that character a few steps further, but there wasn't much hope she'd last beyond the twentieth level. Roscoe felt a little regret. She'd gotten attached to xXRoscoeVersion13Xx and those empty turquoise eyes.

Kazumi guided her avatar toward the front door of the house.

"You ready?" he asked, with a quick smile.

She nodded vigorously. "Ready!"

But her enthusiasm didn't last. Once Kazumi had warmed up her avatar on the test course, making her jump over obstacles, climb trees and walls, and slash wooden targets with her knife, he entered the first floor of the house and began the real game. And that was the same frustrating, discouraging melee she was forced to sit through every day.

Still, something was different about the way Kazumi operated. Where Roscoe charged in recklessly, waving knives and guns at everything that twitched, he planned his moves in advance. He hid behind corners, made use of the shadows, waited until the right moment to surprise his enemies. He seemed to recognize something about the game's style that she never had—that stealth was rewarded and enemies acted like real people, which made them fallible. They were on edge, aware of the danger surrounding them, susceptible to trickery. Kazumi could make her avatar pick up an empty can and utilize something nearby to create a rattle. That would catch a guard's attention, and the avatar would spring out from a direction the enemies weren't expecting to get the kill.

Something had also changed about the way her character worked. Roscoe hated using guns in the game. It was fiendishly difficult to hit the right spot for a one-shot-one-kill, especially with shaky hands on the controller and a low-level avatar. But the upgrade solved that problem. The avatar's hands—and Kazumi's—were firm like ice. Not a bullet was wasted.

Twenty minutes later, Kazumi had cleared all eight floors and left her character standing victorious on the rooftop.

"That was amazing." Roscoe's eyes were wide.

"It's all thanks to the upgrade," Kazumi said modestly. "I never thought the mechanics could be so smooth. Do you mind if I keep going?"

"Not at all."

Over and over, he cleared the eight primary levels and emerged on the rooftop. The game's fatigue system was slowing down her avatar's movements, but that didn't seem to affect Kazumi's skill. After nearly two hours of play, Version 13's health was still at 83 percent.

Roscoe replenished his sandwiches and sat down to watch—on the other end of the sofa, this time, instead of the chair.

Kazumi played until her avatar was too fatigued to move. And even then, he seemed reluctant to give up the controller. She saw him fidget with his pocket, where the corner of his handheld gaming device peeked over the fabric.

"I'm sorry I drained your avatar's energy." He returned her controller to its stand and settled back into the sofa. "I just can't believe how good that upgrade is."

"You were amazing," Roscoe blurted. "You've got the system figured out. I thought this was one of those games where you just charge in and shoot on sight, but you made it look so much easier than that."

"You think?" Kazumi's eyes glowed. "We should play together more often. In fact—" He paused and fished in his pocket. "You could play on my account now, since I drained your avatar's health." He offered her his console.

Surely she wouldn't have such bad luck that she'd kill Kazumi's avatar in one round, especially with all the health upgrades he must have collected.

"Are you sure?"

He settled back into the sofa. "Don't worry about it," he told her. "Think of it as my thank-you."

Roscoe swallowed to relieve her dry mouth and plugged Kazumi's console into the cable dangling from the back of her TV. If only she didn't have to play in front of him, she wouldn't feel so nervous, and her hands wouldn't shake so much, and she wouldn't risk pressing a wrong button that would cost Kazumi his character and her the game. If only—

She detached the controllers from the console and sat back on the sofa. Her hands were sweaty, and the controllers slipped against her palms. Kazumi didn't have grips on his joysticks, and she was used to those. But it would take too long for her to pair her own controller with Kazumi's console. She could switch the grips, but that seemed lame.

She scrolled through Kazumi's games list. He had quiet taste. Most of the installed games, aside from the shooter they'd been playing, were pixel RPGs. Maybe, like her, Kazumi got as much violence as he could stand from his work and didn't want to see it in his free time. In the middle of the pixel designs was the one she was looking for, a red-and-black icon shaped like a house. Under the icon was the provisionary title of their game: *Permadeath*.

Roscoe pulled her blanket tightly around her shoulders. This, she thought, was a prime example of Kazumi's character. He had the longest winning streak among the beta testers, and now he was willing to risk letting her ruin it. All to show his appreciation.

He was really the best coworker anyone could ask for. She'd have to bake him cookies for his trouble. See how long she could keep the string of thank-yous unbroken.

# 07

# HALLEY

"SHE'S PROBABLY STARING AT THE wall. That's about all she can manage this early in the morning. But you might knock just in case."

That was all the information Cal gave me before he shuffled off through the dust and darkness, toward what looked like it might be an undignified kitchen.

The ceiling creaked, and I felt the fuzz on my arms standing straight up. I didn't wait around for permission to let myself through the door Cal had indicated, and I didn't knock, either. I wasn't going to risk getting a non-answer or even a "no."

The room I entered was just as cheerless as the entry to the House. The only furniture was ten or fifteen empty cots lining the walls. Each had a tan-colored blanket and pillow that might have originally been white, and not one was properly made. The floor was hideous bare tile that was probably gray, but it looked green, and I could almost feel the cold in my feet through my thick boots. The grout between the tiles was black with mold. The air reeked of metal, which reminded me of the glue the doctor had used for Petra's prosthetic.

On the bed farthest in the corner, someone sat cross-legged, leaning against the wall.

"Why are you here?" Petra's scraping voice was unmistakable.

"The doctor—you know, my father—he wanted me to check on you." He probably would have said that if he'd been awake to think of it.

"Nothing has changed."

I scuffed my shoes, mesmerized by the cloud of dirt and debris I kicked into the air. The light from the window made pointed shadows on the floor, and I couldn't help thinking that in a strange, sad way, it was rather pretty. A reminder that nature would eventually take over the House and turn it back to the dust it came from, and we could all hope that would happen soon.

"You should get back to the village before play hours start." Even the Mercenaries, the only ones who knew the truth, had adopted the village slang of calling everything a game.

"About that . . ." I hesitated.

She'd given me the chance to leave gracefully. I could rinse that metallic taste out of my mouth with water from the stream. I'd be back in time to get breakfast—maybe I could even worm some pancakes out of Mother—and I could escape the House. Down the mountain, out in the fresh air, I was invincible. Here, I was as vulnerable as one of the fragments of dust I had stirred up.

Or I could stay and ask Petra to show me the reality behind the dream I'd had. Ask her why I'd dreamed of her hands covered in blood. Why the villagers wanted her left to die. What happened in the House, and why she'd shown up at our doorstep so horribly injured. All the things the doctor would never tell me, which I could only find out from her—the girl I'd met by coincidence, who wouldn't be here to advise me much longer.

This was my last chance to settle up with my conscience.

"The villagers were cruel last night." I twirled my hair between my fingers. "Anyone could have helped you, but they were scared to get close because you're a Merc. I want to fix things between the village and you."

An odd smile twisted Petra's lips.

"If you come back tomorrow, I'll do you one better. I won't tell you what we do. I'll show you."

"Really?" I'd expected her to make me work harder than that.

"I'd rather you heard the story from one of us. I don't know what myths you villagers tell each other, but I'm certain they don't resemble the truth. Don't be late. And don't expect to like what you hear."

"I'll be here."

I waited for her to say something else, but she didn't, and it didn't take a socialite to know that I had been cordially invited to show myself out. Thirty seconds of visiting was apparently enough for her.

Cal was leaning against the wall bordering the front door. He had acquired a bowl filled with some orange, porridge-like mush, which smelled like lighting compost on fire. I noticed something black on the back of his hand. Something symmetric and regular, a design stamped into his skin.

When he saw me staring at him, he held out the bowl. "Want some?"

I shook my head and tried not to gag. "I'm going back to town," I told him, dropping an indecisive half curtsy. "Sorry to intrude."

"I'll walk you home." He placed his bowl on the floor, apparently unconcerned about the bugs and rats and who knew what else that might sneak a taste while he was gone.

"No thanks." I edged toward the door. "I'd rather the villagers not find out I came."

"Then why come at all?" Cal laughed, a bubbly laugh that made me want to smile in spite of myself. "Didn't I hear you say something to Petra about how you want to fix things between the Mercs and the villagers? It won't work if you don't publicly associate with us."

How was I going to explain myself if someone saw us? Mother was not above cutting a switch and chasing me down the street for an offense like this. And that would be the least of my social disasters. The villagers would shun me, I'd become a pariah, and then I'd have no choice but to become a Merc myself.

Still, Cal was right. I had no reason to refuse his offer if I wanted to play diplomat.

We didn't talk at first. Cal was humming some tune, if you could call it that, which I knew was going to get stuck in my head. I tried to focus my attention on something else—the noise of our steps, the birds chirping, the rustling leaves—but nothing was going to drown out his voice or my nerves. At any moment we might be spotted. And then I'd never taste Mother's delicious soup again . . .

"When is Petra going to play her next match?" I asked, my patience worn ragged by his musically challenged humming.

"Most of us play every day," he answered, "or nearly every day. That's standard procedure in the House. But what we enjoy most is visiting the village." He looked at me with a guilty grin. "It's pleasant by comparison. Despite the glares."

It didn't seem polite to agree. *Your house is horrible. I don't know how you survive that. I wouldn't want to be you.*

"I'm using you as an excuse to get out." He laughed and skipped ahead, playful once more. I almost got a glimpse of the black mark on his hand, but he moved too quickly for me to focus on it. "You villagers don't like seeing us when we're off-duty, so I never go alone. Besides, if I were to get called into a match and not turn up, I'd be electrocuted by my chip. So I don't take the risk often."

"*What?*" I gaped. "What on earth are you doing here? Why aren't you back at the House? I don't need you to walk with me!"

He had the audacity to wink. "What would life be without a little risk?"

"Much better," I told him firmly. "Go back."

"I think you were about to ask another question."

I didn't want his untimely demise on my conscience, but it wasn't my fault that he refused the out I offered. Before he got electrocuted, I might as well make the most of this rare opportunity to cross-question a Merc.

"Why does everyone hate you?" I cleared my throat. "We see you every day. I'd think people wouldn't care anymore."

Cal stopped in the middle of the road and waited for me to catch up. "If you don't hate us, you don't know enough about us. That's why I was surprised to see you. Fancy that old geezer letting his daughter come up here alone. He must have gone senile."

The doctor's extraordinary mental powers were so self-evident that Cal's insults hardly seemed worth arguing over. "Everyone has a guess about what you do," I said, ignoring the rest. "But we're controlled by the chips too. We understand that you don't have a choice. So, why—?"

"Guess what we do? Meaning you don't know?" I detected malice behind his fixed smile. "Well, do you hate us, peacemaker?"

I knew what everyone else thought. The Mercs were supposed to be liars. Cheats. Thieves. Murderers. The list of names went on and on. Their character was so firmly rooted in public opinion that I had never thought to consult my own thoughts on the topic. Mercs were depraved. This was how things had always been, and *what has always been, always is.* So the adage went. I didn't think Cal would produce a knife while he was walking me home, but I wasn't certain enough to let my guard down.

"No one hates us," Cal continued. "But fear and hatred look the same. Everyone down there treats us like axe murderers, but it's not because they think we are. They're just afraid we might be."

"Are you?"

"I suppose you'll find out. Meanwhile, I'll be heading back to spare you the pain of watching me die by electrocution."

"Thanks." My face went hot with embarrassment, and I stammered, "For walking me, I mean. Not for leaving. I'm not thanking you for going away. I'm sorry, I'm—it's just—"

He nodded and turned to head back up the mountain, tossing me a wave over his shoulder with the inky hand. Maybe it was my imagination, but it seemed like his steps were slower this time. Reluctant, maybe.

As I turned back toward the village, mentally slapping myself for my awkwardness, my wristwatch buzzed. That meant I didn't have time to worry about Cal or Petra or what went on behind those staring windows of the House, or to reproach myself for leaving them behind. I had to run.

I took hold of my skirt and sprinted down the hill, my ankle screaming from where I'd twisted it the night before—but there were worse punishments than that. Breathless, I scurried from bush to bush, hoping I wouldn't run into either the doctor or Mother. If they happened to notice which direction I was coming from, I'd have an awful lot of explaining to do. I ducked behind walls and between houses and under shrubs until I emerged in the village square.

Everyone was already congregating, laughing and chattering as they prepared for their daily business. This was a different atmosphere from the one I'd left up the hill. It was cheerful, bright, happy, content. We didn't spend much time worrying about what went on outside our little town. After all, things had always been this way, and life was still going on. *What has always been, always is.*

I wondered if Petra was going to shatter my happy illusion. If I would ever see this place glowing and thriving again.

"There you are!" cried Mother's voice from somewhere behind me. Before I knew it, I had an apron tied around my middle and an iron ladle in my hand. "Get to your post! Quick!"

Five minutes left. Four. Three. Two.

Just as it always happened before I fell asleep at night, I could feel control over my own limbs slipping away, and my proper consciousness left my mind on autopilot and drifted away to dreamland.

One.

I opened my mouth, and my lips said: "Lemonade, one coin per cup!"

The Mercs would come to me—that was the only time Mother didn't mind that I talked to them—and drink the bitter juice I offered, reciting some programmed line about how refreshing it was. Lies, all of it. Mother made it in the cooker the day before I sold it, and it got stale overnight. I had sneaked a taste once, before I was old enough to worry about the punishment for stealing.

Ten seconds. Locked inside my mind, I sat back to watch myself work.

"Lemonade, one coin per cup!"

That evening, just like every other evening, I rinsed my sticky hands and plodded to the village square. The rankings billboard updated every night at nine o'clock, just before we were released from our tasks, and the Mercs' scores appeared on an electric sign next to the vegetable stand. Everyone checked the rankings before they went home, not because they cared, but because it gave them something to talk about. They heaved a sigh of pity for the names that had been there yesterday but were gone today, shared a few last tidbits of gossip, and went their separate ways.

That evening, though, I had to fight my way through chattering housewives to get close enough to read the numbers. I had never seen the square so jammed. Just when I was starting to wonder whether all the scuffling was worth it, I heard someone mention a familiar name.

*Petra.*

I whipped around and eavesdropped on everybody within listening distance until I spotted the source of the gossip—an old lady whose job was planting and harvesting potatoes. Her face, usually fixed in a sunburnt frown, now registered nothing but a *tch-tch* kind of surprise.

"I never would've guessed it from her," she was saying to her friend, drawling over the vowels. "I never would've thought she could do something like that. Such an unfriendly girl, too. A shame it wasn't someone more deserving. Like that lovely young man who was at the top yesterday, who buys my baked potatoes. I never would've thought—"

I shoved my way forward until I could read the board.

Cal's name had been at the top the day before, but now he was in second place. Right above him, shining white letters had a huge "#1" scrawled beside them . . .

I thought I was dreaming. I had to be dreaming, or else there was a mistake. Nobody—and by nobody, I mean not a single soul in the history of our village—had climbed from the bottom to the top of that list in a single day.

But there had to be a first time for everything. And Petra's name was up there to prove it.

# 08

## ANDY

**ANDY'S ALCOHOL TOLERANCE WAS** zero. Zilch. Nada. He'd begun feeling tipsy after his first sip of Rilo's cheap beer, and the sensation worsened as the evening progressed. The voice inside the radio didn't seem so important now. Maybe it was only a product of the alcohol, and he'd been imagining it all along. He hadn't heard it since Rilo had arrived, and he was about to stop caring.

"You should've gotten a permit for this radio." Rilo's drink slopped on Andy's shirt, but instead of feeling cold, though it had just come out of the refrigerator, it seemed to burn his skin. "Then we could have friends over and make this a party."

"You know I couldn't have gotten it approved," he grumbled. "Aliens don't exist. And nobody on earth uses a radio anymore."

Rilo's eyes shot open. "They mi-i-ight." He gestured lazily at the radio. "You might be hearing people. Or those could be aliens. You never know. You're too closed-minded."

Andy knew there was no point in trying to decipher what Rilo meant by that, if indeed he meant anything at all. They were both too far gone for rational discussions about life. But despite his haze, he couldn't deny that the words struck a chord. *Closed-minded.* People who were so set in their ways that they didn't dare change the worse ones. He wondered if he fit that description. So dedicated to what he couldn't have that he never stopped to think about what he could.

*Where exactly is your place in the world, Andy? The thing you're meant to do—what is it? Is there even such a thing as "meant to"?*

Rilo tugged Andy toward the radio. "It's all static," he complained, twisting the first knob he touched—which happened to be the volume. Andy clapped his hands over his ears.

"Get your grubby fingers off that dial," he ordered, pushing Rilo's hand away from the radio. "If you're trying to tune it, you're doing it wrong."

He lowered the volume and yelped. When he'd made that dial, he couldn't think of anything convenient to use as a knob, so he'd sawed off the bottom half of a soda can. It remained jagged around the edges. He stuck his finger in his mouth and sucked the wound irritably. If Rilo hadn't touched it, he wouldn't have had to retune it, and he wouldn't have gotten his finger cut. Conclusion: Rilo was the cause of all his problems. QED.

"Can you trace the broadcast?" Rilo hovered behind him. "Can you find out if it's aliens?"

"Aliens don't exist." After his third can of beer, Andy was only half-sure he believed that. "Don't touch the knob. That's as clear as it's going to get." He stepped back and wrapped his bleeding finger in the hem of his sleeve.

Rilo plopped down in a heap on the floor with his ear next to the speaker. "It's not working."

"That's because no one's talking." Andy rested his head against the wall. "But the static is quiet, so I know it's tuned to the right frequency. Wait, why am I explaining this to you? Don't you know—?"

"Shhhh." Rilo put a dramatic finger to his lips. "The broadcast could start any moment."

Andy was starting to regret letting him get so drunk. Now he'd have to stay overnight, which meant Andy wouldn't have a bathroom to throw up in when morning came and the hangover he could already feel looming knocked him out.

"Why did you get involved with radios in the first place?" he mumbled to himself, sliding down the wall until he was sitting, legs sprawled out before him. "You should've picked an easier hobby. Quantum mechanics. Telemetry. Rockets. Anything but radios!"

"Don't spoil the fun." Rilo, apparently bored of the static, crawled toward Andy on his hands and knees. "If you didn't have a radio, I wouldn't have a radio."

"You want a radio now, too?"

"I can't risk my job. So, if you have a radio, I have a radio. Easy as pie. Speaking of pie—"

"You're in as much trouble as me if somebody finds us," Andy interrupted crossly. "And no, we don't have any pie. Go to sleep."

Rilo coiled up obediently on the rug. Before Andy could ask if he wanted a blanket, his snores mixed with the gentle background static and the hum of traffic outside the window.

Andy glanced around the room. They'd tried to be quiet, though they couldn't help a few drunken bumps and scrapes, but Andy didn't dare take any risks. He had to hide the radio. In the event that a burglar came, or the police knocked at his door, or the building caught fire and firefighters burst into his room with a hose, at least the radio would go undetected.

He tiptoed to the bathroom and found some spare towels. He spread them over the radio, dusting it off affectionately, then knelt to disconnect the power.

But a reedy voice stopped him.

"WSG, do you read?"

Andy froze with his fingers glued to the dials.

"There's been a change in the rankings. Do you see that on your end?"

Rilo rose from the blankets, a wide-mouthed mummy. "Aliens speak *English?*"

Andy shushed him.

"This frequency is for emergency broadcasts only," the voice continued. "You are not to use it again unless you need to contact me immediately. Is that understood?"

Static.

"I can't believe it." Rilo tugged Andy's sleeve. "You were right! You really *did* hear something!"

"Shh!" Andy pleaded, pushing him away. "No noise complaints today, please."

"It's not like they'd know what it was if they found it." Rilo's voice was only getting louder. "This is the moment you've been waiting for since you first started talking about that radio. Why aren't you excited? You've done it! You've made the whole project worthwhile!"

Andy wished he could stuff Rilo's mouth with the towel he was still holding. "I *am* excited. But we shouldn't be careless until we know the broadcaster won't turn us in to SAFE."

"Sovereign . . . no . . . strategic alliance for financial . . . engagement," Rilo slurred. "Or freedom or whatever. That sounds like a bunch of dudes in suits." He slammed his fist into his palm. "I bet we could take them."

"That's not what you said when I started this project." Andy handed him a blanket and prayed he'd use it. "We'll talk in the morning."

Ignoring Rilo's objections, he tucked himself into his bed and pulled the covers over his head.

Rilo, who had never known a sleepless night, reverted easily to snoring. Andy tossed and turned for hours. The pressure in his head blossomed into a throbbing migraine, and his thoughts dissolved, growing less and less coherent. He felt like he'd be sick if he didn't sleep. Sick if he did.

*They'll find you.*

*They can't find you if your apartment doesn't get searched.*

*But what if you've been accidentally broadcasting? SAFE could trace that.*

*How on earth—or off it, for that matter—would you accidentally broadcast with a radio you made yourself that doesn't even have a microphone?*

At last he'd had enough. Rubbing his burning eyes with the back of his hand, he stumbled into the bathroom, where he'd left his sweatshirt, and pulled it over his head. On his way out, he tripped over Rilo's inert body, which had rolled from the window to the hallway. That idiot—Andy's preferred endearment—was snoring luxuriously and didn't seem to realize that he'd gotten separated from his blanket. Andy gave him a comradely shove out of the way, earning a sleepy snort in return, then left, locking the front door behind him.

Andy was on a first-name basis with everyone who worked the convenience store shift from midnight to eight. A few of them had asked what kept him up so late, and he told them the truth: that he was an astronomer working on his telescope. He left out the part about how he had been trained as a radio astronomer before that kind of research was banned, and that his "telescope" was a radio he'd managed to build out of spare parts he'd stolen from the observatory. They probably would have written him off as a psychopath. Or called the cops to have him arrested for operating illegal equipment.

But what they didn't know couldn't hurt them, and tonight's clerk—a young man with friendly eyes and a bright smile—greeted him as though he'd been waiting all night for Andy's arrival.

"It's great to see you again!" he chirped. "Is there anything I can help you find?"

Andy couldn't place the man's face. *Is he new, or am I still drunk?*

"Nice to meet . . . I mean, see you," he stumbled, looking up at the ceiling, pretending he'd seen a bug. "The store looks different tonight."

"We've rearranged," the clerk agreed. "The ramen's in the back now."

He disappeared into the break room, and Andy wandered through the aisles, hoping he could fool anyone who happened to be watching into thinking he was buying ramen as an afterthought. He wasn't proud of the eating habits he'd developed as a bachelor, and the remnants of alcohol in his bloodstream convinced him that the convenience store staff were judging him. For what or why, he didn't know. There were probably plenty of judgment-worthy things to notice.

He picked up a pack of fluffy donuts as a decoy, then zipped over to the ramen section. Then, shifting the donuts from hand to hand, he lurked between the chips and the cookies, waiting for the clerk.

He paced and read all the labels on the gum packets ("Teeth whitening!" "Overcome your nicotine addiction!" "Not FDA approved!"), and still the clerk didn't come back. He rocked back and forth from his toes to his heels, studied his reflection in the window, jogged up and down the front of the store, picked up and put down a hundred snacks, hummed along with the dusty song that tinkled though the ceiling speakers. Still nothing.

He pulled his phone out of his pocket, balancing his ramen and donuts on his left arm, and scrolled through his messages. He hadn't checked them in days, and his notifications were clogged with old news articles, spam emails, and advertisements. Impatiently, he swiped these away. *Into the junk bin with you, you, and you!* Out with the old advertisements for things he didn't need and in with the new for things he also didn't need.

There was only one recent text message. From 3:05 a.m., ten minutes ago.

Sender: Rilo Walsh.

Andy grinned. Rilo was the type to notice that he was gone and panic like he'd witnessed the Second Coming. "Did the Rapture happen? Did aliens come? Where are you, man?" Andy could practically hear his whiny voice all the way from his apartment. He clicked on the message.

Rilo: Sorry, Andy.

What a definite, startling period. Andy's face tightened into a frown.

He glanced at the clock on the wall. Two more minutes. If the clerk didn't come, Andy would leave.

The second hand seemed to take forever to make its weary journey around the clock face. *One, two, three . . .* Andy tried to stop himself from counting, but he couldn't switch off his brain. *Twenty, twenty-one . . .*

He abandoned the donuts and ramen on the closest shelf and left the store. The bell attached to the door tinkled merrily as he rushed down the street, his breath forming a cloud in front of his face.

*In the morning, I'll make Rilo buy me ramen and donuts. To pay for scaring me.*

He walked so quickly that the wind burned his eyes, and he could feel the tears freezing to his eyelashes. It was only October, too early for snow, but plenty soon enough for the wind to whip through the city and make some poor passersby miserable. A plastic bag wafted across the sidewalk in front of his shoes, making Andy jump to avoid it. Who knew what it had touched before it had ended up here. As he fumbled to balance himself, he stepped into a true Seattle puddle and soaked his ankles.

*Just my luck.*

Ten minutes later, he bounded up the stairs to his apartment and opened the door.

Then he paused, still squeezing the handle. He'd locked that door before he left.

He tiptoed forward, starting when the floor creaked under his feet. A beam of orange light filtered through his curtains, reflecting off the lump of white blankets piled on the floor in the hallway. They were suspiciously flat. Andy kicked the pile, but there was nobody inside.

His attention was caught by something moving in the corner of his eye. It was his curtains, fluttering in the wind. The window behind them was open, flooding the room with freezing nighttime air. Andy hadn't cracked it in years.

His first thought was to check the radio, which he had left underneath the window. It was still covered by the towels, and nothing had been moved. How had Rilo gotten by without disturbing them?

Andy pressed his shoulder against the pile of radio equipment and, tennis shoes scraping the floor, slid it out of the way. Stumbling over the field of tangled wires, he peeked out into the street. If Rilo had recently left through the front door, he should have remained visible. But Andy didn't see anything moving. Even the traffic that usually flowed all night long seemed to have ebbed. It was like staring at an empty stage. There should have been something, some trace of activity somewhere. But there wasn't.

Directly below him was a bright red car, an attractive color amid the nighttime shadows. The roof was crisscrossed with a strangely shaped splotch. Could it be one of the trees lining the street, reflected off the roof? They didn't seem to be in the right position relative to the nearby streetlight to produce a shadow that looked like that.

A shadow that looked like . . . a man?

Andy sucked in his breath.

Across the roof, draped like a child's forgotten stuffed animal, lay Rilo's motionless body.

# 09

## HALLEY

**A SHRIEK OF EXULTATION BUILT IN MY** throat. I could barely stop myself from grabbing the closest grandma and squeezing her in a hug. I wanted to run all the way back up the mountain just so I could congratulate Petra, but I didn't dare try something so brazen in front of the entire village. So I hustled home and burst through the front door, eager to share the news with whoever would listen. I knew the doctor would be proud that his prosthetic had not only helped Petra survive, but also raise her rank so dramatically. And I couldn't wait to be the first to tell him.

Mother poked her head out from around the kitchen wall and shushed me before I could open my mouth.

"Your father wants to talk to you," she said sternly.

My throat tightened. Had they discovered that I'd gone to the House that morning? I glanced around the kitchen to see if she'd gotten out the broom, but it was still safely tucked away in the pantry.

There was nothing to do but confront this, whatever it turned out to be. I tapped on the doctor's door and entered his office.

He was sitting at his desk, facing the window, his back turned to me. There was no hope of reading his face to see if he was angry or concerned or both or neither. With a gentle *click*, the door closed, and I seated myself in his fluffy, velvet armchair.

His pen scratched noisily on a notepad.

I waited, getting more uncomfortable with each infinite second. I thought he was going to make me sit there forever and reflect on my sins, and though that might have been an effective punishment, I was desperate for it to be over already.

Just when I thought I couldn't stand it any longer, he turned his chair around.

"I received disciplinary measures because of what I did for Petra," he told me, as if I'd know what that meant. "I was also told that you went to the House."

"Oh." I gulped. Who besides Cal or Petra could have seen me?

"You don't need to worry about the discipline because it doesn't directly affect you. But you need to realize that we're being watched. And you shouldn't go stirring up trouble by visiting that girl when she's not in the Alliance's good books."

"I just wanted to make sure she was alright."

"So did I. And look where that got us."

I had difficulty commiserating. I had no idea what the "disciplinary measures" were, and it didn't seem like he was planning to tell me, and nobody had come along with a scythe and axed us yet—so all things considered, it didn't seem like much was wrong. Still, I could tell he was disturbed. I wished it hadn't been my fault.

"I'm sorry." For causing trouble, though not for what I had done. "She had a major operation, and I guess she's scared, and maybe it hurts. She can't even come see you for a checkup without upsetting the Alliance. Why shouldn't I be a messenger?"

"How did you grow up to be so naïve?"

Perhaps he thought that would shut me up, but my body stiffened with irritation. "You kept me away from the House, and you refused to tell me what happens there. All I've heard are whispers from the village grandmothers. There's no one my age for me to ask who's not a Merc already. There's nobody I can get information from but you, and you won't tell me a thing."

His eyes fixed blankly on the desk in front of him.

"I don't understand the reason for the restrictions," I added, worried by his silence. Maybe I had been too blunt. "I don't even know what they are. I don't have the seven hundred pages of rules memorized. Why do I have to live by a book I can't even read?"

I always cried when I got frustrated, but the conversation would be over the moment I let my tears show, so I pretended to have something stuck in my eye and tugged at the corners to dry them.

"You want freedom?" he said at last. "You already have all the freedom Maria and I can give you."

"You're not free yourselves."

"Why haven't you said anything about this before?"

Because Mother cut me off whenever I tried to bring it up. Because I'd been afraid I'd find out some horrible secret. Because I hadn't wanted the neighbors to think I was crazy. Because everyone seemed to assume that I already knew.

"I . . ." I fumbled my words. "I didn't think you'd tell me."

"Haven't Maria and I always said you can come to us about anything?"

"Then will you tell me what goes on in the House?"

Usually he answered with some variant of "I'll tell you when you're older," or "You're too young to be worrying about that." Maybe it had finally occurred to him that I was older now.

"You'll be putting yourself in danger."

"Why?"

"You said it yourself. Without knowledge, we can't change the way things are. We're not supposed to change anything, so we're not supposed to have knowledge. If you're caught, I can't guarantee that you won't be forced to become a Merc. And . . ." He adjusted a paperweight on his desk instead of looking at me. "You're a strong girl. But you wouldn't last an hour in the House."

"Who would catch me?"

He leaned forward. "We're under surveillance since what happened with Petra."

I was about to suggest that we go for a walk, but he beckoned me to come nearer. I bent my head to him.

"I don't know what piqued your curiosity about all this," he whispered. "I'm giving you permission to investigate. You may be the only one of us who can. Just be careful. And don't tell Maria I said this, not even if she nags you. She'll worry."

His smile was half-hearted.

"An old man like me would be a more serious concern to the Alliance," he continued softly. "If I got involved, they'd have me killed. You might be able to slip by unnoticed. And the consequences if you're caught might, maybe, be less severe."

As I straightened, he rolled his desk chair back, a frown gathering on his forehead.

"I forbade you to visit the House, and you went anyway," he thundered, as loudly as his gentle voice could manage. "I have no choice but to ground you outside of work hours."

Clever old doctor. I returned his frown with a grin.

"Yes, sir. I'm sorry. I was wrong."

"You're putting your family in jeopardy with your actions." This time I could tell he meant the words. "Think about what you're doing."

"I will." I meant to keep that promise, but I felt so light I could barely breathe. "Thank you!"

"Go. You're *grounded*, you hear me? You won't be leaving the house except for work."

I jumped up. "Yes, sir!"

I hadn't been out of his office for ten seconds before I found myself standing in the kitchen, a broom in my hands, with orders from Mother not to budge until she could see her reflection in the floor. I started to protest, but it occurred to me that obeying was the least I could do after all the trouble I had caused. So I swept diligently, focusing on my work to shut out the nervous thoughts that crowded into my mind, and stole scraps from the counter whenever she left the kitchen. The work was light, and the food refreshed me.

*Maybe I can do this*, I thought, dancing around my broom, pretending to be the girl from the fairy story my mother used to tell me. Cinder-Halley. This was a silly little game that I should have abandoned in childhood, just a way of making my chores more bearable. But now, it gave me hope. *Maybe I can be the adventurer my village never had. Ask the questions no one ever did.*

An hour later, I peeked out the window to find Mother chatting with the neighbor. Her hands were swirling around her head, and her friend was laughing. When they got like this, they could go on gabbing for hours. Mother would forget all about me, and when she came home, she'd be in a good mood, likely to overlook any little shortcomings I had displayed in her absence.

I left the broom in the pantry and headed for the House.

With my ankle feeling better, and with the relief that came with the doctor's approval, I made short work of the climb. Running uphill was so far beyond my abilities I might as well have tried to fly, but I was always late for everything, and I had mastered the art of speed-walking.

"Didn't expect to see *you* today," someone shouted.

I squinted and held up my hand to shade my eyes. Despite the chilly evening breeze, someone—two someones, actually—were sitting on the patch of grass on the left side of the House. That angular silhouette and those flashing blue lights along the arm were Petra's. And the person next to her, with the telltale peek of red at the neck, had to be Cal.

The former best and worst Mercs. Now, there was an unlikely friendship.

"Did the doctor send you back to check on Petra?" Cal waved me over to join them, and I complied, eager to be off the road before the blinding sunset was replaced with darkness. "Twice in one day. He sure does take a lot of interest in her." Conspiratorial wink.

Petra's gaze flitted away from mine like our eyes were similar poles of a magnet, and she ran a hand over her rumpled black hair. Bits of grass floated onto her shirt.

"You should have waited," she said. "There was something I wanted to show you."

Cal clicked his tongue. "You weren't planning to show her around the House, were you?"

"Do you think she'll take our word for it otherwise?"

"Why shouldn't she?" Cal returned. "You of all people should know that some things are best left to the imagination."

She didn't answer.

"Look," I began, clearing my throat, "I don't know anything about you. I don't know why this place exists, or who the Alliance is, or what they want with us, or what happens in the House. I'll believe you, but I'd prefer to see for myself."

"Are we a charity case?" His tone implied that he didn't quite mean that, but his expression was hardly encouraging. "Well, you're the kind of person who's bound to find out. The Alliance will conscript you if you talk like that."

"Cal!" Petra reprimanded.

He raised his hands. "Fine. Enjoy your lofty ideals. But I think Halley already knows what goes on inside the House and she just wants someone to tell her if it's true. What have you heard?" Condescension oozed from every lazy syllable. "Or should I say, what lies are the villagers spreading?"

"They say you fight each other." My voice dwindled. "They say that sometimes you . . . you kill each other. That's the role the Alliance assigned. Nobody's blaming you for it, or if they are, they shouldn't be. We all know you can't help it, and we know you'd never hurt any of the villagers, not intentionally, but—"

"Then why are you here?" Petra interrupted. "You'd be a brave girl indeed if you came alone and unarmed to a house full of killers."

"I'll tell you why," Cal remarked, eyes leveled at me. "Halley knows that what she said might be true. But she won't believe it, not even subconsciously, because if she did, she'd have to intervene or live her whole life knowing she's partly responsible for the deaths of the people she didn't stop us from killing. Pretty selfish! Pretending to despise us so you don't have to bother feeling guilty for letting us continue to exist."

I'd never hated anyone as bitterly as I hated Cal at that moment. I wanted to choke him, strike him, force him to take back what he'd said.

Because, of course, he was right.

"The upper floors of the House are locked outside of match hours," Cal said. "There's no way you could come inside unless you played hooky from your lemonade stand. I don't know how Petra was planning to circumvent the security measures."

"Can't we at least try her hand on the sensor? Maybe a villager could get through."

"She was curious enough to come inside. She's got some pluck, I'll give her that." He crossed his arms and grinned. "But after I let her in, I thought she was going to be sick. And so I doubt her dainty nose can handle the stench of reality."

"Don't speak to her like that," Petra snapped.

"I'll come," I said quickly. It was hardly a choice. If I turned back now, I'd prove what Cal had said about me.

Petra's response was interrupted by a buzz from somewhere in Cal's coat pocket.

He groaned. "And here I thought I'd have a relaxing evening." He got grudgingly to his feet, offering me a mock salute. "Duty calls, as it always does at the worst-possible moment."

"Where are you going?" I asked.

"I thought you said you knew."

"Wait!" Petra was also on her feet, wavering to find her balance on the gentle slope. "It's after hours. Look at Halley, she's not even on duty. Why should you go?"

"Do you want to find out what happens if I don't?"

"I never said that."

"Then don't try to stop me."

The flashing blue lights on her prosthetic arm sped up. I remembered what the doctor had told me once, that they were synced with the wearer's heart rate, since the pulse couldn't be read on a damaged arm.

"Come back safe."

"I will," he said gruffly. "I always do." He turned toward me. "Are you coming?"

I shifted my gaze off Petra's arm. "Coming where?"

"You said you wanted to see what we do."

"You said I couldn't."

"Cal," Petra began, "maybe now isn't the right time. Especially when we don't know why you were called after hours. Maybe you were right about—"

"It's up to Halley."

It wasn't. It never had been. If I didn't go, they'd send me away for good, and I'd never learn the truth.

My neck muscles tightened when I nodded, as if to hold me back. My instincts knew what I stubbornly wouldn't admit: that I was going to regret this, that I was no hero, and that I didn't belong.

"Come on, then." Cal resumed his climb up the hill.

"Cal!" Petra shouted at our backs. "Shouldn't we tell her first?"

He waved at her and kept going.

"Cal?" I asked tentatively. "Should we wait?"

"The biological scanner will shock her if she tries to enter the upper floors without being enlisted for a match. She can't come with us."

"Cal!" she yelled again, and there was a shrill edge to her voice. "Alright, you've convinced me! I changed my mind! Can't you see? What more do you want me to say? Do you always have to prove you're right?"

I stopped. "What's she talking about?"

He grabbed my wrist. "You wanted to find out what we do here—well, you will." There was no amusement in his expression now. "Petra's trying to protect you. I'm going to show you the truth. Isn't that what you said you wanted?"

# 10

## ROSCOE

**KAZUMI'S CONTROLLER WAS TOO BIG** for Roscoe's hands. And where Kazumi's playing had been miraculously skilled, hers was miraculously awful. The more she played, the worse she got. Waves of self-consciousness washed over her like a cold bath and made her palms sweat.

Kazumi was nothing but encouraging. "There's a guard over there." "You might be able to sneak through that gap." "I discovered a vent in that room the other day." Roscoe tried to follow his advice, knowing she'd probably win if she did, but her reactions were sluggish, and Kazumi's avatar was losing HP with every mistake.

Finally, she returned his controller. "I'm sorry," she told him, trying to hide her embarrassment with a laugh. "I don't want to kill your avatar."

"Actually, in one of the developer meetings last week, one of the other beta testers said that it might be hard to attract new players because of how steep the learning curve is for this game. It's not just you—it's everyone. And losing avatars is perfectly normal. That's how the game got its name, after all. *Permadeath*. Kind of has a ring to it."

"The game is so . . ." Roscoe didn't want to sound prudish. "It's so realistic. The guards act like they can hear my character's footsteps, and there's no safe distance because they're all a little different. Sometimes my avatar makes a mistake. She trips or drops something or slams a door a little too loudly, and the guards react. I can't stop it. It just happens. Things don't work like they do in a normal video game."

"That's what makes Warsafe Games unique. We're on the cutting edge of technology. Realism is our specialty."

Roscoe liked how he spoke as if Warsafe was a team. It had been a long time since she'd felt like she was on the inside, but maybe there was a chance she could get back there. She managed a self-conscious smile.

"That's not the only cool thing about us, though," Kazumi added. "It seems Warsafe has a trade secret."

"What's that?" Roscoe sat up, intrigued.

"You know how we had to get those SAFE-approved ID badges to get inside the programmer offices?"

Roscoe nodded.

"Didn't you ever wonder why?"

"I figured it was just because the SAFE badges are manufactured to a standard quality. And maybe the programmers know some of Warsafe's trade secrets. I'm sure the company doesn't want proprietary information getting out."

"Maybe that's part of it, but there's more. I heard that Warsafe has a government contract now. I don't know the details, but it sounds like they might have people in the company working on that project without knowing it. Which means some of us could be spies."

"Spies?" Roscoe had to laugh. "CIA, here I come! I know my résumé doesn't say I have any experience with, uh, spy stuff, but I worked at Warsafe Games, so you know what *that* means. Oh, yes, that sounds legit."

"I'm serious." Kazumi was grinning too. "But you can't tell anyone I told you. I don't think I was supposed to know."

She settled back into the sofa. "Well, you can't just leave the story there. What kind of 'government project' is it?"

He thought for a moment. "I overheard a one-sided conversation, so take the details with a grain of salt. It sounded like they're working on something similar to that old *America's Army* game, but for virtual reality."

"Never heard of that."

"A.A. was put out by the U.S. Army. Sort of like *Call of Duty*. They thought that getting the kiddos excited about playing the game would make them sign up to join the army in real life." He raised an eyebrow. "It worked about as well as you'd expect."

"Why remake it, then?"

"This new project is supposed to be more like a simulator. It would tell the player how well they'd handle real-life combat. And it could identify their strengths and weaknesses. Say they're good at coming up with strategy, but bad at executing it. And if the person played often enough, they'd get desensitized to violence, theoretically making them better-suited for a military career."

"Sounds like you're invested." She didn't add that his enthusiasm was contagious, and she was starting to feel a bit less like a lowly tester and more like a super-secret highly classified secret soldier. Or agent. Whatever. "How'd you find out? That didn't make the gossip rounds."

A sly grin appeared on his face. "I happened to walk by someone's office at the right moment. It's amazing that Warsafe has the technology for a project like this, don't you think? You and I started off with some glitchy old version of Windows."

"True. But I'd still rather work on something lower down the chain," she admitted. "There's so much to worry about with this game because of all the details, and it's exhausting to play all day."

Kazumi's brows furrowed. "I'm sorry. I shouldn't have made you watch me for so long."

"No, no!" Roscoe regretted her tactlessness. "It's not that. It's just . . . well, it's like watching an action movie over and over. It takes energy."

"You don't like the violence?"

"I guess not."

He looked at her curiously. "Then why work at Warsafe? We've been making shooters since the Sega days."

Roscoe sighed. "I love how realistic Warsafe's art is. When I was little, I watched my brothers play their games, and I tried to draw the characters. Working at Warsafe seemed like a dream come true when I thought I'd be working in design. But now I'm not sure I'm cut out for it."

"You're a good artist. Why did you switch to beta testing?"

*Because of you, moron.* "I made a mistake and took a demotion. I had a few applications in at other studios, but nothing came of them."

He nodded. "I understand. But I hope you don't leave. It's nice having you on the team."

"I hope I don't either." For a moment, she meant it.

Kazumi unplugged his console from Roscoe's TV. "It's getting late. I should head home." Roscoe thought she detected a hint of regret in his tone. "Thanks for inviting me. I'm sorry I hogged your console, but this was fun. We should do it again."

"And I'm sorry I almost killed your avatar," Roscoe replied with a self-deprecating smile.

"Don't worry about it," Kazumi assured her, sliding his controllers back onto his console. "I was ready to mess around with something new. I'll probably finish that one off tomorrow and make another."

He promised he'd bring coffee next time she showed up to work, in exchange for her hospitality. And then he was gone, hurrying down the stairs to his car, before she could thank him. Not that her thoughts were moving at high speed. To Roscoe, the whole day already seemed like a dream.

She glanced at her watch. It was after eleven o'clock, and the game was supposed to be closed to beta testing after nine. She had just returned Kazumi's controller about ten minutes ago. Odd. But that was a mystery for another day. And it was going to be another day all too soon if she stayed up much later.

Feeling suddenly weary, she collapsed on her sofa, taking in the rosy scent of her pillows, a hug against her hot cheeks.

As she burrowed deeper into their fluffiness, something felt unexpectedly solid. Sitting up, she dug through the pillows until she found something that felt like plastic. She held it up to the light.

It was a rectangular black box, about the size of a cell phone but without a screen. There was a little folding antenna tucked into the side and an unmarked dial on the front. A piece of crumpled notebook paper was taped over the short edge.

The proper thing to do would be to leave it untouched and send Kazumi a text to let him know he'd dropped something. But curiosity would never let her be so passive. Almost before she could think, she was unfolding the paper and trying to read the pencil scribblings. Half the writing was smudged as though it had been in Kazumi's pocket for a long time, but she could still make out a set of coordinates. She recognized the format of the numbers, but who used those nowadays? Coordinates were the stuff of pirate treasure maps.

There was a blue button under the paper. She pressed it, and the box hissed, a quiet, staticky sound that reminded Roscoe of older technology that wouldn't work right. The sound was comforting and nostalgic, a calm background noise like the patter of rain or the rush of a river. Maybe the device was a noisemaker. Absently, she played with the blue button, turning the static on and off several times in succession.

Her lights flicked off as they always did at midnight. But the room didn't go dark. Red and blue flashed outside her window, sending crazed shadows across her ceiling that made her eyes hurt. Annoyed, she got up and peeked outside. Ambulance lights. And police lights, and fire truck lights, and bobbing flashlights and headlamps.

Irritated, she whisked the curtains closed and reached over to her nightstand to set the alarm on her phone, not bothering to get ready for bed. She was too tired.

Eight and a half hours of peace, and then it would all start over again.

# 11

# HALLEY

"TAKE THIS." CAL HELD OUT A SHORT black knife, hilt-first. His palms were encased in gloves that had the fingers cut off, and he had the knife by its blade. "Actually, forget it. You won't need a weapon." He flicked it closed and placed it into the pocket by his knee.

I wasn't so sure. The scoreboard had once ranked Cal at number one among the Mercs, but I didn't think he had ever played with someone else before. Especially not someone who was probably going to be useless baggage.

That aside, we'd skipped right over the important thing.

"Why would I need a knife?" I squeaked, edging back against the wall. It was too late to escape. Cal had locked us both into a small square room, devoid of furniture or windows or air vents or electric lights. If I panicked, I had the wild idea that I might be able to break through the wall as a last resort. Maybe.

"What you *will* need," he said, ignoring my question, "is this." He pulled the bandanna free from his neck. "Put this over your face. Make sure you cover as much as you can. We don't want anyone recognizing you."

Numbly, I obeyed.

"Now, then." He tugged his gloves. "Shall we?"

"Cal," I stammered, "where are we going? What are we doing? What is—"

A previously invisible door suddenly opened in the wall, letting a sliver of blessed light penetrate the dimness. It was so brilliant that I had to peer through my fingers until my eyes adjusted, and by then, Cal was already halfway down the hall. Straight and narrow, with windows on one side and another light bulb at the end, it stretched onward like a gaping throat.

He held his finger to his lips. "All you have to do," he said in a low voice, "is stay behind me. Don't bother being quiet." His finger tapped against the pocket that held his knife. "And don't repeat anything about this to Petra or anyone else. If you do . . ."

"Yes, yes, okay, whatever you say." I whispered quickly. "Where are we going? What are you looking for? What are we—"

I gaped. Cal's back arched like something had yanked him to the ground, and he fell backward with an echoing *thwack* against the floor. My forward momentum was too much for me to stay balanced. With a small cry, I stumbled over his prone body and careened into the wall, smashing headfirst into what looked like a glass windowpane. Cal's face contorted, and he threw his arms out in front of him, as though he was making a tremendous effort to lift a weight off his chest. His right fist was clenched around nothing, but he swung it down toward his chest and stopped abruptly about eight inches away. Stars danced in front of my eyes, but I saw beads of sweat form on his forehead. With a final heave, he rolled himself over to his front and repeated the peculiar motion with his wrist.

He let his head drop. Gasping for breath, he stayed balanced on his elbows for a few seconds. I blinked, trying to clear my head—since when had there been fireflies in this hallway? When the glowing spots in my vision finally congealed into one electric light, he was on his feet and extending a hand to me.

"What did you see?" he asked, wiping the back of his hand across his forehead and flicking a few stray pieces of hair out of his eyes. "Not much, I hope."

He tried to pull me up, but my legs had turned gelatinous.

"Come on," he said, with a touch of good-humored mockery.

"We're ten feet down the first hallway, and there are eight more floors. If you'll excuse me, I'd rather spend my evening with Petra."

"What was that?"

"What was what?"

"That." I waved my finger in the general direction of his . . . seizure. "What were you doing?"

"That," he said, "was a man about my height, with brown hair and eyes, blue uniform pants and a white shirt, and a shiv."

"A what?"

Faster than I could blink, he had the knife out of his pocket and balanced in his palm. "A knife. A shiv's a knife. Even you should know that."

"But I . . ." Maybe this was what a brain hemorrhage felt like. Or maybe I was psychotic. The doctor's neuropsychology textbook would probably have something to say about the current state of my brain—at least, I hoped it did. I hoped none of this was real. "There was . . . I didn't see . . ." I gestured vaguely at the floor. "There was nothing there! Nothing. You and I were alone in this room the whole time."

"Something knocked me down, didn't it?" He folded the knife with a *click*. "Or do you think this is all just a pageant?"

He jabbed his fingers into the top of his jacket and tugged it down, exposing his collarbone. It was sliced from one end to the other with a dark, shining line. Blood dripped down his chest, disappearing into his shirt.

"He tried to kill me." Cal opened his right glove, clean and empty, and pressed his left fist downward toward it. Six inches away, it stopped, and a red mark appeared in his palm. "So I killed him."

I stepped closer to examine the wound on his neck, my instincts as the doctor's daughter triggered by the blood, but he flicked his collar back into place and turned away.

"Maybe you got that when you fell?" I suggested weakly.

"They're lasers." Apparently my suggestion wasn't even intelligent enough to refute. "High-frequency light. Can damage human tissue. Visible if you have the right optics embedded in your eyes. Which you villagers don't."

Cal dropped to his hands and knees and crawled down the hallway. I crouched timidly behind him. He'd said not to worry. He'd said not to even bother being quiet, but he'd said an awful lot of things, and some of them were beyond the bounds of sanity.

Before we reached the white bulb in the room at the opposite end, he opened a side door and motioned for me to enter. I peeked around the corner. Of course there was no one, not that I could see. There wouldn't have been much space for them. This was a tiny bathroom with a decrepit toilet in one corner, an adjacent tub with a shower, the door to what I presumed was a closet on the other side, and a shattered porcelain sink that revealed the plumbing underneath.

Cal was getting impatient, and he pushed me inside before my eyes adjusted enough to see into the darkest corners. He darted in behind me and shut the door. Much to my relief, he didn't immediately crumple over the way he would have if we'd been ambushed. Instead, he hoisted himself onto the toilet and reached for a vent in the ceiling.

"Not so glamorous now, is it?" Cal balanced himself with one foot on the toilet paper holder and the other on the toilet tank lid. "Bet you thought it was going to be chandeliers and glitzy wallpaper all the way."

It had been about an hour since I'd had a comprehensible thought, but I couldn't formulate the words to say that aloud. There was no telling what we'd find on the next floor, and I decided to sit on what was left of the counter and catch my breath.

The vent squeaked as he pried it free from the ceiling, scraping against one of the screws he hadn't fully loosened. He stiffened, glancing over his shoulder as though he expected someone to come barreling through the door.

"Halley," he murmured, lips motionless, "get into the shower. Cover your head."

The cold porcelain chilled through my clothes as I crouched, shaking, in the corner of the tub.

A long wail of hinges caught my attention, and I lifted my head just enough to see over the edge of the tub. The bathroom door was opening. All by itself.

Cal leapt down from the toilet like a cat, and he landed above the floor. For a split second, he hovered there, his arms coiled tightly around nothing, until the nothing broke loose and shoved him into the closet door. The wood splintered and cracked behind him. I was close enough to see his pupils dilate. His breath caught in his throat, and his eyelids drifted shut.

But only for a moment. The next, he had them open again. He dived away from the door, tugging shards of wood free with him, and leaped onto the countertop. His fist was raised again, but in a different shape this time. His index finger was pointed outward, his thumb cocked high above it. He was holding a gun—at least, he thought he was, though I couldn't see it. Pointing it right at me, pointing it at the tile above my head, shaking, wobbling, drifting back and forth.

I squeezed my eyes shut.

When I opened them again, his arms had fallen to his sides. He slid down against the mirror, and a streak of blood remained on the glass.

"Cal!" I shrieked. My feet slipped on the smooth enamel. "What happened?"

"That door happened," he wheezed. "Got a shard of it in my . . . I hope you aren't squeamish. You're going to have to help me if we're"—he coughed, burying his face in his collar—"if we're going to get out of here."

"Help you? Me?" My eyes went wide. "No, no, not me. We have to get you to the village. To the doctor. You've probably got a collapsed lung. Or a punctured artery. That's a lot of blood. No, I can't help you. How could I help you? What could I—?"

He handed me a syringe from somewhere in his cavernous pockets.

"I'm afraid of needles," he told me, his face grave. "Can you inject this?"

I burst out laughing. And crying and breathing, and breathing too much, and I was going to scream, and if someone didn't stop me I was going to stab myself with the needle—where did the pointy end go? Had I dropped it already? Cal was going to regret asking me to help him, we were never going to get out of here, we were stuck forever, we were—

Something brushed my fingers, and I felt the syringe leave my hand. I fumbled to catch it, but Cal had already plunged it into his thigh.

"Ouch," he remarked ruefully, and for some reason that set me off again.

He pinched my arm. "Halley. Look at me."

I still had an ounce of pride. I refused to let him see my teary eyes, even if most of my face was covered by his bandanna.

"I'm going to get you out. So calm down. You're not in danger."

"Cal," I urged, "you shouldn't do anything for me. You should just leave me. You should get yourself out. You should—"

"I signed my death warrant just by bringing you here." From the corners of my blurry eyes, I saw his expression soften into a smile. A very sane smile, rimmed at the corners with red. "I knew that. Don't make me regret it. Focus. We have seven floors to go."

"You can't die because of me," I choked. "You can't. I could never face Petra. I could never face myself. I'm not like you, Cal. I don't see this every day. I've never seen anything like this. How could you think I'd be able to do anything for you?"

His arms crept around my shoulders, and he pulled me into an awkward hug that jammed my stomach against the granite countertop. I cried into his shoulder, trying to forget that the sharp little things poking my face were shards of the wooden door buried in his chest.

"If I die, it will be because God has decided I'm ready, so you don't have to worry about it being your fault. Now, Halley." He eased me back, hands on my shoulders. "If I sit here any longer, I'm going to fall asleep. And then we'll be in real trouble. So let's go. Let's make it to the roof."

He pulled me up through the vent by my wrists. He had to, or I would have stayed in that bathroom, catatonic. His chest rasped, and he was struggling to stifle his coughs, but with tremendous effort he succeeded in yanking me into the air ducts. He screwed it shut behind us.

Huddled against the metal walls, jammed into a space that was much too small for both of us, I watched through glazed, burning eyes. Every so often, something clicked. Drops of blood, striking the floor of our prison. They collected in a pool by Cal's shoes as he worked. I tried to pick up the rhythm between drops. It seemed to my hazy brain that it was getting slower.

"And we're off," Cal declared. He glanced at me as I stared at the narrow duct. "It's all right, Halley. The first part is always the worst."

My shoulders scraped the sides as we squirmed like rats through the air-conditioning system. My hands were coated with dust and a tinge of Cal's blood, leaving sticky prints on everything I touched. The texture of the metal under my fingertips made my teeth ache.

We passed ten or twenty intersections in the ductwork, none of which caused Cal a moment of hesitation. Then he stopped beside a spot of pale white light. Before my muscles had time to stiffen, he had unscrewed a vent that opened into an exterior room and heaved himself, then me, through it. I emerged with a gasp like a drowning swimmer.

He looked around the room and nodded, satisfied.

"That wasn't so bad, was it?" he asked as he replaced the vent cover. "You're a real Merc now. We navigate vents all the time. It's the only way to get between floors without having to attack the guards on the main stairs."

I squeaked out some nonsense.

With a ragged sigh, he seated himself against the wall. I sank down beside him.

"Are you squeamish, really?" he asked. "I could use some help if you aren't."

"I'm the doctor's daughter," I replied bravely.

His eyes twinkled. "That wasn't a 'no'."

"I'm not squeamish." I had a feeling we were about to find out.

"Then would you pull the shard out of my back?"

"That . . . no, no, I won't." The doctor's textbook said something about this, and I remembered the one time I had impaled myself on a particularly long and vicious blackberry thorn. Never had my hypochondriasis come in so handy. "If I take it out, the wound will bleed more. And if your lung is punctured, you could suffocate. I think. I don't know. I'm the doctor's daughter, not the doctor, and we need to get you to him."

He winced and gingerly crossed his arms over his chest. "The painkillers didn't do a thing. We'd better hurry."

"If I could see them, those people . . ." I'd try to help. I'd try to keep watch. I'd try to defend myself so at least he wouldn't have to worry about me.

"I'm glad you can't." Bracing himself against the wall, he got himself to his feet, and then magnanimously offered a hand to me. I declined it. He seemed so precariously balanced that the slightest change in weight might knock him over. I stood on my own. "Whatever you're seeing must be horrible enough, but you'd better thank God you don't have Petra's eyes. Or mine."

I offered my shoulder for him to lean on, and with my assistance he limped toward the door.

"Why?" I asked. "What's the purpose of this . . ." I couldn't think of a word besides the one the villagers always used. "Why do you play this game? Who are these invisible people, and why are you killing them?"

His laugh went short and sharp. "This is how things have always been."

"Why?"

"If I don't play the game, my chip will electrocute me. Now you know as much about it as I do. If only I could—"

The impact came from behind. He stumbled forward, crashing face-first into the wall, then whirled himself aside just in time for something invisible to form a dent in the drywall where he had just been leaning. He fell hard on his back. He struggled, but he didn't get up.

"Where are you?" I screamed. I held my arms out in front of me, thrashing at the air, searching for something I could neither hear nor feel nor see. "Leave him alone!"

Invisible pressure forced the air from his lungs in a cough. He rolled to the side and slashed his wrist sideways. Once, twice, three times. Then he brought it down, but it halted abruptly six inches from the floor. His grip slackened, and his hand fell.

And I was alone with Cal's seemingly lifeless body.

Pulse. That's what you should always check first. I knew that much. I placed my fingers lightly over his wrist. Nothing. I wrapped them around and pinched and squeezed, but there was no movement under my fingertips. I tugged at his collar and put my hands to his neck. There it was—thin and thready, but there.

He was going to hate me for this. I took a deep breath, raised my hand, and slapped him hard across the cheek.

"Cal!" I shouted. "Wake up! Can you hear me? Wake up!"

His eyelids twitched.

"You can't stay here!" Another slap. "Wake up, Cal. Petra's waiting for you. Come on, that's it, open your eyes!"

His eyes flicked open, and he coughed in my face. Not that I minded, I was so relieved he was alive.

With a grunt, he pulled himself to a sitting position. He would have fallen over his knees if I hadn't caught him, but between the two of us, we somehow got him on his feet. Using my shoulder as a crutch, he hobbled across the room. All I could think about was how his footsteps must be audible to everyone within three floors of us.

"There's a shortcut to the roof by a ladder on the outside of the House," he croaked. "If it's guarded, I don't know what we'll do. It usually is."

The next two rooms were mercifully empty. Through the doorway to the third, I spotted light. Moonlight, peeking through a window high in the wall.

"Look!" I seized Cal's hand and pointed. "The moon!"

Cal didn't answer, but his easy smile had returned. It didn't matter that the dried blood at the corners of his lips cracked when it did. We were almost there. Almost safe.

I knew someone was going to jump out from behind a corner and catch Cal by surprise again. I knew we were going to be ambushed. I knew the window would be guarded. Because the last part was always the hardest. Still, with the moonlight in sight, and an escape to the outdoors so close, it was hard to feel hopeless.

Cal's weight shifted off my shoulder as we approached the final room. He scanned all three entrances—the one we'd come through and two additional doorways to the left and right—before he stepped inside. I trailed behind him, holding my breath. Just in case those invisible things could hear me. We had to make it. We had come so far.

Cal pressed his hand against a scanner in the wall. It flashed for a few seconds, then illuminated green.

"Congratulations, Calhoun," said a robotic voice from somewhere in the ceiling. I started and spun around, trying to figure out where it was coming from, but there wasn't even a stick of furniture in the room for someone to hide behind. Were the invisible beings in here too?

"You may exit the building," continued the voice. Cal's mouth moved along with the words, as though he'd heard this message a thousand times before.

The window opened by itself, and a cloth ladder that had been folded into the frame unrolled itself and fell at Cal's feet.

"No one's going to attack us?" I blurted out, staring anxiously at the doors. "Are we done?"

Cal gave a wry smile. "Unless you count the descent, yes, it's over."

"Descent?"

"Better not to worry about it until we get there."

With that comforting remark, he grabbed the bottom rope of the ladder and held it steady while I climbed up to the window. The night air struck my face, its chill delicious and refreshing. I hadn't noticed that there was no air circulating inside the House. I had assumed that if it had ductwork, it had air-conditioning. As I gulped in one invigorating breath after another, I wondered how I hadn't suffocated in there.

The stars glittered through the eternally green trees above my head. So far away. Somehow they seemed closer when I was down in the village than they did on top of this cursed hill.

I swung my feet out over the ledge and looked up. Thank goodness

I had never been afraid of heights. The brick wall towered high above me, and the rope ladder I grasped went up, not down. To get to the bottom, it seemed, we had to start by climbing.

That was fine for me. But Cal was going to have a much harder time.

"Are you sure you can—?"

He cut me off. "Don't talk, Halley. You have to get far enough up so that I can get out too."

He'd just have to do it, then. I pulled myself up. One rung, then another. The ground grew dim beneath me, obscured by the evening mist gathering above the grass. Up and up, and my arms were starting to ache. I had to rest. I hoped we were safe enough to pause.

I glanced down between my shoes. Cal's head was there, but he didn't look up to see why I'd stopped. He was clinging to the side of the ladder like his life depended on it—because it did—and his head rested against the wall. I didn't want to make him hang there, so I tightened my grip around the ropes and hoisted myself up. One more rung, then another.

At last, I made it to the top. Tightening my hold on the ladder, I hooked one leg over the edge. Then one arm, then the other foot. I let go of the ladder and rolled onto the roof with a hollow *thud*.

I could have lain there forever, staring up at the stars. But Cal was right behind me. I sat up and waited for his head to appear.

I held my breath when he lost his balance on the last rung, but he grabbed the frame and swung himself over the edge. His legs collapsed under him, and he lay there for a moment, then grinned.

"The earth is still spinning, the wind is still blowing, the trees are still green. Life really does go on, doesn't it?" He picked himself up. "Are you afraid of heights?"

"No."

"Excellent. I'll help you with the harness."

The towering hill behind us and a few stray, overgrown bushes cast a stark shadow over the back of the rooftop. In the darkest corner, the one farthest from where we had emerged, lay a pile of black objects I had assumed must be extra shingles or some other maintenance paraphernalia. Cal approached this pile and pulled out a knot of thin black straps. I could have spent the whole night trying to unravel that mess, but he seemed to know what he was doing, and he had it undone almost before I had time to check my watch.

Without a word, he took one of my ankles and fit it through a hole in the straps. Once I regained my balance, he did the same with the other, then he pulled the whole contraption over my shoulders. A buckle clicked on my right side, then my left. My skirt had gotten awkwardly hitched, and I had to walk with my feet close together to prevent a wardrobe accident. That's always how it is with adventurous things. It's not the escaping murderous enemies or surviving a brutal death match that worries you; it's the minor inconveniences along the way.

Somehow, this ridiculous thought cheered me up, and I relaxed a little while Cal was climbing into his harness.

He looked much more comfortable than I did. Not that anything could have made him look anything besides what he was. Tall, athletic, battle-scarred—but I digress.

At the edge of the rooftop lay another strap with a silver hook on the end. Cal fitted this into a metal loop on the back of my suit. He pointed to the edge of the roof.

"Jump."

Jump. Not climb? Heights were one thing when I had both feet firmly planted on something, even if it was just an edge or an outcropping in the brick. The key word was *on*.

Still, I'd rather jump than stay trapped on the House's rooftop. I stepped over and lined my toes up with the edge. I inched forward until my feet were half on the roof, half on empty space. I could feel sweat forming on my forehead. It was hard to breathe. Another second, and I wouldn't be going anywhere.

I realized Cal was talking. "It's alright," he was saying. "I've done this a thousand times. Just ask Pe—"

I launched, and Cal's voice disappeared. For one glorious moment I hung in the air, perfectly balanced between my upward momentum and gravity. Then my body slipped out from under me. I tried to scream, but the air collided so violently with my face that

I couldn't get a breath. The ground was flying toward me, faster and faster and faster, so close I could see the breeze blowing in the grass, my face about to land on a stick that had fallen from one of the eternally green trees, and what if these ropes had been made for the Mercs, who were taller than I was, and that didn't make any sense because they were mostly my age, but that didn't make sense, either—

Something jerked hard against my chest, and I bounced up with a gasp. Then down, then up, then down again, getting softer with each additional landing, until I was bobbing gently back and forth with my nose three inches above the dirt.

I nearly dislocated my shoulders trying to get the strap off my back, but I finally succeeded, falling with a soft *thump* and brushing a patch of nettles. With a yelp, I was on my feet, pulling my shawl over my shoulders to avoid touching those nasty green leaves. Of course the House had stinging nettles. Of course it did.

I looked up, and there was Cal's head, silhouetted against the sky. He spread his arms out questioningly, and I gave him a thumbs-up. Hand over hand, he retracted the bungee cable, and soon he had landed safely beside me.

I turned toward the door, ready to run and find Petra. She'd have bandages. She could help me get Cal down to the village to see the doctor, and she'd know what to say to him. It didn't matter if I got into trouble with Mother. *Do no harm* and all that were far more important today.

"Halley!" snapped Cal.

"I'll be right back!"

"Halley." It was no request, no suggestion, but a command.

I felt myself seized from behind and pressed into the rough brick wall. I tried to scream, but his hand was over my mouth. He bent until his eyes were level with mine.

"Listen to me." His grip pinched the base of my neck, constricting my throat. "Everything you saw today, you have to keep secret. Especially from Petra."

I could barely manage a nod.

"You must never tell anyone what you saw, what you heard, nothing. Don't say a word about what you experienced tonight."

The wall now compressed my spine, locking my neck in place.

His hand slipped from my mouth, but his breath was still hot against my ear. "If you tell her, I'll kill you. Understood?"

"Yes. Yes, Cal, you're choking me." I tried to swallow.

His grip slackened, and my hands went to my throat.

"Sorry, but I had to be sure." His voice sounded like it was traveling through water. "You're going to miss curfew if you don't leave."

"Forget about curfew!" Anger and fear weren't enough to make me forsake my duties as the doctor's daughter. *Do no harm. Into whatever house you enter, help the sick.* There was no "unless." Just orders. Just our oath. "We have to get you to the village."

"The chips, Halley, the enforcement chips. I can't leave the House tonight." As though I'd forgotten, as though I didn't live under their threat every single day, as though I wasn't willing to challenge them just this once because why would the law be more important than a person's life? "Thank you for the sympathy, though. Petra was right about you. You're stronger than you look."

"I can't leave you here," I insisted.

His shoes scraped the ground. "Petra will take care of me."

"I said I can't—"

He continued past me onto the porch and pressed his hand over the sensor.

"You will leave," he said as the door slid open, "because after everything, I won't let you die from some careless accident."

His eternal smile had vanished, replaced by stubbornly pinched lips that reminded me of Petra's.

"Good night, Halley."

He slammed the door so hard that I could feel the vibration. The bolt slid into the lock, and the sensor in the wall went dark.

In ten short minutes I was back in the village, limping along the mercifully flat ground with my weary ankle in tow. It was twenty minutes till curfew, and the only people still outside were some scraggly kids who liked to push their luck and flustered parents trying to shoo them inside. The moon was banished behind a cloud, and the lonely cobbles were illuminated with ugly white light from the streetlights. The neon signs on the surrounding shops and buildings were flickering. Soon they'd go out. I had never seen the street in complete darkness.

In the square, the ranking billboard radiated into the mist. Like a bloodred moon signaling a night of battle and death, with a dreary halo to crown the winner.

My curiosity got the better of me, and I spared it one last glance as I sped past.

Cal's name, which had been in the #2 spot that morning, was now at the bottom.

And it was my fault. Mine alone.

# 12

## ANDY

"DID YOUR FRIEND EVER TALK about death?"

"Was he withdrawn?"

"How much do you know about his family?"

"Relationship problems?"

"Did you know him well?"

"Do you think he would have told you if he was having issues at work?"

It didn't matter how Andy answered. The paramedics, the doctors, the police, everyone who asked him those questions had already made up their minds. Their sympathetic answers to his pleas for information betrayed what they were thinking: *We know you don't want to admit that you missed the signs. We know you feel bad. It's okay. We won't force you to say you should have known.*

But things were not okay. Not okay at all.

Andy's legs were going numb from the stiff hospital chair. Every time he blinked he was tempted to let his eyes stay closed. But he was too nauseous to eat and too terrified to sleep. The image of his friend's face, neck tilted back over the shattered windshield, eyes wide and frightened, jolted him into a cold sweat whenever he let himself relax. Never again, not one more night in his life, would he sleep without seeing that specter.

Maybe Rilo had stumbled drunkenly to the window and fallen before he knew what was happening. That was the explanation Andy had given everyone who asked. But nobody believed him, and Andy wasn't sure he believed himself. To get to the window, Rilo must have climbed over the radio equipment—Andy called it a television set—so there was no way he could have fallen accidentally. Furthermore, he couldn't have landed on the car unless he'd launched himself over the street. That didn't fit with the fact that he was supposedly blackout drunk. Stumbled, maybe. But leaped?

What really happened must have been much worse.

When Andy gave his witness report, he omitted the detail about his front door being unlocked because he didn't want the police to search his apartment before he had time to hide his radio. But he hadn't forgotten it. There was no reason for Rilo to unlock the door if his goal was the window, which meant that someone must have entered the apartment while Andy was away. And that was what had happened to Rilo.

Why hadn't the intruder finished the job? Maybe they'd been planning to rob the apartment, thinking Andy was the only occupant, and Rilo had gotten in the way. But why would they go to the effort of shoving him out the window when a knock on the head would be just as effective? For that matter, how did they get Rilo to the window without disturbing the radio?

Rilo stirred, tearing Andy out of his thoughts. His gaze fell on Rilo's face. Swathed with fluffy gauze and black stitches and dried blood, his friend looked like a mummy from a low-budget horror movie. Andy swallowed and fixed his attention on the rhythmic beeping of the heart monitor.

A gentle knock sounded on the door, and a policewoman holding a clipboard entered the room.

"Good evening," she said. Andy wondered if the dark circles under his eyes were as pronounced as hers. "I need to ask a few more questions."

*Not again.*

"Were there any signs of an intruder at your house?"

"I don't think so." He blinked. "Sorry, what did you say?"

Her expression softened. "I know you must be tired. We're going to search your residence, and we need to know what to look for."

"You're going to *what?*" Now she had Andy's full attention. "Don't you need a warrant for that?"

"Mr. Robinson, you have nothing to worry about," she assured him. "The clerk at the convenience store testified, and we've reviewed the camera footage. You're not suspected of committing any crime. We just want to make sure there was no foul play."

From the legal tidbits Andy's mind was scrambling to retrieve, he realized there might be as little as a few hours between the time the paramedics were called and the time a search warrant was signed. That was if the police needed a warrant, and he suspected that the severity of the potential crime was such that they didn't. There had been cases like that. There were always inconvenient precedents for this sort of thing.

"T-thank you," he stammered.

He was usually prepared for his apartment to be raided, but he had been incautious. Just once, but once was enough. It was Rilo's fault for suggesting the drinks in the first place. In his stupor, Andy had left radio equipment—just parts and pieces, but a SAFE-certified police officer would know—scattered around his living room. He'd thought he'd have at least a day to clean up, maybe two. He had never imagined that bureaucracy could move so quickly.

"Mr. Robinson?"

Words emerged from somewhere beyond his conscious thought. "Can I get some clothes from my house?" he asked slowly. "If I'm going to be staying at the hospital with Rilo for a while, I'd at least like one other thing to change into."

"Of course, Mr. Robinson."

"Thanks." For some reason, Andy really did feel grateful. He wondered what this dutiful policewoman would think if she knew about the radio set in his room. She'd know in a few hours. Could he try offering a bribe? He probably didn't have anything a police officer would want. A plea of ignorance? He'd fall apart as soon as the prosecution shoved his coaxial connector under his nose. No, he had to get creative. Or yield to the inevitable and accept that he was stuck in the frying pan. Forget about the fire.

Then he formulated an idea, an idea so insane and outlandish that it made him want to weep.

*There'll be time for tears later when you're rotting in prison. 'Cause that's how this ends.*

"Can I answer your questions outside?" Andy asked. "I'll say goodbye to my friend and check with the nurses about his condition. Then I'll meet you in the lobby. I don't want to wake him up if he's sleeping."

Her long fingernails clicked against the clipboard, but eventually she nodded.

"Please don't take long."

"I won't."

When she left the room, and when he was satisfied that the door was closed securely behind her, he ran his hand across Rilo's forehead, weaving his fingers through the bandages and the blood.

"I'll find that stupid radio. I'll get the reward, and I'll pay your medical bills. You'd better wake up so I can tell you about it, you hear?"

Rilo wasn't going to argue. He wouldn't complain about getting lonely, nor would he offer to watch Andy's apartment while he was gone. Not a word would sink in through the tightly shut eyes and hissing oxygen mask.

With a brief clasp on his friend's arm, Andy let himself out into the sterile hallway. The noise of the machines keeping Rilo's heart beating faded in the distance behind him, and for a moment he was blinded by the white fluorescent lights sparkling on the laminate floor.

The policewoman was gone, presumably following his instructions to wait in the lobby. If Andy had been given an extra five seconds to think, he would have asked her to wait somewhere else because he didn't know another exit. But there was no helping it now.

With difficulty, he pulled his thoughts together. The hospital must have at least two exits on the ground floor in case of fires. The problem would be getting there from the ICU on the second floor without passing through the lobby. There was only one stairwell that visitors were supposed to use. The rest were reserved for doctors and nurses, and there were enough staff moving about the hallways that Andy doubted he could sneak by unnoticed. That left him only two options: disguise or diversion. Andy's paper-white features and black, messy hair were unmistakable, so he settled on diversion.

He considered screaming and beating his head against a wall, pretending to be an escaped psych patient. This seemed like an appropriate response to everything that had happened that night, but it would probably only earn him a padded cell. Or he could pull the fire alarm, but with the surveillance cameras on every side, it would only be a matter of minutes before the hospital staff figured out who did it. Officially, he wasn't being investigated for a crime. Yet. It seemed safest to keep up the charade.

In the end, for what felt like a long time, he did nothing but stand anxiously in the hallway, staring in agony at everyone who passed him and wondering which of them would be the first to turn him in.

A nurse with her nose glued to a folder trotted past. She was the first person who hadn't looked dubiously alert, and she seemed busy enough with the charts she was studying that she might not notice anything amiss. Andy tried to calm his pounding heart as he tapped her shoulder.

"My wife had a baby," he babbled, going along with the first plausible nonsense that came to mind, "and my in-laws are in the lobby. They're having a fight about what we're going to name the little one, and I just want to . . . uh, get my wife a sandwich. She asked for a specific brand of tuna sandwich. You know how pregnancy cravings are." Andy certainly didn't. "Can you let me out the back? Please, for a tired father. New father, I mean. Please. I'm begging you."

The nurse raised a pair of bleary green eyes.

"You're not supposed to bring food after hours," she sighed, "but I guess an exception could be made. Follow me."

The nurse led him down the staff staircase to the ambulance exit, past a team of paramedics—luckily none of them looked familiar—and out a garage door that led to the street. A few minutes later, he was half a block away. A free man. For the moment, anyway.

All he needed was an hour, some equipment from his apartment, and extensive good luck. He was certain he could get the latter two, but how could he buy enough time to hide from the police until he decided where he was going? Having been out of work for several months, he didn't own a car, and running from the cops in a taxi sounded like something a low-budget action-movie villain would do. "Oh, those flashing lights behind you?" he'd say, with the inevitable nervous giggle. "That's weird. I wonder what they want. Could you drive just a tiny bit faster, please?" The cinema had shown him a hundred times that being unnecessarily dramatic didn't pay. Necessarily dramatic, on the other hand . . .

Before he had figured out how he was going to get back to his apartment, he found himself on his own street, having absentmindedly covered the distance. The crushed car outside his apartment window was still surrounded by emergency vehicles, police tape, and a host of curious onlookers. Andy tried to avoid looking at them. Not that anyone from his building would recognize him. He wasn't the neighborly type, which he'd never, until now, considered to be one of his strengths. But better safe than sorry.

Slipping through the outer barrier of police tape and pulling his hood snugly over his head, he used what he thought was the last of his energy to climb the stairs. Several policemen were loitering in the hallway, subjects of awe from a wide-eyed neighbor or two, but they all seemed to assume that Andy had permission to be there.

When he reached his apartment, he locked the door behind him and rummaged through his closet for a change of clothes. Sweatshirt after sweatshirt was tossed aside until he finally reached the unsettling conclusion that his choices of disguise consisted of either sweatpants or a suit. His limited wardrobe was one of extremes. And since he'd worn a sweatshirt to the hospital and all his others were the same color and style and brand, the choice was obvious.

Reluctantly, he pulled on the suit. It had been so long since he'd worn it that he couldn't resist checking his reflection in the mirror to see if he looked as dapper as he felt. If he was going full James Bond villain-style, running from law enforcement and "taking matters into his own hands"—the only action-movie quote he vaguely remembered—he might as well look the part.

His eyes were hollow, his face was pale, and his hair stood straight up, forming a jagged ridge along his head as if he'd trimmed it with an old-fashioned weed eater. But what did that matter so long as he looked different than he had when he left the hospital? He found a bottle of gel in a cobwebbed corner of his cabinet and smeared it through his hair until it shone.

Disguise complete, he turned away from the mirror and dug through his shelves of electronics. Odds and ends of circuitry spilled out into the hallway, and parts crunched under his feet. He barely spared a moment to think about how much they'd cost to replace. His attention was focused on a small black box on the top shelf, just out of his reach. With a lunge, he seized it by the edge and pulled it down, dislodging a basket of transformers.

This was his magnum opus. He'd spent more time, money, and energy on this box than on his radio. That had been an outlet for his curiosity, a reminder of the old days in college, back when he'd studied radio astronomy. This was the device he'd made betting on the slim odds he ever picked up a signal. It was the bridge between his homemade radio and a true scientific endeavor. A radio locator. With it, he could trace the source of the broadcast he'd heard, whether it was a hundred miles away or a thousand.

Once he found that, he could go to prison happy. He'd spent all this time working on his radio in secret, sharing the details only with Rilo, worrying about whether he'd be caught and what would happen to him if he was. Well, now he could stop wondering. It had finally happened, or was about to happen, so he might as well make the most of the opportunity. The radio was too unwieldy for him to carry while on the run. But he could try to find the source of that broadcast, and if he succeeded, he might earn himself a lighter prison sentence and a cash reward. Rilo's bills would be paid.

The red light of the locator flickered for a moment, then died.

Andy couldn't remember the last time he'd turned it on. He never thought he'd need it. But he kept a collection of batteries in his desk because irrationality was less depressing than the alternative.

As he bent over the drawer, rifling through stacks of paper clips and sticky notes and pens, he heard a commotion outside. Voices. Footsteps. They weren't outside his window; they were coming from the landing right beside his door.

He grabbed the first set of batteries he saw, and by pure luck he ended up with enough of the kind he needed. He discarded the extras onto the floor, vaguely imagining the police tripping over them while he was fleeing and thus buying him time. With stiff fingers, he slipped the rest into his radio locator and flipped the switch. This time, the light flickered and stayed on, bright and clear.

Satisfied, he tiptoed to the window. There was no one in sight. The sounds he'd heard must have been coming from around the corner, which he'd have to walk around to get down to the street. Perhaps it was best to wait and see if the route cleared. What if they came knocking on his front door? He was starting to feel nauseous. He needed time to collect both his thoughts and his belongings.

To keep his mind busy, he matched the locator's frequency to that of the radio. The red light on the locator faded for a moment, but then it began to blink so rapidly that Andy could hardly look at it. It went steady for a few seconds, then blinked again. The arrow on the directional dial swiveled toward his door.

That signal was close. All but under his feet.

He opened his door slowly, gripping the precious locator in sweaty palms, and peeked out onto the empty landing. Nothing. The door swung closed, and he locked it behind him.

The locator dial spun frantically, then slowly reversed its direction, pointing back at his apartment. He was on the wrong floor.

He remembered the policemen loitering in the stairwell. The only direction he could go without being noticed was up. There was one floor above Andy's, which gave him a fifty-fifty shot of finding the signal without having to go downstairs. Except that there were multiple floors below and only one above, so it wasn't quite fifty-fifty, unless the radio operator could fly. But for once, Andy wasn't bothering with accurate statistics.

The voices he'd heard around the corner piped up again, slightly louder this time. Someone was coming. Someone with a deep, official voice, who sounded like the kind of person who wouldn't be embarrassed by asking personal questions. *What are you doing here? Did you murder Rilo?*

There was no time for strategizing. Andy dashed up the stairs, praying he wouldn't have to stop and catch his breath. He had no plan for what he'd do once he reached the roof if he found nothing there. Rilo had survived his jump. Maybe Andy would too. A little trip to the hospital never hurt anyone if they were desperate enough. And rich enough. Which he wasn't.

He pressed the locator against the first door he saw. The light had vanished. Whoever was operating the radio must have turned it off.

"I want a good story to tell, Rilo," he muttered under his breath, picturing his friend lying in the hospital bed. "We promised we'd do this together, but if we can't, I'll do your part for you."

*Here goes nothing.*

# 13

## HALLEY

**A PAIR OF THICK CANVAS CURTAINS** were pulled across the only window in the Mercs' communal room, dissolving the brilliant exterior light to a fuzzy spot on the wall. As my eyes adjusted, I began to make out the rows of cots. There were ten in total. One was occupied. Petra's sticklike silhouette was bent over the bed, conversing softly with someone I couldn't see.

I was walking on tiptoe, trying not to disturb anyone who happened to be napping, but my movement caught her attention. She fixed me in a glare that I felt like a knife to the chest—though that was becoming a sensitive simile these days, and I banished the thought the moment it appeared.

"Why are you here?"

I sat on the nearest bed. "To check on Cal. He is here, isn't he?"

A snort of laughter resounded.

"It's nice to know that someone cares," Cal remarked from somewhere under a pile of blankets. "You should be grateful, Petra, that you have such a nice friend."

"Stupid," she admonished. "If you think this is funny, why don't you spend your time trying to get off this island rather than playing the Alliance's games?"

"Harsh words, doc. I take issue with being killed on the spot, so I come and go when I'm . . ." His words died off in a rasping cough.

I had a safe home to go back to, and I didn't have to worry about my rankings. Cal had been injured when I was with him. Moreover, I couldn't say a word to defend myself. Couldn't say I hadn't seen the enemies. Couldn't say I hadn't been given a weapon. My presence had to be rubbing salt in Petra's wounds, and I didn't blame her for looking at me like she wanted to eject me with violence.

"Tell me again," Petra said, brushing a stray piece of hair out of Cal's face. Her pale hand lingered on his forehead. "Tell me exactly what happened."

"I tripped on a banana peel. Alerted a guard, and whoops, I was done for."

"There's nothing funny about this."

"Right." Cal struggled to half-sit, half-lie against the thin pillows piled under his head. His face had turned a drained, yellowish tan, the same color as the worn-out coverlet tucked under his chin. "I don't know what happened. I couldn't play as well as usual. It's hard to explain." He picked at the sheet. "I don't know. I just wasn't myself."

"But you've never come back in this condition before." Petra clearly wasn't satisfied.

"Nothing about yesterday's play-through should have been different." He gestured vaguely at his chest, and I could see that one of his arms was bandaged from shoulder to wrist. I wondered what other injuries I'd missed in my blindness. "It wasn't Halley's fault. She never got attacked. I guess the guards didn't recognize her." He shot me a look I pretended not to see, a look of *don't you dare open your mouth*. "It's my fault. I just don't know how."

"You can't afford to mess up." Petra's words were sharp, but her voice hid a quaver. "Someone from the village will have to take your place if you die."

Cal's lips twitched. "And it wouldn't be the same for you if I wasn't here, I guess."

"Worry about yourself."

"I am. That includes worrying about you." He raised a hand disarmingly, before Petra could snap at him. "I think we should all be worried about what happened last night. I think it had something to do with the chips."

"That's an old wives' tale," she scoffed. "And you're the one who convinced me of it."

At last I knew what they were talking about. These "chips" weren't the kind we had with fish. Each of the villagers, and apparently the Mercs too, had a little scar behind our right ears. Rumor had it that an electronic device had been implanted there when we were born. I'd asked the doctor about mine when I'd first noticed it in the mirror, but he told me he didn't know how I'd gotten it or where it came from. Whether that was because he really didn't know, or because he was under surveillance at the time, I couldn't say. What I did know was that the chips were the Alliance's way of enforcing the island's laws. Steal something? The chip could shock you. Kill someone (if you weren't a Merc)? The chip could kill you. Or so I'd been told. I'd never encountered anyone eager to test that theory.

Cal fidgeted with his cross necklace, twisting it back and forth and rubbing the clasp between his fingers. For the first time, I got a clear glimpse of the back of his hand. I'd been right about that mark: a strange black-and-white design inked into the skin. A *W*–or an *M*–slashed through with a cross, bordered on each side by a pair of wings. *M* for *Merc*, maybe?

"I've seen the villagers while they're working," he was saying. "They get this blank stare, and they never seem interested in their work. If the chips can make them act like that, why shouldn't they have some control over our perception too?"

I tried to think about my own experience with my work. I had never tried to deviate from my lemonade script, which didn't mean I couldn't. Still, why hadn't I thought of trying it before? How about: *Lemonade, three coins per cup?* It would be nice to have a larger allowance.

"But if the Alliance can control our minds, why wouldn't they stop us from thinking about escaping?" objected Petra. "Why wouldn't they make us happy to be here?"

"Well, maybe they can control our actions, but not our thoughts.

Or maybe they can only control certain things. Or maybe you're right, and there's nothing to what I'm saying. I was just trying to explain what it felt like. You asked. But don't worry about it right now." Pulling the blankets up to his face, he stifled another bout of coughing. "Why don't you go outside? I didn't mean to ruin your plans for the day."

"I never have any plans."

He tousled her hair with his good arm. "It's not like I can run off while you're gone. You don't have to worry about leaving me here."

"But if you have to play?"

"I'm too beat-up to get called in."

"But if we need to take you to the doctor?"

"I feel fine right now."

"But you can't possibly—"

"No more buts. Enjoy the weather. Put your head together with Halley's and see if you can figure out what happened to me."

She gazed at him for a moment, unwilling. He gazed back, and I stared at both of them, too mesmerized to realize that I wasn't wanted. The three of us sat there—one as out of place as a third wheel on a bicycle, but I wasn't going anywhere—and looked at each other, and looked and looked and looked, but nobody moved. All I could hear was a gentle humming in my ears.

"For goodness' sake, Petra," Cal muttered, "can you make this any harder?"

Her face tightened. "Me?"

"Please go," he told her, his voice quiet. "I'm sorry. I need to think."

The bed swayed on its fragile legs as she rose. "Let me know when you're done introspecting."

"Petra—" Cal swallowed the rest of his sentence. "Thank you."

She nodded and let herself out into the living room.

Cal rolled over, turning his back to me, and burrowed down into his pillows. "That wasn't an invitation for you to stay."

"Yes, well." I stood up. "I was going to say thank you."

"For what?"

"For taking me into the House. For protecting me. For getting me out."

"So I solved a problem I created." He remained turned away from me. "Leave or I'll get up and throw you out."

I wanted to say something about the easy availability of psychiatric care at the doctor's office in the village, since Cal was in desperate need of intervention for his obvious bipolar disorder, but I couldn't bring myself to be rude to his face. Not after everything we'd gone through together, not after the pain he'd endured because of . . .

Was it really because of me?

I wouldn't be able to live with myself if I started asking questions like that. Cal didn't seem to blame me for what had happened yesterday, and that would have to be enough. I didn't have the luxury of a conscience strong enough to accept the kind of guilt these people carried.

"Thank you, anyway," I said to his back. "I'll talk to Petra. We'll figure something out."

"Halley."

I stopped with my hand on the doorknob.

"Tell Petra . . ."

I turned to find him picking at the edge of the blanket. His face was highlighted on the stack of pillows Petra had left him, exposed in the dull sunlight seeping into the window.

"Tell her I didn't mean what I said. Tell her I haven't—what's the expression?—haven't had my coffee yet."

I nodded. But I wouldn't do it. It was best that he tell her himself, especially if they were—well, I couldn't fathom why anyone, especially the levelheaded Petra, would be stupid enough to fall in love with an emotional tempest like Cal. But everyone made mistakes, and it seemed that she was as susceptible as the rest of us. No, he owed her honesty, and that couldn't come from me.

I wondered what their relationship looked like to those who lived in the same House with them. If it had ever been any healthier than this. If it was possible to have a relationship even distantly resembling healthy when you lived on a knife's edge.

As I left the Mercs' sleeping quarters, I noticed three Mercs, all boys—or men, but barely—huddled in the corner of the living room. They were chattering in low voices, so engrossed by whatever they were looking at that they never noticed me. Thank goodness. I doubted they'd ever seen a villager up here, and I didn't know whether their reaction would be positive.

"Could the Alliance technicians have come in the night and installed it?" one of them asked.

"Or did we just not notice it before?"

I strained to see what they were talking about, but it was too dark for my eyes to focus. The best I could make out was some sort of glassy rectangular object, suspended from the ceiling and hovering about eight feet off the ground. A powered-down screen, maybe.

Petra wasn't in the common area, which meant she had to be either in the kitchen or outdoors. There was no way I was going to snoop around the House without a guide, so I decided to check outside first. Sure enough, I found her seated under an oak tree, fingers playing idly with a slender fallen branch.

"You wanted to see what happened in the House." She didn't have to look up to know it was me. Merc's instincts, I supposed. "Well, now you have. That's a chance no villager has ever gotten, not in my memory. What do you think?" Petra's shocking turquoise eyes regarded me with amusement. "What are you going to do now that you know the truth?"

I sat down next to her and curled my legs underneath me. There were thistles growing abundant in the close-cropped grass, and I tried to balance myself on the sides of my boots to avoid getting pricked. And to take my mind off what I was going to say next.

"The villagers." We who should have held ourselves and everyone else responsible. "Why do we let you do it?"

She ripped a leaf off the branch, crumpled it, and tossed it to the winds. "The Alliance forces us to play in the same way you're forced to work."

"Couldn't we fight?"

"Against what? There is no Alliance in any definite sense of the word. It's a colloquial term to say that the 'Alliance' gave us our chips and enforces the rules, but who knows if it means anything?

Its members are secret, and if they are here on this island—which I doubt—you can't talk to them, can't hit them, can't hold them at gunpoint. How would we start?"

"Where else would they be, on a boat?" I couldn't imagine spending more than an hour or two on a boat. We villagers explored the water occasionally, usually because we were feeling peckish for fish, but the ocean was infinitely vast and infinitely deep and could swallow us all whole, and that was enough of an incentive not to tempt it for long. We kept our feet planted in the sand. Boats were generally forbidden anyway, because—well, that was the way things had always been.

Petra leaned back against the tree. "Have you ever asked anyone what they did before they came here?"

"Before they came where?"

"I wasn't born on this island." This made about as much sense as if she'd claimed to be born on the moon. "I don't think most of the villagers were. But I've asked around, and none of them remember what happened before they arrived. Most of them think they were born here, and the few who don't know nothing about the outside world."

"You remember something?"

"I remember getting sick," she said. "I think I was very sick. I was in a hospital. There's a voice in my head. An older man. I can hear him saying, 'Your daughter is going to die,' as he's standing next to my bed. He seems tall, far away. I must have been young."

She had lost me near the beginning of her story. "What on earth is a 'hospital'?"

"You don't know the word?" Petra flashed me a puzzled glance. "It's . . . it's like a doctor's office, but for hundreds of people. Maybe even thousands."

"But there's only one doctor."

"Not out there. Not beyond the island. If there are hospitals, then there must be many doctors."

I frowned. The doctor had rescued Petra with a lifesaving injury in just a few short minutes of surgery. I didn't think many people could claim skill like that. And imagine having enough doctors to treat thousands of people at once! Enough nonsense for a whole novel.

But Petra seemed sincere, so I kept my doubts private. "What else do you remember?"

"I remember two people coming to visit me. They used to bring me things. Maybe toys, maybe food. I don't remember exactly, but I was always happy to see them. One of them, the woman, she cried often. But everything after that is black until I arrived here as a Merc. By then, I was an adult."

"But I remember growing up here," I protested.

"Well, you might have been born on the island. You're younger than me, aren't you?"

It was hard to tell. Petra's face was as smooth as a child's and as angular as an older woman's.

"What does any of this have to do with Cal? With the House?"

"Everything. If a world exists outside this island, the Alliance must be there. That could be the beginning of our fight."

Her metal hand reached out and tightened around my shoulder. She probably intended it as an affectionate gesture, but those alloy fingers were hard and strong and cold. I wiggled out of her grasp and pasted on a smile.

"Thanks for telling me." That was the best I could come up with, but at least it gave me a moment to think about what I was going to say next. "Are you sure about this? It seems like our current problem is more immediate. We have to figure out why all this is happening and what we're going to do about it. We can worry about how it happened later, can't we?"

"I wouldn't have told you any of this if I didn't think you'd try to do something. I don't waste time like that. We Mercs don't have any to spare."

She was about to explain what she meant, but she was interrupted by a yell from somewhere behind us. In a second, Petra was on her feet and pulling me up by my shoulder. I tried to find my footing, but she didn't wait, just dragged me up the hill as my heels scuffed in the dirt.

"What happened?" I gasped, clinging to her slippery metal elbow.

"Cal. They said Cal's name."

She opened the door to the House with a few taps of her finger against the invisible sensor and bolted into the gloom. I barely had time to follow before the door slid shut behind us and the world faded into abrupt darkness.

As my eyes adjusted, I spotted a horde of silhouettes crowding around a dim screen on the opposite wall. So that was what the younger Mercs had been looking at when I'd left the House earlier. There was nothing to differentiate it from the myriad of similar screens we had down in the village, except the fact that it had appeared seemingly out of nowhere.

Petra squeezed her way to the front of the crowd, her childish figure dwarfed and nearly invisible except for the glare of the screen on her upturned face.

The screen displayed eerily overexposed black-and-white footage that looked like it might be coming from a cheap security camera. The feed was grainy and glitchy, occasionally interrupted by whirls of vibrant color. At first, the pixelation made me dizzy, and I couldn't figure out what I was supposed to be seeing. But it only required a few seconds of adjustment to get a better view. Then I realized I was looking at a large interior room with only one source of light, a blinding white bulb on the ceiling, crisscrossed by whirring fan blades. This room was empty of furniture, and it was difficult to tell whether the white spots were windows or just dusty spots on the camera lens.

In the center, directly under the light, knelt Cal. Despite the low-quality video, I had no trouble recognizing him from his reflective hair and red necktie, which formed a dark spot in the sea of white.

"What's he doing in there?" Petra snapped, but the other Mercs shushed her.

"You knew I wasn't recovered." Cal's voice, replete with wheezes and coughs, echoed from the screen. The sound they produced was so tinny that it made me wince. "Are you trying to get me killed?"

There was no one else in the room. And so, when the high-pitched voice emerged from the speakers, we all jumped.

"Suicidal maniacs aren't tolerated here."

The Merc closest to the screen, a tall girl with her hair in a ponytail, put her hand on Petra's back. The same black design imprinted on Cal's hand was on hers too. That got me curious, and I looked around. It was everywhere. On right hands, on left hands, on everyone. They were all stamped with that strange cross and wings and *W* or *M*, but then, everything was upside down.

Except Petra. She had lost her dominant hand, and with it, the Mercenaries' mark.

Petra shook off the girl's arm and approached the screen. If I had been a little closer, I could have watched the video from its reflection in her eyes, they were so wide.

"You were in control, telling me where to go and what to do. It's not my fault I ended up looking like this." For a moment, Cal glanced up at something on the opposite end of the room, but he quickly let his head drop. "I won't be fit to play for weeks, and you've only got yourself to blame."

"I wouldn't have let it happen if you had stuck with the plan. You were supposed to make sure the other Mercs stayed away from the villagers. And now I find out one of them has been coming inside the House for the past two days. What part of your orders didn't you understand?"

"I agreed to that before I . . ." Cal's voice trailed off. Maybe he knew that whatever he said, no matter how watertight his excuse, that lifeless voice would never show any humanity. Instead of finishing his sentence, he lifted his head again, propping himself on his hands and knees, and said, "I'll do anything else. Anything. But not that. Nothing that harms her. You agreed to that condition."

"You're hardly in a position to be talking about conditions."

A man dressed in a patterned green suit, carrying a rifle across his chest, stepped into the frame from the left side of the screen. He paused in front of Cal, tapping his boot against the floor. I could almost feel that tap through the ceiling. Low, monotonous, level. Uninteresting. Faint.

Despite the camera's low resolution, I could see Cal's body tense. "You—"

"Are real," the man interrupted, hefting his weapon into his right hand. His voice was deeper than the one we'd heard before. "What kind of war would this be if there weren't lives involved? Who would think the cost was high enough?"

He stepped toward Cal, who shifted defensively back onto his knees and inched his hand toward his waist. But before he could grab whatever weapon he had concealed there, the other man darted toward him with nimbleness contradictory to his heavy equipment and smacked his head with the stock of his rifle. With a groan, nearly drowned in the hissing of the camera audio, Cal collapsed.

"Are there cameras in that room?" the disembodied voice asked.

The man looked around for a moment, and his eyes came to rest directly on the camera through which we were watching. For one panicked moment, I imagined it was a two-way camera, and he could see us too.

"How do I know if it's recording?"

"You'd see a red blinking light at the bottom."

"Then we're safe." He yanked the device off the wall, and our screen flickered to black.

My ears rang as though the static was still playing. I thought I could still hear that voice through the ceiling. I could hear the *crunch* of his rifle against Cal's head. I could hear him groan as he fell. The feed was still playing. It had never stopped. It never would. It ran in a loop on and on inside my head, and it was never going to stop.

Then there was a *crash*. A *boom*. It rattled the floor. It burned our ears. It shook us all awake.

The Mercs nearest Petra, heaving one collective breath as the silence shattered, murmured what had to be empty words of comfort.

"I'm sorry." For what? "Let us know if you need anything." What would they do? But they had seen all this before. They knew better than I did what they would want to hear if they were in Petra's shoes. So they said that, quietly, and moved on.

Soon they had dispersed, and Petra and I were left alone in

front of the blank screen. I couldn't even see her breathe, she was holding herself so still.

"Petra?" I whispered.

No answer. No movement, not even a twitch.

A hand reached out of nowhere and seized my shoulder. Before I could scream, I was pulled into a dim side room that turned out to be the kitchen. There were six or seven Mercs in there, sitting on the counter, leaning against the walls, crouching on the floor, the most I had ever seen in one place.

One of them, the ponytailed girl who had been standing next to Petra, offered me a chair.

"That was a livestream from the fourth floor," she told me. "I'd know that room anywhere. A few minutes after you and Petra went outside, Cal was summoned to a match. He told us to pay attention to the screen, and . . ."

"He told us not to tell her what was happening until it was over," someone from the corner finished. "Maybe we should've listened."

"Of course we shouldn't have," Ponytail snapped. "Can you imagine if we'd had to explain all that to Petra? She would never have believed us. At least, in a way, she was there for him. That's better than nothing."

"If Cal was a spy, Petra should know," came a hoarse male voice from beside the refrigerator. "She can help us do damage control."

"But Cal was the one who told us about the live feed." The ponytailed girl was pacing up and down now, her boots tapping an anxious rhythm on the wood floor. "Why would he go to such effort to make sure we all find out he's a spy? And besides, who would he be spying for? Who were the other people in the video?"

"The Alliance, obviously," replied the refrigerator voice. "Who else?"

"Why would the Alliance need spies when they have the enforcement chips?" I objected. The Mercs had brought me in here, so they were getting my opinion whether they wanted it or not. "Besides, if Cal was a spy, it doesn't make sense for him to give himself away. He turned himself in to both sides at the same time. Surely he'd pick one to stay friends with."

The girl shrugged, but one wrinkled man, sitting cross-legged on the kitchen table, was ready with an answer. "I'd guess it's because the Alliance doesn't just want to force us to play their game. They also want to influence events organically and figure out who is and who isn't willing to work on their side. They must think coercion will yield a better result than force. There's that. I don't know the answer to your second question."

"What's the desired result?" said one of the other men—boys?—leaning on the counter. "Playing the game can't be an end by itself. There must be a reason we have to play a certain way."

"So . . ." I was struggling to keep up with their rapid-fire assumptions. "You think that Cal might know what that reason is? Because you think he's a spy? And he somehow managed to turn on the video feed so we could find out that he knew? If that's true, why didn't he just tell us? He didn't have to go to all this trouble. He didn't have to get himself caught."

"If he just waltzed in one day and said he was a spy, we wouldn't have believed him," Ponytail explained. "We had no idea there were Alliance members in the House. We've got no room either for lunatics or traitors, and we would have kicked him out. Then he still would have been killed, and we'd be none the wiser."

"I think Cal wanted to knock out two birds with one stone," the boy leaning against the counter suggested. He numbered off his points on his fingers. "First, by hacking the video feed, he showed us that he's really working with the Alliance. No one who wasn't affiliated with them could've figured out how to do that. Second, by forcing the Alliance to say that Cal hadn't been doing his job properly, he showed us he's a double agent, but on our side. Maybe he knew he was about to get in trouble, so he took this as his last chance to tell us."

"Which means," I put in, "we have to find out where that soldier took him. Now that we know he's working with us, it's safe to bring him back here. And once we do that, we can find out if our guesses were right."

Silence met my words.

"Didn't you hear the gunshot?" Ponytail's tone was gentle. I might have bristled at the condescension if I hadn't been so startled.

"Gunshot?" My voice was high-pitched. "What gunshot?"

Then I remembered the echoing vibration that shook the floor and sent a tremor up my spine. I had chalked it up to another mystery of the House, perhaps a slamming door or window.

"Cal's . . ." I swallowed. I couldn't say it. It was like calling the moon a square or the sky green. Those two words were so ridiculously mismatched. Cal and death—they didn't fit.

I waited for someone to contradict me.

No one did.

Ponytail kicked the counter with her steel-toed boot. "One of us has to find his body. We can't assume he didn't have anything with him. And we need to go through his belongings."

"We should let Petra do that," someone suggested.

"But will she? She and Cal were—"

"I'll do it." Petra had appeared out of nowhere, silhouetted in the dim light of the doorway. I could barely see her face, but there was enough light from the noncommittal kitchen lamp to reveal that she hadn't been wasting time with tears. "After I escort Halley back to the village. It's nearly curfew."

She grabbed my hand and pulled me out of my chair. "Let's go, Halley."

Petra kept her hold on me until a few hundred meters or so away from the House. Then she stopped in the middle of the road and let go.

"Are you alright?" she asked.

"You're asking *me*?"

"My fingers left marks on your arm. Does it hurt?"

"Oh." I glanced at the handprint stamped into my skin and rubbed it absent-mindedly. "I'm okay."

I wanted to ask her why she was acting like nothing extraordinary had happened. Why everyone was acting so . . . practical. Why I couldn't process what I'd seen, not even enough to feel sad or sorry or even angry. I wanted to ask her if the feelings would all hit later. If she'd ever experienced something like this before. I wanted to ask—

"The Alliance will find out that all the Mercs saw what happened. When they do, they'll have us killed. We have to act before then."

I gaped at her. "Killed?"

"We can only hope they never find out you were here to see it." Her face was inches from mine. "Don't tell anyone you were here tonight. Not a word. Not to the doctor, not to your friends. No one. If the Alliance finds out, they'll kill you, too, and no one will be left who remembers."

I couldn't even stammer out a response, but she seemed to take my silence as agreement.

"I'd say we have a few days." She resumed walking, slower this time. "They'll probably assume Cal has been feeding us information, so they could investigate. It might be best if you don't visit the House for a while."

She stopped again, finally noticing that I wasn't following.

"Halley?"

But I couldn't. I couldn't do it. I couldn't stand to make plans and run about our business like everything was fine when we both knew someone was missing. I couldn't stand to see her face empty and blank just the same as it had been before Cal's death. She was the only one who shared all my secrets. We weren't friends, but we had to work together. To see her so distant, a casual observer of an experiment, made me unbearably lonely. She could say she'd seen death before, that she saw it every day, but she *hadn't*. Not with Cal. Not with the man I thought she loved.

"Are you used to everyone around you just leaving one day and never coming back?" I said, my voice cracking. "Are you so used to it that you can't even cry anymore?"

"You think I don't feel anything?" Her face creased, but I couldn't tell whether she was frowning or smiling or crying. "That I don't care? That this is all just another day for me?"

I shook my head. What I'd meant was—I didn't know what I meant. That I wanted her old self back. That I wanted things to go back to how they were before.

"I couldn't expect anything more of you, could I?" The tight smile reminded me of Cal's. "Come back tomorrow. We'll look through Cal's things. He had a lot of papers, and I don't want the other Mercs to see them until we know what happened. There might be something he didn't intend anyone else to see. Or don't come if you don't want to."

Her hands deep in her pockets, she walked past me, back up the hill, back to the House that had killed her best friend.

As her silhouette faded against the dark green trees, I saw her pull something from her pocket—a long red piece of cloth. A red bandanna. It fluttered briefly as she pressed it to her lips. Then I lost sight of her.

# 14

ANDY

**ANDY KNOCKED ONCE, THEN TWICE,** then three times. The silence in the hallway was loud enough that he was about to give up—though whether that meant go about his business or break down the door, he hadn't quite decided—when the handle turned, and the door opened just a crack.

"Who are you?"

"I'm—uh—" *I'm your neighbor. I just have a few questions for you. Oh, also, don't worry about the sirens. Those are unrelated.*

He ended up standing there, tongue-tied, until the door started to close. Without thinking, he shoved his fingers in the crack, yelped in pain, then pushed against it.

The stranger's one visible eye widened in alarm, but Andy was stronger, or at least more awake, and he managed to force the door open enough so he could see whom he'd been talking to. Messy pink hair, strawberry-patterned comforter tucked around her shoulders, dark marks under her eyes, cat-paw slippers visible from the bottom of the comforter. And behind her, pink walls, a pink fur rug, pink everywhere.

He wasn't sure what he'd been expecting—maybe some sort of government super-agent—but it definitely wasn't this.

It occurred to him that the sleepy fear in the girl's eyes was converting to anger, and she looked as though at any moment she might find the energy to kick him out and call the police. Before she did, he had to convince her that he didn't mean any harm. A preposterous task, given that he'd just forced his way into her apartment at midnight.

"Get into the bedroom," he said huskily, pulling his suit collar up around his face. "Don't come out until I say so."

"This is a studio apartment. There is no bedroom."

Andy cleared his throat. "The bathroom. I meant the bathroom."

"I have my phone in my hand. I could call the police."

Andy ruffled his hair, annoyed. She was sharp, much sharper than he was this late at night. Curse those night owls. As fast as he'd gotten sleepy, she'd woken up.

"You might start by explaining what you're doing here," the girl suggested, pointing to the sofa. "Then I'll decide whether you're going to spend the night in jail."

Wondering when exactly he had lost control of the situation, Andy accepted her invitation and sat on the sofa. But his attention was immediately caught by something on the coffee table, a small black box with a metal antenna folded on the top.

"Where'd you get that?" he asked sharply.

The girl had stepped into her kitchen—or, as she had pointed out, the area of the single room that functioned as a kitchen—to boil water for tea, but she glanced over her shoulder to see what he was talking about. "Don't touch that," she said. "It belongs to a friend. He left it when he came to visit, and I'm going to give it back to him tomorrow. If you're thinking about robbing me, don't."

Andy picked it up and turned it over and over, opening and closing the antenna and tweaking the dials. His hands were shaking with excitement.

"This is what I came for," he said, trying to keep his voice steady. "I was picking up the signals from my apartment."

"Signals? What signals?" She padded back to the sofa and offered him a cup of tea, which he took without noticing. "Is it a cell phone?"

"It's a radio." Andy was so engrossed with his discovery that he just said whatever came to mind. It didn't seem like there was much point in lying to this girl anyway. She had to be psychic if she could keep calm in such a questionable situation. "How long ago did your friend leave? The signals only stopped about ten minutes ago."

"I might have turned it on by accident. What do you want with that thing?" She was sitting on a beanbag chair across from him, back poised stick-straight, her hands around her cup of tea. "Don't damage it. I have to give it back."

Andy reluctantly placed the radio on the table. "Do you know what a radio is?"

"No."

"It's a device for long-distance communication, the same as telephones. Only, unlike telephones, they're illegal. A few years ago, the government collected all the radios they could find, and there haven't been any available for public use since." He could barely keep his hands off it. If he had a screwdriver, it would have already been pulled apart and spread inside-out across the table. "I picked up radio signals from my apartment tonight for the first time in years, and when I tried to trace them, they led me here."

"So?"

"What do you mean, 'so'?" Andy couldn't believe her nonchalance. "So, if I turn you in to the police, you'll get a longer sentence than me. You have a functional radio. Professionally designed, if I had to guess. That's a felony."

"But the thing's not mine."

"Prove it."

They sat in silence for a few moments, until the girl commented: "It seems like you're offering me a way out."

"Someone has been communicating with your radio," Andy said. "I want you to give me this device so I can find out who it is."

"That'll get my friend in trouble. Besides, how do I know you're telling the truth about all this radio stuff?"

"I used to be a radio astronomer."

Her mouth quirked. "Prove it."

Andy sighed. "Look up the radio laws on the SAFE website. You'll see I'm telling the truth about that, at least. Don't try to find out anything about me, though." His social-media profile picture was something he preferred to keep between himself and—ideally, nobody. He wasn't even sure why he bothered with those sites, except that he'd once thought they might help him make friends.

The girl pulled her phone from the depths of her strawberry-colored comforter. "You don't make a good robber," she observed. "Most of them start by taking the phone. It's pretty much robber protocol."

"If you call the police . . ." He grimaced. "Well, I'm already in trouble, so it's not like you could make things worse."

She looked up from her screen. "All these cop cars are here for you?"

"No." Andy tried not to groan aloud. He wasn't an idiot, not ordinarily, or else he never would have gotten an A in that one professor's organic chemistry class. He didn't even like to talk, so how was this girl worming information out of him? "Sort of. My friend had an accident, and the police think I had something to do with it."

"Did you?"

"Do you really think I would be here if I did?"

"Why aren't you with your friend?"

"Just look up the laws." It had finally occurred to him that that she might have already notified the police and simply be killing time until they arrived. It had taken him far too long to think of that. "And then give me your phone. You're right, it'd be inconvenient if you turned me in now."

Obediently, she scrolled through a few pages.

"I believe you on the radio laws," she said at last, closing the app and handing him the phone. "You want to take this radio from me? You might be doing me and Ka—I mean, my friend—a favor, since it sounds like we could get in trouble for having it. I didn't know that, and I doubt he did either."

"That's how I hoped you'd see it." Andy let out a sigh of relief. "Yes, give me the radio and I'll leave. And apologize."

The moment the words left his mouth, he caught a shifty flash in the girl's eyes as they flicked toward the door. It wasn't hard to guess what she was thinking. When he left, if she hadn't already, she'd turn him in. The police would catch him long before he found the source of the broadcast, in which case he might as well have cooperated and gone to jail without kicking up such a fuss. Maybe then he would have gotten a shorter sentence. Maybe they would have let Rilo visit him.

Now he was in too deep.

"Actually," he said, wishing he'd majored in criminology or psychology or anything that might help him now, anything besides physics, "I'm taking you with me."

"What?" For the first time, she looked frightened. "You can't. I've already called the cops."

Andy powered on the phone, grabbed her hand, and pressed her thumb against the sensor. There were no records in the call log from the past hour. She was a good liar. She'd had him ready to bolt.

"We'll take your car," he said. "You do have one, right?"

"Why would I tell you?" The girl's voice was sullen.

She had a glint in her eye like she might kick him where it hurt at any moment. Andy lacked the physique to defend himself, even against this short, pink-haired girl—who was built like she had a membership at the swanky gym down the road and drank kale smoothies on the regular.

"If you turn me in, I'll turn you in. We'll both be in prison for the rest of our lives."

That froze her just long enough. He backed into the kitchen, keeping his eyes on her, and found a knife in the drawer.

"You can scream," he answered, his hand around the handle. He coughed, and, almost blushing, added, "But it won't do you much good if I—if I were to stab you afterward."

Her eyes widened. "You wouldn't." Her words trailed off, and Andy fancied that he had made her believe, at least for a moment, that he would. He deserved a sense of exhilaration from all that bluffing, but he felt a little sick inside.

"What's your name?"

She bit her lip, but a glance at the knife seemed to change her mind. "Roscoe."

"Nice to meet you. I'm Andy."

She sat staring straight ahead at nothing, her comforter wrapped tightly around her shoulders. She didn't look frightened anymore. In fact, she had the audacity to look offended.

Andy couldn't stand another second of the chilly silence. "Alright." He tightened his grip around the knife handle and picked the radio up from the table. "Remember what I said. Go downstairs."

Knife in one hand, radio in the other, he paused before the door. What if he was recognized? It had been nearly two hours since he'd promised to meet the officer in the hospital lobby. By now, there was probably a statewide search for him (or his body), complete with drawings, descriptions, photographs. Maybe his own personal satellite. Grannies everywhere, watching the nightly news channel, would be shaking their heads, clicking their tongues, mumbling a few words of pity for the young man who'd tried to outwit the police. If he sashayed down the stairs of his own apartment, the odds were a hundred—no, a thousand—to one that he'd make it exactly ten steps before someone raised the alarm.

He heard rustling behind him and turned to find that Roscoe had stood up from the sofa and shed her strawberry comforter, revealing silk pajamas. Pink, of course.

"Can I go put on daytime clothes?" she asked, her eyes fixed accusingly on the knife.

"Yes—I mean, no. You can't go where I can't see you."

She opened her mouth to make what Andy was sure would be a scathing remark about his personal morals, but he plunged on. "Once you give me your car and we get out of the city, you can go shopping on my dime." A rash suggestion, since his dime wasn't much more than ten literal cents, but he had a confused idea in the back of his mind that wealth might impress this unimpressionable girl. "It's the least I can do."

The corners of her lips puckered.

"I can get anything I want?"

Andy gave a hesitant nod. "No overdrafts, though."

"You're the worst robber." Roscoe's laughter echoed. "Isn't that like . . . reverse robbery? Like pickpocketing, but putpocketing?"

Something scraped. Andy could barely hear it over the sound of her voice, and he'd ignored it at first, but now he was certain. Someone was turning the front door handle, slowly, cautiously, as though they knew he might overhear. He'd left that unlocked after barging inside, curse his foolishness. If only he'd had a coffee before he came.

A crack of light from the hallway appeared on the floor. She'd left him no choice.

With a surprisingly smooth swoop, though Andy had never been much of an athlete, he wrapped his free arm around Roscoe and drew her to the window, tucking them both in a corner behind the curtains. They were four stories above the ground, and Andy had already seen firsthand what a shorter fall could do. But he was running out of options. If the worst happened, which it would, because it always did, it was best to have some way out of the apartment. If worse came to worst, maybe he could launch the radio out the window and at least save that.

Before Roscoe could scream, he clapped his hand over her mouth and waved the knife in front of her eyes, careful not to let the blade touch her skin.

"Miss Bradley?" came a voice from the front door. A flashlight beam struck the curtains, then drifted away.

"What are you going to say?" Andy hissed in her ear. He meant for the words to sound like a threat, but they shook and squeaked.

"Let go," she whispered, fighting his arm.

That was the point at which he should have used his knife. Instead, he forgot he was holding it until it was too late.

"Then go." He released her so suddenly that she stumbled out into the room. All he could do was hope he'd gotten through to her somehow.

"Officer," she said politely, a tremor in her voice. "Sorry about that. I was looking out the window." Though he couldn't see, Andy knew she must be pointing right at him.

"I understand," said the officer. "Go into the hallway, Miss Bradley."

His slow footsteps drew closer as Roscoe's faded, and Andy heard the jolting sound of metal scraping on metal. A gun being loaded.

Before he could think, he had stuck the knife into the wall and hooked his leg over the windowsill, holding the radio awkwardly under his arm. The officer shouted for him to stop, but to Andy, the warning might as well have been given in ancient Hebrew. He'd hold on to the windowsill by his fingers until everyone left, then climb back inside. He'd find a way to climb up from the window to the roof. He'd—

A *bang*, and a flash, and a tidal wave of pressure and sound. Andy lost his balance.

He didn't wake up for . . . three days? Four days? A week? A year? Or possibly three.

He sat up groggily, wondering what kind of prison cell was padded like this. A sort of hard cushion underneath, something low and stretchy and soft above that brushed the top of his head, and an irritatingly smooth texture wrapped around his shoulders.

"Officer?" he mumbled, lying back down. But he discovered that he couldn't stretch his legs, nor could he lie flat without bumping his neck against something that felt like plastic. All this made him unreasonably angry.

"What am I doing here?" he demanded, sitting up and once again smacking his head.

"Calm down," said a voice. "You're not in jail."

He was so surprised that he momentarily forgot the English language. "Who . . ."

"I know you don't have amnesia. That only happens in romance novels. Which this is not."

"Are you taking me to jail?"

"No. I put you in my car like you asked, and I've got the radio . . .

thing. Locator. That black box you were carrying when you walked in. Broke in, I mean."

Her words were clear enough, but Andy couldn't seem to figure out what they meant. "Why didn't you turn me in?"

"You said you'd turn *me* in if I did. I'm not stupid. I don't want to go to jail."

Andy rubbed his throbbing temples, wondering if he'd finally lost his mind. "That doesn't make sense. Start from the beginning."

There was a long, drawn-out sigh. "I called the police the moment I let you into my house. By the time you made that threat about the radio, it was too late for me to change my mind. Well, when the officer was in my house, you tried to jump out the window. He yelled at you to stop, but you didn't, so he shot at you."

Andy's heart stopped. "Shot me?"

"Shot *at* you. You panicked and took a nosedive into an open dumpster. If it had been closed, you'd be dead. As it is, you're alive, but you reek of garbage. You had a banana peel in your hair, and I had to pull it out. You owe me for that."

"I fell out a fourth-story window and didn't get hurt, but Rilo fell from a third-story window and almost died?" Andy found himself speaking his thought aloud. "That's not fair."

"I'm sorry." Her voice, so steady before, became uneven. "About your friend."

"How do you know about Rilo? Did I tell you?"

The car slowed, then swerved and squealed to a stop.

"It's my fault." There was a choked sob. "It's my fault that happened to your friend."

Andy untangled himself from his seat belt to lean over the front seat. Roscoe was hugging the steering wheel, shoulders shaking, crying like she didn't know or care that he was watching.

He patted her awkwardly on the back. The car was swaying like a cradle, and he couldn't tell whether that was a draft from the cars that were passing them or if he had horrible vertigo.

"So," he asked. "For real, this time. Why did you decide to take me with you?"

# 15

## HALLEY

**IF YOU'D ASKED ME WHAT CAL'S** favorite song was, I couldn't have told you. I didn't even know if he listened to music, or if there was a player in the House like the one we had at home. I didn't know his favorite color or what cot belonged to him or if he liked cats or dogs best. I didn't know his favorite book—I didn't even know if he had any books—and I didn't know what he really thought of Petra or his fellow Mercs or the House or the Alliance or the game he played. I had known him for less than a week.

So it was strange that when I fell asleep, I dreamed about him.

I found myself crouched in the corner of a hideous room. The walls were covered with brown-stained paper, torn and peeling. The floors were tattered carpet, the original color of which remained a disgusting mystery. The lights on the ceiling were flat, rectangular, yellow instead of the usual white, and they droned on and on in an endless hum. I wanted out. I tried to run, but my feet were glued to the floor. I couldn't even close my eyes or turn my neck. All I could do was look straight ahead.

There was a window in the wall in front of me, through which I could see that the sky was dark. Silhouetted against the inkiness was the soldier from the video, tall and still and almost majestic in his uniform. As sometimes happens with lucid dreams, where you know more about the scene than what you see, I was aware that he was waiting for someone.

I heard the squeak of a door opening, though I couldn't look around, and Cal entered the room as though he'd walked right through me.

"I saw you with her." The sergeant did not turn.

"You were right when you said Petra would get in my way," Cal answered. I had never heard his voice so dry. "She did."

"So? What will you do?"

"Nothing."

"'If your eye causes you to stumble, gouge it out and throw it away,'" the sergeant quoted. "'It is better for you to enter life with one eye than to have two eyes and be thrown into the fire of hell.' Believe me, hellfire is what you'll get if you don't back down."

"What a horrendous perversion. I won't stop if you're going to profane things that way."

"Why won't you stop? Finish. Go free."

"I work for you. Fine. I'll do anything you want—nearly anything. But I can't be a spy if it means betraying Petra. All the others—well, that's another thing, if it keeps her safe. But not her. If she's taken a liking to this girl, and if she wants to help her, and if that makes her feel better about herself, it's none of my business. Now, my head is still aching, so if you'll excuse me, I'm going to bed."

He rose to leave, but the door seemed to have locked behind him, or it was blocked from the outside. Cal rattled the handle.

"You're a man," the sergeant jeered. "You're stronger than that village girl."

"That's why I can't do what you're asking."

"We'll kill her."

"And you'll destroy the natural balance"—he emphasized those words as he turned back to the sergeant—"of the game. Isn't that what you said?"

The sergeant's rough-gloved hand smacked Cal's face, but Cal only smiled. "I didn't think you'd stoop this low," he remarked, rubbing his cheek. "You must really be desperate, hitting a man who can't fight back. All because he refused to commit a murder. How noble of you."

The sergeant grabbed Cal's coat collar. They stared at each other, and I tried to shriek, but I couldn't make a sound. The sergeant threw Cal backward, and he crashed against the wall.

"You have twenty-four hours." The sergeant reached for his holster and placed a pistol on the floor. "If you don't, we will."

"You can't deny you're doing this to be cruel." Cal licked blood off his lips. "Why would you want me to kill her when you could just do it yourself?"

"I'd be more than happy to do the honors, but you'd lose your chance to prove you're loyal to the Alliance. Be thankful." His voice went low. "You made me swear when you took this job that our motives are pure. Why bother if you were never going to believe us? What you're doing is for the greater good. Now, get to work and kill that girl before she ruins everything."

Cal picked up the gun and racked the slide. A cartridge clinked on the floor.

"What's to stop me from killing you?" he suggested.

"The fact that you and Petra and the girl would all die anyway. Maybe slower, depending on who takes my place."

That was the first time I'd seen Cal's ever-present smile flicker.

"Then I'm not loyal to the Alliance." He placed the gun on the table. "I could never be loyal to anyone who fights so dirty. You can take that as my final answer, and you can kill me if you don't like it."

"You won't do it?"

"No."

"You won't kill her, and you won't tell us anything else about what Petra, or the villagers, learned from her when she came to the House? You won't even tell us who she is?"

"Still no."

"God help you, then," sighed the sergeant. "God help us both. I'll make you talk, and then I'll find her."

Cal wiped the back of his hand across his mouth. "I hope you try."

The lights blurred, their voices got quiet, and the hum of the lights got louder. I yelled, or at least I tried to yell, but the lights drowned me out, and the louder I shrieked, the less I could hear my own voice rasping in my throat.

I woke up in my own bed.

# 16

## ROSCOE

**ROSCOE DIDN'T KNOW WHETHER TO BE** pleased or annoyed that she'd made Andy believe she was that much of a simpleton. Was it the pink hair? The pink comforter? The pink pajamas? Or was it Andy's own stupidity?

Not that it mattered. The moment he'd let her pick up her phone to "look up the radio laws," she'd texted 911. It was the logical thing to do. Anyone would have done it. A few minutes later, she'd heard boots in the stairwell, and she'd laughed to cover the noise. Andy had once again let her out of his grip and away from the knife. Mission accomplished. Rather nicely too. Now, if only she didn't feel lightheaded with terror—"excitement," she told herself—she could go back to sleep and forget any of this ever happened. She'd hoped Andy would have the good sense not to mention the radio, but if he didn't, she'd deny possession and burn it the moment she was left alone.

Not until the gunshot did she feel a pang of guilt. She had never heard a gun fired so close. It echoed around the landing, repeating a thousand times between the enclosing walls, louder than she had thought possible. In the movies, it wasn't like this. It was clean. Quick. Simple.

For some reason, she had almost pulled away from the first responders wrapping her in a blanket to run back into her apartment and scream at the officer to stop. The paramedics mistook her start for fear and tried to hold her back. Slowly, she relented, reminding herself that Andy deserved all that was coming to him. His story about the radio broadcast reeked of artificiality, and for all Roscoe knew, he'd wheedled his way into her apartment to kick her out the window. Like he'd done to his friend. Once a window kicker, always a window kicker.

"Roscoe!"

She whirled around. She'd know that voice anywhere.

"Kazumi!" She waved, and the blanket slipped off her shoulders. "Over here!"

In an instant, she was wrapped in a bear hug.

"Thank God," he breathed, replacing the blanket and tucking it cozily around her neck. "I thought something terrible had happened."

"How'd you know?"

He ruffled her hair, and in the interest of possible romance, she let it slide. "I heard someone tried to steal my radio. I remembered I left it with you, so I wanted to make sure you were alright. And when I got here, I saw all the ambulances, fire trucks, police."

"You came for your radio?" Roscoe was flustered. She hadn't even told the police about that, worried he would get in trouble. "I . . . I guess that's true, someone did try to steal it." His story didn't explain how he knew.

"Do you have it?"

"What?"

"The radio."

Roscoe pointed to her apartment. "It's in there on the coffee table."

Kazumi whisked past her, past the police—who, she noticed, didn't try to stop him—on into her apartment. He was only gone for a few seconds before he emerged triumphantly with the radio held aloft.

"Did it make noise?" he asked, turning it over in his hands like he was afraid she'd damaged it.

*You're not entitled to him caring about you.* But she couldn't help feeling jealous of the little black box in Kazumi's hands, which seemed to interest him far more than she did. Common human decency, she groused, ought to make him ask her how she felt about almost being murdered before he asked for his radio. Maybe she had misjudged him.

"Well? Did it?" he prodded.

"No."

Roscoe was a poor prophet. She had hardly shut her mouth before the radio crackled to life and a staticky voice emerged from the speakers. This caught the attention of several police officers standing nearby. Much to Roscoe's relief, none of them seemed to know what Kazumi was holding.

"WSG, come in please," the tinny voice said.

"I'll be right back," Kazumi promised her.

"Alright."

He seemed to be trying to smile, but his eyes were shadowed with worry. "Wait for me, please." Gripping the radio, he disappeared around the corner.

This kind of eavesdropping, Roscoe figured, could be filed under the excusable heading of "Checking Out Potential Dates Before Meeting Them Alone." Not to mention that she was desperate for something to distract her attention from the fact that she had almost died. *Which is dramatic. But true this time.*

So, hugging her blanket, she waited until the paramedics were distracted by an order from a police officer. Then she followed Kazumi down the hall.

He hadn't gone far. Though she didn't dare round the corner, Roscoe could clearly hear words and the radio's response.

"We've taken care of your avatar as you ordered," Kazumi's radio voice was saying. Any expression it might have carried was muffled by the weak speaker. "And you were right. It seems he was a double agent, spying for both the Mercs and Warsafe. It's impossible to tell whose side he was really on. He might have changed his mind halfway through. I think he betrayed us to keep that girl safe."

"Of course he did." Roscoe could imagine the way Kazumi was

presumably grinding his teeth, a habit of his when he was tense. She'd seen it before when someone on his team missed a deadline. "We let them get to know each other because we thought Petra would be a stabilizing influence, and she was. Only she stabilized him out of being a soldier."

"I'm sure someone will replace him as our agent. Besides, we still have Sam."

"She can't mingle with the other Mercs the way Cal does. There has to be a way to get him back." The breeze picked up, rustling the trees that overhung the apartments, momentarily veiling Kazumi's voice.

When Roscoe could hear again, a third voice came through the radio. A woman's, this time, low-pitched in an evident effort to speak quietly.

"We have to start fresh," the woman said. "We can tell the beta testers there's another bug, and we can apologize that their accounts got deleted. It's more important that we make sure the player characters can't mess this up. Remind them that they're just that: characters. Not real."

"But there are thirty of them." Kazumi spoke so quickly it was almost an interruption. "And they're real to us."

"What about it?"

"That's . . ." For the first time, there was a trace of hesitation in Kazumi's voice. "We can't just 'start fresh.' We can't kill thirty people."

"Many more lives than that will be saved if Warsafe is successful." The woman's voice rose, as though someone had turned up the radio volume. "Have you forgotten why we're doing this? Do you remember how strongly you believed in this project? We knew there would be sacrifices. We had to reprogram the digital prototypes when they collected too much information. We knew the first batch of real ones would likely be destroyed for the same reason. Don't pretend you weren't warned."

The male radio voice started to say something, which dissolved into a soft *hiss* of static.

"Sergeant?" Kazumi said.

There was a long pause, and then: "I'll need help," the man said. "It'll be a few days before I can get a team out here."

"Fine." Kazumi paused. "You have five days. Got that? Not before, not after. You will do it in exactly five days. Notify me before you start and when you finish. I want to be monitoring everything."

"Copy," the male voice said.

The radio clicked and went silent.

Roscoe clutched at the wall behind her as her legs wobbled. It was far too late now for her to be feeling like this. Far too late for her to be paying the price for her own ignorance. Far too late for her to do anything about it.

Far too late, she understood why she'd hated her work for so long.

The realism.

The secret project.

The way her avatar moved after she turned the game off.

*Did I kill Kazumi's avatar?*

*Did I kill . . . a real person?*

She wanted to scream.

*What have I done?*

*What do I do now?*

"Roscoe?"

Her eyes traveled upward from his shoes to his chest to his face, wearing an expression of innocent puzzlement. Her acting was overdone. His eyes met hers, and she knew she hadn't managed to keep her thoughts a secret.

"The radio . . ." She could do one last thing for those doomed souls. She could snatch the radio from Kazumi and smash it on the ground. She could pay for the pain she'd caused. The violence she'd watched without a second thought. Maybe that would delay their execution for a day or two.

He flicked it out of her reach. "Talk to me. What did you hear?"

"Police!" she shrieked. "He's got a radio! A radio! A—"

"Now, wait a second, Roscoe—" Kazumi started.

But she had fled.

Down the stairs, through the halls, shoving her way past

incurious policemen, trying not to make too much noise so she could hear if Kazumi followed her, Roscoe ran, tripping over the corners of the blanket she still clutched mindlessly. She didn't even stop to question if what she'd heard Kazumi say was true or if the conclusion she'd drawn from his words was reasonable. Of course it wasn't. It never would seem reasonable no matter how much proof she had. But Andy would know. Andy had known something about that radio all along. And thanks to her, he was probably dead. Maybe the police had found him, and she wouldn't get to talk to him. Maybe she'd never know the truth. Maybe she was hallucinating everything. Maybe this was all a horrific dream and she was on her way to the psychiatric ward in a straitjacket. She almost hoped so.

When she rounded the corner and looked up and down the street under her window, she saw no one. No police, no Andy, no nothing.

*So, this is a dream after all. A godforsaken nightmare.*

There was no way he could have walked away from a fall like that. And it was too soon for his body to have been moved—the same two ambulances were still waiting nearby, empty. The police would be down at any moment to look for him, or at least to clean up his splattered remains. She looked up to her window and saw a face framed by a uniform collar. Its mouth moved, and a voice yelled to her to come back.

In her head, she drew a straight line from her window to the ground and followed its path with her eyes. The trajectory ended in an open dumpster.

Her car was parked across the street, and Roscoe, a reckless soul, usually left her keys inside to save herself the trouble of forgetting them and having to walk back up four flights of stairs. She had often scolded herself for this habit, but now she had never been more grateful for her own carelessness. The voice from the window hadn't finished speaking before she had the car unlocked and the engine started and the back door open. Then, still ignoring the shouts, she hoisted herself up on the side of the dumpster and peeked inside.

It smelled like a thousand wheels of cheese. She gagged, but as her eyes adjusted and her nose became numb, she heard a whimper.

"You'd better not be dead," she warned, sliding down into the dumpster feet-first. Eggshells crunched under her shoes, and something slimy brushed against her. She told herself it was her imagination, then spotted an arm and seized it. "You'd better—not—be—"

With a tremendous effort, she hoisted Andy out of the dumpster and almost dropped him on the sidewalk below. But his legs caught on the edge, and he wouldn't move no matter how hard she tugged, so she let him dangle there while she pulled herself out. She'd have a better chance from the other side.

"Hey! You! What are you doing?" This shout was traveling toward her, and when Roscoe turned to look, a solar-bright flashlight made her eyes squint. "Stop!"

She grabbed Andy's legs and pulled him into her shoulders. His weight almost crumpled her, but driven by adrenaline, she staggered across the street and bundled him into her car.

"Stop!" The flashlight wavered wildly. The person holding it was running.

Roscoe didn't wait around to chat. She fumbled with the seat belts, slammed the door on Andy, and flung herself into the driver's seat. Half a tank of gas left. That would be enough to get her out of town, and then she could worry about how she was going to hide her gasoline purchase from the police. That kind of thing probably wasn't possible, but there had to be a way. There always was. Criminals existed no matter the century.

The flashlight glittered in her rearview mirror as she put the car in gear and barreled down the road, swerving to miss the vehicles parallel-parked in front of her. Since when were there so many neighbors? They were probably all standing at their windows now, clicking their tongues at the poor young girl who'd had such a bright future, ruining her life by getting arrested for aiding and abetting a murderer and spending the rest of her life in solitary confinement. They couldn't do that, could they? Solitary confinement would only be temporary—which might be its own punishment. What was she going to say if one of the neighbors asked where she'd been? How do you tell someone you've been in jail for the past twenty years? Reintegration was not an option.

Maybe this was all a misunderstanding. Running from the police, kidnapping a possible murder suspect, abandoning her job and her home and her friends—she had done all this without even sparing a second to think about the consequences she'd face if she were wrong. What if she'd misunderstood Kazumi's words over the radio? Worse still, what if this had been some kind of elaborate prank that had gotten out of hand? What if Warsafe was trying to come up with an excuse to fire her? Even in her half-panicked state, Roscoe managed a grim smile at the last possibility. There were much easier ways they could have tried first if they were that determined to get her off the payroll. She ought to feel honored she was getting this much attention.

But there was one thing Kazumi had said that she couldn't forget, and when she replayed the phrase in her head, it was hard to come up with an alternative interpretation. *I should have killed her when Roscoe gave me access to her account.* That *her* couldn't be anyone besides Roscoe's avatar, who, apparently, had a name besides xXRoscoeVersion13Xx. That *her* was a girl, a real girl.

And then there was someone called Petra. Or maybe those were the same person. Such an odd name, Roscoe thought, although she was hardly one to talk. What kind of person was Petra? Had she joined Warsafe Games willingly? Did she look anything like Version 13, with digitally enhanced eyes and a trim prosthetic arm? Was she one of the other beta testers' characters?

Roscoe let out a shaky breath. If the real-life character had any resemblance to her appearance in the game, then Roscoe had an awful lot of apologizing to do. Scratch that—apologies wouldn't be enough. And groveling with her forehead to the floor wouldn't make any difference now, anyway.

When she was certain no one was following, at least not closely, she pulled over to the side of the road and looked back at Andy. He was draped across the seat with his arm wrapped around a headrest. His lank figure was crumpled and squished against both doors, so she tugged at any limbs she could reach until he looked a little more comfortable. He never woke up, no matter how hard she pulled. He might have to go to the hospital, and there would be police at the hospital. There always were.

A quick search of medical sites informed her that he had severe brain damage and a hemorrhage and was going to die in the back seat of her car. But his pulse seemed steady, and the only exterior damage she could see was harsh purple bruises on his forehead and elbow.

So she kept driving, murmuring incoherent prayers under her breath that she wouldn't become a murderer and that Andy would wake up.

And, eventually, he did.

Andy was still groggy. That must have been why he couldn't immediately determine whether he had gone insane.

"Wait, wait, wait. Stop," he said, putting his hands up in the air. "Hold on. You're telling me that this video game company you work for is using *real people* in a game? So what? Doesn't every game use human models these days?"

"They're not models. They're real people playing the game. They're the characters."

Andy couldn't think of a reply.

"Don't you get it?" Roscoe demanded. "You need to use your radio locator to find the source of the transmission. And then we have to go there, and we have to save the people."

He didn't get it. He hadn't thought that far ahead. He was still stuck on the details, a great number of which continued to escape him. "How is the game played?"

Roscoe kept her eyes fixed straight ahead. "The player starts out on the bottom floor of an eight-story house. There are guards on every floor, and the player has to either knock them out or sneak past them to get to the next floor. Once they get to the roof, they win, and then just start all over again."

"So it's a standard, combat-based RPG?" Andy, who had never played a video game in his life, was a great lover of technical terms. "But don't the player characters just regenerate after they die in games like that? How could a real person regenerate?"

Roscoe shifted uncomfortably. "Not in a permadeath game."

"A what?"

"A permadeath game. Player characters die permanently when they're killed."

"Oh." He didn't want to think about what that implied, and his fuzzy head was doing a great job of making sure he couldn't.

"But are you certain?" he asked. "Are you sure you heard your friend correctly?"

"Are you *sure* radios are illegal?" Roscoe mimicked. Andy thought, from the catch in her voice, that she must be close to losing her temper. "Are you sure I had a radio in my apartment? Are you sure you heard someone talking through it?"

"Let me put it this way." Andy took a deep breath. "We sound insane. Are we agreeing to believe each other no matter how little sense our stories make?"

"I believe you," Roscoe told him. "I don't have a choice. I need to find out what's going on, and you're the only way I can."

"Then I believe you too." Andy decided his head was already starting to feel better. Reconciliation was a charm.

He felt around in his pockets for his radio locator, which he had stuffed away shortly after entering Roscoe's apartment. Despite the abuse it had endured when he fell from the window, it powered on, but this time the red light held steady.

"We should find a place to rest," he told Roscoe. "Someplace where the cops won't think to look for us. I can't do anything with the locator until there's a broadcast, so we have to wait."

Manicured fingernails tapped the steering wheel. "Alright. But I'm new to this whole criminal thing. I think we should keep driving until we have to stop for gas."

"Do you have cash or a credit card?"

"Uh . . ." Roscoe cleared her throat. "I was in a hurry."

"I think I have a credit card," Andy said. "But if I know anything, I know the cops can trace electronic transactions."

"Why don't we stop somewhere now and withdraw some cash?" Roscoe suggested. "By the time that's discovered, we'll be miles away, and we'll keep driving until we need to refuel. I don't think anyone can trace paper money."

"Probably not," agreed Andy, who had no idea. "Where are we?"

Roscoe was about to pull out her phone, but Andy stopped her. "They can definitely trace that."

She slammed a palm against the steering wheel in frustration. "Once we find the source of the radio transmissions, what are we going to do? How are we going to go back to our normal lives? You're probably a felon, and I'm a co-felon or something. Are we ever going to be able do basic things like use credit cards and make phone calls?"

"We'll emigrate." It was the only solution Andy had come up with so far.

"Thirty people's lives are on the line. We could get there faster if we took more risks. Like buying food and water and whatever else we need."

"We won't get there at all if we get caught. We can take turns watching the locator and driving to make it faster."

"You're not driving. You got knocked out. The medical site says you have a concussion. Or a contusion. I forget which one is worse."

"But—"

"We won't get there at all if you wreck the car."

Andy was forced to concede. "Did you get any sleep before I came barging into your apartment?"

"No."

"Then we have to stop somewhere, and soon. Let's find a parking lot where there are lots of other cars. While you're sleeping, I'll switch our license plates."

"You'll do what?"

"If we can find a supermarket, there'll probably be an ATM inside I can use right before we leave. I can also buy some batteries for the locator. I'll get you up after you've slept for a while, or if I get a signal."

"You seem to have this all planned out." Her eyes narrowed. "Are you sure this isn't a setup?"

"Frankly," Andy observed, immensely pleased that he was finally winning a point, "your story sounds a lot crazier than mine. Yours has cyborg humans. Mine just has radios."

That silenced her—for a moment, anyway.

"I see a sign for a Walmart," she said. "I'll pull in there."

"Park in the middle."

She did as he suggested, then leaned her seat back with a *thump*. "I'm exhausted," she admitted, yawning. "And it's so bright in here. Why'd the only empty space have to be directly under the light?"

"You know what they say about that being the safest place to hide." Andy took off his jacket and tucked the sleeves into the front-seat handholds, covering the windshield and casting a shadow over Roscoe's face. "Sleep tight."

Roscoe's head was already nestled into her shoulder.

There were exactly two things Andy knew about being a professional thief, both of which he'd learned from action films. One: The police were ridiculously inefficient when the thief was the good guy and marvelously efficient when he was the bad guy. Andy was not yet certain which category he and Roscoe belonged to, so that didn't help much. Two: Police had eagle eyes that could read license plates and model numbers from half a mile away. He could work on that.

Wincing at the chilly night air, he climbed out of the car to do some petty thievery. He didn't have a screwdriver, but he scavenged an old bottle cap that had been crushed flat by a car wheel. This bit of ingenuity inflated his ego, and his headache improved rapidly as he distracted himself by using the twisted metal cap to unscrew Roscoe's license plate. Then, pulling his suit collar high around his neck, he stood up and scanned the parking lot.

Roscoe's car was as basic as they came, and he had only been searching for a few minutes when he found one of the same make and model. A different color, unfortunately, but he had to count his blessings.

Working quickly, terrified of wasting time by looking around to see if anyone was watching, he removed its license plate and replaced it with Roscoe's. No one, he thought, would be likely to notice such a minor change. The digits weren't even that far off. And maybe if Roscoe did end up getting pulled over, the cop would only notice that the license plate was registered to a car that almost matched Roscoe's and ignore the slight difference between the black car he'd stolen the plates from and Roscoe's bright red one.

He started humming as he screwed the stolen plate onto Roscoe's car. Only a few hours before, he'd been resigned to spending the rest of his life in prison. Now he was squatting in a parking lot, having committed his first official robbery, keeping the promise he'd made to the unconscious Rilo, and running off to see the world and have a little adventure. A science fiction–sounding adventure that he only believed because he'd promised that he would. Exactly the right thing for a depressed, overworked twenty-something-year-old to be doing.

It was tempting to just give up already and turn himself in.

Roscoe's deranged claim that thirty people were about to be murdered, all for the sake of some unreleased video game, had gotten stuck in processing and wasn't likely to sink in anytime soon. For one thing, Andy wasn't sure he hadn't hallucinated the whole story. It was just that preposterous. And even if he had heard Roscoe correctly, it didn't seem like she had much foundation for her belief. One innocent conversation about video games and one eavesdropped conversation could easily be misunderstood. Besides, what kind of civilized modern person could justify killing to develop a video game?

Something flashing caught his attention, and he twisted to look at his radio locator. The red light was blinking with aggravating slowness, and the arrow was swinging to point across the parking lot. He automatically followed it with his eyes, though he could tell from the speed of the blinking that there was no way he'd see anything. The signal was too far away.

With an old man's grunt, he stood up and peeked in Roscoe's window. He hadn't been gone long, but she was sleeping peacefully, lips parted, breath even and steady. It would be a shame to wake her before she'd had a true rest.

Andy made a mental note of a light post directly in front of his locator arrow. He was glad he did, for the red blinking light went solid a few moments later, and the arrow swiveled back to its resting position.

Suddenly chilly, he snuggled against the tire, not wanting to get back inside the car for fear of waking Roscoe. He had forgotten he was wearing a suit, and for a split second, he agonized about how dirty it must be. But then, when had he ever cared about that? He tucked his feet up under him in case a car got close and rested his head against the wheel well, rocking thoughtfully.

The next thing he knew, he found himself being shaken awake by a disheveled Roscoe. Her pink silk pajamas were wrinkled, and her pink hair made a wild halo—tinged with pretty orange from the sun, Andy couldn't help noticing—around her face.

"Get up," she ordered, irritation plain in her voice. "I thought you said you were going to wake me up, not sit there with your legs stretched out in an empty parking space. What if you'd been run over?"

Andy blinked and rubbed his hand across his aching forehead. "Is it time to go?"

"You tell me! You were supposed to be paying attention!"

"What time is it?"

Roscoe had to start her car to find out that it was already after eight. This, in turn, reminded them that no matter how much of a hurry they were in, they wouldn't be going far. The gas light was on, and the needle was at the bottom of the gauge.

"They'll know it's us as soon as we walk in front of a security camera. We stand out too much," Roscoe fretted, examining herself in the rearview mirror. "You look like you got drunk at a Nobel Prize committee, and I look like someone you kidnapped on your way home. I'll go inside and get us some cash and normal clothes. You . . ." She had a doubtful look, like she didn't think there was much Andy could contribute. "You're a scientist. You know something about cars. Make sure this will get us to wherever we're going."

That was a mistake. Andy could grasp the principles of the engine, and he understood the purpose of the battery, and he had a vague idea of which hole the windshield wiper fluid went in, but he had no idea how these things worked together to produce locomotion.

Trying to look professional in case Roscoe came back while he was working, he flicked the gas cap to make sure it was tight, fumbled with the air conditioner to check for blockages, and tried to open the hood to analyze leaks. He couldn't get it open, though, and if he couldn't even see the engine, the battery, or the wiper fluid, he was at a loss. Since Roscoe still hadn't come back, he opened the trunk to see if there was any food. Breakfast. Everybody liked breakfast.

A stack of exuberant pharmaceutical advertisements flew up in his face, caught by the breeze. Apparently Roscoe had garden-variety allergies. Why keep all these pamphlets, he wondered, but no food?

Annoyed, he brushed them aside. They scattered to reveal a dusty video-game console.

He thought it wouldn't be charged, but to his surprise, it turned on readily when he flipped it over and pressed the power button. The controls didn't take much getting used to, and he managed to navigate to the main menu.

The first game on the list, the most recently played, was *Permadeath*. The icon was too small for Andy to make out exactly what it was, but it looked something like a child's sketch of a house.

*So, the game's real, at least.*

He navigated to the icon and launched the game. The splash screen flashed "WARNING!" in bright red text, and he almost dropped the console. But it was only a reminder that he was playing a beta version not intended for the general public and that distribution was forbidden by the terms of the nondisclosure agreement. Andy didn't consider himself the public, so he continued.

A simplistic loading bar appeared, and a white slogan was printed across the screen: *Safety requires the many to sacrifice the one.* Interesting. Ominous. It hovered there, flashing, until Andy wondered if the console had frozen. Just when he was about to turn it off, the screen flickered, and he found himself looking at a dark room. A closet, more like. In the center stood a girl—the playable character, perhaps? She was short, pale, dark-haired, and sickly. Her eyes were an unnatural shade of turquoise, and they were half-closed, sullen, and unhappy, seeming to look right at him through the screen with a hateful glare. He found himself looking away. He felt as though he'd done something horribly wrong already, just by making her appear.

"Hey, you," he said uncomfortably. "Are you real?"

The girl on the screen crossed her arms and leaned backward, letting her head rest against the wall.

"Are you tired?"

Andy couldn't even tell if she was breathing.

"You can't hear me, can you?"

The girl's head dropped to her chest, and she started to slide down the wall.

"Hey, wake up!" Andy urged.

She did, just before she hit the floor, and stood up with a soft grunt. Her hands reached for her eyes, and she rubbed them.

"What are you doing?" asked a very real, very loud voice that made Andy jump about a foot into the air. Roscoe had appeared out of nowhere with her arms covered in plastic grocery bag handles. "Where did you find that thing? How does it even have any battery power left?"

"Who is this?" Andy turned the screen toward her.

"How did you—?" Roscoe snatched it from him and powered off the console. "I warned you about this. That's not just some fantasy character that lives in a server somewhere. If I'm right about all this, that's a person. A real, live human being that you just put in fear for her life."

"What? How did I do that? What did I do? I was just pushing buttons to see if I could find the game you were talking about."

"I thought we were taking each other on faith."

Andy looked at her. "You're telling me that a major company is committing mass homicide. You have to admit, it's a little hard to believe."

The wind ruffled the plastic bags, and Roscoe let them all drop to the concrete.

"It's hard for me to believe," she said, kneeling and digging around in the bags. Either her voice had gone quiet, or the rustling had gotten louder. Andy could barely hear her. "Do you know how many people I had to give up on when I gave up on Warsafe last night? My younger self, for one thing. Some guy I thought I might be in love with. Not that you care, but it all mattered to me."

"I'm listening." Andy crouched beside her and pretended to be helping her find whatever she was looking for. Which was probably, if he had to guess, something pink.

She rocked back on her heels. "I'm accepting that all these people are murderers. Sixteen-year-old Roscoe didn't know she was going to grow up to kill people." Her eyes welled with tears. "Three . . . three of them . . ." She could barely talk as tears rolled down her nose, dripping down to her chest and leaving wet spots on her pink pajama top. "Three . . . before . . . her. And I almost . . . if it hadn't been for Kazumi . . . she'd also have been . . ."

"But she isn't. I just saw her. She's alive, and she's . . ." Andy couldn't think of a positive synonym for "functional enough not to pass out cold on the floor," so he swerved: "She was ready to go to work. She's not so overwhelmed that she couldn't keep doing what she's good at."

"Killing. If you had pressed the start button, that girl would've started killing. *That's* what she's good at. That's what I—" Roscoe began to shake uncontrollably. "That's what I'm good at. Making her do it. And I'm not even very good at that."

Andy wished he could explain how ridiculous that statement sounded. Huddled in the middle of a Walmart parking lot, crying until she could barely catch her breath, burying her pink head in her hands, Roscoe hardly looked the part of a murderer.

"You didn't know, Roscoe. You couldn't have known."

"I should have guessed. I should have found out. I should have—"

"The more you worry about your conscience, the less likely it is that you can save these people. Stop thinking about what happened in the past. Start thinking about how we're going to get over there." He pointed toward the lamppost. "This light isn't blinking fast, so we have a long way to go."

She wiped her eyes with her thumbs, stuck in the habit of trying not to smear her makeup. "Help me pick these up," she muttered, turning away from him and filling her hands with bags. Somehow, although she had carried them all by herself when she'd left the store, she could only collect about half of them now before she was overloaded. "Are you just going to sit there?"

He scrambled to obey, slightly daunted that she hadn't had a better reaction to his profound philosophical observations. Science could only go so far when it came to tackling emotions. That was why he was so bad at writing essays, which was why he had no job. Which was why he lived in a shabby apartment, which was why someone had been able to break in, which was why Rilo had been injured, which was why Roscoe's life had been uprooted.

Sunlight struck him in the face as he stood, able to look over the hood of the car. Its brilliance nauseated him, and he stumbled backward.

"Roscoe," he wheezed, holding up his hand to block the sunlight, "I don't feel so—"

He didn't think he could lower himself to the ground, but gravity did the job for him. He was on his back, first looking up at the sky, then grateful to close his eyes and lie back and let the sleepiness win.

*The pavement feels cool.*

Something struck his cheek, and he summoned the energy to flinch. "Andy!" called a faded voice. "Can you hear me?" Another strike. "Open your eyes, Andy. Open your eyes and look at me!"

*Not even for you, I can't.*

It was so warm here. So comfortable he never wanted to get up.

"I didn't risk my career and my future to let you die in a parking lot," said the voice, so faint that although Andy somehow got the gist of what it was saying, he couldn't recognize a word. "If I have to call an ambulance, I will. What will we do then? Andy, wake up! Stay with me!"

Andy couldn't remember why calling an ambulance would be such a disaster.

But he did remember how Rilo had looked in the hospital.

*Pale.*

*Sick.*

*Dying.*

*Not dying. I have to help him. I have to—*

His eyelids were so heavy. Like they were weighted down with lead. One push, then another, and a sliver of light poked into the comfortable blackness, sharp and blinding. He blinked and decided that it wasn't so painful as he expected. Something cast a shadow over his face, something fluffy and pink, something with a halo.

*An angel.*

"Get your sorry self up," snapped a high-pitched voice, "or I'll leave you in the parking lot."

*What kind of angel would—?*

He opened his eyes again, incredulous, and discovered that he was looking at Roscoe.

She rocked back, leaning against the stack of bags he had dropped. "We have to get you to a hospital," she said, gathering the bags and tucking one of them under Andy's head. "You're still sick from your concussion. Somebody needs to take a look at you. Don't worry, Andy. I'm sure we'll come up with something. Some other plan. You don't have to go with me. Don't worry about what I said."

He sat bolt-upright, head swimming. The haziness cleared after a few seconds of blank staring, and he took a deep breath.

"No." He put his hand on Roscoe's. She had taken out her phone and was about to power it on. "Don't call anyone. I'm fine."

"You're not fine. You fainted in a Walmart parking lot."

"That's a new low," he admitted. "But I was conscious the whole time."

"You were not."

"I was."

"No, you weren't."

"Roscoe, we're sitting in the road. Can you help me get up, and then can you pick up the bags?"

She helped him to his feet, and he balanced himself gingerly against the car.

"See?" Andy held out his arms. "I'm fine. Standing and walking. What more do I need?"

A tense giggle escaped Roscoe's lips. "The med site says you're going to die."

"It's not like the hospital can do much. They're not going to give me a magic cure, and they'll probably keep me overnight for observation. By that time, the cops will have caught us. In fact"— Andy squinted at the sun, successfully this time, and ran a quick mental calculation—"it's already getting late. We have to get out of here."

"You did not just look up at the sun and figure out what time it is. They only do that in books."

"I need this, Roscoe. For Rilo. For myself too." He blushed, suddenly aware that he was confiding in the person he had kidnapped, who had dragged him out of a dumpster and pulled a banana peel out of his hair.

Roscoe managed a shaky smile. "Alright, then. This bag is yours. Get changed, and then we're off."

"You'd be passing out, too, if you went all night with no sleep," Andy flung back over his shoulder. He hoped that was true. *Passing out is normal, isn't it? There's nothing special about me, is there?* "I'll be back in a few minutes." Hopefully in one piece.

Everything was alright. Everything would be alright, as long as the blackness didn't come again. If it did—well, he'd just have to figure things out when it happened.

# 17

## HALLEY

**CAL'S PERSONAL BOX SAT IN THE** middle of the room. It was made of cardboard, well-used, square, about sixteen inches to a side, and it was stacked to the brim with papers. I'd never seen so much loose-leaf in one place, for it was a rarity in the village. Perhaps that was the reward Cal got in exchange for his spying. The money we used on the island, shiny copper coins, was already plentiful enough that he wouldn't have asked for more.

*Don't speak ill of the dead. Cal must have had a reason for what he did.*

Looking at a dead person's papers makes you feel despicable. You don't deserve to know what they were thinking just because they're gone. As Petra sifted through the box, handing a few sheets to me and setting others aside, I smelled the dust and the ink and the paper, and it made my throat sore and my eyes water. I was already crying, and I hadn't even been in the room five minutes. As always, I was useless.

Petra's eyes bored holes in the side of my head, and I knew what she was thinking: I wasn't cut out for this, and she should just send me home. So I wiped my eyes stubbornly and picked up the first of the papers she'd handed me.

"Chapter Sixteen, *With Love from the Past*," ran the heading at the top of the page.

I skimmed the text, which described some kind of futuristic detective fiction. Not bad, I thought. Not bad at all. Had Cal wanted to be a writer? I would've liked to read his novels. His writing wasn't technically polished, but it possessed an artless charisma that made me feel like I could hear his voice through the words on the page.

I wondered if Petra was thinking the same thing. I hoped she was.

"Poems," said Petra, tossing a stack of paper into the corner with, I thought, unnecessary violence. Her prosthetic hand was shaking—an electrical malfunction, perhaps. "That's why he was always taking notes."

She buried her nose in a spiral-bound notebook, and I crawled across the room to examine the papers she'd thrown away. They were crinkled around the edges as though Petra had pinched them while reading. And when I smoothed them out, I understood why. The poems were about her. Not directly. The actors were flowers and leaves and clouds and sunlight and other natural things, but they were pale and small and had blue eyes and were quiet and shy and kind and gentle. All the things Petra would have been if it weren't for the House and what it had done to her. For all Cal's bitterness, these little stories were as cheerful and lighthearted as warm sun and fresh air. Somehow, they were very like him. And although I hadn't liked much I'd seen of Cal, I found myself liking these.

A crinkled paper clipping slipped from between the pages, drifting down and vanishing under one of the cots. I scrambled to retrieve the paper and a handful of dust bunnies, smoothing the creases across my knee.

It was a photograph. So sharp and clear that it was barely an image, almost the real thing. Gray stone walls, monumental in height, crowned by a steeple and a gilded cross that, from the camera's viewpoint on the ground, looked at first like a glimmer of sunlight. The walls were trimmed with heavy glass windows, pictures themselves—colorful pictures of a dying man, of doves, of mourners, of the letter *A* and another that I couldn't read, of hands clasped in pleading. Pictures that caught the sunlight and threw bursts of sharp, reflective color over the street, decorating the pitted steps leading to the door.

One of the doctor's old books had a picture like this. I'd found it as a child, and curiosity made me struggle through the caption I could barely read. In some fictional world, or in some world that no longer existed, was a building meant for people to worship God. God being, of course, some kind of divine entity who was still human enough, or interested enough, or something enough to wonder what His congregation was up to and present Himself at those events. Sometimes. Though the people never admitted whether they could see Him or whether His presence was more like air or wind, undeniable but invisible. Because what would God look like if you could see Him? No one could say exactly, except that a God deserving of such a monument must be wonderful indeed.

I knew about religion. Nothing specific, but at least I knew what it was—belief in something other than the Alliance as the determining factor of our lives. Some of the grandmas used to murmur little prayers before they opened their booths in the morning, a blessing over the food they sold or over the Players who would eat it and die. Prayers that asked little and accomplished less. The enforcement chips had never punished anyone for that kind of quiet talk, but it was vaguely understood that any attempt to worship in groups would be considered an act of sedition and, thus, punishable by anything between sudden death and conscription as a Mercenary.

I wondered, briefly, if Cal had been religious. He was already a Mercenary, so he had little left to lose. And he always wore that cross necklace. But there was something paradoxical about a Cal who got down on his knees beside his bed before he went to sleep.

When I looked at the picture again, wondering whether those walls would be cold or warm to the touch, and what those glass windows would look like from the inside, I wondered if maybe there was more to his spirituality than nighttime lullabies.

There was something else too. The picture I'd seen in the doctor's book had been a drawing. This was a photograph, and nothing could be photographed if it didn't exist. If the building wasn't here, and if it never had been, maybe Petra was right, and there were other islands. Somewhere out there, somewhere we couldn't reach any more than we could hop into this picture and make it our reality.

I folded the poems gently and put them back inside the box. Petra, fixated on the notebook, didn't seem to notice I had taken them.

The next paper in my stack was folded and thick. I shook it. Out fell a cream-colored envelope made of some lush material I had never seen before. I flipped it over, and there was Petra's name scrawled in a messy stripe of ink.

I held it up. "This one's for you."

Her titanium fingers were cold against mine as she took it from me and slit open the envelope.

"Go over there," she ordered, sitting down against the wall.

I retired obediently to the opposite corner of the room, dragging the rest of my papers with me.

"Chapter Seventeen, *WLFTP*," said the next one. I wondered if I could find all the chapters and have the doctor help me bind them into a book. Maybe Petra would like that. Maybe it would be a nice surprise for her. Or maybe it would just make things worse.

There was a quiet gasp from Petra's side of the room. It was all I could do not to inquire, but I knew better than to interrupt her while she was reading Cal's letter.

I skimmed Chapter 17 in silence for a few minutes, wondering idly if Cal had left some kind of secret code in his novel. Maybe the first letter of each paragraph spelled out something simple and obvious like "Go to the beach at sunset and there will be a boat to get you off the island." He could've just written that out without bothering to encode it. After all, he had been reckless about revealing to both sides that he was a spy. He hadn't seemed afraid of getting caught.

I swallowed. Cal would like to be remembered as idiotically brave. He'd probably crack a morbid joke about it that would make Petra worry, and he'd be the only one to find it funny.

I glanced up at Petra, half-expecting her to have crumpled the letter and tossed it across the room like she'd done with the poems. But she hadn't, not yet anyway. Her eyes were still fixed on that scrap of paper, wide open, filled with silent tears that began dripping onto the page.

Once again, I crawled over to her on my hands and knees. I put a tentative hand on her. I had never expected to see her cry.

Petra let the letter slip to the floor and buried her head in her hands. "'You're real?'" She drew in a deep breath and lifted her head. "I heard him say it. He was so surprised. I should have known."

"Known what?"

She shook her head. "I can't explain. It can't be true."

I picked up the page she'd let fall. "Can I read this?"

She nodded.

I stretched my legs out in front of me and spread the paper across my knees.

> Dear Petra,
>
> If you're reading this, you either suspect that I'm a spy and are going through my belongings (how dare you read my secret papers! Just kidding, I'm in no position to say I mind) or I'm dead and you want to know how it happened. Either way, this letter is coming too late. But I have a secret to tell you before I'm gone for good.
>
> We've talked about the chips. Do you remember? You used to tell me that you think the Alliance can control our minds, and I'd laugh and tell you that's impossible. I did that because it was my job to make sure you never found out the truth. And back then, I wanted to work conscientiously because I thought I could keep you safe that way. I think I succeeded in changing your mind.
>
> The truth is what you thought at the beginning. The chips do control our minds when we're in a match. They're designed by the Alliance, and they're tricking you. Tricking you to think you're fighting real people. But you're not. Do you hear

me, Petra? Read this part carefully because it's the last and most important thing I can give you. You're not a murderer. Neither am I. None of us are. We haven't killed a single person. All those guards are laser-generated holograms that your mind, controlled by the chip, thinks are real. They can inflict real damage, but they're not real themselves. If you were to take any of the villagers into the House, they would only see you fighting with thin air. Don't get angry with Halley for keeping it a secret; I swore I'd kill her if she told you. Just theatrics, of course, but she wouldn't have known.

You're not a terrible person. I am. For knowing and not telling you. At least let me explain why I didn't. If I had, you would have pitied the other Mercs and told them the truth. And there's at least one other Alliance spy besides me, so you must not tell anyone, Petra, not even now that I'm gone, because if it gets to the wrong person, I'm sure you'll all be killed. I hope that my death or my treachery, whichever it is that has happened, will show you I mean what I say.

You're free. Free from all guilt. You don't have to worry about what to do with me, either. I won't get in your way after this. Whatever you choose to do, I'm sure it will be right.

Thank you for making my time on the island a little less miserable. I'm sorry for everything I did to make yours worse. In another life, I'd have done better for you. But I tried my best in the only way I knew how. That's God's honest truth. You know I love you so I won't say it again.

Cal

# 18

## ROSCOE

**THERE WAS JUST ONE OBSTACLE ANDY** had failed to factor into his calculations: the Pacific Ocean.

"Maybe . . . a boat?" Roscoe suggested, spitting a strand of salty hair out of her mouth. Ocean water and dyed hair made a crunchy blend.

"How are we going to rent a boat? Do you know anything about boats?"

"I kayaked once."

The distance indicator on the radio locator flashed. They looked down at it, then out at the water, then back at the swiveling red arrow, then at each other. There wasn't much else to see—the beach was flat and rocky in both directions, and intermittent rain had eliminated sunbathers. On another day, Roscoe might have made a dive at that crab or poked one of the anemones clinging to the offshore rocks. As things stood, all she could do was shiver and wish she had a warm blanket.

"It really is pointing directly out into the water."

*Leave it to Andy to state the obvious*, Roscoe thought uncharitably.

"We've got to get there somehow," she said aloud. "We don't have a choice. You're a wanted man, and I'm probably going to be sent to a mental hospital if they catch me. It's do or die."

"Surely people rent boats. Seattle is a seafaring city, isn't it?"

"Why are you asking me? How long have you lived here?"

"I was born here."

"Then act like it." Roscoe took a deep breath and dug her toes into the sand. She couldn't start an argument, not now, not while she still hadn't found Petra. "Of course we can rent a boat. The question is, how will we learn how to use it? The other question is, do we have enough cash to pay the rental fee?"

"It can't be that hard to drive a boat." Andy patted her shoulder. "You can figure it out, I'm sure."

"Excuse me? Why does it have to be me?"

"Because I don't know how to drive a boat, and I will never learn. I hate the ocean. I hate water. I hate boats. I hate things that move underneath me."

"Great," she huffed. "So you're going to be seasick the whole time."

"But look." Andy pointed to the blinking red light on the locator. "It's flashing quickly now. We're close. Whatever we're looking for can't be far offshore."

"Could we take the ferry?"

"You tell me. Do you think War—what did you call it? Warsafe?— would have their secret operations somewhere so obvious that the ferry can get to it?"

That was a surprisingly coherent thought for Andy, and Roscoe had to admit he was probably right.

"Besides, we don't have time to waste," Andy continued, pocketing the locator. "If we get on a ferry and go to the wrong place, we'll lose hours."

A sharp gust of wind blew sand in Roscoe's face, and she coughed. "Can you estimate how far away the thing we're looking for is?"

Andy squinted at the blinking light. "Maybe fifty miles?"

"Fifty miles!" exclaimed Roscoe. "Is that what you meant by 'not far'? You really want me to drive a boat *fifty miles* into the Pacific Ocean? Have you lost your mind?"

"Well, what else are we going to do?" he retorted, flinging his hands in the air. "I've got to show Rilo that he didn't get almost murdered for nothing, and you think that thirty people are about to get assassinated. Neither of us has much of a choice."

Roscoe snapped her fingers. "That's right! I forgot we're criminals!" She clapped her hand over her mouth and looked around, wide-eyed and guilty, but they were still alone on the beach. "We can steal a boat," she went on, keeping her voice just loud enough to be heard over the waves. "We can just get in somebody's boat and take it. What are they going to do, put us in prison?"

"That's a terrible idea. For starters, I'm not a criminal. Except for the radio thing. But I don't even know for sure if the police found out about that. Plus, you're not a criminal if I'm not a criminal. The last thing we need right now is a real record."

Roscoe rubbed her temples. "Why do you always think of things I don't?" she groaned, plopping down in the sand. She looked up at him. "How hard can it be to drive a boat? It's just like driving a car, right? Do you even need a license?"

"Probably, and I'm sure a car license won't help you drive a boat," Andy said, but added optimistically, "Let's keep looking until we find a place that doesn't require it."

Without her phone to use as a GPS, stuck in an unfamiliar part of the city, Roscoe had no idea where to start. They wandered along the shore, entering any dockside shop that had "boat" in the name, getting turned away at each when Roscoe admitted that she didn't have a boating license. In they went, and out they were kicked, until Roscoe's cheap shoes began to feel like they were made of concrete.

"The more people see our faces, the more likely we are to get caught." She pulled the floppy sunhat from Walmart over her face to keep the drizzle out of her eyes. This wasn't what she'd been hoping to use it for. "We need to figure out where to go before we keep walking."

Andy didn't respond. His eyes were fixed on the sidewalk, and he was clearly daydreaming. Roscoe didn't even want to imagine what he was thinking about. Probably some lengthy mathematical equation. She just hoped it had some relevance to their current predicament.

"Hello." She snapped her fingers under his nose, startling him so badly that he jumped. "Are you paying attention? You're the one who's going to jail if we don't find this boat."

"Yes, well, I'm probably going to jail, anyway, even—I mean, especially—if we find a boat." He looked around, and his gaze landed on a waterfront building constructed like a warehouse. "What about that one?"

"Electric Boats?"

"Is that what it—I mean, yes, I was going to tell you to go over there once we got a little closer. I've had my eye on it for a while. Electric boats sound like a great idea. Where are we going to stop in the middle of the Pacific Ocean to get gasoline?"

Roscoe sat down on a bench and crossed her blistered foot over her knee. "Where are we going to stop to plug in the boat? You're a scientist. Can't you come up with some kind of salt-water-powered generator?"

Andy's whole face went beet red, and for a moment, Roscoe couldn't tell if he was angry or embarrassed.

"Do you know anything about science, Roscoe?" he finally asked, drawing a deep breath.

"What are you going to do to me if I say no?"

"Science isn't random knowledge. Science is a way of thinking. Science is a lens through which we view the world. Science is—"

Roscoe got to her feet, swaying reluctantly. "My scientific worldview tells me that I won't be able to walk much further, so if we want to rent a boat, we should give this place a shot. Let's go."

"—the way in which we approach a problem, trying to think practically about it and eliminate all the—where are you going?"

Roscoe was already across the street, half-walking, half-limping her way through a traffic jam. She raised her hand and motioned for Andy to follow, but she didn't look back to see if he was. If he wanted to go on talking about science while the court processed their warrants, he was welcome to his cell.

A speaker crackled to life as Roscoe opened the warehouse door. "Welcome to Electric Boats," said the prerecorded message. "We thank you for choosing us, and we wish you a comfortable voyage."

With a burst of energy, Andy caught up to her and tried to hold the door open. He arrived a moment too late and found himself standing awkwardly in the street while Roscoe approached the salesman.

"How can I help you today?" he asked, his attention fixed on the receipt he was writing. Then he looked up, and something about Roscoe's face convinced him he might be willing to try a little harder. "We have a wide selection of luxury boats," he began, straightening, "that are available for tours along the—"

"Do you need a boating license to rent?"

"No, ma'am." He glanced at Andy, who had made a belated entrance.

"I want your fastest boat." Roscoe leaned in, and the salesman's attention quickly reverted to her. "I want to see surf. I want to make waves. I want speed."

Andy grimaced.

"That would be the Speedy. She goes seven miles per hour." The salesman fished a stack of papers out of a drawer behind the counter. "As I was saying, she's a luxury craft, equipped with bass-boosting speakers, a refrigerator, cushioned seats—"

"Seven miles per hour?" Roscoe's eyes went wide. "So it's going to take seven hours?"

"Ma'am? You can't keep the boat for seven hours. We'll be closed if you stay out that long."

"She's not talking about your boat," Andy broke in, shooting Roscoe a glare that was as eloquent as a ten-minute speech. *Shut up. Don't say another word, or he's going to kick us out like everybody else did.* "She's talking about how long it would take us to get around the lake in our hometown. We were thinking about purchasing a boat just like this, which is why we're renting yours."

The salesman frowned, but he pushed the paperwork across the counter.

"Sign here, please," he said, indicating a blank at the bottom of the page. "And here, and here, and please initial here, and—"

"I can read," Roscoe snapped, and then regretted it. "It's been a long day."

"You could say that again." Andy nodded sagely.

Roscoe ignored him, burying her nose in the paperwork.

How suspicious would it be if she wrote down her driver's license number and credit card number "from memory"? She didn't have her wallet or phone, so she couldn't even pretend to be looking at the numbers. She would just have to hope that the salesman wasn't too observant, and that sixteen digits was the right amount for a credit card. Did driver's licenses have twenty? Twenty-four? Did it vary by state?

Six pages deep in legalese, she reached the final signature line. There she paused, pen hovering over the paper. If the salesman ran the fake credit card number she had written down, they would be caught before they could even escape the store.

"Do we have to pay up-front, or do we pay when we get back?" she asked.

Andy stepped in front of her, pretending to reach for a business card, and discreetly pointed toward the street. Two men in police uniforms were standing beside the bench Roscoe had been sitting on, and they were talking to a woman with a neon-yellow grocery bag who had walked past them several minutes before. She pointed at their warehouse.

One of the cops glanced over, and Roscoe accidentally made eye contact with him through the glass.

"You pay when you return the boat." The salesman looked like he was having second thoughts, and Roscoe had to tug to get the keys out of his hand. "You'll be taking the boat on the second dock. Do you need me to show you how to—?"

"We've got it." Andy was dragging Roscoe to the dockside door, wounded foot and all. "We've done this plenty of times before. We're Seattle natives. Have a nice day."

"That's the wrong door," the salesman warned them, and Andy course-corrected with a jerk. He opened the door and pushed her out, then shut it tightly. He had no key for the lock, so he dragged a trash can in front of it and tucked it under the handle.

"Let's get out of here," he said. "Are we really taking the boat?"

"Are you kidding? After we went to all this trouble to get it?"

"There are so many problems with this situation," Andy complained, huffing and puffing, barely able to keep up with Roscoe as they strode down the dock. "First of all, what on God's green earth is an *electric* boat? Did nobody think that putting humans on a generator and then submerging them in a large body of water might be dangerous? Second of all—"

"You get what you get, and you don't pitch a fit. We got a boat, and that's more than I expected, and we're going to save those people. Besides . . ." Her bright blue eyes narrowed. "I thought you said it was a good idea. You were the one who pointed out the electric boat rental."

"Yes, well," he said awkwardly. "I'll only take credit for it if it works."

The trash can rattled.

"And it had better work," Andy added, breaking into a run, "because we're stuck with it now."

# 19

## HALLEY

**I SHOULD HAVE STAYED WITH HER.**
But Cal had been right about me. The overwhelming presence of the House had sapped my courage and turned me into a child again. I had to get away from it, even if it meant leaving Petra there, alone in a sea of papers and tears and questions and painful, bittersweet memories.

So I left when she told me to, and I pondered questions of my own.

*If they can control the Mercs' minds, can they control ours too?*
*What if the game hasn't been going for as long as we thought?*
*What if none of this is real?*
*What if this is all a dream?*

The one question that never entered my head was: *Is it true?*

Because it didn't matter if Cal was telling the truth. It didn't matter if what he'd said about the Mercs fighting holograms was right. What mattered was that he knew, or at least had thought he knew—because who would willfully lie in the last letter they wrote before they died?—and he had never told Petra. Worse still, he'd told me not to tell her, implicating me in his lies of omission.

I had never guessed the magnitude of the secret I was carrying. I had never guessed that Petra thought she was a murderer. I thought they all knew they were only killing ghosts. Invisible, electronically generated ghosts that looked real and could inflict real injury, but critically weren't real themselves.

What I read in that letter turned my world upside down. It must have shattered Petra's.

I wondered what she was thinking, how she was taking the news. What she had decided to do with what she knew. But I didn't get to ask. For days, she didn't come to the village, and I couldn't bring myself to go near the House. I wasn't sure Cal's parenthetical had been enough to convince her that I was an unwilling, unknowing accomplice, and I was afraid of what she might do to me. So I told myself, and I was cravenly grateful for the excuse. If I didn't see the House, maybe I could forget all about this. If I never saw Cal's memorial, that lonely stack of scribbled papers, maybe I could go on living like I had never met him so that I would never have to mourn him.

*Papers.*

I could forget the poems. I could forget the plot of his book. Try as I might, though, I couldn't forget the secret he had unveiled in his last letter.

It was obvious why the Alliance would have holographic guards instead of real people. Perhaps it was so obvious that it was surprising Petra hadn't thought of it herself. Lasers were replaceable. Humans were not. There weren't as many Mercs as there were guards, so the Alliance could afford to replace the latter.

It was all very logical, very rational. If it was conveniently forgotten that the Mercs had souls.

That got me thinking about what role the villagers played in the scheme, since Cal's letter implied deception that went far beyond the Mercs' game. Most of the people in the village assumed that we had all been here forever and that the game had been going on for eternity. I had thought that too until Petra suggested some of our memories might be fabricated. *What has always been, always is.* No one thought to question the status quo. But now I knew there were a lot of somewheres. Cal was getting his paper and his orders from somewhere. The man who had murdered Cal must have come from somewhere. The Alliance had to be located somewhere. If

Petra was right and they weren't on the island, there must be a way of traveling back and forth, which meant that we should be able to make the voyage too. Why hadn't we?

Had we been deceived into thinking this island was all that existed?

To imagine a world outside our little land, a village outside our self-sufficient town with people I had never met—it was like learning that fairies were real. But now I had a reason to hope they were.

Two days later, I was manning the lemonade stand. My mind had wandered far from my body, and I was fantasizing about how I was going to explain to Mother why I was locking myself in my room immediately after work, and why I didn't want dinner, and why I'd had to take anti-nausea medication for the past two days. The doctor had forbidden her from asking questions. But dear old Mother really did love me. Seeing my distress and being unable to do anything about it hurt her gentle heart. I wished I could tell her the truth. I had started to do it, but the doctor reminded me with a significant finger across his lips that he and Mother weren't the only ones listening.

"Excuse me. Do you live here?"

I blinked. Two customers had appeared in front of the lemonade stand. One was a woman with blue eyes and pink hair. Pretty, I would have said aloud, if I could say anything. The other was a disheveled man with wacky curls that stood up in points. They were an odd pair.

Odder still was the fact that I'd never seen either of them before.

"Do you live here?" the man repeated.

Nobody had ever asked me that. My mouth opened, then closed, then opened again. I knew what I wanted to say: "Obviously. Where else could I live?" But I couldn't get the words out.

"Of course she does," the pink-haired lady scolded. "If this island belongs to Warsafe, everyone must live here."

Reverting to my programmed routine, my mouth grinned widely and said: "Lemonade, one coin per cup!" while I choked on my embarrassment.

"Lemonade?" the man asked, raising one perplexed eyebrow.

"Coin?" He fished in his pockets and handed me a small brass object. There was a face on one side and a grand building with columns on the other.

"Sorry, honored customer. It seems like you want to barter, but this shop only accepts coins."

"But that *is* a coin."

"Not everyone is American," the woman observed dryly. "They have their own currency."

American? Another island like ours?

I could hear my heartbeat in my ears.

"Can you tell us where to find Petra?" asked the man, replacing his "coin" in his pocket. "She's got dark hair and blue eyes."

All that came out of my mouth was: "Sorry, honored customer. I don't understand the question."

"P-E-T-R-A." He sounded annoyed. "Petra. You must know her."

"Sorry, honored customer. I don't understand the question." I opened my mouth frantically, willing my lips to move, but I couldn't say anything more.

The pink-haired woman drew closer. "Do you know what you're saying?"

"Sorry, honored customer. I don't—"

"The game can't be played after nine o'clock Seattle time," she said, turning to her companion. "If we wait until then, we might be able to get more than preprogrammed responses out of these people. But there's an error-prevention mechanic that prevents players from going off-script. It'll crash if you keep triggering the same response over and over, so we have to stop harassing her. Besides, I'm exhausted. Don't you want to give those heated leather seats a try?"

If they knew about the House and about the game, they knew too much. Enough to be the Alliance spies Cal had warned us about.

"I wanted something to eat," the disheveled man groaned, "but I don't think I could keep any of this stuff down. It smells awful."

*Well, thank you.* Not that he was wrong. I was pretty sure the sun had fermented my lemonade, and there was no telling what it had done to the seafood.

"Let's go back to the boat, then," said the pink-haired woman.

"Goodbye, honored customers!" I chirped.

The customers, who were not really customers since they didn't seem interested in the lemonade, walked away, and I was left to scream silently inside my immobile body. For three hours, I sat there in agony, until I finally felt the iron vise on my mouth slip and the door to my booth unlock. The chip had let me go. In a flash, I was on my feet and sprinting up the hill.

At the crest, right in front of the House, I paused, panting, and rested my hands on my knees. I was getting good at this climb, but I had never beaten my previous record of ten minutes. Below me, laid out in a dismal panorama of dark-colored roofs and winding streets, the village glowed in the fading orange light. Two dark specks were moving between the first house and the base of the slope. I had a head start thanks to the fact that none of the villagers had been able to give the visitors information, but I didn't know if it would be enough.

I gulped in a deep breath and stumbled into the House. Luckily, the door was unlocked, though I didn't see anyone nearby. Strange. It was the first time I'd seen it that way. Thank goodness one of the Mercs had gotten careless on the very day efficiency required it.

A disembodied voice spoke from the shadows. "Petra isn't here."

I turned toward the sound, and after some blinking, identified the speaker as Ponytail, the girl who'd led the discussion about Cal. Today, her hair was in a bun, specifically to confuse me.

"We haven't seen her all day," she continued.

"Haven't seen her?" I groped for the wall, feeling dizzy. "Is she in a match?"

A bony hand grabbed my shoulder and steadied me. "She's not here. Aren't you that girl who was visiting her the other day? It's me, Sam."

She hadn't told me her name when we'd met before, but I pretended to remember. "There are strange people in the village," I told her. "Two of them. A man and a woman. I've never seen either of them before. They came up to my booth and asked me questions

I didn't know it was possible to ask, and I couldn't answer them, and they wanted to know where Petra is."

"People? How could there be new people? Where could they have come from?"

I described their appearances and tried to recite exactly what they'd said to me and to each other. With every detail I added, Sam grew more and more agitated. Even before I was finished, she'd started pacing, and her response to my story came out in an anxious murmur.

"We have to find Petra before curfew."

"Wouldn't she come back before then?"

"What if she comes at the last minute? You wouldn't be here to explain."

The obvious response—that Sam could relay what I'd said—occurred to me and was promptly dismissed. She'd been so quick to dismiss it herself. Evidently she had other things to think about, though I couldn't imagine what those might be.

"Then we have to look for her."

Sam shook her head. "We Mercs can't just leave the House. If we're called in for a match, we have to be ready within five minutes, or we'll be shocked by the chips."

"Petra wasn't afraid to leave."

"Would you be thinking straight if your best friend had just died?"

"You can't leave, then. But I could."

"That's what I was hoping you'd say." Sam smiled. It had the same flashing brilliance as Cal's, and for a moment, I thought I saw his face in hers. It was only my imagination, though—they looked nothing alike. "You don't know your way around, but the forest isn't that big, and once it gets dark, you'll be able to see the village lights to find your way back."

As I let myself out the front door, I glanced at my watch. Work had ended at nine and curfew began at eleven, so I had about an hour and a half left before I'd have to start running down the hill. The mountain was huge, I was alone, and Petra knew how to keep herself hidden if she didn't want to be found. I didn't stand a chance, but I couldn't think of a better alternative.

Something hard hit me in the face, and I stumbled backward and landed hard on my backside. My vision blurred. I discerned the pink-haired woman and her peculiar friend, looking down at me with friendly concern.

"Oh, it's the lemonade girl!" cried the man, extending his hand with a smile that certainly looked kind and a little shy. Much less alarming than I remembered. "I'm sorry about that, I didn't see you opening the door. I'm Andy."

"And I'm Roscoe," said the pink-haired woman.

In a daze—possibly from my fall, or just from the shock of running into them—I took Andy's hand and let him pull me to my feet.

"I'm Halley," I told him. Then I wished I hadn't. Hoping they'd forget if I rushed to another subject, I added politely, "I don't have time to talk."

"Wait!" said Roscoe, grabbing my arm. "You haven't answered the question we asked earlier. Do you know anyone named Petra? We asked around in the village, but everyone told us to come here."

I started to say no. Then I had an idea. This pair had waited for hours to talk to me, and they were still just as determined as ever. Having their help might be better than going to look for Petra alone, even if they turned out to be hostile. A girl with pink hair and a praying mantis—the spindly man with glasses—didn't stand a chance against Petra.

So I told them, "Petra's usually here, but she's wandered off. If she's not back by eleven, she'll be killed by the enforcement chips."

Roscoe's breath hissed between her lips. "Where do we start?"

"Andy, you can look along the road," I suggested. "Roscoe, if you go left, I'll go right. We have a little over an hour. If we can't find her by then . . ." I forced a smile. I had no idea what we'd do, but I wasn't going to admit it. "Let's hope it doesn't turn out that way."

They nodded, and we started off in opposite directions.

The mountain was dark at night. Not dark like the village, which was always lit up with ugly white streetlights that made a few hard shadows, but dark like only wilderness can be, with surprising noises bursting out at every step and only pale starlight to hint at where they come from. Points near the ground glowed, that might be eyes, but they didn't move. If they were eyes, they just stared, watching your every step. The mind conjured up the worst possible things and placed them in the bushes, where you couldn't quite see them, but you suspected they might see you. Each rustle and stir and crunch underfoot reinforced fear, and soon there would be the shaking and shivering and the thinking you couldn't go on.

Having lived in the village my whole life, I had never seen true darkness. Up here on the mountain, with the wind tossing my hair and the branches catching my sweater, I had never felt so trapped, though I had never been so free.

My watch ticked. My clothes were torn because I couldn't see to avoid the brambles, and my feet were aching and wet through my boots. My throat was sore from shouting Petra's name, and my eyes were crossed from straining to see what was lurking in the bushes. Maybe Petra didn't want to be found. Maybe—and I was upset at myself for thinking it—she didn't deserve to be found.

She was, after all, a killer. Or at least she thought she was, and that hadn't stopped her.

"Petra!" I shrieked, my voice rasping in my throat. One last time. "Where are you?"

Through the crunching of my boots in the underbrush and my own heavy breathing, I thought I heard a distant voice say: "What are you doing here?"

Suddenly the underbrush vanished, and I discovered that my feet were planted on solid rock. And instead of darkness, the horizon was splendidly lit and glowing against the evening fog.

I had found a natural overlook, rimmed with trees and bushes in three directions, but steep and barren on the fourth. Below my feet, which had strayed dangerously close to the edge, was the village, all lit up in its evening splendor. At least it looked splendid from up here.

Perched on the edge, legs dangling over the precipice, was Petra.

I sat down beside her, halfway to tears from relief. "I've been looking for you forever," I said. "I thought I'd never find you."

Her prosthetic arm threw a cold turquoise glow across her face as she turned to look at me, surprised. "Why were you looking for me?"

"Why do you think?" The words came out in a rush. "Petra, something's happened. People have come. From the Alliance, I guess. You were right. This island isn't all that exists. They came from somewhere. They're probably here to kill us."

"You haven't been killed yet, have you?" Why must everything remind me of Cal? Even Petra's gentle mockery seemed off-kilter for her, more a reflection of her so-called friend than her own thoughts. "How did you meet these people? And why did you come looking for me?"

I explained how they'd visited my lemonade stand, and what they'd said, and how Sam had suggested I search the forest, and how I'd decided that having them look was better than having no help at all. Her reaction, much like Sam's, was surprise and horror. But her first question was quite different.

"Are you alright?" she demanded, seizing my shoulders as she knelt and looked at me intently. "Did they hurt you? Did they ask about your family? Do you think they'll try to follow you?"

I was glad she cared enough to ask, but I had no more answers than she did.

She let go, staring straight into my wide eyes. "Let's get you home. Tomorrow we'll figure out what to do about those two. You should be safe after curfew."

As she walked along the path, her steps firm and determined as though she knew exactly where she was going, I trailed a little behind. Not far enough to get lost or spooked by the noises, just far enough that she couldn't hear me mumbling. I had to talk myself down from my panic before we met up with Roscoe and Andy.

"Hey!" Petra's voice made me flinch, and I broke off in the middle of reciting a poem Mother had once forced me to memorize.

She grabbed my wrist and yanked my arm up to her eye level.

Her face paled. "That's it," she whispered. "It's past curfew!"

No. Impossible. Absolutely impossible. I had watched the time as though my life depended on it—because it did. I'd had a whole half hour remaining to get home after I heard Petra's voice. That should have been more than enough time to get to the village and back if we economized.

But with our conversation and Petra's exhaustion and my naïve carelessness and the forest's comforting quietness and the cliff's lovely view . . . could time really have flown so fast?

I maneuvered my wrist out of Petra's grip and checked my watch. 11:03.

"I'm not dead," I breathed, awed. "Neither are you."

"Are you sure your watch is right?"

I tapped it with my finger and shook my wrist up and down and blinked a few times and tried to read the display upside down. I knew how to account for my own occasional idiocy. But the hands ticked steadily onward, and now it was 11:04.

"It's never been wrong before." I held it up for Petra to double-check, though the bright turquoise numbers were as clear as the moon in the sky. "How did we do it?"

Our conversation was interrupted by a rhythmic *crunch* of underbrush. It wasn't the kind of stealthy crunch that could be a late-night squirrel or bird or raccoon—it was heavy and careless. And it seemed to have started out of nowhere, not far from where we were standing.

Petra put a finger to her lips.

Someone shrieked: "PETRA!"

I almost collapsed with relief. At least we didn't have to go looking for her too. The voice belonged to the pink-haired girl. Roscoe.

She came barreling out from behind a tree, and before I could respond, she slammed right into me, knocking us both inelegantly to the ground.

By the time I managed to get my wind back, Roscoe had already moved on. I peeked up from the underbrush to see her and Petra standing across from each other, eyes locked, both motionless. It looked like an old-fashioned standoff, the kind described in the doctor's novels where the cowboys stand with pistols and wait until one of them makes a move. Roscoe's back was to me, so I had no idea what she was thinking, but I could tell from the rapid lights on Petra's prosthetic arm that she was tense.

"It really is you." Roscoe was the first to speak. "You were the one Kazumi talked about."

She reached a tentative hand toward Petra. Petra flicked it away. "Who are you?"

"Roscoe, where'd you go?" complained a drawling, masculine voice from somewhere near the nettles. "We shouldn't have listened to that girl and gotten separated like this. I don't know anything about being in the woods late at night. Are there bears here?"

Apparently getting bruised and banged up wasn't enough punishment. *That girl* was a definite demotion.

Roscoe's wild-haired companion emerged into the clearing. Petra tensed, evidently ready for a fight.

"Wow." Andy's attention was immediately caught by Petra's arm. "You must have had a serious accident to end up with a bionic limb like that."

"Don't touch," Petra snapped.

Andy's eyes widened, and his jaw slacked. He pointed shakily at Petra's black metal hand. "Did . . . did you just *move* that?" Ignoring Petra's protests—which were half-hearted because it was easy to see that Andy's curiosity was about as threatening as a seagull—he took her hand and held it up. "Can you feel this? Can you move your fingers? Can you—?"

"She's my avatar." Roscoe glanced at Andy.

"Observe the incredible juxtaposition between high technology and primitive style." Andy was oblivious to anything but his own glee. He turned Petra's hand over and over, waving it up and down, playing with the lights, sticking his fingers into the elbow joint. I was surprised at how patiently she endured it. "She's dressed like a French peasant, but she's got this amazing functional prosthetic. Did you see the machines they had back in the village? Automatic vending machines, automatic shops, automatic everything, but the buildings were barely out of the Stone Age."

I glared at him. Did Stone Age humans have music players in

their *buildings*—otherwise known as *homes, thank you very much?* How about automatic dressers?

"We don't have technology like this back on the mainland. I could spend a hundred years in a lab and never come up with something so intricate, so purposeful. Why, these people are—"

"Andy," interrupted Roscoe more loudly this time. "She's my avatar. She's the character I play in the video game."

Video . . . game. A game on video? A video of a game? What a strange combination of words.

One of them I understood with no trouble at all. Game. *The* game. So Roscoe and Andy were somehow involved. That made them dangerous, no matter how friendly they seemed.

Andy's mouth clamped shut. In the pause that followed, I managed to struggle to my feet and dust off my leaf-encrusted knees. I thought my sudden resurrection from the underbrush would startle at least one of the pair, for the silence had become tense and uncomfortable, but they had eyes for no one and nothing besides Petra.

She snatched her titanium hand out of Andy's grip and took a few steps back, eyeing them skeptically. "You seem to know more about what's going on than we do."

I got ready to run, in case—in case—well, I wasn't sure, but I could imagine at least fifty ways things could go south. Maybe a hundred. Maybe more.

Unfortunately, none of them was the right one.

"It's . . ." Roscoe looked doubtfully at Andy.

"It's a long story," he finished hastily.

And one that I didn't get to hear.

Something soft slipped over my mouth, and before I could lift my hands to investigate, my head spun, and the ground became as attractive as a magnet. I opened my mouth to scream, but my eyes were already closing.

No sound escaped that tight blanket.

# 20

## KAZUMI

"NO, I'M NOT RELATED TO HIM. No, I'm not his father-in-law. No, I'm not his legal guardian. The man is in his twenties. Can't I just talk to him for a moment?"

"He's asleep."

"For heaven's sake, why? It's eleven thirty in the morning."

"I can't discuss a patient's personal information without—"

"When he wakes up, will you tell him to call me back?"

"I'll leave a note."

"Fantastic." Kazumi's face was getting hot with frustration. He wasn't used to arguing to get his way. "Goodbye."

Six hours later, he still hadn't gotten a return call. He dialed the hospital again, and after an unnecessarily long argument with the front desk, he was transferred to the room phone.

"Hello?" answered a groggy voice.

"Hello. This is Kazumi Sato, calling from Warsafe Games. How are you today, Mr. Walsh?"

"Walsh?" In the silence that followed, Kazumi was almost certain he could hear the man's joints crack as he stretched. "You can call me Rilo. Everybody calls me Rilo. Are you calling to tell me how I ended up here?"

"I'm calling to offer you a job."

"A what?"

"Would you be interested in working for Warsafe Games, Mr.—Rilo?"

"I honestly have no idea what that is. I'm not big into that board-game stuff. Though I did play Monopoly once when—"

"We provide excellent medical insurance."

"Oh?"

"Your hospital bills would be fully covered."

"Oh?"

"We're a video-game development company, and we're looking for a full-time computer technician. It is my understanding that you are currently in the hospital and are expected to remain there for another week or so. You could start work when you're feeling better, but you'd receive insurance and other benefits right away."

"This sounds like a scam." Rilo's good sense hadn't quite been knocked out of him.

"It's no scam." Kazumi caught a glimpse of his grinning reflection in his glass window. "Your friend Andrew is an acquaintance, and he asked me to pull some strings to help cover your medical costs."

"Andy." Rilo became suddenly mournful. "How would I know if you're telling the truth about being Andy's friend? He hasn't come to visit me. Is he afraid I'm going to be mad at him for letting me get so drunk that I jumped out of a window?"

"I'm not sure if this counts as proof, but I can tell you that Andy goes to his corner convenience store almost every night around two a.m. and buys the same box of spicy ramen noodles. He used to be a heavy smoker too. He's not proud of either habit, so how would I know unless we're friends?"

"Hmm. Maybe you're right." Rustling noises in the background interrupted him, and then he continued, in a milder tone, "I'll have to think about your offer. They've got me so dosed up on some medication . . . what was it again, nurse? F . . . fexofenadine?"

"Fentanyl," came a faraway voice.

"Yeah, that's right, fentanyl. Anyway, I can't think straight. Call me back later. Or email me some paperwork. I'll get back to you as soon as I can, thanks. Have a great day."

"What's your email address?"

Kazumi scribbled his loopy answer on a pad, holding the phone to his ear with his shoulder. "I'll send you papers to sign. Remember, Mr.—er, Rilo, your hospital bills will be paid if you accept this job."

"You sound like the Good Samaritan."

"I hope you feel better soon."

"Good . . . Saaa . . ."

*Click.*

Kazumi couldn't quite keep his lips from twitching as he hung up the phone. Rilo and Andy were such polar opposites, he reflected, that it was a wonder—and lucky for him—they had ever become friends.

Bad form. A would-be assassin couldn't start ruminating about his targets.

Not that Kazumi had volunteered for this job. He just happened to be President Samantha Aeron's errand boy. Saying no to a direct order from Aeron was risky at best, the kind of mistake that got you kicked out of a window much higher than three stories. *Defenestrated*, Kazumi had written in his report. The word for that punishment of the ages.

Kazumi had pointed out how Rilo's death would probably motivate Andy to fight harder. Of course he had said nothing about how he didn't want the mission. He thought his logic was airtight enough to get him out of committing the murder, but Aeron had disagreed.

"If Rilo gets hurt," she reasoned, "and Andy thinks it's because of his radio, he'll back down. His personality type is averse to physical pain, and he won't want to share his friend's fate. We can't have him intercepting and tracing our transmissions. That was the whole point of using radio communications in the first place. No, we have to either kill Andy or Rilo, and Rilo is easier because we might need Andy's help if one of our radios breaks down."

*Look who turned out to be right.*

It had been difficult to find a car with a crushable roof that might provide some cushioning, but Kazumi had succeeded. The rest . . . well, he had connections, and he didn't mind getting his own hands dirty or putting on a convenience store clerk's apron when it came in handy.

But Kazumi was tired of hurting people. Leveling up Petra, Roscoe's avatar, had been an exhausting task. She looked so miserable as her energy meter drained, he'd almost caught himself feeling sorry for the pixels on his screen. And Calhoun. Kazumi could only imagine how hungry he would be for revenge if he knew that Kazumi had allowed Roscoe to walk him so close to death.

But it had to be done. If Petra's arm hadn't been wounded, she wouldn't have been able to get her prosthetic, and she would never have met Halley. She would never have formulated a plan to free herself from the House's constraints. If someone hadn't played her until her rank increased, Roscoe would have killed her and never known the difference. If Calhoun hadn't been injured, no one would have been able to take him prisoner, and Petra wouldn't have been incentivized to investigate the House's secrets. It was all a magnificent puzzle, and it was Kazumi's opinion that there were too many moving parts. He was no psychoanalyst, though he was playing the role as best he could.

It occurred to him that he was starting to get moody, and when he got moody, he didn't get any work done. He glanced at the special edition Warsafe Games poster pinned to his office wall and tried to focus his eyes on the words President Aeron had written when she signed it:

*If you forget everything else, remember this: Safety requires the many to sacrifice the one.*

"Forty days," Kazumi reminded himself. "Forty down, forty to go, and the game will be complete."

Forty days and his task would be over. *One way or another, this, too, shall pass.*

## 21

### HALLEY

"HEY."

*What if I dyed my hair pink?*

"Wake up."

*Wake up?*

But I was already awake.

*Then act like it.*

I opened my eyes.

There was Cal.

*I'm dead.*

I let my eyelids drift closed. No point in trying to keep myself awake if I was dead.

"You're not dead," Cal assured me.

His telepathy only reinforced the conviction that I was, in fact, dead. Because what kind of normal human could read thoughts like that?

"In fact, you're in the House," he said. "Somewhere on the eighth floor."

I peeked out through half-closed eyes and noticed that he was sitting in a chair. This seemed like a prosaic choice for a ghost. If someone could float, wouldn't they want to do it all the time? At least I could confirm the village legends about the House being haunted. Cal and I were here to prove it.

Even though he was a ghost, I was unexpectedly delighted to see him again. I tried to get up so I could give him a hug on Petra's behalf—where was she right now? I wondered. Did she know about my untimely demise?—and a smack for personal gratification. But I found that I, too, was sitting in a chair, and my hands were tied to its arms.

Strange. What kind of sorcerer was powerful enough to tie up a ghost?

I settled for saying, "I missed you." There was a pleasant, lingering lightness in my head that kept me from realizing it might be time to panic. But the sensation was fading, and my thoughts cleared with a jolt. "No, wait, that's not it. I mean, Petra missed you. She read your poems."

"Did she read my letter?" He leaned forward slightly. His hands must have also been tied, because he came to a rough stop. "Did she tell anyone?"

"She read it. No, she didn't say anything." That I knew of, anyway.

"Did it make her feel better?"

"I don't think so."

*Why did you force me to lie?*

I couldn't let that be the first thing I asked him, not after everything he'd gone through on our behalf. Once the words left my mouth, there would be no taking them back, and I still wasn't sure how I felt about what Cal had done.

My eyes were beginning to adjust to the shadows, and I tried to map out the room. It was long—about twenty feet, by a rough and dim guess—but not wide. So it was a hallway. Cal and I were sitting across from each other, and a white bulb, heavily obscured by dust, was hanging between us. The chairs we were sitting in looked like they had once been white plastic, but they were a dirty, flaking cream now. They didn't seem very ghostly. Quite solid, in fact.

I might not be a ghost after all.

But what about Cal? There was the problem. If his wounds hadn't killed him, the gunshot certainly had. Yet he was sitting across from me, and I could talk to him, which meant that I had either developed magical powers or we were both dead.

I tried to rub my eyes to clear up the confusion, but of course, I couldn't move my hands. In the absence of alternatives, I decided to be direct.

"Are you a ghost?"

He chuckled. "Why would you think that?" Then his eyes widened. "Don't tell me. Did Petra think I was killed?"

"Everyone did. Back there in . . . real life . . ." I blinked and tried to clear my head. If Cal wasn't dead, then I wasn't dead, either. But what if this was all just a cosmic trick to make me *think* I was alive? What if I was really dead after all?

This confused me so much that I fell silent.

"Halley," Cal said. "If you'll listen, I can explain."

Well, I could at least hear him out. If I was a ghost, I had all the time in the world and then some. If I was alive, I wasn't going anywhere, anyway.

"Did you see the video where I confessed to being a spy?"

I nodded.

"The Alliance didn't know I set that up. So they weren't supposed to realize I'm a double agent, but I wanted *you* to know, just in case I wasn't able to escape and come back to tell you." He gave his head a shake. "I didn't think you'd jump to all sorts of conclusions. I wasn't dead, just a prisoner. Didn't you see that ugly soldier brute knock me on the head with his rifle?"

"We heard a gunshot," I told him. By some miracle, his words were starting to make sense. I could dimly begin to see how it had all happened, although the why was still elusive. My fingers were tingling, and I clenched my fists to get my blood flowing. "One of the Mercs said it meant you were dead."

"Who?"

"Ponytail. That is . . ." It took me a moment to remember her name. "Sam."

"Interesting." He stared thoughtfully at the ceiling. Then looked back at me. "But what about you? How did you end up here?"

"Well, assuming I'm not dead . . ." I tried to think about what had happened before I'd woken up, but I couldn't remember anything after I'd found Petra. I explained what little I did recall as best I could.

"What a strange chain of events," Cal mused. "And to think I've been within two hundred feet of you and the grieving Petra—she *was* sad, wasn't she?—this whole time."

"Does the Alliance still not know you're a double agent?"

"Well," Cal said. "I may have confessed under . . . duress."

"Duress?"

"Don't worry. I doubt you have any information they need." Reassuring. "The Alliance has been trying to figure out whose side I'm on and how much of a liability I am."

I stared hard at Cal, trying to figure out what he meant. All the blood that had lingered from his injuries during the match he'd played with me had been cleaned away, and he was sitting up straight and proud. His chest wound had healed remarkably, almost like it would have if the doctor had treated him.

Perhaps the Alliance had its own doctor. Perhaps they knew how to make him scream without leaving a mark of their cruelty.

"Anyway," he went on, observing that my thoughts had wandered, "I knew my letter would make Petra happy. I'm glad she read it. I almost wanted to fake my own death so she'd read it sooner, but I couldn't risk her knowing."

"Then why wait?" This was a question that had been bothering me since I'd read the letter. "If you were planning to tell her all along, why not do it right away?"

"Well." His smile vanished. "I shouldn't have told her at all. The Alliance would kill her if they had any idea she knew. But I couldn't stand thinking she'd never find out. And I couldn't trust the other Mercs, because one of them might be a spy, too, so I wrote it down. Besides . . ." He paused. "I honestly thought she knew. I dropped hints. I thought she'd guess."

I wondered about that. She had reacted so strongly to Cal's letter. But was it because she hadn't known what it contained, or because it was proof Cal had been lying to her?

The wall to my right flashed white, dazzling me until all I could see were light and dark spots. I blinked and blinked until I could bear the brightness. Then I saw that the wall was illuminated with a projection showing the same overexposed, grainy video I'd seen on the House surveillance cameras. Except this time, I was looking at the front room on the first floor of the House. Instead of Cal and the sergeant, there were three people in front of the camera: Petra, Roscoe, and Andy.

"I should have known dear old Sergeant Porok had something else up his sleeve," Cal muttered, leaning forward as far as his bonds would let him.

"Why should I have to play?" Petra demanded. Her voice rasped from inside the screen. "You can't force me when there's no operator on the other side of the screen. What do you want me to do, stand here forever until someone comes and kills me?"

"You won't play for yourself." A booming voice crackled to life through what sounded like a loudspeaker. "But will you play for someone else?"

Another light flicked on, this time shining in my face. I jerked my arms to cover my eyes and failed miserably. But my motion was so sharp and sudden that it knocked over my chair. With one last desperate attempt to correct my balance, I toppled off to the side, unable to stifle a cry of surprise that echoed Cal's.

"Where did you find her?" Petra stepped closer to the camera. "Where is she?"

"She's on the eighth floor," said the loudspeaker. "It'll be easy for you to get her back. All you have to do is come get her."

"No, Petra!" cried Cal. "Don't do it!"

The light went out before he could finish, and our camera must have switched off with it.

Petra pointed to Roscoe and Andy. "Leave them out of this. They're not Mercs. They have no place in the game."

"Bring them with you."

"I can't fight for three."

"Cal told you that the enemies in the House aren't real, didn't he? You'll only be fighting for yourself. Think how funny you'll look to those two!" The voice dissolved into a chuckle. "We'll broadcast everything to Halley. If you don't make it, neither will she. I'm sure she'll be hanging on your every move."

"We're not done!" called Petra, seizing the camera and shaking it so violently that the video made me dizzy.

No one answered.

Cal groaned. "So they know I told her about the holograms. How did they find out so quickly?"

A fourth figure entered the video, a girl with her hair in a bun. It looked like Ponytail—Sam. From my sideways position on the floor, it was difficult to hear what she said. Through the broken words and phrases that reached me, I teased out that she was trying to convince Petra to start the match. And Petra wasn't having it, at first. I saw her eyes narrow in suspicion—*why would Sam want me to go?*—but one word from Sam was enough to make her forget her doubts.

*Halley.*

Desperate, kindhearted Petra didn't think she had a choice. If Sam had ulterior motives for persuading her to start the match, there was nothing she could do about it. Because the Alliance had me.

"I knew they had a second spy." Cal swore.

My eyes drifted shut. Maybe he had guessed, but I should have known. It was Sam who had convinced the other Mercs that Cal was dead. Sam who had convinced me to wander into the woods and search for Petra. Sam who had appeared here and there and everywhere, influencing our actions in ways we barely noticed. Just enough to change the course of our story.

Petra approached the door on the back wall.

"Don't do it. Don't . . ." Cal's voice trailed off. He knew it was no use.

She typed in the code, and the door swung open. Roscoe followed her inside, with a reluctant Andy in tow. There was a brief delay before the camera angle switched to the inside of the . . . for lack of a better term, the waiting room where Cal and I had started our match. The three of them could barely fit.

"You won't see the people I'm fighting." Petra fished a short piece of twine from her pocket and pulled her thick hair into a makeshift bun. "You have nothing to worry about. But stay close to me."

"They *do* have something to worry about," Cal corrected. "The lasers from the holographs can do real physical damage. That's why I had you duck into the bathtub that one time. Since those two don't have chips, they can't be perceived, so the holographs won't target them. But if they accidentally get in front of one . . ."

"This time, you won't be controlling me," Petra said, looking at Roscoe. "We'd better hope I learned something from you."

"You were the one doing the work. I only gave directions."

Tugging her leather gloves, Petra crept out into the hallway.

The camera angle switched again, and for a few agonizing seconds, we watched as she crawled beneath the row of windows that opened between her hallway and the next room. Then, for no reason that I could see, she reached up, wrapped her hands around an invisible obstacle, and dragged it to the floor. She must have met the same guard that Cal and I had, because she fell in exactly the same place.

"That was a nice takedown," Cal commented.

Petra turned to Roscoe and Andy, who were tiptoeing behind her at a respectful distance. "Did you see that?"

"See what?" Andy's face crinkled. "See you imitate a jack-in-the-box?"

"Andy!" Roscoe poked him. "Stop being rude."

Petra's face relaxed into the first real smile I had seen from her. "I suppose Cal was telling the truth." The realization must have felt good to her, but good didn't begin to express the look on Cal's face. Relief, amusement, and playful frustration alternated in his eyes, which finally closed in a sigh. I supposed, after everything they had been through, it felt good to be believed.

Petra rifled the invisible body and held her fist in the air. "Can you see this?"

Roscoe and Andy shook their heads.

"She's holding a knife," Cal whispered. "A long silver knife with a black rubber handle. But you can't see it at all. Technology is amazing, isn't it?"

I shook my head. "No, it's not. Not like this."

Petra and Company rounded the corner into the next room. The moment the camera angle switched to follow them, Cal sucked in his breath. It took Petra only a split second longer to identify whatever he was seeing. She dashed into the center under the light and hovered for a moment in midair, wrapping her arms around—something. She and her enemy tumbled to the floor, and after a few seconds of struggle, she got up and dusted off her hands.

Roscoe gave her a thumbs-up. "You're better than I am. You play with a combination of stealth and speed. I was always in a hurry to get things over with."

"Yes, well." Petra was already looking around the next corner. "I wish you'd slowed down. This"—she tapped her prosthetic—"hurt." Her tone was mild, but despite the camera's poor resolution, it was impossible not to notice her jaw tighten. She had her back to Roscoe, though, and she was quick to add, "My trigger finger is steadier now. Having a bionic hand isn't so bad."

"Oh, you bet I noticed!" cried Roscoe, excited for a moment. Her gaze dropped. "But I'm sorry. If I had known what I was doing to you—"

"You didn't. You're not to blame," Petra interrupted. Without giving Roscoe a chance to respond, she waved the group forward.

"Personally"—Andy's interruption earned him an eye roll from Roscoe—"I don't think we should destroy the House. I mean, look at all the technology in here! Invisible laser holographs—are they ultra-high-frequency? Why can't we see them? Neural implants, 3D food printing machines—"

"You don't want to eat the food."

"—hackproof biometric locks, watches that never need batteries replaced, fully functional prosthetic limbs—"

Petra's hands flew to her throat.

"—plants that never stop growing, automatic dressing machines—why can't you just dress yourselves? And why don't you have dishwashers?" Andy did not seem to notice that Petra was thrashing on the floor. His gaze roved the walls, which were lined with old, broken automatic cookers. "Amazing medical advances.

You must have healed up pretty fast if Roscoe was able to keep playing with you. And why would the buildings look so shabby and old? Couldn't you make new ones out of some kind of fancy—"

"Would you shut up?" Petra, having shaken off her assailant, was creeping on her hands and knees along the edge of the wall. "I can't hear if someone's coming."

"Sorry," he whispered. He switched to talking to himself, with his lips moving but no sound coming out. Roscoe shot him a scornful glare.

They continued along the room, Roscoe and Andy walking upright, Petra creeping on her hands and knees, until they came to a small wooden door in the wall. A familiar door to me—the same one that Cal and I had entered during the match we'd played together.

Petra put a finger to her lips and let herself into the tiny bathroom, ducking around the corner as though she expected someone to be inside. Cal and I both sighed, relieved; the room was empty. With a satisfied nod, Petra hoisted herself up onto the toilet lid and pulled a screwdriver from her pocket. There was a vent on the ceiling directly above her, and, standing on tiptoe, she began loosening it.

"Are we supposed to tell you if someone's coming?" Andy asked nervously.

Besides this remark, Petra's work went uninterrupted. In half a minute, she had the vent cover off the ceiling.

She placed one hand on either side of the hole and hoisted her slender body inside. She fit, but it was a tight squeeze. Roscoe, who, unlike Petra, wasn't built like an anemic twelve-year-old, had a harder time. They were stuck entirely when it came to Andy, who was as inflexible and brittle as a tree branch. They both tried tugging him through, but he made such a fuss about twisted joints and pinched extremities that they were forced to give up.

"I guess you can take the stairs." Was it just my imagination, or were the dark circles under Petra's eyes more pronounced than usual? "But you'll have to find them, and us afterward, by yourself."

"Do you know where the stairs are?" he asked, eyes like a lost puppy's.

"I never go there." Petra replaced the vent cover. Through the bars, she whispered a ruthless: "Good luck!"

"Even I fit through the vents." A smile flitted across Cal's face and vanished. "That guy must really hate tight spaces if he'd rather wander around alone."

My right arm, which was squashed between the side of my chair and the baseboard, was starting to cramp. Or bruise, or maybe I was tearing a . . . but there was no point in speculating, not when the doctor was miles away and probably searching for my dead body.

With a terrific tightening of my stomach muscles and a series of inelegant kicks, I managed to scrape my sideways chair around until my arm was free and I had a better view of the screen. By the time I got myself positioned to look up, the camera view had split into two separate scenes—Petra and Roscoe on the second floor, and Andy stranded on the first floor. The latter was wandering the halls, looking terrified and directionless, while Petra and Roscoe were already far from the vent they'd climbed through and heading toward what looked like a central room.

I had just started to think the worst was over, when a nondescript dark shadow jumped around the corner and seized Petra's shoulders, bending her frail body backward at almost a ninety-degree angle.

My stomach tightened, and nausea rose in my throat. I wasn't supposed to see that. I couldn't see them—the holograms—the fake people who couldn't be killed.

But I could see real people.

In a flash, Petra was out from under the attacker. She managed to lodge a kick behind his knee, crumpling him like his legs were noodles, and then she raised her fist and sliced it across the back of his neck.

But her hand, which still appeared empty to me, didn't connect. The shadow was up again in a moment, shoving her back against the wall and raising a knife—a knife that was visible to me as a silver flash under the white fluorescents. The light cut across his face, giving me a brief glimpse of his expression, knotted in fear and hatred and intense concentration. As he stepped away from the wall, he solidified into a shape. A human. Just as real and alive as Petra, dressed in a dark green military-style uniform with a patch above the breast pocket. Four letters were embroidered there—but he moved too quickly for me to see what they were.

She grabbed his wrist, and the blade hovered above her skin. The man was too strong for her, and it was only by a well-timed squirm that she avoided being stabbed in the chest.

Roscoe hovered just around the corner, watching in spellbound horror. Petra's hairbreadth escape seemed to startle her back to her wits. She crept into the room, and when she was within arm's length of the man, she grabbed his neck, twisted around to his front, and kicked him where it counted. With a shrill cry of pain, he collapsed, and Petra tore the knife from his grip and knocked him on the back of the neck with its handle. That was the end of that.

"You saw him?" Petra whipped around to face Roscoe. "You saw that man?"

Roscoe's face was the color of seaweed, but she gulped, brushed her hair out of her face, and nodded.

"He was real," Cal said tersely. "Besides the sergeant, I've never seen real people in the House before." His eyes were dark with worry. "Petra's never had to fight a real person. And people don't act like programs."

My eyes darted back to the screen.

"Stay quiet." Petra turned back to Roscoe. "The holographs won't hear you, but people will."

"But Andy!" Roscoe seized Petra's sleeve. "He doesn't know that!"

Petra glanced back at the vent, and her mouth set in a line. It was easy to guess what she was thinking; they couldn't go back, and they couldn't catch Andy's attention. There was nothing they could do but wait until he figured it out himself.

A quick glance at the second camera angle proved that he remained as clueless as ever. He was still wandering on the first floor, mournfully calling Roscoe's name, opening doors, sighing, and closing them again. Every step he made echoed through the halls, audible even through the camera's weak microphone.

Cal grimaced. "Rest in peace."

The words were barely out of Cal's mouth before Andy was attacked from behind.

He let out a shriek and toppled with a crash that I could have sworn I felt through the floor. But, by some miracle of gravity, he landed on top. That gave him enough time to push his assailant away and flee, screaming for help, busily pursued by the camera, tripping over his own feet and narrowly escaping a nose-first collision with every corner.

Despite his angular limbs, Andy was shockingly fast. His assailant was up on his feet in a moment, and even through that thick green uniform—the same as Petra's enemy had worn—I could tell he was taller and more strongly built than Andy. But, somehow, he kept falling farther behind even as the camera lost them altogether. Soon, even their pounding footsteps, which I thought I could feel through the floor under my left shoulder, died off into silence.

It didn't last long.

The door behind Cal burst open, slamming into the drywall with such force that it left a handle-shaped dent. There, in the doorway, stood the soldier from the video. The one whom I thought had killed Cal.

He, too, wore the green uniform, but his was formally styled. Gilded silk epaulets shone on each shoulder, and the double corners of his collar were stabbed through with a little gold pin, the image of a laurel wreath. Over the right-hand breast pocket was the same white patch, and now I could see the letters embroidered there: S.A.F.E.

Instead of a rifle, he held a syringe.

"This has nothing in it," he informed me, long before I'd had time to worry about the minor details. I wasn't at all certain how much difference that would make, and the sergeant's next words confirmed my fears: "Petra won't know that, though."

I lurched myself forward and smacked his shins with one of

my chair legs. The blow didn't even shake him. He looked down, and I braced myself for him to hit me. But he only shook his head and held up a warning finger. I dwindled like I was twelve again, being reprimanded by the doctor for sampling the lemonade I was supposed to be selling.

He fished a remote from somewhere in his cavernous pockets, pressed a button, and stood under the light. It cast a black shadow across his eyes, which were sunk so deeply into his face that I could only see the outline of the sockets.

"Your attention, please!" he announced to the bulb. "Your friend is about to get a dose of sodium thiopental. If you aren't up here in fifteen minutes, you're going to watch her scream." He depressed the plunger, slowly, suggestively. Though I could see there was nothing in it, I could believe there was. I could see it dribble down the needle, onto his hand, down his arm . . . no, I couldn't, because it was just a trick of the light and the cruel smile on the sergeant's face. "Trust me. I know how much this hurts."

I strained my neck to get a better look at the video feed. Petra made a dive at the wall where the sergeant's image was projected, but with one quick press on his remote, the video disappeared, and her fists beat uselessly against the rotting wallpaper.

"Truth serum," Cal remarked. "It's always truth serum with the bad guys. Why would you even want to interrogate her? Can't you get a little more creative?"

The sergeant waved his needle so close to my arm that I imagined its metallic chill against my skin. He held it in front of me, studying my tense face with the curious eyes of a five-year-old child, then buried it in his pocket.

"No one likes needles." He nodded politely. "Sorry to make you sit through that."

Taken aback by his change of manner, I found myself mumbling, much against my will: "That's alright."

"It's not alright!" Cal declared peevishly, stomping his heavy boots against the floor. "Why are you in such a hurry? Why do you need Petra up here? You could just as easily go down there yourself and kill her. You know where she is. You've programmed the cameras to follow her. Why don't you do your own dirty work?"

The sergeant grabbed hold of my chair, and with a dizzying sweep, I finally found myself upright again. The blood returned to my head in a rush, and I gulped in a grateful breath.

"The Alliance, as you call it, may not be in a hurry. But I am." He seated himself with his legs outstretched and his back against the wall. "There was a time when I would have trusted you with my plans, Calhoun, but you lost that trust a long time ago. I'm glad the Alliance has decided to get rid of you."

Cal snorted, but for once, he didn't seem to have a comeback prepared.

I peeked over my shoulder at the projection, wondering if the sergeant was trying to distract us with his pointless conversation. Andy had finally stopped running, allowing the cameras to catch up. He was rubbing his arm, twisting his neck around like an owl to see if anyone was following him. Petra and Roscoe were tiptoeing along a hallway in perfect sync with each other. So far, none of them looked much the worse for wear. Petra's lights, which had been blinking so rapidly before, had slowed down to an even, steady tempo. Things were going well—for now, anyway.

"You've fought in a war," said the sergeant.

"What's that?" Cal raised an eyebrow. "Are you trying to make small talk? We don't want to chat with you. Especially after you so eloquently told me you're planning to kill me."

"You know how awful it can be." The sergeant rested his head against the wall. "You read the briefing before you came here, so you must understand how high the stakes are."

"What are you talking about?"

"Aren't you glad you can prevent it?"

"Prevent what? War?"

"Of course."

"You bet I would be," said Cal, glancing back to the screen, "if war wasn't exactly what we do here every day, and if I had any hope it would ever end."

"Of course, that's your job," the sergeant conceded.

"Excuse me." Cal's voice was dry. "Now, there's the misunderstanding. I only play the game because you'd blow my head off with your little mind-control chips if I didn't. I strongly suspect that's the other Mercs' reasoning too. If you're trying to imply that I enjoy war, well, I'd like to see you fight. Lay off your cushy little office job and pull the trigger yourself instead of handing me the gun. Then we'll see how you like it."

I tensed, certain the sergeant would take Cal at his word. But his voice remained mild as he answered, "Nobody likes war. If you can wait until they replace the rest of the holographs with real people, war as we know it will be extinct. You're religious, aren't you? You can thank your God for that."

Cal let out an incredulous snort.

"Re-replace the holographs?" I stammered, my mind scrabbling to formulate a coherent question. Cal was obviously ready for the conversation to end, but we couldn't waste this chance. We had the sergeant and everything he knew right there in front of us, and we couldn't let him leave until he explained what he meant. "Is that what will happen next?"

"Instead of hundreds of thousands of soldiers fighting, it'll just be you versus them. Well, not you. You're not a Merc. *Them.*" He bent his head toward Cal. "The ones with the tattoos on their hands. That will be a world worth living in. A world without war." He smiled—actually smiled, revealing a pair of tiny dimples. "Congratulations to you both on your participation in such a wonderful experiment."

The only thing I could hear in the silence that followed was the light bulb buzzing. Or was that my ears?

Cal's face had turned an odd shade of olive green, mimicking the color of the rosebud leaves scattered across the faded wallpaper. "Experiment?" he managed with a bitter laugh. "This is your experiment? Before I started spying for you, back when I thought I was a murderer, back when . . ." He glanced at me, and his voice sank. "When you tortured me, tried to force me to kill Petra. That was a science project?"

"I apologize." The soldier bowed his head gracefully. "You're right, it is no longer an experiment. It's the real thing now."

"The real what?" I blurted. My fear dwindled. I had no hope left for us. All I wanted was to know the truth before the sergeant did—whatever it was he planned to do. Before I lost Cal. Petra. The doctor. Mother. Everyone. The last thing I could do for them was to learn the truth and take it to my grave.

"War simulator." He barely looked up, as though he hadn't just said something that might have changed everything we'd ever done. Every plan we'd ever made. Every little rebellion we had imagined and had never dared to attempt. "Once again, congratulations. And thank you for your sacrifice."

This flustered Cal so much that he could only sputter.

"Congratulations? Sacrifices?" I echoed.

"Are you saying," Cal demanded, regaining his voice, "that we're fighting entire wars on someone else's behalf? All the killing we do here is for someone else? Someone we've never met, who has reasons to fight we'll never understand, and never even be told? Are you saying that our deaths are somehow supposed to mean something to *you*, but never to us?"

Over the course of Cal's outburst, the sergeant's expression had gone from confused to surprised to alarmed.

"But you knew." His voice was faint. "Warsafe told me you knew. They must have told you."

"Yes, well." Cal drew himself up the best he could. "That's the thing about the Alliance. They lie."

# 22

## KAZUMI

**THERE WERE FEW THINGS KAZUMI** hated more than noise. He had turned down the volume as far as it would go, but that did nothing to make the agony in his headphones any more bearable.

"For the love of . . ." The cries faded to gasps. "You wouldn't have had to do this if it weren't for Petra. I would have told you anything you wanted to know. Why did you bring her here? Why did you make me start to question myself? Why, why did you make me have second thoughts?"

"Do you regret it?" a second voice asked, gruff but quiet by comparison. "There's no need. You can have her and your happily-ever-after, too, if you'll just tell me what I want to know." It dropped to a hushed tone. "You were *programmed* to love her. You can't help loving her. You could never stop, even if you tried. This is how we made you."

A crazed cackling sent static flowing into Kazumi's ears. "Do you think I remember what you were asking? I'm too busy trying to figure out if I'm bleeding out or if you're only making me think I am. I haven't got time to think about anything else. I haven't even got time to think about her."

"This is electrical stimulation. Your body is not being harmed."

"A whole lot of difference that m—!" The word broke off into a scream, then a shuddering breath. "Can't you give me any warning?"

"Tell me what you leaked to Petra."

"Stop asking me to do the impossible."

"Why is it impossible?"

A cry of anguish, and the voice came, weaker this time. "Your deal was with me. Not her."

"Are you admitting you told her something we would kill her for knowing?"

"I'm only saying that she has nothing to do with this, so would you stop talking about—"

Another scream. An awful sound. Kazumi waited a couple of seconds—or perhaps they were only tiny fractions of seconds—and then, before he knew what he was doing, his finger was on the intercom button, and he was speaking.

"Stop. Stop!"

A series of cries died into a whimper.

"What do you want?" The sergeant's irritation was plain in his voice.

"We'll come back to him later." Kazumi was vaguely aware of his shaking hands. He could barely hold down the button. "I want you to get Petra in a match so we can prevent her from leaving the House."

"You swore!" cried the voice somewhere in the background. Even more faintly this time.

"I told you to stop—"

There was a crash of static, and the voice went silent.

"Whatever you say," the sergeant agreed sullenly, returning to the receiver. "But I could do both."

"It's more important for us to get Petra where we can watch her than it is to get answers out of Calhoun. Take care of her first, then finish with him. Don't hurt either of them."

"Yes, sir." There was a *click*, and the line went dead. Sergeant Porok had never been one for small talk.

Kazumi sank back into his chair, letting his head rest against the back. He had to think consciously about making his muscles relax or he'd end up with a headache. And he didn't have time for that. He had to think clearly. He was running out of opportunities to intervene. Already, he was cursing himself for putting it off so long. But who could blame him? It was no small decision. He didn't like to think about the weight he'd bear if he got it wrong.

"Excuse me." His administrative assistant tapped on the glass that separated his office from the cubicle farm. "You have a board meeting in five minutes. Should I tell them you'll be late?"

"No, no." Kazumi gulped the last of his coffee. "I'm on my way."

As he skirted the cubicles, he wondered what Roscoe would think if she could see him now. He had pitched the idea to her, half-heartedly hoping she'd take the bait and agree to work with him, but he hadn't forgotten the look on her face when she admitted that Warsafe's game was too violent for her. And that was back when she thought it was a game. She would never have held herself still during Calhoun's tortured screams. She wasn't that kind of person, had never been. She couldn't have done it even if she'd wanted to.

So what if he had enjoyed their little workplace flirtation? It had all been built on lies—the lie that he was just a beta tester, that he knew nothing about Warsafe's secret project, that he was a kind and honorable man. She'd fallen for it all so easily.

It had taken hours to disable all the sensors that would have warned the security team about intruders on the island. Even so, he couldn't answer for what would happen if Sergeant Porok found her and her little scientist friend.

Kazumi didn't like to remember the names of people whose deaths he was going to be responsible for.

He couldn't let himself think about what he'd done, not with the keen eyes of the nine board members fixed on him. They'd see right through his habitual confidence. They wouldn't have earned their seats at this table if they couldn't do that. Right now, in this room he had just stepped into, Kazumi was the president's right hand. Just that. Nothing more, nothing less.

"So," he began, seating himself in the soft chair at the head of the table, "what progress have we made besides backward?"

"We've got a real mess on our hands," said a young woman seated off to his left. Kazumi racked his brains for her title: chief debugger? chief beta tester? Whoever she was, she was as sharp as a tack and about as comfortable. "The Mercenaries have probably received enough information from Calhoun to realize they aren't isolated on the island and that a world exists outside their village. If this stimulus is strong enough, it could overturn the psychological code we constructed that makes them believe their current state is how things have always been and how they always will be."

"Can't we shock them with the chips if they start trying to leave?" someone else suggested.

"Abuse would only make them more anxious to escape," Kazumi replied, and the chief debugger nodded in agreement. "The chips are helpful in maintaining basic discipline, but we don't have the funding to keep eyes on everyone all the time. If one Mercenary wanders off into the forest and chops down a few trees each day and one obscure villager ties the logs into a raft, there's not much we can do. They'd likely drown before they reached the mainland, but there are no guarantees."

"So much for being the world's most powerful company," grumbled a man who, Kazumi remembered for no particular reason, had once stirred his coffee with his finger and wiped it on his suit jacket. "We should never have started working on a project of this scale unless we were certain we could control it."

Kazumi noticed the chief debugger looking as though she had something to interject, so he nodded at her.

"We could reprogram the Mercenaries' memories and erase their knowledge of the past week," she said, hesitantly. "But someone has to be present on the island to perform the operation. By the time we figure out who needs reprogramming and design all the replacement memories, there might be resistance on a large scale, and then we'd be in trouble. Besides, this same situation could always happen again unless we find out what catalyzed it in the first place."

"What if we used the chips to order the Mercenaries not to resist?" someone suggested. "Similar to how we use the chips during the game while they're being controlled by the person playing."

"Do you think we wouldn't have done that if we could?" she shot back. Kazumi was perversely relieved to see he wasn't the only one exhausted and angry from the week's fiasco. "The chips can only incentivize the Mercenaries. Nothing about their actions can be forced. Ultimately, what they do is up to them. The key, until now, was making sure they never became aware of that."

"There are only a few hundred of them," noted the coffee stirrer. "Warsafe is connected with the government. A battalion of soldiers—"

The chief debugger stopped him. "If we killed them, Warsafe would have to spend several more millions trying to find replacement Mercenaries and villagers. We don't have the resources for that, not if we're going to have the game finished in time. Besides, there may not be enough eligible candidates who all speak the same language. The prerequisite condition, as you know, is rare."

"I don't know," the coffee stirrer said. "They were all chosen before I was hired."

"Amnesiacs," someone explained. "They're all natural amnesiacs. We pulled them out of hospitals, promising them an experimental treatment. That's how their minds were conditioned to accept the chips."

"We don't have time to scour the hospitals again," Kazumi agreed. "We're headed for full-scale war in Iceland, and right now, SAFE doesn't have the leverage to stop it. We need results, and we need them now."

"But what option do we have besides wiping the slate clean?"

"What if . . ." piped up a small voice. Kazumi looked down to the distant end of the table.

The interrupter turned out to be a twenty-something graphic designer in a bright-yellow button-up shirt and floral tie. His evident nervousness to speak up in front of the group made him look younger than he probably was. Curious about this innocent-looking little man, Kazumi indicated for him to keep talking.

The designer took a deep breath and said, "What if we didn't kill the Mercs outright? What if we tried to distract them with something unexpected? Something that makes them have to fight so hard, they don't have time to worry about resisting us?"

That hadn't made the short list of things Kazumi was expecting to hear from this sleek little man with a cappuccino at his elbow.

The head of security snapped his fingers. "Sir"—Kazumi turned his head—"I think this is an excellent idea. It sounds like it's time for us to update you on our progress with the prisoner program."

"Oh?" Kazumi said absently. His eyes had gone back to the graphic designer, who, released from the spotlight, was now talking excitedly to the girl sitting next to him. The man's tie was crinkled. He probably barely knew how to tie it, maybe had to ask someone to do it for him. But he had done the impossible. He had thought of a way to solve the little problem of the Mercs that might be even worse than killing them outright.

"We're ahead of schedule." Security's voice broke in on Kazumi's thoughts. "As of this morning, approximately twenty percent of the holograms we have been using as Merc opponents are now real people."

Kazumi had to fight the urge to bang his head against the desk. "Congratulations. Why didn't you tell me?"

"We thought it would be a nice surprise." Security beamed. "We wanted to implement the program first."

"And they're convicts? All of them? Death-row prisoners?"

"That's right. To save the expense and legal hassle of executing these criminals, and to . . . well, to put it less delicately, execute them cheaply. It was President Aeron's idea, which she documented before she left for the island. Do you recall?"

At least they'd stuck to one part of the plan. Only using people who were going to die anyway.

"Don't make changes like that without telling me," ordered Kazumi feverishly. He was sure he was going to have a stroke at the ripe old age of thirty.

"This could be the opportunity we were looking for," the graphic designer exclaimed, knocking a pen off the table in his excitement. "Surely it will be harder for the Mercs to fight real people. Our holograms were good, but they were at least somewhat predictable. Real people won't be that way. This is exactly what we need to keep them occupied so they don't start figuring out how to leave the island."

There was nothing Kazumi could say against that.

"Let's not overanalyze the situation. Ultimately, we only have two goals." Kazumi ticked them off on his fingers. "One, we want to make a game that has a high cost to play. The cost being, of course, the lives of the Mercenaries and opponents who are killed during a match. Two, we want to make it realistic. If we can meet those two conditions, we can make a game that will replace wars. We don't want to get lost in the weeds and forget where we're aiming."

"Of course," agreed the debugger, much to Kazumi's relief.

"Keep working on your assigned tasks, then. I like your idea for the Mercs"—this with a nod to the debugger—"but don't worry about that right now. I'll take care of things from here." He pulled himself to his feet to indicate that the meeting was over. That was one of the perks of his position—no meeting ever had to outlast his attention span. Nodding, then straightening his tie to give his hands something to do, he made a beeline for the door. "Don't worry about it. I'll make sure everything turns out alright. I'll . . ."

He was still talking as he shut the door behind him and ran—actually ran, shiny shoes tapping briskly on the linoleum floor—down the hallway to his office. Those glass windows never let him have a moment of privacy, but he was not above crouching on the floor behind his desk in moments of weakness.

He had done this. He was responsible. All the Mercenaries who were doomed to meet violent ends, all the villagers who were going to squander their lives in wasteful poverty on the island, all the opportunities that were lost, all the stories that were ended—all of it was his fault. He slammed his fist onto the floor.

"She said it would never come to this. She said we'd always be better. She said we'd let the Mercenaries choose for themselves."

*She said a lot of things. She lies. That's all she does, to you, to them, to everyone.*

"She went to the island herself. She believed so strongly that we were right."

*No one else got a say. Not the villagers, not the Mercenaries, not you.*

Someone tapped lightly against his window, and Kazumi hauled himself up from the floor to meet the eyes of his administrative assistant.

"There's a suspicious charge on your company credit card," she said, as unruffled and soft-spoken as ever. "Would you like to review it?"

"Is it three thousand dollars to some boat company?"

"Yes, that's right. Did you notice it already?"

"It's authentic." Kazumi steadied himself against the desk. "Would you note on the schedule that I won't be available tomorrow? There are a few things I need to work on at home before I return to the office."

"Yes, sir." She dipped her head and disappeared.

It was time. Time for someone to step up and do something. Although he had no idea what. He hadn't thought this would all happen so soon.

He pressed the red button on his keyboard. "Sergeant Porok, do you read me?"

No answer.

"Sergeant?"

Still nothing but a faint hiss of static. Kazumi released the button and left his desk.

# 23

## HALLEY

**I MEANT TO BE STOIC LIKE CAL AND** stay awake. But I couldn't remember the last time I'd eaten, drunk, or slept, and my eyelids were so heavy that I doubted I could hold them up with my fingers even if they had been free to try. Slowly, my head drooped, and I drifted in and out of a doze.

I couldn't have been out for long before the door to the room reopened and the sergeant appeared with the empty syringe in his hand. Seeing me eyeing it, searching the tip of the needle for telltale drops to show he'd put something in it, he smiled reassuringly.

"I'm just sending your friends a reminder," he said. "They're on the seventh floor now. But Petra is looking winded, and I need her to hurry."

"Petra? Winded?" Cal scoffed. "She's stronger than all three of us put together."

The sergeant shrugged. "See for yourself."

We looked up at the screen. Petra and Company were reunited, so only one angle was shown and Petra's back was to the camera. But when she turned around, I heard Cal's sharp intake of breath.

With the video's low resolution and chronic overexposure, Petra had gone so pale that she was positively glowing—except for her eyes. They looked like holes drilled into her face, hollow and expressionless. Roscoe and Andy had her arms draped across their shoulders, and she leaned heavily on them for every step. The scratch across her face, a relic of her fight with the "real" guards, draped a sheet of blood across her left cheek that, through the ugly camera video, looked like a solid black mask.

I closed my eyes.

"She's not winded." Cal struggled against his ropes until his chair scraped against the floor. "She's injured." He glared at the sergeant. "And you're going to make her go even faster?"

He might as well have been talking to the moon. The sergeant was filling the syringe with plain old water from a bottle—a bitter reminder that my lips were cracking from dehydration—with as much care as though it was a priceless drug. He squirted a few drops in the air, refilled it, and emptied it again. He paced up and down the room, rubbed his gloves across the camera lens hidden in the light bulb, watched the video feed for a few seconds, and paced again.

Finally, he seemed to make up his mind, and he grabbed my chin in his hands and tilted my head back. I squirmed, barely able to breathe through those strong fingers. But he ignored my struggling, forced the syringe in my mouth, and depressed it. I let out a stifled shriek, expecting to feel the needle's bite. Cool, delicious water poured in a tiny stream down my throat.

"What a bizarre creature you are," Cal observed to the sergeant's back. "Make up your mind whose side you're on!"

"More?" the sergeant asked me.

I nodded desperately, and he poured straight from the bottle into my mouth. Ice cold and gloriously refreshing, it ran down my chin and soaked my shirt and cooled my sweaty skin. My stomach, which had been rumbling angrily, quelled as the chilled water filled it.

Something else was happening, too, something that gave me even more relief than the water. Over the sergeant's stooped shoulder, I could see that Cal's squirming had stopped, and he was holding his hands triumphantly in the air. They were patched with dried blood and emerging blisters from the ropes, and one of his fingers had swollen and turned an ugly purple. But he was free.

With the silent steps of the former best Merc on the island, he crept toward the sergeant, who was still occupied with the water bottle.

As he came within arm's reach of the sergeant's neck, Cal reached out with the same catlike grace with which Petra had executed her first takedown of the match. I thought it would work. It would have worked on anybody except the sergeant, whose neck was as thick as a tree trunk. But Cal's boots left the floor as the sergeant jerked backward, treating me to a faceful of water and shaking Cal off like an inconvenient fly.

Cal rolled off the sergeant's shoulder and past my head. I ducked on reflex to give him room and bit my lip to keep myself from shrieking. Miraculously, Cal landed on his feet. The sergeant was between him and the door, but Cal didn't have to overpower him to make it there. He only had to outsmart or outrun him.

My fingernails dug into the arms of my chair. Cal had a way of faking things, but he hadn't yet recovered from his injuries. He had to be exhausted, and his movements dragged. There was only one way I could imagine this fight ending.

They circled each other cautiously, the sergeant in front of me and Cal behind, neither of them any more aware of my presence than they would have been if I was a scarecrow. I was tactical advantage, soon to be collateral damage. The sergeant's heavy steps shook the floor. Cal's breath was hot on the back of my neck. I thought they might keep tiptoeing forever.

In the time it took me to blink a stray drop of water out of my eye, Cal darted across the hallway. Past me, past the sergeant, past the light, past his chair. He yanked open the door and stumbled straight into the arms of a girl.

It was Ponytail. Sam.

And she was pointing a gun at me.

Instinct took over, and I barely had time to feel a stab of terror as I shifted my weight in the chair to topple out of the way. But this time, of course, when my life depended on it, I couldn't tip it far or fast enough to fall. I saw Cal grab the gun and jerk it upward. Slowed down by his injuries, he was just a little too late. Someone seized the back of my chair and sent me spinning and crashing across the room. There was an explosion so overpowering that if I did scream, I couldn't even hear myself—and then a burnt chemical smell.

There was silence for a moment. Silence so loud and horrible that I could hear it through the ringing in my ears and that cursed light bulb's buzzing.

Then, from behind me, came an abrupt curse.

I took my eyes away from the doorway and twisted my head around. The sergeant, hands pressing the left side of his chest, was sprawled across the floor on his back. His mouth hung open, and his breaths came uneven and ragged.

Cal had managed to wrest the gun away from Ponytail, and he jammed the barrel into the side of her head. "What were you doing?" he yelled hoarsely. "You almost killed Halley!"

I couldn't keep my eyes off the sergeant. He dragged himself across the floor until he was able to rest against the wall, barely holding his head upright, chest rising and falling with as much distress as though he'd just finished running straight across the island.

*He saved me. But why?*

Maybe I should have stayed quiet, but for one moment, he wasn't our enemy, and we weren't his prisoners. We were all just people who hated suffering.

"Cal," I cried. "The sergeant!"

Torn, he glanced back and forth between the sergeant and Sam, reluctant to leave her unguarded, yet reluctant to leave our captor to die. Perhaps he was thinking the same thing I was. That possibly in his own twisted way, the sergeant wasn't so evil as he had seemed. Or perhaps he was just incorrigibly kindhearted. Or he knew that this was a real person's life in question, not a holograph that could respawn on demand.

Pity won over doubt. He shoved the gun into my hand and knelt beside the sergeant.

I kept the weapon dutifully trained on Ponytail, twisting my wrist under the rope to hold the weapon steady even though I couldn't move my arm. She raised her hands, looking bored, and my finger hovered over the trigger in case she tried to run. I knew I had to keep her there, but my gaze kept straying back to Cal.

"I still don't know whose side you're on." Cal unzipped the sergeant's green uniform jacket. His eyes rounded as he took stock of the injuries, and his breath whistled through his teeth. "There's a doctor in the village. We'll take you right now if you'll let us out—"

"Stop the war." The sergeant seized Cal's wrist, gripping until a white mark appeared. "Stop the—" He was interrupted by a choked cough, which sprinkled blood over Cal's face. "Then you can leave the game." His words came in ragged gasps. "But first, please, stop the war. Stop the—"

"What war? This war? The *Permadeath* game?"

Cal bent close to the sergeant's mouth.

"Eye . . . ss . . . la . . ."

Cal sat back on his heels, slowly wiping his bloody cheeks with the back of his hand.

"I never thought I'd be sorry to see him go." The irreverent remark carried a tone of unusual sobriety.

A tear slipped down my cheek, making my dry mouth sting with salt.

"I think he might deserve to rest in peace," Cal said, drawing his hand in a cross shape over his chest. "May God forgive him. He certainly needs it."

My weapon drooped. I had almost forgotten about the prisoner I was supposed to be guarding. My eyes were fixed on the sergeant's limp hands, so large and callused with rough use, the same hands that had pulled me up from the floor, that had swung the rifle stock into Cal's face, that had given me water, that had forced Petra to fight for her life, that had pushed me away from Sam's bullet. Neither perfectly good, nor perfectly evil. A persistent glimmer of humanity's past perfection and its present destruction appeared in everything he did, but good intentions alone weren't enough to save him.

The book had closed with a snap. Just like that. No warning, no way to go back, no way to change what we'd done.

I thought I knew what death meant, I thought I was ready to die if I had to, but I realized then that I was wrong. How childish and naïve I had been. Of course it didn't matter how much I'd thought about it and read about it and even dreamed about it. I would do anything to live. To not look back from the afterlife and see my own face shining with sweat and waxen, drooped on my chest, powerless and helpless and at the mercy of my worst enemies.

No. I'd fight. I'd fight until I learned the truth about life, death, my purpose in life. I didn't know where that man had gone, but I knew I wasn't going there with him. Not until I was ready.

Cal's brief moment of reverence vanished long before I was ready to let go. He climbed awkwardly to his feet and took the gun from me, sparing a brief nod of approval when he saw that I'd managed to keep Ponytail in the room.

Or maybe it wasn't me. She could have escaped if she'd tried. Maybe she just wasn't done with us.

"I could understand if you had tried to kill the sergeant." Cal racked the slide with a *click*, letting the unspent bullet drop heavily to the floor. "You probably thought he was keeping us prisoner. But your laser was on Halley's chest."

Sam lowered her arms. "I didn't mean to shoot at all. If you hadn't grabbed my hands—"

There was death in the room because of what she insisted was an accident. But she might as well have been talking about the weather for all the remorse she showed. Her eyes were dilated and sly and darting, searching for an escape. And there was a slight tilt of her body to her right side, barely noticeable, that suggested she might have a second weapon hidden there. I hoped Cal saw it. There was no way I could warn him.

Cal started to argue, but Sam was faster. Her hand flew to her waist and seized the handle of a knife. Not an imagination induced by the chip. A real knife with a silky blade and a point so sharp it blended with the wall behind it. I saw it flash through the air and come down on Cal's neck.

I squeezed my eyes shut. I couldn't bear to watch him die again.

But I couldn't keep my eyes closed forever, and when I opened them, it was as though the scene had frozen. For that one split second, no one stirred. Right above Cal's neck, less than an inch above his skin, a hand had seized Sam's wrist. A thin, wiry, delicate hand, with pink polish on the nails.

And then the spell was broken. Cal dodged out from under Sam's knife, putting her briefly out of commission with an elbow to the stomach. She didn't stay down, though. In a lightning-quick move, she grabbed the pink-polished hand and hoisted herself back to her feet, swinging the knife like a windmill. A third person appeared out of the darkness of the hallway, but that person was useless, collapsing on the threshold after having hit no one and having been hit by no one. I couldn't tell what had made him—her?—fall, but that someone was in for a bad time. The standing combatants couldn't avoid trampling them.

I fought against my ropes. I sapped the last of my energy squeezing my stomach muscles, fighting to bend forward far enough to gnaw the bonds at my wrists with my teeth. It was no use. I was too weak, and they were too tight. I yanked and pulled and kicked and let the ropes saw into my skin, screaming as though that would make the ropes untie themselves. Of course it wouldn't. Of course I was trapped here, unable to save my friends. Even if I could get loose, what would I do besides get myself killed?

Cal had the gun in his hand, but he couldn't shoot in such close quarters. Instead he rested his finger on the trigger guard and swung it at Sam's head like a club. The pistol was heavy, and Sam had time to duck out of the way. Knife in hand, she was halfway to Cal's throat, seizing at his collar with her other hand and all the venom of a rabid dog.

The person on the floor, who hadn't yet moved, now grabbed Sam's ankle and yanked her foot out from under her. Once again, she smacked the floor, and this time her knife clattered out of her hand. A bright pink orb had appeared in the doorway, and with a surprisingly athletic leap, Roscoe cleared Sam and Cal and scooped up the knife, which was sliding toward my boots. She held it like she was ready to carve up a turkey. There was a glint in her eye that suggested she'd take the chance if she got it.

Fortunately for everyone involved, the fight was mostly over. The person on the floor now had hands around Sam's throat. She madly tapped her opponent's shoulder, but only in a weak spurt, and only for a few seconds. Then she went limp.

Cal bent down and put a finger to Sam's wrist. "You didn't kill her." I couldn't tell if that was a compliment.

"And you," he said, getting on his knees to address the sprawled form, "you owe me an explan—" He went still.

That tragic pile of clothes and bones was Petra. Her face was covered in red—her nose had been ground into the floor, and her wound had reopened—and her breath emerged as a thin, high-pitched whine between lips sealed shut. Her skin was tinted an unhealthy blue, and the dark circles around her eyes were sunken and nearly black.

*Sickly pale.* Those were the first words I'd thought of to describe her, back when we first met, but there was nothing sickly about her. She was just sick. She had been this whole time, and none of us had noticed.

A quick glance at Roscoe must have satisfied Cal that she wasn't a threat—or if she was, they were on the same side. His eyes drifted to her knife, but instead of filching it from her, he said brusquely, "Untie Halley and find the door to the roof. I'll be in the village at the doctor's house. Halley can help you find your way there." With that, he gathered Petra in his arms and hurried out through the open doorway.

A cherry-red, sweaty face framed with greasy curls peeked around the corner, and Andy surveyed the room with undisguised horror.

"Where were you when we needed you?" Roscoe demanded. "Not that we did. You heard that man. Untie Halley."

Andy dug a red knife from his pocket and sawed me free. He hovered to my left to do so, staying as far as his lanky arms would reach. I knew why. Two steps farther, and he would have had to step over the sergeant's body to reach my wrists. I was grateful he gave me an excuse to look the other way, though I hoped he had good leverage on the knife for my wrists' sake.

Free at last, I stood up, massaging my forearms and stretching my neck. The water that had been spilled on my shirt hadn't nearly evaporated yet—that was how fast everything had happened—and I shivered, irritable and achy and soggy. I wasn't afraid, not anymore. I had seen so much horror in such a short amount of time that I couldn't dredge up the energy to turn my daze into any recognizable emotion.

Roscoe dragged the limp, twitching Sam to one of the chairs and, with the leftover rope from Cal's and my bonds, tied her firmly to the seat. We could only hope that Roscoe's knotting skills were better than the sergeant's, which Cal had been able to escape. Sam was going to wake up hungry for revenge, and we would make for an excellent meal.

"There's a utility closet in the hallway," Roscoe said. "Halley, can you help me?"

With much grunting and scraping, we managed to drag Sam and her chair into the utility closet and shoved the door on her with a satisfying *click*. Being in complete darkness might make it at least a little harder for her to get free. With an extra shred of rope, Roscoe tied the handle of the closet door to another handle around the corner, creating a makeshift lock.

"Nice." She held up her hand for a high five but withdrew before I could reciprocate. "I guess you don't like me," she mumbled, turning away and wrapping her arms nervously behind her back. "I wouldn't either, if I were you."

She looked so small and sad that I could barely resist the urge to pat her head. But I had my dignity to preserve, so I said, "You fought on our side. Why would I be angry with you?" I had been steadily losing track of whom to hate.

"You don't know everything," she mumbled. But a shy smile crossed her face as she ducked her head.

Funny. There was a vast difference between the knife-wielding Roscoe, who was ready to turn Sam inside out, and the self-conscious one, who couldn't accept the idea that everyone except herself had forgiven her. Even Petra. Even me.

When we reentered the long hallway, we found Andy staring at the screen.

"Hey." He spoke without turning around. "This . . . this is . . . interesting."

The camera view had split into eight different screens, each just large enough to make out the larger details. Every scene was a war.

Some fought with fists, some with bats, some with knives. I saw blond hair and black hair and red hair and everything in between, both men and women, ages varying between sixteen and thirty. With bizarre ferocity, they leaped on each other, beat each other off, ducked and dived and smacked and slapped and bit.

This, I realized with horror, was no mere practice round with pretend weapons. If I could see them, they were real.

"Grand," Roscoe observed. Her face had drained of color. "The Mercenaries finally lost it. Not that I blame them."

We huddled around the screen in the upper-right corner, where the combatants were closest to the camera. Through the chaos, I managed to discern a familiar face. One of the boys who'd been sitting in the kitchen after Cal's supposed death had another Merc by the throat. His expression was different now. The fright I'd seen before was gone, replaced with bruised and twisted anger.

"How are we going to get out?" Andy asked bleakly. "Don't we have to get through them?"

"What about Cal and Petra?" Roscoe said quietly.

We stared silently at the screens. I couldn't get that boy's face out of my head, and at last I had to look away.

They were all doomed, and I couldn't bring myself to do anything about it. Run down there. Pull them apart. Get between their knives and knock some sense back into their computerized, remotely controlled heads.

"We're fine," came a voice from the hallway.

My heart leapt.

Cal staggered through the doorway, with Petra draped across his shoulders.

"But we're stuck here," he added. "Not just us, but all twenty-seven of the other Mercs too." He propped Petra's head on his wadded-up jacket and eased her body to the floor.

"What about the lock?" Roscoe wanted to know. "You're a Merc, aren't you? Can't you open it with your handprint?"

"Yes, ordinarily, but right now it doesn't work." Cal brushed Petra's sweaty hair off her forehead. The Mercs' aggressive movements onscreen caught his attention, and he shook his head. "I knew the

Alliance would have something up their sleeve. I suppose making the Mercs kill each other is easier than sending out people to kill them in a fair fight. But I'll stop them myself if I have to."

"You can't," I broke in. "You're bleeding."

He glanced down at his chest. "Petra's."

The screen flickered in the corner of my eye, and when I glanced at it, a ninth angle appeared. The newest one showed the main room on the ground floor of the House, where a man was swiping a key card in the door. One of the mini screens switched to show him entering the tiny room where Petra and Company had started their ascent.

"Is this one of the Mercs? Do you know him?" I pointed at the screen.

Cal glanced at it. "No."

Roscoe cleared her throat. "That's my fr . . . I mean, that's Kazumi."

"The guy who owns your radio?"—Andy.

"The head of the Alliance?"—Cal.

"Who?"—Me, helpfully.

"The head of *what?*" Roscoe's eyes went huge. "Cal, what did you just call him?"

"What else would he be?"

"He's not the head of anything. Let alone any kind of Alliance. He's a beta tester at Warsafe, like me."

"I have no idea what that is. All I can tell you is that he's the one who asked me to start spying for the Al—I mean, Warsafe. What we call the Alliance—or something to do with the Alliance, anyway. He said he was the . . ." Cal hesitated. "CFO? CSI? He told me it meant head."

"CEO?"

"That's it."

Roscoe pushed back her fluffy pink bangs. Her skin shone with sweat. "That's not supposed to be true, but if it is, he's in charge of the whole project. He could probably press a button and blow us all to the next dimension."

"Then the only option is for me to go down there. I'll . . ." Cal's expression had turned bitter. "I'll either stop the Mercs, or I'll kill that man. Heaven knows he deserves it, and"—he glanced at Petra—"I think I might too. Either way, I'll buy time until you find a way to get out."

"No!" I croaked. "Cal, you can't leave. What are we going to do if we don't find a way?" It was a poor excuse, the only thing I could think of that he might consider a valid reason to stay.

"You will," was his answer. "You have to."

Just as he was about to leave the room, the lights flickered. For a moment, they came back to full power, then flickered again, then went out altogether. We were left in opaque darkness until the screen rebooted itself with a crackle of microphone static and switched back to the nine camera angles it had shown before.

Except this time, where the twenty-seven Mercs had all been fighting, there were now bodies scattered across the floor. The one exception to the stillness was Kazumi, who was quietly picking his way through the mess.

"What did . . ." I could see the screen reflected in Cal's horrified eyes as he took a step closer. "What did he do to them?"

Roscoe let out a choked sob. Andy put his arm awkwardly over her shoulder, but she shook him off and covered her face with her hands. I stood there and watched her cry, numb. Exactly as I had done when I'd thought Cal was killed, wondering what we had done to deserve this special kind of torture.

"Maybe they're not dead," Andy offered quietly. "Maybe there's another explanation."

This roused Cal from his shock, and he turned his gaze away from the screen. His face looked more like Petra's than his own. Expressionless still. I'd seen that look from her before. I'd never expected it from him.

"When Kazumi gets here, we'll find out what happened." His hand traced the outline of the weapon in his pocket. "And there won't be one secret left when he's gone."

# 24

## KAZUMI

### STEP ONE: RENT OUT AN EMPTY FERRY.

Do it on the company credit card.

Step Two:

That was where things got tricky.

He was on the island. Boots—or toes—in the sand, so to speak. So far all he had done was stand on the beach and look back and forth between the path that led to the House and the path that led to the village. One old grandmother with an assortment of carrots clutched in her hands had seen him and run away screaming. This had hurt his feelings more than he cared to admit. More importantly, it had shaken his confidence that he was going to be able to do anything besides cause more problems.

"Sergeant Porok," he said into his radio, "do you read?"

Still no answer. There hadn't been one since he'd left his office a few hours ago.

"Sergeant Porok, this is WSG. Do you read?"

Porok, who wasn't answering; Samantha, who wouldn't answer at all; and Cal, who would answer with a bullet straight to the eye socket or some other unpleasant and vital location. Those three were his only hope for assistance with his monumental project.

He might as well pack it in.

But he'd come this far. It was physical torment if he kept going, legal repercussions if he didn't. Either way, everything was already in flames. Why not add gasoline to the fire?

He took out his laptop from his briefcase and sat down on a log to do some investigating. One of the perks of being a higher-up in the Warsafe company was that nobody paid much attention to what he did on his computer. He had already been able to get away with a lot. No one else could have programmed Halley's dreams without getting the nth degree from Security. But it was only a matter of time before someone thought to check where he had gone. The more time he spent accessing the Warsafe servers, the higher the chance some security officer somewhere would notice an IP address that originated on the island. Then the sensors would come on, and the live soldiers in the House would be alerted.

It was worth the risk, however, to check the cameras and see what Sergeant Porok had been doing besides not answering his radio. Kazumi pulled up the first-floor feed, but nobody was visible. He started to click away, and then it occurred to him how strange that emptiness was. Thirty Mercenaries lived in the House. What were the odds that all of them had been called to a match at once?

He clicked to the second-floor video and groaned. He knew at once what had happened. That sadistic young designer from the meeting had proposed the bright idea of making all the Mercenaries fight each other, which would keep them distracted while the holograms were switched out with real people. The kid probably thought he was showing initiative, lining himself up for a promotion, when he had found someone smarter than him to execute the programming required to make it happen. Kazumi wondered when *initiative* had gotten confused with *disregarding authority*. He should have run a tighter ship. Made sure there were no leaks like this, no one venturing out on their own to make the project "successful." He was certain he hadn't given anyone permission to run this script. He was also certain no one had directly asked him.

They all thought they knew him. Knew what he would and wouldn't approve. He had kept up his ruthless and conniving façade for so long that they had all come to believe it. It had been months since he'd let himself feel any shred of pity or remorse, fearing that the moment he let the thought into his mind, those around him would sense his change in demeanor.

If he was fired—or if anything worse happened to him—he wouldn't be able to stop this project. So he had let them all believe he was the kind of person who would cheerfully sign off on this death match. And these were the results.

His administrative assistant answered the phone on the first ring. "Mr. Sato?"

"Tell whoever is making the Mercenaries fight each other to knock it off."

In the eloquent silence that followed, Kazumi watched a hermit crab skitter across the beach and disappear into the water. Part of him wished he could do the same. One coherent or half-clever question from her, and he was dead.

Her throat cleared. "Excuse me?"

"Someone in the programming department sent a signal to all the Mercenary chips that is making them fight each other. Tell them to stop. We don't want to risk the Mercenaries getting killed. Tell them they're beyond fortunate I happened to look at the video monitors, or else they might be out of a job and into a lawsuit."

"How awful."

Kazumi was pretty sure she had no idea what that word meant.

"Tell them that, if they need to do something while the Mercenaries aren't paying attention, they can simply put them to sleep." All except Calhoun and Petra, whose chips he had disabled before he left headquarters. And Samantha, who had no chip at all. She didn't need controlling when she was so perfectly self-controlled.

"Yes, sir," said his assistant.

Kazumi ended the call and turned back to his computer. He had already called up the program that would permanently disable the chips, which he had convinced an unsuspecting junior programmer to build several months ago. It hadn't been difficult. All Kazumi had to do was send a jumble of radio signals from his computer, which would scramble the chips' processors and render them permanently unusable. He couldn't do that right away, though, because someone back at headquarters would notice the moment the signal was lost. And he needed at least a few hours before they found out what he had done.

"Sergeant Porok?" He raised his radio to his mouth again. "This is WSG. Do you read?"

Static.

He turned off the radio, closed his laptop, and put them both into his briefcase. No one was going to help him now. It was time to take responsibility for what he'd done, time to fix everything that he had broken. At last, he could think the thoughts of rebellion he had scarcely dared to indulge before.

*Roscoe, Calhoun, Petra. That other guy.*
*I'm coming for you.*

# 25

## HALLEY

**MY HEARING WAS DAMPENED BY THE** sound of Roscoe's half-stifled crying, but I was the first to hear a faint moan from Petra's side of the room. I uttered a cry and pointed a trembling finger in her direction. Cal started up like he had wasps after him, and I scrambled after him as fast as my aching legs allowed.

He said her name, then held up his hand before Petra's face. "How many fingers do you see?"

Her eyes were dazed and half-closed. But when Cal's face came into view, her whole body jerked. I knew exactly what she must be thinking—*this is it, I'm dead, I'm seeing ghosts. Am I a ghost too?* She glanced over at me, but one glance was all I got before her eyes reverted to Cal. She'd known I was alive, but the sergeant's video had been angled away from Cal, so his presence was a complete surprise.

"Yes, it's me." Cal reached out as though to touch her, but she flinched and squirmed away. *Ghost.* He tried to catch her eyes. "Petra, you must have had a lot of questions, and I wasn't there to answer. I'm sorry. Really sorry. I'm sorry I left you. I'm sorry I didn't tell you. I'm sorry you had to see me like that. *Sorry* isn't going to cover it, but it's the best I've got short of getting you out of here."

Her forehead crinkled. One pale-blue hand slowly reached up

and brushed his cheek, running down his neck and grasping the red bandanna at his throat, damp with sweat, undeniably real. Her eyes widened. She tried to speak, but all that came out was a choked gasp.

Cal took her hand in his. "I'm not dead. Neither are you. We're okay. We're both okay." His voice dissolved into a rough whisper. "You did it. You made it. Roscoe and Andy and Halley are here, and they're safe too." He had positioned himself between Petra and the screen, bending his head over her so that all she could see was him and me. "You saved everyone."

"I hate you," she whispered back, her lips barely moving.

I grinned and blinked, rapidly swallowing and focusing my thoughts on hermit crabs and lemonade. I hadn't come this far just to let the others see me cry.

"Did you know?" he asked her. "Did you know before I told you?"

She coughed. Cal wiped the corner of her mouth with his shirt and waited anxiously for her to speak.

Faint and nearly indecipherable. "Yes."

Cal's head lowered. "I knew you would figure it out. I thought that if they found out you knew, they'd kill you. I couldn't tell you directly. It wasn't worth the risk." A tinge of pink crept into his cheeks. "I couldn't. You understand. I hope you do."

A tight smile lingered on her face, the kind that didn't express anything except an inability to think of some other expression. "Hurts to . . . breathe." She eased her hand from Cal's and pressed it to the left side of her chest. "Lightheaded . . ." Her eyes drooped closed, but she quickly opened them again. "Halley . . . where did she go?"

"I'm here." I leaned over Petra, smiling like an idiot. "Thank you. I mean, I'm sorry. I'm glad you're awake. You look terrible—I mean, you look great all things considered, but—"

"I think you're beautiful." Cal was watching the screen.

"And there's water if you want it," I chattered on, holding up the bottle with what remained of its contents. "But you probably don't feel like—"

"Why isn't she going crazy?" Trust Andy to say the right thing at the best possible time. "Why isn't she behaving like the other Mercs?"

Roscoe shot him a horrified look, and Cal gestured wildly out of Petra's sight line, but the damage was done.

"Other . . . Mercs?" Petra shakingly raised herself on one forearm. "What happened to them?"

"It's nothing. You need to go back to sleep, Petra." Cal's tone had turned gentle. I pretended to be deeply interested by the light fixture, but I didn't miss when he leaned forward and pecked Petra on the forehead, a shy, short kiss like a schoolboy in mischief.

"You've done everything you needed to do," he said, brushing a piece of sweaty hair from her cheek, "and I'll take it from here."

She buried her head in Cal's jacket. A few minutes passed, and her breathing grew even and steady.

My skin prickled with jealousy. I wished I could sleep, too. I would have liked to have skipped this horrible day, stop planning, and let the future be what it would. Here and there and sometimes everywhere, on every blank wall and in the dark corners and on the insides of my eyelids, came sparks of memory that sent nauseating shivers through my body. The black around Petra's eyes. Scattered papers, crumpled and torn. A distant gunshot. Blurred, grainy video. A syringe, water dribbling from the needle. A surgical knife and the smell of burnt flesh.

And there was still the dark corner of the room where my chair had been sitting. I hadn't looked over there since Andy had freed me.

While Petra slept, the rest of us gathered in front of the screen, watching silently as Kazumi ascended. He weaved his way through the Mercs, who were oblivious to his presence, and the guards—the real ones Petra and Company had encountered—who let him pass with deferential nods. One of them pushed a notepad under his nose, which Kazumi signed with an embarrassing attempt at nonchalance. That scribble could have been an autograph, or it could have been an authorization on an order to kill us all. By my watch, it had been exactly seven minutes and thirty-three seconds since he'd opened the door to the waiting area, and he was already on the seventh floor at the base of the staircase to the eighth.

"I've watched Kazumi play. He's the best," Roscoe said. Her

tears had dried up, but only barely. "Especially if you're right, and he is Warsafe's CEO. They designed every nook and cranny of this awful building. I helped them do it. He knows the game better than anyone."

"Then we can't sneak past him. And we can't get out through the roof. I could go down and meet him, but I doubt I'd have the element of surprise. He must know we're cornered."

"What if we wait until he gets up here and then sneak down to the seventh floor?"

"He can move between floors faster than we can. He'd catch up. And I'd be surprised if he hadn't locked the front door."

"We could lure him into a room with a lockable door and trap him for a little while. Give ourselves time to break out."

"That—" Roscoe broke off suddenly, but it wasn't until the first metallic *click* that I realized why. While they'd been talking, Cal had retrieved the pistol he had taken from Sam. Now he absent-mindedly cocked and un-cocked it, sending the unspent bullets rattling and rolling across the floor, until the magazine was empty. Empty—probably. There was room for hope.

The same kind of room you'd find between electrons in an atom.

"It would be a lot easier to shoot this Kazumi person," Cal said at last, setting the pistol and magazine on the floor and flashing Roscoe a grin. "Have it over with and start again tomorrow. Oh, you don't like that idea? But you played along with it during the game when you let *us* get shot."

"Cal!" Petra's voice admonished. All four of us startled, surprised to discover that she was awake. "Roscoe didn't know what she was doing."

"Ignorance is no defense. Besides, what if she's lying?"

"I know the difference between the truth and a lie." Her voice was stronger now.

He grinned. "You never seemed to notice when I lied. Maybe I'm just that good at it."

Roscoe took a small step forward. "If there's anything I can do to prove how sincere I am, I'll do it, no questions asked. If you want me to go down there and confront Kazumi myself, you might give me the gun first, but then I'll—"

"Stop apologizing," Petra insisted, hoisting herself up until she was sitting reasonably upright with her back against the wall. I expected Cal to help her, and when he didn't, I started toward her to do it myself. But she had balanced herself before I could reach her. "She saved my life on the way up here. Roscoe, don't take it personally. Cal's . . ." Her wheezes turned to coughs, and she choked: "He's worried about keeping us safe."

When she pulled her hand back from her mouth, she paused for a split second. She hadn't meant for us to see, but her hesitation was enough for me to notice spots of red on her palm. The doctor's textbooks would have said something about that, but I hadn't gotten that far in my studies. I'd finished *Ten Most Common Deadly Illnesses* and *How to Cure the Common Cold*, but I hadn't completed *The Surgical Approach to Trauma Wounds*. I'd gotten nauseous long before I reached the chapter on lungs.

Cal started to untie his bandanna, but Petra waved him away and coughed into her sleeve. "No one dies, Cal," she said, voice raspy. "Neither of us has killed anyone, and we're not going to start now."

I thought this would close the argument, but Cal's smile didn't fade.

"What's the difference between thinking you're a murderer and actually being one? I knew the truth. But you didn't. You went on killing even when you thought you were killing real people."

I gaped at Cal while he retrieved the pistol and jammed the magazine into place. "Just because I decided to keep you alive in the end doesn't mean I'm not the traitor everyone thinks I am." Metal scraped on metal as he racked the slide. "Why aren't you angry with me, Petra? Why won't you just curse me and be done with it? I've done everything I can to make you hate me, and still you won't let me go."

"Oh, how stupid!" Roscoe burst out. "Cal, you're a bitter, ugly narcissist, and everyone thinks you're the worst person they've ever met. There you go. Is that punishment enough?"

I made a mental note that if we were ever chased by a bear, I could in good conscience run away and leave Roscoe to fend for herself.

"Say it back to me if you want," Roscoe continued, crossing her arms defiantly. "If we can just work together for five whole minutes, maybe we can get out of this alive and continue this stupid discussion elsewhere. Over coffee and scones."

"Hear, hear!" I responded. Not aloud. Just in my head. Cal was gripping the gun in both hands, and he looked like a thundercloud.

I still wasn't properly afraid, not the knees-knocking, sick-to-my-stomach kind. Cal had gotten the chance to hurt us all many times before, and he'd always come out on our side in the end.

That didn't tell us much about what was going to happen in the middle.

In one bound, he was across the room and had seized Roscoe, pinning her against the wall, pressing his gun against her head. "Don't preach to me about things you don't understand!" he growled. She flinched, but then she lowered her chin stubbornly and squirmed in his grip. "You're a stranger on the island. If I had been in Petra's place, I would have killed you before you ever set foot in the House. I might have betrayed the Mercs once, but I won't be a traitor again. Now that I've chosen sides, I won't go back."

Nothing short of a miracle and a hefty dose of adrenaline could have gotten Petra back up on her feet, but she was built for desperate times. Avoiding the mangled chair I'd been sitting in, she bumped me out of the way and wedged herself between Cal and Roscoe. It was inspiring. On impulse, I started after her, catching Roscoe and knocking us both away from Cal. By the time I made a rough landing in the corner, I realized I had done something remarkably brave. I felt briefly pleased with myself until I remembered that he still had the loaded gun and all we had were bruises.

"Stop acting like you know her!" Petra stared up at him stubbornly, a kitten in front of an enormous dog. "You'd die here as a Merc if Roscoe and Andy hadn't come. You can hate me all you want, and you can say I'm a murderer. I don't care. But leave Roscoe and Andy out of it."

Roscoe knelt by me, and her fingernails dug into my arm. "I'm fine, I'm fine," she whispered, nodding frantically at me. "Halley, get out. Don't wait until he remembers you're here."

But Cal wasn't the forgetful type. He swung the gun in my direction.

"My orders were to keep villagers out of the House. Yet here you are, and I didn't even try to stop you. The Alliance was right to punish me. I should never have let you see the inside of this place. Not if all you ever meant to do was drag more people into the game and let them die because you're too persistently *good* to kill someone in self-defense. After everything else we've done, this is where you draw the line?"

I couldn't move. I couldn't take my eyes off his face, couldn't say a word in response. Trying to run would've revealed that my legs had gone limp—even if I could get to my feet. I could only huddle in the corner, petrified, as he raised the gun. Right between my eyes. A round black circle that would kill me in a second or two. I'd gotten through that section of the *Trauma* textbook. I knew in anatomical detail how it would happen, and how much it wouldn't hurt.

"Stop it before you do something you'll regret!" Petra demanded. "You weren't a traitor to the Mercs! You left me that letter! You gave us all those clues about the chips! You—"

"Hush!" begged Roscoe, jumping up from the floor and clamping a hand over Petra's mouth. "Petra, don't say it!"

"Hello?" said a small voice from somewhere at the back of the room. Andy, probably, though it didn't quite sound like him, not that I had any attention to spare for such unimportant details. Where had he been while we were all trying to convince Cal to let us live?

If I didn't have much time left, I didn't want to spend it thinking about that.

Cal's gun was black and a little rusted around the edges, so close to my face that I could almost see the grooves inside the barrel. It was small and narrow. It might misfire. Cal's eyes were fixed on my face, but I couldn't return his glare. It wasn't him I was seeing. It was the power of death he held in his hand. The same power that had killed the sergeant, whose body was lying on the floor behind me. I was bound to end up like the solider after all.

All I could do was sit and shiver and wait in dread and hope it happened quickly.

"Uh . . . Roscoe? What's going . . . oh!" The Andy soundalike became alarmed. "Put that gun down!" I'd heard the sound of a gun being cocked enough times to recognize it.

But Cal hadn't moved. Then who—?

"Don't," Petra wheezed. "Stop, stop. Just . . ." Her voice trailed off, and Roscoe dived to catch her as she began to collapse.

As they vanished from my field of view, I got a brief glimpse over Cal's shoulder.

*Kazumi.*

Cal had distracted us for too long. Intentionally or not, he had killed us all the moment he opened his mouth.

And now Kazumi was coming to finish the job.

Well. At least I'd have company along the road to eternity.

# 26

**"IT'S NICE TO MEET YOU IN PERSON."**

Cal's back was to the intruder. But he had been a spy. He must have heard his handler's voice, and he recognized it now. "I hope you can—"

"Put that gun down, and then we'll talk."

Cal did as he was ordered, sliding the weapon along the floor toward Kazumi's feet. As it spun, I noticed that the bottom of the grip, where he had been clicking the magazine in and out, was empty. Hollow.

*Unloaded.*

I took a tentative step back, kicking a cartridge with the heel of my boot and sending it rolling and skittering into a cobwebby corner.

Kazumi brushed past Cal and confronted Roscoe.

"Is Petra alright?" he demanded. "Are *you* alright?"

Roscoe cradled Petra defensively in her arms, glaring at Kazumi.

He took the hint and backed away, hands in the air. "I know what you're thinking, but this time I swear I'm here to help. That's what I've been trying to do for months."

No one seemed inclined to argue. Probably because the point seemed too ridiculous to bother refuting.

Apparently the silence was enough for Kazumi. "I'll prove it. I'll give you my key card." Fishing inside his jacket, he held it up, suspended from a lanyard around his neck. His picture was displayed on the front, fringed by some tiny numbers and letters. A barcode and a stripe crossed the back. "I'll leave. You don't even have to take me with you." He unclipped the card and laid it gingerly on the floor, backing toward the door. "All you have to do now is get out of the House."

"And leave the other Mercs?" Cal scoffed. "Who do you think we are?"

"We?" Andy's dormant temper had finally been riled. Emerging from his corner, dusting off his knees, straightening himself up to his full, lanky height, Andy demanded, "Since when have you been on our side?"

Kazumi ignored him. "Come with me, Calhoun," he said, gesturing toward the door with his pistol. The gun didn't sit easily in his hand, and he almost dropped it. His thoughts might as well have been written on his face: *Cal is a whole foot taller than me. And he's a Merc.* But Kazumi continued, "I'm here to get them out of the House. If you're working with the Alliance, you follow my orders. If you're working with the Mercenaries, this should be exactly what you want. Either way, it's in your interest to work with me."

A smile appeared on Cal's face.

"No one would believe you're here on the Alliance's orders when you talk like that." He grinned, retrieving his gun from the floor and sliding it into the pocket at his knee. Stepping back toward the wall, he sat down and let his head loll back against the paneling. "Mercy isn't their thing. Roscoe, tell them what I told you earlier. When I was treating you devilishly and all that."

Roscoe was obviously more relieved than annoyed. "Cal said everything was an act. He wanted Kazumi to think he was still on the Alliance's side to gain his trust and get some questions answered. But if Kazumi is really here to help us, it was all for nothing. Just a big show without an audience."

That seemed awfully convenient. Roscoe must have had the same idea, and she narrowed her eyes at Cal.

"Do I believe that?" she asked, as if daring him to deny it. "I'm not sure I do. It sounds like you're known for switching sides, so why would I believe you're telling the truth this time?"

Cal stuck out his bottom lip. "It was a pretty good idea. It worked. Not the way I intended, but it worked."

Even Kazumi looked mortified.

"You had no right to say what you did." Petra could barely croak the words out, but her tone was sharp enough.

"I did whatever I thought would save your life. I'm not saying you need to grovel, but a little thank-you might be in order."

Petra turned to Kazumi. "Put the gun down."

Kazumi obeyed and held up his empty hands.

"Hold on," interrupted Cal. "The other Mercs—"

"Are alright," Kazumi assured us hastily. "They're asleep. I thought that might buy us some time before headquarters realizes something's up."

"So you're saying I have to share some of the thanks with you?" A wave of good humor washed over Cal's stiff face, and he placed his gun on the floor and flicked it in Petra's direction. "Never thought I'd show gratitude to an Alliance member."

"It's not just me you owe. If Roscoe hadn't overheard my conversation, and if she hadn't been able to find her way here, and if you hadn't been a spy, and if Andy hadn't been a nerd, and if Sergeant Porok hadn't been so kindhearted, and if I hadn't disabled your chips, you would never have found out the truth. You could search for a hundred years, and you would never be any closer to finding the 'Alliance,' as you call the Warsafe board of directors and its allies. They exist in a different world from you. A world where half the things you take for granted, like that silly automatic dresser downstairs, don't exist." Kazumi glanced at his watch. "As things stand, it took you exactly forty days, twelve hours, twenty-seven minutes, and three seconds to unravel the whole thing. Well done. You did better than I could have hoped."

"Forty days?" echoed Petra. "I've only known Halley for three weeks."

"I'm not talking about how long you've been trying to escape. That's how long the game has been going."

He might as well have started speaking in tongues.

"The game . . . you mean, the game when it's played with real people instead of holograms?" I said hesitantly. Someone had to say something, and at least if I said it and it turned out to be the wrong thing, it would be considered sufficiently unimportant that no one would get shot.

He frowned. "When I disabled your chips, you should have gotten your memories back. You wouldn't remember everything, of course. Just what happened immediately before you were brought to this island."

No one took the bait. Roscoe, who had shown no sign of surprise until I spoke up, raised an eyebrow.

Kazumi tried again. "Your chips were programmed to make you think you've been here your whole lives. That generations of Mercenaries have played and died and been replaced. Actually, this batch of thirty is the first. They did that so you wouldn't think to question a system you believed you'd lived under forever. So you'd be used to it, in a sense." He turned to Roscoe. "All your prototype avatars before Petra were just that. Prototypes. Digital. Lasers. Not real people. You never killed anyone, Roscoe. Things were getting to that point, which is why I'm finally here. Almost too late."

"Are you telling us," Cal asked, carefully enunciating each syllable like he was afraid of being misunderstood, "that Sergeant Porok is the only person who has ever died on this island?"

"Yes." Kazumi hesitated. "Almost. I just found out that some of the holograms were switched out with real people, but they . . . they were sentenced to death anyway."

"'Anyway'?" Cal mocked, raising his eyebrows. "Well, that certainly makes it all better."

I happened to glance back at Petra, my attention caught by her movement. The blood on her palms reminded me of something. Of yellow flowers with transparent stalks. Of clear blue skies and the whole village yelling at me to stop. Of waking up in a cold sweat from a nightmare.

"If you can program memories," I mused, "did you also program my dreams?"

Kazumi's head swiveled to me. "How much do you know?"

"If it's true, then tell me what my dreams were." There was no way he could know the answer unless he really had been inside my head and had access to the chips. Unless he was a member of the Alliance. Unless he was everything he claimed to be.

"The first two were about Petra. You were standing in a field of dandelions, and Petra was trying to get you to follow her. I tried to make the dreams vivid enough that they'd get you curious about going to meet her." I wondered what other cobwebs he'd been able to dig up inside my mind. Hopefully he could only put things there and not get them out again. "The third was about Cal and a conversation he had with Sergeant Porok. Which was a playback of a real conversation. I wanted you to know that about Cal."

"What did he say?" Petra asked.

Kazumi's only response was a glance at Cal's stormy eyes and a noncommittal shrug. I couldn't blame him. I wasn't telling, either.

"The chips can control people's perception," he said. "They can't make you do something, but they can manipulate you into choosing to do it. If I was controlling the chips from the central computer, for example, I could make Petra think Cal was a guard in the House. I couldn't force her to attack him, but she would probably do that on her own. They can also cause painful sensations of electric shocks. As you might know if you've ever broken the island's laws, this is how Warsafe enforced the rules."

"Why didn't you use that tactic when you were trying to make me kill Halley?" Cal caught the look on Petra's face. "Yes, Petra, I was in direct communication with Kazumi through the sergeant—the one who—the one over there. He ordered me to shoot you and Halley both, and I refused to do it. I thought I'd get electrocuted or brain-fried on the spot, but nothing happened."

"Because it's not healthy for your mind. You Mercenaries have a reputation for being a little . . ." He twirled his finger beside his head. "The effect of the chips is much stronger on you than it usually is for the villagers. It has to be, or else you couldn't be deceived into thinking those holograms are real people. Besides, I didn't actually want you to kill anyone. I just had to say that because Sergeant Porok was going to get suspicious if I didn't."

"Your kindness has undone the trauma I went through. Thank you."

"I also modified the code in your watches," Kazumi continued, his face a well-deserved shade of red at Cal's sarcasm, "so you could be outside after curfew on the night when Roscoe and Andy appeared. I knew they were here within an hour of their arrival. We have sensors all over the island. You're lucky I was watching, because if I hadn't noticed, the chips would have killed you for breaking curfew."

"Impressive," observed Roscoe. "Warsafe can do all this, and yet they can't make money on any of their video-game releases."

"The government isn't a moneymaking organization. Not in the usual sense."

"What does the government have to do with—?"

"I'll tell you," Cal interrupted. He glanced at me, and as our eyes met, I knew we were both thinking about the sergeant's story. His small talk, Cal had called it. There was only one thing that made sense, only one reason for this enormous deception that could remotely be justified.

"This whole island is just a game," he said grimly. "A game that's supposed to take the place of real-world wars. If the sergeant was telling the truth, the government has an obvious interest in supporting it. Though I have no idea how you plan to make this work."

Kazumi nodded. "Porok was a good man. He wasn't supposed to tell you, but I'm glad he did."

So it was true. We were here for a purpose. All along, there had been some semblance of a reason for our suffering. Somewhere in the world, somewhere we were never intended to see, a war was being fought. A war that we could have prevented if only we'd kept on playing the game.

It was all too awful. War was awful. Our lives were awful in equal measure.

But the tens, hundreds, thousands of deaths that actual, real-world war entailed—did we have those on our consciences now?

Cal had more to say. "The game is produced by a company

called—" He stopped speaking to hold up his tattooed left hand, spreading his thumb and pinkie to reveal the broad wings wrapped around the *W* and the slashing cross. It was the first time I had seen the mark clearly and upright. It was graceful and elegant. A mark of ownership. Beautiful in a harsh way.

Suddenly I knew—or perhaps remembered?—what it meant.

*Wings for freedom.*

*A cross for the sacrifice you make.*

*An arrow for the wars you fight and your matchless bravery.*

I had seen those words written down somewhere. But there was no point in trying to remember where.

"*W* for *Warsafe*." Cal closed his fist. "It was never *M* for *Mercenary*. It was never about us. It was always Warsafe."

"I told them about all that," Roscoe broke in—forgetting, apparently, that I had heard nothing of her explanation because I'd been busy getting trussed up and kidnapped. "What I want to know is, why couldn't Warsafe make this information public? People are idealistic. They would volunteer to play the game, just like they volunteer to join the military. Why keep it a secret?"

"Public opinion would never support such a thing. It's horrific, isn't it? When you found out, I saw the disgust in your face. It's too deliberate, too prefabricated. Wars are perceived as a necessity, but is this"—Cal looked at Petra—"is this how things have to be? Suffering on an individual scale, all planned out and designed in advance?"

"If Warsafe had told the Mercs," she insisted, "it might have made their sacrifices seem worthwhile."

Kazumi shook his head. "The benefit of telling them wasn't worth the possibility that the secret could leak."

"If you're done chatting," Cal interrupted wryly, "we need to get Petra to the doctor."

Petra collected herself and clambered to her feet, swaying.

"There's no rush," she protested. "I want to hear the rest of the story."

Cal was ready to catch her if she fell, but she steadied herself against the wall. "Kazumi," she said, "will we have any trouble getting down the stairs?"

Kazumi considered this. "No. That is, I don't think so. If we meet anyone, I'll say I'm here on the board's orders like I did on my way up. But they should have left the island by now. There was a company boat hidden by the shore for them to use in case of emergency, and I sent out the signal as soon as I got up here."

Boats. Water. Sea monsters. There was a reason why we villagers hated going near the beach, and that was the way things had always been. I sighed. I was going to have to get out of the habit of saying that. Because it was *not* the way things had always been. There was no such thing as always.

"If you're sure about that, why don't you go in the front?" Cal gestured toward the door. "I'm sure your friends down there will be a lot more likely to not murder us if they see you first."

I was grateful that Kazumi picked up his pistol and ignored Cal's thinly veiled irritation. All we needed was another fight.

"The one problem could be Samantha." He stepped over the spots of blood that remained on the floor from Cal and Sam's encounter. "She won't be fooled for a moment if she sees me here."

"He has a point. What did you do with her?" Cal asked Roscoe.

"We tied her up in a closet down the hall." She impatiently brushed a wisp of pink hair out of her face.

Kazumi stared at her. "You tied the president of the company up and put her in a closet?"

"The what?"

He shook his head. "I underestimated you. Or overestimated her."

We traded glances, but no one said anything.

Holding his weapon tightly to his chest, Kazumi peered gingerly around the corner. Why he thought there might be anyone in the hallway waiting to see if we'd come out when they could have easily come in, I couldn't tell. But his caution impressed me. I tiptoed after him. Roscoe, who was pinching her necklace chain to keep the charm silent, followed closely. Cal offered his arm to Petra and was ignored. Andy brought up the rear.

The floorboards creaked under our feet. Petra's footsteps landed heavy and uneven. A faint hum from the House's hidden machinery blended with the sound of our breathing into a gentle background of white noise.

Nine floors to go.

The eighth floor was empty. So was the seventh floor. So was the sixth. But on the fifth, Kazumi, despite his theatrical attempts to circumvent the corners, forgot to look at his feet. He stumbled over something lying across the doorway, fading into the next room on his hands and knees. We were behind him, and we didn't see what made him fall—we only heard a *bang*. A sound that was all too familiar. I dove behind the wall as Cal grabbed Petra and shielded her behind him. Roscoe and Andy waffled for a split second—left behind by those of us with other priorities—and then sprinted for shelter.

"It's alright!" Kazumi picked himself up and dusted off his hands as he stood. "It's a Mercenary."

"So it is," affirmed Cal, who wasn't about to let go of Petra. "It's Sara."

Mistrustful, I went on tiptoe to spy over Cal's shoulder. And sure enough, spread out across the floor was a Merc—Sara, apparently, whoever that was—fast asleep, chest rising and falling with monotonous regularity. Thank goodness she was alive. That meant the other Mercs probably were too. And it meant that Kazumi had told the truth when he'd said he hadn't killed them.

Cal prodded her with his foot, but she didn't wake up.

"How did you get here?" he asked Kazumi as he dragged Sara's limp body out of the doorway. She landed like a sack of potatoes in the corner. "Can you take everyone back with you?"

"Yes," Kazumi replied. "But what then? We have things like social security numbers and passports and birth certificates. Without those documents, none of you will ever be able to do anything. You won't be able to get jobs, drive, buy a house, buy alcohol . . ." Roscoe raised an eyebrow. "The Alliance—not Warsafe, but SAFE—writes the rules for all that paperwork, and it's standardized internationally. If you tried to apply for replacement documents, they'd trace you. Who knows what they'd do to stop you from spreading their secret?"

"Then we have to make the situation so public that there'd be an outrage if they killed us. Isn't that what you said would happen if

Warsafe went public with the game? The outcry would be so big they'd have to stop?"

"Nobody would listen. You're not Warsafe. You're not a major company. You're just one potentially schizophrenic individual with a bizarre story that sounds straight out of a sci-fi novel."

"Not one," I reminded him. "There are two hundred of us, villagers and Mercenaries. Roscoe worked at Warsafe, so she can corroborate the story. You, too, Kazumi."

Kazumi's expression grew thoughtful. "We could possibly sue Warsafe for causing Petra's amputation. You could all testify."

I listened to him, bewildered. Sue? As in, Susan?

Whatever he meant, Roscoe caught on right away. "And then we'd have legal jurisdiction to demand records from Warsafe." She snapped her fingers. "Theoretically, since the judiciary and executive are separate and controlled nationally, not by SAFE, we might have a shot at a fair trial."

"No one would take the case." Andy's words fell like a rain cloud over their excitement. "You have no proof."

"We do." At least I could follow this part of the conversation. I pointed to Petra's dimly blinking arm. "You yourself said technology like this doesn't exist on the . . . mainland. So, where else could it have come from?"

"That's not enough. You need documents. Recordings. Hard evidence. Proof."

"Before I left, I took some papers from Warsafe that show . . ." Kazumi looked hard at Andy, and his voice trailed off.

It occurred to me that he had barely addressed Andy since we'd met. And although Andy hadn't known who he was, he had never bothered to ask Andy's name.

"They prove Warsafe was engaging in illegal activities," Kazumi continued, shifting his gaze away. "Forced labor, for example. If I present those to the court, they'll have reasonable grounds to demand other records. Those, combined with Petra's prosthetic, are enough to make a case. The problem is that the documents I have incriminate me too. I'd rather try something else."

No one had an answer.

"Oh, come on." Kazumi eyed us. "Surely we can come up with something."

But we couldn't.

"Alright," he said at last. "I have an idea. I can't tell you what it is, though, or it won't work."

"I don't know if we trust you," Petra said. "Even if you aren't trying to work against us, why should you help us?"

"I agree," said Cal. Petra scowled.

"I promise you, I'm on your side," Kazumi said. "I despise Warsafe as much as you do for what they did to me. And you, of course. Mostly what they did to you."

Petra eased to a sitting position against the wall. "There's one other thing," she said. "Are we trying to save our own lives, or are we trying to destroy Warsafe? Because I think we're making a mistake either way."

Cal looked down at her, frowning. "And they called *me* a suicidal maniac."

"I'm saying we should think about it." Her voice was raspy, and concern flickered across Cal's face. "War, Cal. That's what we're up against. If our lives are all that's required to save thousands of soldiers, why shouldn't we stay here and pay the price for everyone? Of course Warsafe was wrong to lie. But if they had told us why we were here, I wouldn't have been so angry. I might even have played willingly."

Of course Petra would be the one to say what we had all been trying to ignore. Of course she had to ruin it.

"In theory, it's not a terrible idea," Roscoe commented. "The concept of replacing wars with video games. I understand that if it didn't work that way, conscience would be the only thing preventing the loser from sending out their real army for revenge or to change the outcome. But why wouldn't Warsafe use volunteers? Why did they make us play? None of those beta testers had any idea what they were doing." Her voice trembled. "Were you trying to turn us into killers?"

"I can explain that too," Cal told her. "People volunteer for wars because they don't know if they're going to die. But all the Mercs are bound to die eventually, because the cost of the game isn't high enough to prevent wars from being fought over every trivial dispute."

"Correct," Kazumi agreed. "When the *Permadeath* game is finished, no one will survive it. All the players will play until they're killed. And that—it won't take long."

"Isn't it always better for only a few people to die?" Petra's voice sounded faraway, and her chin drooped to her chest. "The number of Mercs lost won't be anything close to the number of soldiers who would die in even just one war."

"Petra. Stop following your heart and start thinking with your head," Cal warned. "Sacrificing yourself in the most obvious way isn't always the right thing to do. A system like this could never work. The cost is too low, and it's misplaced. Those who fight the wars won't be the ones whose lives are sacrificed or whose families are inconvenienced. They would want to fight wars and kill Mercs over unimportant things. It's not just *you* who would die. It would be thousands of others."

"And every country would be forced to do it," Kazumi said, "by—"

"Let me guess," Roscoe interrupted. "That was why we had those SAFE badges. Because this is SAFE's war simulator. Warsafe was working with them, and they're the ones who will enforce participation."

"Enforce? How?" Andy asked. "SAFE likes to say membership is mandatory, but they don't technically have legal power without consent of the member governments."

"Do you really think all those countries would cede power voluntarily?" Kazumi asked wearily. "You bought their lie about nuclear disarmament, didn't you? You thought that the world gave up its weapons to the arsenal of common defense, like a good little child, because SAFE was promising us a better life. But they had stockpiled stronger weapons already, and everyone knew it. They kept the nukes we gave them, and now they can make credible threats to wipe any country that resists them off the map. Working with Warsafe, letting governments have this small burst of violence inside the game to settle any serious disagreements, they can ensure that no one will have or even want an army strong enough to fight back. It's a peaceful regime, alright, until you start resisting."

"But they could come up with a lighter punishment," Petra argued. A little of her usual energy seemed to return as she spoke, though she hadn't yet gotten back to her feet. "There has to be some other way to force countries to abide by the rules of the game. Some other weapon. Some other threat that wouldn't create so much destruction if it did have to be used. And besides, wouldn't people comply voluntarily if it meant there would be no more war?"

"If you lose the *Permadeath* game, and if the stakes are high enough that you're willing to sacrifice the manpower and resources, a real-world war will be fought no matter what," Kazumi said. "That's economics. Game theory. Math. Human nature. SAFE knows it, and that's why their threat has to be enormous."

"I agree. It would be different if we had chosen this place," Cal said slowly. "Maybe it would be a good thing, a noble effort, even if it didn't work out. But if we don't destroy it now, it will always be inhabited by people who didn't choose to come. Children will eventually be born here, Petra. Raised in the belief that their life purpose isn't good for anything except killing. They'll all live like us, and for what? For a system that might not work? For a system that might cause more deaths than it prevents?"

"Did you not see that sergeant sitting in a pool of his own blood?" Petra pointed back up the stairs. "Do you want to see that happen ten thousand more times over the course of a single year? Or would you rather see it happen over generations? Tell people what they're sacrificing their lives for, and some of them will choose to stay."

"But we can't tell them," Kazumi said, "because then the secret would leak, and I'm telling you, Petra, a single photograph of you in this state and a well-written news article about the horrors of *Permadeath*, and the system would be terminated for good. Even SAFE wouldn't be able to defend themselves against the outrage."

"Have there been no photos and no articles about war? And yet it still exists."

"Time's ticking." Kazumi tapped his finger against his watch. "I didn't sabotage headquarters and my own career for things to end in a fight about whether or not to leave."

"He's right." Roscoe nodded. "The choice will be made for us if we stand here and argue. We have to act now and decide later, even if . . ." She swallowed. "Even if it turns out there is something to this idea of Warsafe's."

"If we make the wrong choice," Andy said, "we could be responsible for the next world war." He said it calmly, with a scientist's precise statement of fact.

"No matter what we do, that might be true," Roscoe admitted. "But Kazumi is right. We can't just stand here."

"Anonymous ballot," Cal proposed. "Whatever the majority decides is what we all do."

He took a small leather notebook and pencil from one of his bottomless pockets. The sheets of paper, I noticed, were about the same size as the ones on which he'd written his poems about Petra. But there was no sentiment about the way he tore two pages free and ripped them into six evenly-sized shreds.

"Write your answer on the paper and put it in Petra's satchel. We'll mix it up so no one knows what belongs to whom. No one will ever know what you voted, so vote honestly. The goal is to have no regrets. We don't have room to doubt ourselves."

He passed out the slips of paper.

"You've always thought this was wrong." He paused in front of Petra, stooped, and lowered his voice. "You've always fought so hard against this system. Don't give up now, just because they hold out one glittering promise of a peaceful world that might not be true. Fight against death, Petra, not for it. Don't give up on free will."

I took a shred of paper from him. It was translucent, soaked with sweat from his palms.

"I'll go first." Cal gripped the pencil between his left thumb and forefinger and pressed the fragment of paper into his hand. "It's 'go' for leaving and 'stay' for letting things go back to how they were." His scribbling finished, he looked up and handed the pencil to me.

"Does it have to be just the six of us?" My voice caught. "Aren't we deciding for the villagers in the same way we don't want the Alliance to decide for us?"

Silence met my question. I was right, of course. We all knew it, but what else were we going to do? There wasn't time to trot down the hill, explain the whole situation, and run a poll. There were only the six of us and these slips of paper that were about to decide our fate once and for all.

I stared down at the paper and pictured the two words scrawled across it.

GO.

STAY.

If I wrote GO, I carried the fate of an army in my hands. If I wrote STAY, Cal and Petra would die. Probably all six of us would die here in this House, like the sergeant. Buried in our blood, our deaths changing nothing. All our work, everything we'd done over the past forty days, would cease to matter.

I closed my eyes. In my head I could imagine a thousand Mercs lined up in regular ranks and rows, like I had seen described in the books I sneaked from the doctor's shelf. They had weapons in their hands—rifles, shotguns, swords, axes—and they were ready to fight. And die, if they had to. Unlike me, they had somehow looked straight into the face of their own demise and had found it bearable. I could never be like them.

The difference between my imaginary army and the Mercs standing next to me was that in the best of those books, the soldiers had chosen to be there. Chosen to join, chosen to fight, because of something they believed important, something they cared about.

We had never chosen. We cared about nothing. Stood for nothing, meant nothing, were expended like nothing.

But we were meant to be free. We all possessed that divine spark of past perfection that had made the sergeant save me before he died. That had made him misguidedly sacrifice his morality and our lives to keep the game running, to stop the faraway war. We had that kind of love and sacrifice and desire in us too. We had the right to make our own choices. And if that meant that we died fighting, so be it. But that would be our choice and ours alone. It had to be, or else it meant nothing. It was not a sacrifice, not courageous. It was just more meaningless death.

I might be wrong, or stupid. Or selfish. But right then, I had to choose.

I scrawled down the word "GO" and handed the pencil to Roscoe.

Slowly it made the rounds, until all six of us had voted. Petra passed around her pouch, and we all slipped in our papers, folded or wadded tightly. I was certain we would agree. We had to. One disagreement, and our little group of six could be irreparably broken apart. Those of us who left would know that we had killed whoever stayed, and whoever stayed would know that we had abandoned them.

Cal withdrew the first vote and smoothed it out on his palm. "Go," he read.

I held my breath.

Then the second. "Go."

And the third. "Go."

Then the fourth. "Stay."

My stomach dropped.

Fifth. "Go."

Sixth. "Go."

He looked up expressionlessly and returned Petra's satchel. "So we're going. If whoever voted no wants to stay behind, they're welcome to it."

No one moved.

"Alright, then." He pocketed the notebook and pencil. "Let's get started."

# 27

**ROSCOE WAS THE FIRST TO MOVE. SHE** positioned herself in the center of the circle and started directing. "We can split up into three groups. Andy and Cal, you figure out how to destroy the House. No objections"—this was addressed to Andy, who had tentatively lifted his hand—"and you're a scientist, so you should know something about explosions if it comes to that. Kazumi, you help me figure out how to convince the villagers to get on the boat. And Halley, you take Petra to the doctor."

I was more than happy to get started on a concrete task. Anything to take my mind off the decision we had just made.

I glanced at Petra, still leaning against the wall. Except for her brief participation in our discussion, she had hardly spoken. I had a feeling she would have liked to say more if she could have found the energy. She had been lagging behind as we'd walked, frostily refusing Cal's attempts to steady her and assuring Roscoe that she was, to use her own descriptive word, "fine."

The years I'd spent believing I was the doctor's daughter—or at least the programmed memories of those years, if what Kazumi said was true—hadn't gone to waste. I knew a dying patient when I saw one.

"Are you ready?" I asked her.

She started as though she'd been asleep, slowly got to her feet, and leaned on my proffered shoulder.

We didn't talk much on the way down the hill, except my pointing out a loose stone or a patch of slippery gravel to save her from a quick trip to the bottom. Petra was exhausted, and I was out of breath. She was putting more weight on my shoulder with each laborious step, and I was afraid I'd be carrying her by the time we got to the village.

Fortunately for my aching spine, she straightened up the moment we came within sight of the first house. Her pride wouldn't let her stumble into the village of people she hated. I was ready to catch her if she collapsed, but despite some wobbling, she remained upright.

After we'd been walking for a minute or so, she gathered enough breath to speak.

"Cal and I have been Mercs for three years in my memory."

So that was what she'd been thinking about. Not her injuries. Not our precarious moral situation. Just him.

"We've known each other for two and a half years," she continued.

Which was impossible if Kazumi had been telling the truth.

"Do I really know him?" she asked peevishly. "Cal the spy could have been his true personality, since apparently it only took forty days for him to switch sides twice. What if he was only trying to sidle up to me so that he looked like an ordinary Merc? What if he was programmed to treat me the way he did? What if this is all something one of the technicians at Warsafe invented?"

"Surely Kazumi would have told you if that were the case." I didn't think he would, though, and my explanation didn't seem to satisfy Petra.

"What if I asked Cal about it?" she said hesitantly.

"Right now, you should focus on getting well."

"And if I don't recover? What if I leave him up there now and we never see each–?"

"Stop it, Petra. The doctor says that half of getting well is believing you will." I began to hurry her along. I didn't care that I was going too fast for her. I just wanted to get there. He would know what to do. He always did.

When I reached the threshold and opened the door to my house, I expected to see the doctor nestled in his armchair like he was every afternoon and to hear Mother bustling in the kitchen fixing a homemade dinner. But I had barely gotten out the preliminary "hello" before I was enveloped in an overwhelming embrace.

"Thanks be, you're home!" Mother breathed, squeezing my ribs until I thought I was going to explode. "Where have you been? How did you avoid the curfew? Why didn't you tell us you'd be gone?" She stepped back, putting her hands on my shoulders to look at me. Tears welled in her eyes. "Oh, Halley, how could you do this to us?"

I had been so busy thinking about how to stay gone forever that I hadn't thought about how long I'd been gone. My best guess was two days and a night. And, like everyone else in the village, I had never been out at night before. The doctor and Mother couldn't have known how I had magically avoided death by curfew, and they had probably been scouring the woods for my body.

"I'm so sorry, Mother." I fell back into her hug, mortified at the suffering I'd caused. She stroked my head as I clung to her, and I fought back tears. Maybe she'd been right when she'd told me to stay away from Petra, and I should never have gotten involved. What had I contributed besides providing an extra set of eyes to witness all the destruction? But it was too late now. "I'll explain everything later, Mother, I promise. And I promise I did the right thing. Right now, I need to see the doctor."

She nodded and let me go, teary-eyed, one hand still stroking my hair. But as she spotted Petra for the first time, her expression hardened.

"You can't come back here," she said, voice bitter. "You have no idea what we've had to go through because of you."

"Mother!" I tried to move her back inside, away from Petra. Or whatever it was she saw when she looked Petra's way. "Please. She needs to see the doctor. Where is he?"

"He's not here," she began, but she had always been a bad liar, the kind who told tales with eyes fixed firmly on the floor. I craned my neck, and I spotted the doctor's head peeking around the corner.

"There you are!" I exclaimed. "Petra needs your help."

He hesitated. The good old doctor hesitated. The doctor who had never turned away a patient, who had risked his life to save others, who was awakened at all hours of the night to take care of some ill villager, hesitated, hiding behind the wall like a frightened child.

I looked back and forth between him and Mother, waiting for one of them to give in and say it was all right. They would. They always did. Things had never worked the other way around.

They avoided my eyes.

"I'll go," came Petra's voice from behind me. She had wrapped her jacket around her tightly, chilly in the evening breeze. "They're right, Halley, I'm putting you in danger."

"Wait." The doctor emerged and inched toward the door. "Your lips are blue."

Petra tucked her chin into her collar.

"Your face is blue." His voice was strained. "I can't let you leave like that."

I turned to her, but she was already several paces away.

"Petra!" I called. "Come back here!"

She ignored me.

Ashamed of my family, ashamed of myself and the empty promises I had made, I vented my frustration on Mother. "Look what you've done!" I rounded on her for the first time in my life without picturing the bristly end of her broom. "She saved my life. She saved two other people's lives. She saved all our lives. She's done everything for us. And now you–"

A distant sound, fluttering fabric and a *thump*, caused me to whip around. Petra had collapsed.

Both the doctor and Mother shoved past me, rushing into the street to catch her.

A tide of unbearable nausea washed over me. I galloped to

the bathroom and opened the lid of the toilet through an ever-darkening circle around the edges of my vision.

This time I didn't get the doctor's Instant Cure for an Attack of Nerves. Cold tile pressed against my head revived me a little, but I could barely crawl across the floor to reach the sink. I managed to splash my face with water and slurp straight from the faucet. After a few minutes of listening to my heart pound in my ears and mentally drafting my last will and testament, I found myself able to stand up and hobble toward the living room.

The sofa and chairs were haphazardly shoved into a corner, and a surgical cot had been placed under the lamp in the center of the room. Petra was sedated, an intravenous tube connected to her hand, feeding her some murky yellow mixture out of a bag. The doctor was waving a plastic-looking wand over her chest, and a grayish image of her insides appeared on a screen that Mother held up beside him.

"She's a blue baby," he announced gravely. "I'm glad you brought her here when you did. A few more hours, and—well."

He had to be joking. I was familiar with the oddities of doctor-speak, but this was a whole new level of crazy.

There was a glossary of medical terms on his bookshelf. I skirted the piled-up furniture, found the book, and scanned the "B" section. Sure enough: *Blue Baby Syndrome*. A genetic condition that stole oxygen from the blood, filtering it weakly around a heart that was blocked, then pierced straight through the muscular walls.

Petra had been walking around with a hole in her heart. No wonder she was never in a good mood.

Cal and Andy were trying to engineer an explosion. Just everyday problems, Andy grumbled to himself, although with surprisingly everyday solutions.

"We have every chemical you could possibly want," Cal offered, pointing to the kitchen. "There's baking soda, detergent, ingredients for the auto-food-maker-thing, fizzy drinks . . ."

Andy went into the kitchen without deigning to reply and threw open the cabinets one by one. Six plates. Eleven bowls. One fork. A bottle of solidified milk. One toothpick all alone in a three-foot-square cabinet. A small box of flour. And, finally, a broken cracker.

At a loss, he sat cross-legged in the middle of the floor and pressed his fingers to his temples. "Ammonium nitrate . . . gunpowder . . ." he mumbled. "EDDN . . . flares? No, those don't explode . . . fireworks . . . dynamite . . ." He wasn't going to find any of that. Not on an island where, so far as he could tell, every precaution had been taken against escape. "Most houses don't have flares. But some houses still catch fire." Just like his high school days, spent poring over Aristotelean logic because his counselor said the class would give him a better chance at getting into the science program in college.

Maybe, Andy realized with a start, Aristotle had one good idea. Maybe all that logic had been good for something after all.

He got onto his hands and knees and crawled toward the automatic cooker, sniffing the floor like a dog, tracing the smell to a knob on the cooker's base. He rotated it with a quick flick of his wrist. The room flooded with a sour smell, and he whooped.

"I've got it!" he cried. "We'll create a gas explosion!"

Cal poked his head around the corner and raised an eyebrow, pinching his nose. "Shouds like fun."

Andy closed the valve. "We've got to get all the Mercs out. Everyone has to be at least a hundred yards away from the House, and we have to be ready to go farther, in case the trees catch fire."

"Got it."

"Second, we'll need to turn on the air conditioner. You do have climate control here, don't you? Those vents you crawled through on the way upstairs will be perfect. I'll turn on this valve and leave the fan running, which will cause the gas to dissipate. That should take . . ." His voice died away, and he fished a wrinkled napkin and pencil stub out of his pocket. "Assuming we're at sea level . . . and the temperature might be about fifty-five degrees Fahrenheit . . . what's the concentration of gas? . . . ah. It should take about two hours."

"I don't know what an air conditioner is, but we have fans, if that's what you're asking."

"Then I'll pull some wire from this cooker thing and set up a fuse. One millijoule of energy will be more than enough for a spark." Andy rubbed his hands. "We'll have what's called a toothpick explosion. All that'll be left is toothpicks."

Cal's expression brightened. "I'll get Kazumi to wake up the Mercs. You set up everything else."

"Is there anything you want to take with you?" Andy asked. "Papers, pictures, books, dishes? Food? You won't be able to get anything back."

"Nothing. Go on, we don't have much time."

Andy opened his mouth to explain the risks—there were a few minor considerations that he thought might be worth a few seconds' extra discussion. But before he could say anything, Cal had darted back up the stairs, disappearing in an echo of clattering boots. So much for teamwork. Lucky Cal didn't have to stick his face in a leaky gas line.

There was no danger of an immediate explosion, so Andy loosened the valve and let the gas flow into the room, standing near the door until the smell was so strong that he had to breathe through his mouth. He hadn't expected the island variety of natural gas to have such a high concentration of sulfur. It was probably for safety. Maybe the islanders had bad noses.

It was then that Kazumi disabled the Mercs' chips. It was an anticlimactic and minor victory. Over the next twenty minutes, with bellowing yawns, groans, and complaints about the hardness of the floor, they stumbled into the kitchen. The room filled, much to Andy's annoyance, until all twenty-seven were there without a brain cell to split between them or a glimmer of an idea about what they were doing. Some of them sat on the counter. Some lay on the floor. Some cursed. Some mumbled nonsense. One of them—an eighteen- or nineteen-year-old boy—opened a cabinet, discovered it was empty, then sat down on the floor and cried.

Cal dusted off his hands, pleased at the result of his work, while Andy hovered shyly in the corner and tried not to make eye contact.

"Everybody," Cal announced, hoisting himself onto the dinner table, "we're leaving."

He received only groggy stares in response.

"The game is officially over. We are blowing up the House. The end."

Addled by sleep and an utter lack of backstory, they would have jumped off a bridge one by one if Cal had told them to. As it was, none of them had much of a reaction beyond a few faint and half-hearted okays and sures and miraculously creative expletives.

"Tell them to go outside and stand away from the House," Andy said in a low whisper from his corner.

"Hey! Everybody! Get up and go outside away from the House so we can blow it up." Cal herded his sheep toward the door. "Twenty-six, twenty-seven . . . there should be twenty-eight, not counting Petra and me." He paused. "Ah. Sam."

"You forgot one?"

"What am I going to do, politely ask her to come with me?"

"You can't just leave her."

"I could."

Andy paused to consider that. There wasn't such a thing as a right response with Cal. The only thing that had ever remained consistent about him was his infinite variety.

"Whatever you think." Andy went back to fiddling with the gas line, but his fingers slipped, and a belch of rotten-egg smell filled the room.

Cal grinned. "You're the judgmental type, aren't you?" He clapped Andy's shoulder. "If Sam kills me, tell Petra that at least I tried. Maybe then she won't look like she bit a lemon every time she talks about me."

"Just don't flip any switches, or you might ignite the gas!" Andy shouted at Cal's receding back.

Once Andy had confirmed that the other Mercs had evacuated the House, he mounted the steps leading to the porch and cleared his throat. This attracted no attention. He did it again louder, and still nobody noticed. At last, resigning his dignity, he shouted: "Everybody!" in a voice about forty decibels softer than Cal's.

One or two bleary faces glanced his way.

"Don't go near the House," he cautioned. "Stay at least a hundred yards away. And be ready to run in case the foliage catches fire."

The Mercs who weren't dozing off nodded in lazy agreement. A few of them even started down the road toward the village. Satisfied that he had done his duty as a chaperone, Andy returned to engineering.

He had to think of a way to make a slow-burning fuse to ignite the gas in the house, and his only idea required parts he didn't have: yarn and alcohol. Specifically rubbing alcohol, but any strong liquor was a viable option. He'd scoured the House and found it blue-collar and free of knitters. He did, however, find a broken shoelace. That was too short for comfort—much too short. He scanned the Mercs' clothes. If he asked all the girls to remove the strings from their French peasant-style collars, he might be able to get about ten feet of fuse. But that was still a long way short of a hundred yards.

What about rope? Strips of sheets could be an option, too, but they wouldn't burn the same way an ordinary string would. If only he'd paid more attention in chemistry class.

By the time he'd made up his mind, the Mercs had drifted down the road until the last of them was almost out of sight around an outcropping of trees. For lack of any better ideas, Andy trotted after them to ask about borrowing the girls' collars.

He felt the heat first. It hit him in the back as solidly as a bat, sending him soaring in a graceful arc down the road. He made a scratchy landing in a bush of thistles, blinking and rubbing the back of his head, which had suddenly grown hot to the touch. Then he heard the explosion, and he was so disoriented that he thought at first it was somehow the sound of his own fall that echoed until it felt like his eardrums were about to explode. A piece of fire rained down from the sky, crashing into the bushes beside him and setting them ablaze.

Andy scrambled to his feet, his bare arms needled with spiny leaves, and fled, pursued by flames from heaven that rained down on the road beside him—but, somehow, never quite touched his clothes. He ran and ran and ran, his lungs filling with smoke, until his muscles cramped and knotted and his chest felt like it had been doused with burning acid.

Only then did he look back.

The House was in flames. The House *was* flames, its solid lines vanishing in the all-consuming inferno. The very top of the eighth floor was still visible as a blackened skeleton, and as Andy watched, it collapsed in on itself with a sickening *crack*. A stream of sparks danced into the sky.

"Cal," Andy whispered.

We heard it from the village. Felt it too. It rumbled the floor and discolored the sky and shattered one of the windowpanes in the kitchen.

A few minutes later, after a series of miniature explosions and distant cracks and creaks and whines, the lights went out with a snap. With the lights went the heart-rate monitor, the surgical saw, and worst of all, the IV pump that was delivering Petra's anesthesia. Mother saw it coming, and so did the doctor. But before either of them could reach the manual pump, Petra woke to find the doctor's saw balanced precariously over her chest.

She handled it admirably. Better than I would have, anyway. Licking her lips, she fixed her eyes on the doctor's gloved hands and edged her body off the table until she dropped to the floor. Wincing, she crawled backward until she hit the sofa.

"So it's done," she said, letting her head rest on the cushions. "It" might have been the surgery or the explosion or the damage to her nervous system. Or all three. She didn't explain, and none of us asked.

I ran to the window and tried to see up the hill, but the view was obscured by a thick cloud of black smoke rolling down the road. Something had certainly been done. Well done, at that.

Char-broiled, in fact. I could only hope it wasn't Cal and Andy and the Mercs.

The doctor placed his saw on the table and coughed.

"What did you do?" he asked me, with dangerous politeness.

I looked at Petra, and she looked at me, and we looked at each other.

"He's your father," Petra said.

"You agreed to come here, so you've got to help me out," I answered idiotically.

"I only came because you dragged me," she retorted. "I could have just died up there instead of down here."

Mother was getting a deadly look in her eye, so I gave up the argument and rushed ahead. "Some people from Warsafe—that's who we've been calling the Alliance, or at least they're working with the Alliance, it's a long story—showed up here on the island, and one of them brought a boat to get everybody off. So Cal—he's a Merc, and he's Petra's, uh, it's a long story—blew up the House to stop the game from being played, and everybody's going to leave the island, and we're going to sue Warsafe."

Disturbing silence followed.

"We've been on the island our whole lives," the doctor said quietly. "At least, most of us have. And you want us to leave now?"

"You've only really been here for forty days." I faltered. He probably thought he was going to have to brush up on his psychiatric book for this level of delusion. And what if the information I had gotten from Kazumi was wrong? I'd never be forgiven, even if we were right about the rest of it. "Look, there's no way for me to explain. The bottom line is that we have to get off the island today, because if we don't, Kazumi—that's one of the people from Warsafe, the head of the Alliance—says they'll kill us."

Mother opened the curtains that covered the fireplace area window. Outside was a thick haze of black smoke the streetlights couldn't penetrate, a blanket so dense that it obscured even the cottage across the street.

"What have you done?" she whispered, then, louder, "What have you done?!"

The doctor's face contorted. "I told you to gather information! I told you to be careful!" He slammed a hand into the folding table. "I didn't tell you to blow up the House! Fraternizing with Alliance spies. What were you thinking?"

I had never, not once ever, seen the doctor angry. "I was just trying to—"

"We had all the time in the world! We weren't always happy here, Halley, and I know you didn't like your job, but you don't have the right to put us all in danger just because of your selfishness." Tears sprang to my eyes, but I held them back. The conversation would be over the moment I let them fall. "Maria's right. How could you do something like this without consulting someone first? Someone who could talk you out of it?"

"I'll tell you how," interrupted Petra. The blinking light of her prosthetic had sped up until it looked almost steady. "It's because the status quo is good enough for you. If Halley had told you what she was doing or asked your permission, you would have told her it was impossible or too dangerous or stupid, and nothing would have changed. Cal and I would be dead, and the world would keep on turning. It's because of Halley's incredible naïveté that we might get to escape this prison."

"Forty years this game has run, and you're telling me we haven't lost a life?" The doctor's voice shook. "I've amputated limbs. I've held the hands of dying patients who were younger than Halley. I've operated without anesthesia on people who don't even have enough life left to scream."

"No, you haven't." Petra pulled herself to her feet. Weak though she was, somehow she still looked like more than a match for the old doctor. "But it doesn't matter. Let's say you have been here as long as you think you remember. Don't you know by now that life here isn't all that great? Maybe it's bearable, but that's all. I want more. The unnecessary things. I want to paint. I want to eat homemade food. I want to see what sunflowers look like. I want to sleep in. I want to love someone. I want a child. I want to find my real parents. I want a room that's all my own. I want . . . I want . . ."

"Life," I finished, as her voice trailed off. I managed to meet Mother's eyes. "To live."

"Freely."

"Without the Alliance's threats."

"You have the same kinds of dreams Halley and I do. If you can admit you do and believe us, then everything will change."

My mother's lip trembled. Because if we were wrong, at least we were passionately and sincerely wrong. They had once been the same as we were, and all they had to do was look at Petra's gaunt, desperate face to see that she believed what she was telling them.

"Good intentions don't justify what we've done," Petra added softly. "But if it's worth anything as an apology, we were doing it for you as much as for ourselves."

The doctor rubbed his eyes. "I want hot buttered toast," he said, with a manufactured cough to cover up what I suspected was a sniffle. "And coffee that doesn't come from a machine."

He looked at Mother, but she huffed and said nothing.

"I want a kitten," I volunteered.

For the first time since we'd come, the doctor smiled at me. "Even with the surveillance, we could have figured out a way to talk about this."

I nodded, unable to speak for a moment, and the doctor put his arm around me. "I'll do better next time."

"No, you won't," Mother snapped. "There'd better not be a next time."

Turning back to Petra, the doctor continued, "Thanks to the imaging machine, I know what's wrong with you. But without electricity, I can't perform surgery. Even if I could, you wouldn't be walking on your own for days, maybe weeks. And that sounds like it's not a possibility right now."

"Then we'll just have to leave it."

"If you don't get the surgery soon, you'll die."

"Alright."

I wanted her to be angry about it, to fight it, to keep listing her wants and the things she dreamed of doing. But her transient thoughts of sunflowers and children and painting were already buried so far down now that I was afraid no one would ever see them again.

"We need to find Roscoe and Kazumi." Petra continued matter-of-factly. "They're the people from Warsafe. They're trying to figure out how to convince everyone to leave the island on Kazumi's boat."

"Now?"

"Now."

"Alright." He turned to Mother. "It sounds like we have no choice. Pack up anything we can't do without. Meet us in the village square."

She didn't protest, didn't try to stop him. She just bustled off to the kitchen, leaving me, Petra, and the doctor to figure out what came next.

*He's almost died before.*
*He was fine last time.*
*Everyone thought he was dead when he wasn't.*
*It'll happen again.*
*He'll be fine.*

Working frantically backward through the possibilities—a fine example of inductive reasoning, but much too late—all Andy could figure was that there had been more gas in the air than he'd predicted. Hence, he realized with dismay, the strong smell of sulfur. He had already worked out that it would only take about a millijoule of energy to ignite a gas fire when the concentration became high enough. And an average light bulb used sixty joules per second. There had never been much room for error.

"Are you writing equations in the dirt with your finger?"

Andy turned and found himself face-to-face with Cal—what remained of him. The right side of his face was a mess of fried flesh and tattered skin, and his clothes were speckled with burn holes. Right then, to Andy, even Roscoe's lovely face framed with silky pink hair had never looked so good.

He gave a shout and threw his arms around Cal. "You're not dead!"

"Crickets, that hurts. That *hurts*. Get off me." Injured Cal's temper had a shorter fuse than the shoelace. "Of course I'm not dead. Take the Mercs to the village and meet up with Roscoe and Kazumi. Find out what happened to Petra and tell me when I catch up to you."

Andy did as he was ordered, and Cal followed. But Andy was no great athlete and he didn't get much of a head start, so by the time he got to the bottom of the hill, Cal was right behind him.

That was how the doctor, Petra, and I, venturing into the smog that hung over the street, almost ran smack into them. I gasped when I saw Cal, and the doctor muttered to himself, shaking his head.

"You keep this up, and you'll bankrupt me," he sighed. "I've never run through so many bandages."

"Don't worry about me," Cal said. Too nonchalantly, I thought. "It's not bleeding, so it can't be that bad."

"It's not bleeding because your face got cauterized," the doctor said wryly.

Petra's face turned the color of wilted grass, which seemed to delight Cal.

"You look pretty when you're scared," he teased, twisting a lock of her black hair around his singed fingers. "You should try it more often."

She pulled her hair free.

"You know, Petra," he began, frowning, "just because I had to come up with something while I was trying to keep you safe—"

"You called me a murderer." She stared up at him, eyes hard and expressionless. "Why was that on your mind, Cal? Don't answer. We don't have time."

"Because it was the most believable," he insisted. "It had to sound like I meant it. And if I really wanted to hurt you, that's what I'd say. Besides, I knew it wasn't true. You told me you knew the truth all along."

"Guessed. Not knew."

She looked him over, absorbing his dusty hands and torn collar and half-burnt shoes. Almost unwillingly, her hand brushed his wounded cheek, and she ran her fingers thoughtfully over the patches of skin that were still intact. He flinched when she reached the purple line of his jaw, and she withdrew her hand.

"We barely know each other. It's been a month." She held up her hand to stop his interruption. "Not years, like we thought. I won't be angry with you until I've had time to know if this is what I should expect of you." She turned her back on us and headed for the square.

The doctor was looking at me with one eyebrow raised like he thought I understood what was going on, but I simply shrugged. No matter what I did or didn't know, we had no choice but to bite our tongues and hope the argument died down.

Roscoe and Kazumi had been profiting off the chaos caused by the House's explosion, rounding up the alarmed villagers and straggling Mercs with vague threats of aftershocks and spreading fire. Here were all familiar faces: the elderly lady who grew our vegetables, the wizened old fellow who updated the rankings board, the middle-aged man who rang the bell in the clock tower. The crowd was jammed so tight that we could barely squeeze our way through. How in the world, I wondered as an elbow nicked my chin, were we going to make sure all two hundred of the island's inhabitants boarded Kazumi's ferry? Mercs and villagers alike were mixed into an indistinguishable muddle, and I couldn't tell one from the other. But if we left even one person behind—

Far to my left, a distant speck, I saw Cal trying to shield Petra from the trampling crowd. They were drifting farther away, and I'd never be able to catch them without getting puréed. I couldn't see the doctor or Mother or Andy. I couldn't even tell which direction was the center of the square. I was too short to see over the nearest heads.

Something clanged, and the crowd abruptly went quiet.

"Attention!" cried a voice from somewhere to my left. Kazumi. Hovering on the toes of my boots, I could just barely make him out. He was balanced on the edge of the ranking billboard, whacking a copper kettle with a ladle.

"This is an emergency evacuation," he shouted, handing the

kettle to someone below. "The fire at the House is expected to spread. The island will burn. Everyone needs to get on the boat at the beach and leave. For good."

There was a doubtful silence, and then the crowd began to rustle.

"I've never seen him before."

"We've never left the island."

"Do you think he started the fire?"

"Is this an attack?"

It was exactly what I would have said if I'd been in their shoes. Kazumi tried to explain over the disapproving rumble, but no one was listening. They were too busy trying to figure out how and why they were being bamboozled. And of course Kazumi couldn't convince them. He wasn't an islander. He was a stranger, and we had never seen strangers before, with the exception of new Mercs who came, in our memories, to replace those who had been killed in the House. Liars, cheats, and thieves by popular representation. Never trustworthy.

Someone pushed past me. Through the endless sea of brown boots and stockings, I recognized the tan hem of the doctor's trench coat. The lover of peace and quiet and books was going to try out some public speaking—something I knew must be abhorrent to the depths of his soul.

Did he really believe us now? After we'd burst in his door without a shred of evidence, were our words alone enough?

"Listen!" he called out, grabbing Kazumi's hand and raising it toward the crowd. Everyone seemed to recognize his voice, because the jostling stopped and I was finally able to squeeze in a breath. "He's here to save us from the fire. The island is about to be destroyed. You won't survive if you stay. Get on the ferry and follow his instructions."

My heart warmed. Of course our word was enough. My word was enough. I was, after all, his only daughter.

"Pack only what you can't live without," Kazumi told them. As though anyone had much else.

"What's out there?" someone shouted. "Where are we going?"

"But is there anywhere to go besides here?" another wavery voice cried.

The doctor glanced irresolutely at Kazumi.

"The Alliance is out there," he said at last. "The people who have kept this island running since the very beginning." *The people who started the killing game.* "The people who sustained the village commerce." *The people who forced us to work jobs we hated.* "Now that the House is burning, they've sent us a way to escape. You're right to doubt they have our best interests in mind, but they don't want us dead, or they wouldn't have kept us going all this time. This isn't a trick, and it isn't a game. The island will burn, and you'll burn with it if you don't come with us."

Slowly, the tide reversed. Instead of pushing toward Kazumi, little groups of people broke off from the crowd and ran for their houses. The square emptied, only to refill a few minutes later with people of all ages, shapes, sizes, and colors and their corresponding bundles. No one protested. No one was angry. Some, mostly the very old, were muttering nervously and casting glances at the smoke wafting down from up the hill. The young ones—those in their twenties and thirties, and the Mercs—looked cautiously excited.

After all, there were only two hundred of us. At one point or another, we had all trusted the doctor with our lives. He had never, in the whole forty days he'd been on the island, let us down.

I perched on the neighbor's garden fence and watched the stream of people descend to the beach. Maybe the sand was safe, but it was hard to overcome the prejudice I'd held all my life, and I had no intention of going near it until the last possible moment. Kazumi and Roscoe and the doctor were already down there, just visible through the thickening smoke, taking a head count and offering platitudes to everyone who could hear. I saw Mother get onto the ferry, pausing to say something to the doctor that made him laugh and pat her on the head—a gesture she shook off, marching up the ramp with her chin disdainfully high. She had every right to cry. I'd cried, and I had nothing to leave behind. But she was so brave and graceful and beautiful as her world dropped out from under her.

Maybe she'd been right, and I'd made a mistake. Maybe I'd been too impulsive. Maybe freedom wasn't going to be worth it. Perhaps we'd made the wrong decision back there during the ballot. Maybe whoever had voted to "stay" was right.

I caught a glimpse of Cal and Petra, standing solemnly next to each other and looking up at the billboard. When the power had gone out, its screen went black. No one was number thirty now. No one was first. No one was anything between. They all shared the same fate.

I was close enough to overhear them.

"Where's Sam?" Petra asked.

"I left her in the House."

Petra grimaced and turned away, but Cal grabbed her wrist. The wounds on his face made it difficult to read his expression, but I thought he looked exhausted.

"Do you really think I'd do something like that?"

"I don't know." Petra stopped with her back to Cal. "Did you?"

"She wasn't in the closet where we left her. I checked the eighth floor. The explosion happened before I could look anywhere else. I even tried to go back inside, which is how I got like this."

"You didn't intend to leave her?"

He let go of Petra's wrist and stepped toward the empty board, crossing his arms and resting his head against the cool glass. "I don't know who programmed our memories, Petra, or why. But some of it was real—it couldn't have been made up. When we sat on the lawn after you played your first match and you were crying, do you remember what I brought you?"

"Tea."

He nodded. "The day I was injured, when my ranking dropped, do you remember what I said?"

Petra's face reddened. "No."

Amusement flitted across his face. "Whether our memories are real or not, we share them. And now that I know everything, even though you say we don't know each other, I want to make more memories like those. The memories you have—I have them too. The way you remember me is the way I remember myself. The person you think I am is also the person *I* think I am."

For a long time, she said nothing. Then, "You look like a hero," she said with a tight smile. "I was wrong to assume the worst. The last few hours should have been enough to prove that. I'm sorry."

"Are you saying . . . ?"

"I'm beginning to see the good in what you did."

For one uncomfortable second, I thought he was going to kiss her right then and there, in full view of everyone on the ship. But it seemed he was unwilling to push his luck that far, and he looked away.

"I don't deserve that."

"You forgave me. You loved me even when you thought I believed I was a killer." She paused. "I see a spark of divine forgiveness in you, Cal. You're the kind of person I want to be. A human who makes mistakes but looks remarkably like his Maker. I've never met anyone like that. So I can't let you go."

His mouth had fallen open. "You were never religious. Since when have you seen the divine?"

"Since we figured out we had a chance to get off this island alive, and together. Since things became both dangerous and promising." Her voice dropped. "Since you became the kind of man you couldn't be unless you had a hope I didn't."

He held out his hand. The one with the Mercenary tattoo, which had been burned into a blurry series of black lines and curves that no longer resembled the original design. "Then let's leave together. We'll find what you're looking for."

This time, she took it willingly. Cal flinched when she touched his charred skin, but his hand tightened over hers.

"No more killing," she said.

"No more."

There was a tap on my shoulder, and the doctor helped me down from the fence. "Kazumi's ready to leave." He waved to Petra and Cal, who had spotted us. "You owe me an explanation," he whispered, "and I hope you're right about all this. Because if not . . ."

"I am," I told him. If I wasn't, it was too late. I had made my decision the moment I tucked my slip of paper into Petra's satchel and voted for our escape. I wasn't going to waver now.

The four of us stepped onto the ramp to the ferry, wobbling on the unfamiliar, swaying surface. From his perch in the wheelhouse, Kazumi motioned for us to hurry. Once we were all safely aboard, Cal and the doctor closed the gate and untied the ropes holding us to the dock.

We had no idea where we were going, or what was waiting for us when we got there. All we knew was that for once, for the first time in our lives, we had control over the decisions of our own lives.

We were finally free.

# 28

## KAZUMI

"IT'S A PLEASURE TO OFFICIALLY meet you." Kazumi held out his hand. "I'm the one who pushed you out the window."

Rilo had started to shake his hand, but at the second half of Kazumi's introduction, his arm froze midair.

"No, you weren't drunk. Well, you were, but not that to that degree." Kazumi seated himself in the visitor's chair by Rilo's bed. "I'm responsible for everything that happened, and I want you to listen carefully to what you have to do now."

Rilo glanced at the window.

"The moment I leave this room, you're going to press the call button. A nurse will come, and you're going to tell her that I, Kazumi Sato, pushed you out of a window following a dispute about your salary at Warsafe Games. You're going to say that you recovered your memories from that night. But you will never tell anyone that I came here to visit you, or that we've spoken since the accident. Or I'll defenestrate you again, and this time I'll do a better job."

"Where's Andy?" sputtered Rilo, ripping off his oxygen mask. His throat gurgled as he gasped for air. "Did you—?"

"He'll go home, no questions asked. Your hospital bills are paid too." Kazumi dusted off the back of his suit coat. "For what it's worth, I'm sorry. What have the doctors said?"

Rilo sucked some air from his oxygen mask, staring incredulously at Kazumi over the nosepiece. "That I'll be alright in a week or two."

"Glad to hear it. This is the last time you'll be seeing me, unless we meet in court. I'm hopeful that won't happen." He bowed toward Rilo. "I've arranged for you to get some books from the college library. I thought you might want to get some work done while you're recovering."

He was about to leave, but Rilo started up from his bed, dragging his IV behind him and tripping on the cables of his heart monitor.

"What's in this for you?" he panted, balancing himself against the IV pole. "Who am I covering with this lie?"

"Andy, if all goes well. Goodbye, Mr. Walsh."

Two days later, Kazumi was behind bars.

Becoming a criminal shook him less than he expected. It was undoubtedly a relief to know that Warsafe Games would have a hard time killing him, even if he had to exchange his freedom for safety behind bars. He had lived in fear for his life ever since the thought of treachery first crossed his mind, and now he only had to worry about the fact that his pillow wasn't as soft as he liked. The food left something to be desired, too, but Kazumi had never been a picky eater.

He had been gazing at the wall for nearly an hour, trying to imagine what he was going to say in court, when the peephole on his cell door opened and a clean-shaven face peered in.

"You have a visitor," the officer told him, reading off a clipboard. "Calhoun. No last name on the paper—I'll get him to fill that out later. Would you like to speak with him?"

*What could he possibly—?* Kazumi stopped himself. His fate was anybody's guess, and there was no sense in worry.

"I'd like to see him." The plastic cover on his mattress crackled as he stood up. "Lead the way."

He was taken out of his cell and placed in a viciously clean visiting room. Wall to wall, floor to ceiling, every surface was as smooth and glassy as ice. There was nothing he could possibly use to escape, and the only way he could see his visitor was through a thin, reflective pane of plexiglass embedded into the wall. Refraction made Cal's face look thinner and more pinched than Kazumi remembered. But it also softened the harsh lines of his scars, which were still stretched and pink from his burns.

"I've decided we're not so different after all."

That wasn't the opener Kazumi had expected. "How so?"

"We both meant well. You were our tormentor. I almost got Petra killed. You tortured me—yes, I knew it was you behind that radio, even if it's the sergeant's face in the nightmares—and I kept a secret from Petra that made her wish she was dead. But we meant well. All along, we thought we were doing right. Our good intentions paved the road to hell."

Kazumi's eyes glazed, and he focused on a bubble in the glass that separated them.

"I never liked how you treated Petra. I never even liked how you treated yourself, and what you let us do to you," he admitted at last. "I'd hate to think that if I had been in your shoes, I would have said and done what you did."

"Then tell me I'm wrong. Can you say that honestly too?" There was a hint of mockery in Cal's voice.

"No. I would have been even worse. I was worse."

"Hate yourself, not me. It's best if we don't compare misery."

"You haven't been tempted to do that? Not even once?"

Cal twined his fingers behind his head and looked up at the ceiling. "The main difference between us is that there's someone who doesn't hate me. One person, and one divine. I try to imagine myself through their eyes."

"I have no one like that."

Cal's eyebrow quirked. "Roscoe is the woman Petra would have been if her first nineteen years of memories weren't from the island," he said. "Brave and smart and driven. Magnificent under pressure. But she's clever. She understands you, and she's given up. Petra is too naïve to send me away."

"Petra knows the truth, too, though she might not want to admit it. She knows we're not at all the same." Kazumi leaned forward, and his breath fogged the glass. "When you agreed to be our spy, you did it because you hoped you could get information from us.

I know because I watched, and I let you do it. Do you think you could have learned everything you did about the opponents being holograms without me noticing? Do you think you could have left that letter for Petra without me guessing what you wrote? You succeeded because I helped you. I helped you because I was too much of a coward to fight Warsafe any other way, and I didn't dare speak up even when I thought things were going wrong. You're the reason Petra is free. You're the reason Warsafe's secret is being brought to light, why SAFE is being forced to scrap the program."

"You couldn't possibly know that." Cal's eyes sparkled. "Maybe I really was on Warsafe's side, even if it was only for a little while."

"I know you. I don't believe it."

A burst of noise from the waiting room outside interrupted their conversation, and Kazumi was grateful for the opportunity to look away.

"My point," Cal resumed, when they could hear each other again, "is that you and I are too similar to hate each other. I admire what you're doing now, sacrificing your career for us, and I suppose careers are to you people what our lives were to us. If we're never going to see each other again, which I hope we don't, that's how I want to remember you. It sticks in my throat, but I'll even say thank you."

"Are you saying you'll forget the rest?"

"I'm saying that hating you is tiring at best and frustrating at worst, and I have a life to live." Cal winked. "People like me never change. We're selfish to the core."

Kazumi found himself smiling. "I appreciate it, Calhoun."

"Save your breath and stop calling me that." Cal pushed back his chair with an obnoxious scrape. "Thanks to you, I'll never sleep through another night in my life. Whenever I see Petra, I'll wonder if her heart or her memories will kill her faster. I'll wonder how she would have been different if she had never played the game. I'll remember how I tried to protect her and how I failed so miserably. I'll remember how you listened to me scream. I hate those memories. I hate those thoughts. So I refuse your thanks and your apologies, but I'll forgive you. Heaven knows you're earning it in your own twisted way." He tapped the button on the wall, signaling that he was ready to leave. "I was grateful when someone told me that I disgusted them. I only wish I would have heard it sooner."

"I deserve it. And I'm sorry."

"I'm sorry too. To everyone but you."

The door squeaked open.

"Follow me, Mr. . . . is Calhoun your only name? You must have a last name too." The policeman squinted at his clipboard, mystified. "You need to finish filling out this paperwork before you leave."

"One last thing." Cal glanced up from his forms, pen in hand. "Did you intend for me and Petra to end up together? Did you program that into our chips?"

"I wasn't . . . certain that would happen."

"Come, now. Isn't lying a mortal sin?"

"Not if it's well meant."

The pen froze midair. Cal's smile was unreadable.

"Understood."

# 29

## HALLEY

## WARSAFE GAMES EMPLOYEE PLEADS GUILTY TO ATTEMPTED MURDER.

It was a tight headline, terse and shocking and calculated to grab a reader's attention. Cal was the first to spot it as he walked past a newsstand. He bought a copy of the paper and shared a photograph of the story with the rest of us.

"A Warsafe Games employee has claimed responsibility for an attempted homicide last month. In the early hours of June 5th, Rilo Walsh was pushed from a second-story apartment window. Though he has since made a full recovery from his injuries, he testified to police investigators that someone broke into the apartment where he was staying and, failing to commit robbery, pushed him out the window and fled. The previous suspect, Andy Robinson, was cleared by the employee's admission of guilt.

"This employee claims that Warsafe Games financially incentivized him to commit the crime. He is currently in custody and will be tried on attempted murder charges. Warsafe Games has released a statement saying he was not protecting company secrets and they claim no responsibility for his actions. There is no information yet on whether they will be investigated."

The piece rambled on indefinitely, covering the front page of the paper, but I stopped reading after the first two paragraphs. At last, I understood what Kazumi had done. His confession would bring Warsafe under scrutiny, too, and his trial would become theirs. He couldn't save himself, but at least he could take them down with him.

I wished there had been another way. I wanted to see Kazumi again to ask him more questions. He knew the truth about everything, the why and the how and the who and the eternal *what was it all for*. But he was shut away, and we were left with what we could figure out on our own.

Before we left the ferry, Kazumi's last instructions to us were for the doctor, Mother, Petra, Cal, and me to agree that we would be the only ones to testify at Kazumi's trial. The other villagers and Mercenaries were to scatter, pretending to be immigrants who had lost their documents through various fabricated accidents. It would have been better for us five to disappear into the flurry of bureaucracy, too, but someone had to corroborate Kazumi's story. And technology like Petra's prosthetic arm, as Andy had once explained, didn't exist on the mainland. She was living proof that the story we wanted to tell was true, and she was to be a key witness, with the four of us to support her.

The state of mainland medical technology horrified the good old doctor. Borrowing Roscoe's computer, he looked up videos on "modern" surgery, which left him swimming in tears.

"If I'd attached Petra's arm with that thing," he told me when I happened to walk by, zooming in on some dreadful silver knife-looking object, "she would never have been able to use that arm, and then she would have been killed in the House, and we would never have made it off the island. Why doesn't the same technology exist here?"

I was the wrong person to ask. I was still trying to figure out how to put my shirt on without the automatic dresser's help.

"And this!" He displayed another gruesome photo of what might have once been an internal organ, except that it was decidedly external now. "The damage this instrument causes must be worse than the injury it's meant to cure. The world can't go on like this. People are suffering. They need the tools I had on the island."

"Invent them," Mother called from the kitchen. During the two weeks since we had left the island, we had crashed in Roscoe's apartment. It was a tight squeeze, but everything was so dependably cheerful and pink that no one really seemed to mind stepping on other people's feet. "Invent them and sell them and make us enough money to live on. You can help the world and us at the same time."

Roscoe and I shared a smile. It was an open secret that Mother was as industrious as the doctor was idealist.

"I could never put them together from scratch. I don't even know what half of them were made of." The doctor squinted at the slimy mound of flesh on the screen. "Roscoe, how do people manufacture things here? Back on the island, we were self-sufficient in every aspect but the technology. That, for all we knew, had been there forever."

"I have no idea," she admitted, "but if you can come up with the idea, I'll help you patent it, and we'll present it to some startup med-tech company somewhere."

The rest of us had no idea what this string of words meant. But later that day, the doctor went out and bought a sketchbook, a drafting pencil, and a book of equations and unit conversions. That was the beginning of his quest to give the medical world a properly modern overhaul.

He had his project. Mother had her cooking. Roscoe was up to something, because she was away from the apartment almost every day. During those first weeks, I tried to be good, to show them that after everything that had happened, I was okay. I helped Roscoe look for jobs. I helped Mother cook, and I helped the doctor organize his papers. I did everything that was required of me and nothing for myself, growing so apathetic that Mother had to remind me to wash my face.

It wasn't boredom. In fact, it was a relief to have nothing to do, to let my mind wander and my body rest. It might have been loneliness. I missed the close-knit community of our island. And yet, though the ache grew sharper every day, it barely occurred to me to find out where Petra or Cal had gone. I had lost touch with the other villagers, even the ones I had known well, and I never tried to contact them. I just kept on existing, and I was fine with that.

Mother was not. She told me I was looking too pale and that I should go out and play, which meant nothing to a penniless, friendless seventeen-year-old in an alien world. I spent more and more time wandering the streets, fabricating excuses to leave the cramped apartment behind and search for a sense of purpose among the thousands of signs and books and newspapers and advertisements cluttering the shops. I got to know the area, and I found a host of places where I could hide while Mother thought I was playing—whatever that was supposed to mean.

A few days into my explorations, as I rounded a corner in the shady part of town that lay between Roscoe's apartment and the grocery store, I ran smack into Cal. The impact made me drop a head of lettuce I had been carrying, and it rolled into a ditch where I was reluctant to follow.

"Didn't expect to see you here," he said. He looked a little less ruddy than I remembered, and suddenly I understood what Mother had meant by calling me pale. He was worse off than me, though—I could see the bones in his cheeks, and his skin was stretched over them, feverish red and splotchy where his burns had been left to heal without proper dressings.

"Where have you been?" His voice had grown hoarser since we had left the island. "Petra says she hasn't seen you recently."

"Yes." I looked at my shoes. "To be honest, Cal, I haven't seen me recently either. There's no combat game anymore, no mysteries to be solved. So, what do I do? I can't find my place. I can't figure out what to do with myself."

At the expression on his face, I realized I'd done it again—gone off and said too much. I hadn't even gotten past "hello" before unloading on him.

"Well, you're out a head of lettuce," he said slowly, "but I wonder if I can help with the rest."

"No offense, Cal. It doesn't sound like you're any better off than me."

*You didn't hear from me—but I never heard from you, either.*

"Of course I'm not. You've got friends, Halley. Friends who like you and don't think you should have died. You've got a warm place to stay at night and parents who'll take care of you." He cocked his head. "Be honest, Halley. You hate me, don't you? You hope I never see Petra again, and you think she'd be better off without me. You think I'm a manipulator and a liar, and you aren't sure if the list of things I've told you that are true is longer than the list of lies."

My eyebrows shot up.

He took my silence as agreement. "This is why I became a spy. Because I don't have to be told these things." I thought he was going to add something dramatic, but instead he burst out laughing. "No, I'm kidding. You have dislike written all over your face. It's like you got a mouthful of spinach."

"Carry these back to Roscoe's apartment, and I'll consider forgiving you for the lettuce." I shoved the rest of my grocery bags into his arms. There had been one good outcome from the time I'd spent as a prisoner with Cal, and that was the fact that I'd finally learned how to deal with his bizarre moods. "You're wrong, Cal. I don't despise you. I think you hurt Petra, and I don't like the way you base your self-worth off what she thinks of you. I think she's as bad for you as you are for her. But it's none of my business."

He took the bait. "Why do you think she's bad for me?"

"Everything you do, you do for her. Even the horrible things you've done—and don't try to pretend that some of them haven't been despicable—they've all been for her. You don't think straight when you're around her. And now that we're off the island, you seem to think that your only worth is in what she thinks of you. You're still trying so hard to please her. Has it ever occurred to you that you might not be able to? What then? Who will you live for if it can't be Petra?"

Cal went silent, and for a moment I was afraid he'd hand my groceries back and march away without another word. I'd probably deserve it. He'd asked for directness, not a direct assault.

"Come with me," he said at last. "I have something to show you."

Before I could come up with a polite way to explain that I wasn't going anywhere alone with him, he trotted off with my bags draped over his arms and disappeared around a corner.

If it hadn't been for the groceries, I never would've followed. But he had the celery hostage, and that had to be given to Mother as a peace offering to placate her for the lettuce's loss. Hitching up my pants—I'd borrowed them from Roscoe, and they were a size or two big for me—I picked my way after him, dodging puddles and dirt and other questionable relics of city life. This was the kind of back alley where people probably got murdered every so often. Maybe Cal was going to murder me for my thoughtless comments on his love life.

Leave it to my imagination to make things interesting.

We threaded our way through an ocean of apartment complexes that all looked the same: gray, concrete façades with monotonous windows that were dark like the House had once been. I had lost track of where I was and where I had come from and what direction we were headed, and I was about to ask Cal to lead me back, when suddenly we emerged from the apartment complexes into an open street. Across from us, towering over our heads and blocking the sunlight, was a church. A cathedral.

*The* cathedral—the one I'd seen in Cal's photograph.

Cal swept his arm in a magnificent introductory gesture. "Welcome to Saint James."

It was hard to feel welcomed before such a glorious structure. It was so big, so grand, so elegant, that I felt like a mouse in comparison with its sheer magnitude.

"This cathedral," Cal explained, "and what it means, are what kept me sane throughout my time as a Merc. It's what kept me hanging on to Petra, and it's what will help me figure out what I'm going to do now that I'm free."

Apparently not as overwhelmed as I was, Cal trotted up the front steps and opened the door. He beckoned me to follow, and since I couldn't do much besides stand and gape if I stayed in the street, I obeyed. Besides, he still had the groceries.

A draft of cold air struck my face as I entered, a product of the dark stone walls and the dim, dusty shade. It took my breath away, and I didn't get it back for several seconds. Golden wood on the ceiling, reflected off the perfectly polished floor. Delicate chandeliers so brilliant they rivaled the sunlight outside. Neatly organized benches, perfectly symmetrical, hard and straight-backed and beautiful with a spartan grace. All of this was spread out before me in a vast, chaotic mixture of perfectly blended textures and colors that made it hard for my eyes to focus.

"It's beautiful," I breathed, gawking at the arched ceiling. "How did you find out about this place?"

"I had the picture," he said. "A cut-out from a travel magazine, I think. It was among some of the papers Kazumi gave me as a reward for spying. I've always been religious, but I never knew that the thing I believed in could look like this."

"You don't seem like the type."

"I wish I did." His towering height so close made me feel even smaller. "I wish I reflected this kind of beauty to you. To Petra. To everyone. It's the thing that's most important to me in this life, something I'll have even if I lose Petra. It's the thing that motivates me to keep her no matter what. It's the only thing that has kept me going this long."

"What is religion to you, Cal? Besides a place? Or a . . . hope?"

His words came out slowly. "Religion is the knowledge that something perfect exists. And if God is perfect, then He must have created everything, which means He meant for me to be alive. And if God, the perfect Being, so fascinating and desirable to mankind that we built this incredible monument to His glory, takes notice of me, then what does it matter if anyone else does?" His eyes were fixed on the cross at the end of the aisle. "I intend to marry Petra here. To show her that this is what I'm trying to be. To show her that she and I are not the end of the world, that something exists above us, and perhaps that no matter what happens, we'll be okay eventually."

He turned to me and gave me an impish grin. "Sorry I made

you walk two miles just to prove you wrong. I have my character to defend, you know."

"If that's true, why didn't you defend yourself when we all thought you were going to betray us?"

His laughter was loud after our hushed conversation. The sound made my spine tingle, yet his happiness seemed fitting within these walls. "Are you saying you don't still think I'd do that?"

"I had a hard time liking you," I admitted. "You were cruel to Petra. You were a spy for Warsafe. But I understand now why. Why didn't you make me walk the two miles back then?"

"Because I thought that if everyone hated me, it would be easier for Petra to let me go." He shrugged. "Divine perfection is a long way from being complete in me. Let's go back outside so our talking doesn't disturb anyone."

The sun outside the church was so staggeringly bright, despite the constant gray pallor that belonged to Seattle skies, that I had to stand in the shade for a few seconds before my eyes adjusted. Cal waited for me to get my bearings, and then he set off in the same direction we had come from.

"I acted surprised when you said that Petra thought I was dead," he told me, loosening his red bandanna, "but when the sergeant cornered me that day, I figured that was it. When Petra left my room that day, I thought it was the last time we'd speak. I wanted her to remember me in the worst way possible so that she could spend her energy on something other than what could've been."

"You're evil, you know that?"

His lips puckered. "You don't have to say it quite so bluntly."

"I've been wanting to say it since then," I told him. "Now that I've said it, I'm over it."

"I'll take what I can get."

We walked on in silence until we reached the intersection where we'd met. My lettuce had been filched from the gutter, leaving behind a few brown-tinted leaves that hadn't been worth the thief's effort. I wondered how hungry you had to be to eat lettuce out of a gutter, and I wondered if Cal had been living like that.

"You asked me what you're supposed to do now that the island doesn't exist," he said, returning my groceries. Apparently he had no intention of following me home. "But as you can see, the island never did stop existing. You and I were still at odds because of what happened there. Petra's still wounded. Kazumi's in prison. I'm still a morally anomalous disaster. Just because the scenery changed doesn't mean the enemy is dead."

Once again, I expected him to reach some magnificent and inspiring conclusion, but that inexplicable remark turned out to be the end of his speech. He gave me a mock salute, turned on his heel, and disappeared into the darkest of the sprawling alleys.

"Where can I find you, Cal?" I shouted after him. "Where are you going?"

He either didn't hear me, or he ignored me, and my question went unanswered.

# 30

## ROSCOE

**THESE DAYS, WHEN ROSCOE TRIED TO** get out of bed, she had to hop over the lightly snoring Maria, the sleep-talking doctor, and the stone-cold sleeper Halley, who couldn't be awakened by an earthquake. Roscoe wasn't an ungracious host. In fact, she liked having people she could talk to, people who understood everything she'd been through and had stories of their own. But the current arrangement was unsustainable for several reasons, not the least of which being that Roscoe was out of a job and nearly out of money too.

She had been intending to turn in her two weeks' notice, but when she arrived at Warsafe headquarters with the letter in her hand, she found that the contents of her desk had been neatly boxed up and placed in the hallway. Understandable, she had to admit. Absence for a whole week without a word of explanation would have been enough on its own. Add to that breaking an NDA, trespassing on private company property, and starting a scandal that would probably make the history books, and her job was safely in the bin.

The apartment wasn't going to pay for itself. And there was the small matter of the boat she and Andy had rented to get to the island. It hadn't occurred to them to wonder about the rental fee, since they had been in such a hurry when they signed the paperwork. But upon returning without the boat, they were informed that the rate was $150 per hour, and that they'd had it for seventy-two hours, and that, in theory, since they hadn't brought it back, they still had it. All of this was against policy. So the company had helpfully rounded the total up to thirty thousand dollars—nearly twice the cost of the boat itself.

They'd managed to scrounge up the money by depleting their savings and straining their families' generosity, but it had been a tight squeeze on both sides. A second month of this, and Roscoe wouldn't be able to pay her rent. Or eat, for that matter. Beans and rice only went so far.

"Do you know what you want to do?" Halley had asked, and for the first time in her life, Roscoe didn't have an answer. If she'd been asked the question four, three, maybe even two years ago, she wouldn't have hesitated: "I want to design graphics for video games." But updated Roscoe, who had barely gone a day since she was old enough to sit up by herself without playing a game, hadn't touched her console in weeks. It remained perched beside her TV, unplugged from its charger. The low battery had light blinked sadly until that, too, went out.

"What are you going to do?" prodded Halley. "You have to find something you like, Roscoe, to make up for all the time you spent doing something you hated. The world out here is huge. There has to be something in it for you."

"I doubt it," was Roscoe's only response.

That evening, after she was satisfied that everybody else was asleep, she returned to the job-listing website where she'd applied for the graphic design position at Warsafe. There were so many listings that would have caught her attention before—small indie game studio needs a menu designer, GUI designer wanted, create a game for deaf children—but now she could hardly bring herself to click on any of them without a sharp twinge of shame. How despicable was she for even considering going back to the career in which she had done so much damage?

"It's what you're good at," said a groggy voice behind her, "and it's what you want to do. Roscoe, you can't keep acting like your career choice was the problem. It's Warsafe's fault, not yours."

Roscoe flipped on her desk lamp to reveal a red-eyed Halley.

"Go back to sleep." She turned back to her computer, grimacing. "You have no idea what it's like."

"Really?" Her voice shot up a pitch. Roscoe was afraid she'd wake the doctor and Maria, and then who knew how much unsolicited advice she'd get? "The moment you found out about what was happening at Warsafe, you gave up everything—your entire life—to make things right. I knew at least the bare-bones rumors about the game since I was a child, but it never occurred to me to do anything until Petra was wounded. It wasn't until she came crawling onto our doorstep, dying, with no one to help her, that I finally realized just how evil it was. I wish I had done what you did. Changed the moment I knew it was the right thing to do."

Roscoe hugged her pillow tightly to her chest. *When I was a child*, she'd said. Well, Halley was still a child out here in the real world. She had never had a career, never had to worry about impressing her parents, barely understood the concept of money. She had pronounced "quinoa" like "kwinoah" at the grocery store, which reminded Roscoe sharply of how limited her experience was outside of potatoes, lemonade, and death. She couldn't understand what it felt like to be left with paralyzing fear of everyone and everything, and unrelenting guilt over something she should have prevented.

"I know what you're thinking." Halley pulled her blanket tighter around her shoulders. "You're thinking that my opinion doesn't count for anything since our experiences are so wildly different. But they're not. You and I and everyone who left that island with even a partial understanding of what happened there is stuck with the same kind of guilt. 'If only I'd done something sooner,' you're thinking. Well, so are we. What's going to change if we all sit here and think about it forever? We have to do something to make it all worthwhile. If we aren't careful, if we don't use our lives wisely, then what were we saved for?"

"You don't seem like the kind of person to make a speech like that. No offense, of course," Roscoe added hastily. "It just doesn't sound like you."

"I know, right?" Halley giggled drowsily. "I got it from Cal. Almost verbatim. He said it in the context of religion, and now I'm repeating it to you in the context of—um—this video . . . game . . . career . . . thing." She yawned. "How are they sleeping through this conversation? Do you think they're just pretending?"

Roscoe didn't think so.

"If I get in trouble for this, Halley, I'm blaming it on you."

"Please do. You know enough people aren't already upset with me." She snuggled down into the floor bed that Roscoe had thrown together from spare blankets and sofa cushions. "Go for it, Roscoe. Do something that Warsafe hasn't thought of yet. Be better than they could ever hope to be."

She was a fast sleeper, that one. Her breathing faded to a whiffle, and Roscoe turned back to her computer, relieved to finally be alone with her thoughts.

The website had refreshed itself while she was talking to Halley, and there was a new listing at the top.

*Wanted: Graphic designer to work on an indie "cozy game."*

Roscoe clicked on the listing.

*Work will be full-time, but may be done remotely at the designer's request. Preference will be given to those based in Washington State. Please send your résumé, a personal statement, and a portfolio to this address*—there was an email embedded in the words—*or use the Submit button on the listing page. Genre: Pixel RPG. Platforms: All major, incl. PC. Title: The Pink Surprise (work in progress). Other details: Story-driven, simple design, suitable for children. Projected ESRB rating will be E10+. Looking for a designer who can bring charm and sophistication to the game's GUI.*

No more violence. Roscoe's cursor hovered over the "Submit" button.

*Can I really go back after all the harm I've caused?*

*Will my work remind me of all the things I want to forget? Or will it be a better, more wholesome version of the one thing I love and am good at?*

She clicked the button, adjusted her keyboard, and began typing in the "Personal Statement" box.

# 31

## HALLEY

**I SAID ALL THAT TO ROSCOE. AT THE** time, late at night with my thoughts blurred, it was easy enough to mean it. I repeated Cal's speech as though I had believed him. The next day—the three-week anniversary of our escape—I woke up and watched Mother cook, the doctor leave for a job interview at a local restaurant, Roscoe type up her résumé. And I continued to do nothing.

Stories from the island, vignettes from my memory that were particularly provocative or painful, had been welling to the surface of my memory. With no one to talk to, these stories had nowhere to go. Sometimes they painted themselves onto blank walls, and I would look up from whatever idle occupation I had thought of to see Petra's bloody arm on the operating table. There it would stay until I blinked, frantic, and realized it was nothing more than my imagination. I couldn't focus. I couldn't keep my thoughts from straying into dark places.

Everyone else was finding their place, and I wasn't. I couldn't keep living like this.

I went out that day and bought notebooks. If there was no place inside my mind for these memories, I would put them on paper as the first step toward freeing myself. I curled up on Roscoe's porch with a blanket over my shoulders, shivering in the only privacy I could find, and scribbled for hours.

That evening, when I looked up and discovered that the sun had gone down, I realized I had found something. I didn't yet know what. But it was something more than I'd had before.

Writing became a secret obsession for me, one that I hid guiltily whenever I noticed my parents watching. They were concerned about me, I knew. They wondered what was happening inside my head, and they thought maybe my notebooks could tell them. But I knew they were too generous to try sneaking a peek, and all they could do was watch and worry while I buried my heart in those empty pages.

Word immediately got out, probably by way of the ever-optimistic Roscoe, that I was writing a book. It made me laugh. *If only it were that simple.* But part of me liked the idea, and as the notebooks filled up, I spent hours in my corner of the room, rearranging my notes on the floor in chronological order, dramatic order, reverse order.

It was a good thing I had something to occupy the hours, because I turned out to be otherwise useless. Selling lemonade isn't a marketable skill, especially when you don't get a script. I had no education besides what I'd scrounged from reading the doctor's books, and I hated to waste the time I could have used to work by studying. The pros and cons balanced out, and I ended up doing neither.

The inactivity wore at me. I felt like a hypocrite. I was letting the beautiful thing Cal had showed me slip through my fingers, though the memory lingered constantly in my mind, because I couldn't be bothered to get out of bed in the morning. I had told Roscoe to follow her dreams, but I had none of my own. Since leaving the island, I had been desperately brave, doing my best to support everyone else in their newfound lives. I had entirely forgotten to attend to my own.

No sooner had the doctor gotten his first batch of tips from the restaurant than my parents sat me down at the kitchen table, with grave faces, for what they called a "heart-to-heart."

I joined them with misgivings, and Mother gave me a cookie. I ate it, and she gave me another one. That made me even more suspicious, because she had never let me indulge in sweets before, and I said they had better tell me what they were up to. I already had a guess, but I wanted to hear it firsthand.

The doctor began. "Maria and I are worried about you, Halley."

"I'm more worried about *you*." I was interrupting already. "You're working your fingers to the bone, and I can't do anything to help." It wasn't like I hadn't tried. I was learning new skills. I had borrowed Roscoe's computer and was teaching myself how to use that puzzling set of devices she called a "keyboard" and "mouse," and I was getting pretty good at it.

It was hardly my fault that I hadn't gotten any answers to the job applications I had sent out in a brief frenzy when we first landed. That I was young and had no experience with anything except potatoes, lemonade, and killing. That I had no idea what I wanted to do and no motivation to answer interview requests when, occasionally, they came.

"With everything you've gone through, perhaps you need some help. Perhaps some counsel—"

"No," I interrupted flatly. "I'll be fine. What I really need is something to do. A job." I'd just have to force myself out of this mood. Or force those "book" notes onto an editor's desk, if that was to become my new mission in life.

They exchanged glances. My mother started to say something, but the doctor stopped her. "Alright, Halley," he said. "We'll give this a few more weeks. But may I suggest you engage again—with old friends, at least—and begin sooner than later."

I took his advice to heart. He was right, but even the thought seemed like sludging through mire. And a job. Maybe I *would* focus on potatoes. Or lemonade.

Between writing sprees, I wandered the alley where Cal and I had met. I had more questions to ask, more to learn about the place he'd taken me. The lettuce scraps left unfilched in the drain wilted and disappeared. The weather grew colder. My notebooks filled up, and still Cal never appeared.

If he left, I wondered, where was he going to go? Wasn't there enough in Seattle to satisfy him? Why did everyone want something they couldn't find, and what was it he wanted?

There was only one person who might know where he was. More

than a month had passed since I'd last spoken with her, but my parents had been kinder than me. They had reached out, and they had told me where I could find her when I was ready.

I swallowed my pride and my nerves and a straight shot of Seattle espresso. Then I borrowed Roscoe's phone, and I called Petra.

# 32

## ANDY

"YOU NEVER CAME TO VISIT, NOT EVEN once!" grumbled Rilo. He had a death grip on the hands of his walker, and Andy had a wild suspicion that Rilo was imagining choking him. "Where were you? What were you doing? Why did you disappear that night?"

There were about three things Andy could say, ranging from "Oh, you know, I just felt like taking a spontaneous vacation!" to "I lost my mind and ran away from the asylum," or, for extra flair: "I helped save two hundred people's lives." The only thing he managed to get out of his mouth was a noncommittal laugh, which did not satisfy Rilo.

"I met one of your friends," Rilo told him, apparently unaware that he had stopped leaning on the walker and was now lifting it off the ground, waving it like a flag, "and he said you'd show up eventually. But you're a little late, man. They're about to discharge me already."

"One of my friends? Who's that?" The list of possibilities, in Andy's books, was short.

Rilo regarded him with the same look in his eyes that a child would have who has been caught stealing cookies. "I, er . . . wasn't supposed to mention that." He cleared his throat. "Maybe we can talk about something else."

"If you're going to keep secrets, too, will you stop asking me where I was? You'd better believe I would have come to see you, and I was going crazy every time I thought about you falling out the window." Andy sulked. He hated being so vulnerable, and Rilo had a glint in his eye. "Gloat all you want. I've been miserable this past week."

"Did you elope?" Rilo questioned. The walker still wasn't touching the ground. "Did you run off with some girl? Did you discover how to make a brand-new type of radio? Come on. Tell me everything you can. I don't care if you redact some of it, I just want to hear the interesting parts."

Andy opened his mouth to say something scornful about how not every adventure had to involve falling in love and where'd his friend even get that outdated, hackneyed trope, but he shut it rapidly. He was many things, but a hypocrite was not one of them.

"So you do have something to say!" Rilo grinned. "Spill it."

"She's got pink hair," admitted Andy grudgingly, "and I've known her for less than two weeks."

The ensuing silence allowed Andy to discover that the hospital garden was overrun by crickets. Their chirping resembled mocking laughter, and Andy decided that he wouldn't be sorry if the ground opened up and swallowed him.

"I never knew you were capable of this," Rilo remarked. "I don't know exactly what this is, but Andy, it's good for you. I support it."

"I've spent about twelve thousand dollars on her and her crazy schemes so far." He wasn't sure why he couldn't get his mouth to stay shut. Hopeless, he continued, "And also I tried to kidnap her."

Silence again.

"Well, I don't generally condone violence against women, so I'm not sure . . ."

"She agreed to it."

"Oh!" Rilo's eyebrows shot up. "That changes things! Where in the world did you get the dough for that?"

Andy rubbed his eyes wearily. "I don't know. But we had to have the boat, so . . ."

"A boat? Andy, you rented a boat with this girl?"

"I have no idea. I really have no idea what I'm doing."

"You must be in love." The walker finally made contact with the pavement, and Rilo returned to leaning against it. "I take back what I said earlier about this being good for you. You shouldn't get too attached."

Andy was already in so deep that a few more insignificant details wouldn't hurt. "I saw her grab a knife from a . . . uh, a mugger. She was going to attack him if a . . . uh, a passing policeman hadn't stepped in. Anyone would be in awe of her if they had seen it. I can't tell if I have a crush on her or her coolness."

"Why not both?" Rilo suggested.

"Stop it," Andy groaned. "Stop giving me ideas."

But it was too late. The idea had been given, and now all that remained was for Andy to do something about it.

A few hours later, Andy found himself sitting at his desk, researching the meanings of rose colors.

White was premature. It had only been two weeks, after all, and even the romantically inexperienced Andy was not afflicted with the delusion that he could propose marriage that quickly. He wasn't sure if Roscoe would be able to tell the difference between white and ivory, so it seemed safest to rule both out. Yellow apparently represented friendship, which was the exact opposite of the message Andy was trying to send. Perhaps . . . pink? The site informed Andy that the roses were, in fact, peach and not pink, and that they were usually used to seal business deals.

In the end, he settled on lavender roses. The name seemed like a contradiction in terms to his strictly logical mind, but they were pretty, and the meaning was right. That was the key thing. There was some heat in his cheeks as he pressed the purchase button and arranged for them to be delivered to Roscoe's doorstep. This, he was well aware, was an un-Andy-like thing to do.

Now for the more subtle planning. The roses would arrive, and Roscoe would find them on her doorstep. Because she was a woman, she would know immediately what the color of the roses meant. This would make her wonder if she had a secret admirer, and she'd go through the list of men she knew—which Andy prayed was short—until she reached the most likely suspect. When he arrived a few hours later, suited and booted and shined, she'd either tell him she was in love with him or that she never wanted to see him again. That was how it always worked in romance novels, and Andy, who had never read one, was convinced that real life would work the same way.

All he needed was an excuse to appear gracefully on Roscoe's doorstep by coincidence so she would see a suitable opportunity to confess her admittedly well-concealed feelings. He had a habit of sorting through his paper clips when he was stressed, admiring the different shapes and colors and thinking about all the interesting scientific papers he would someday clip together with them. He sorted the clips five times before he had a flash of brilliance. He could take the essay he'd been writing to Halley and ask her to proofread it. Hadn't she been working on a book lately?

Foolproof stratagem.

Maybe he would've been thinking more clearly if he hadn't been in mourning over his radio. The police who had searched his apartment had found it, but for some reason, the only fingerprints on it had belonged to Kazumi, so it was impounded as evidence against him. No matter how long Andy argued with them, they refused to believe that he had made it. It eventually occurred to him that if they ever were convinced, they would probably also arrest him, and that was exactly what Kazumi had been trying to prevent. He gave up and accepted that he would just have to build another one. He hadn't gotten over the loss. He wasn't himself, not without that mess of wires and coils to keep him company.

The roses arrived on Roscoe's doorstep at 1:02 sharp the next day. Andy had signed up for text alerts so he could time his mission. He dressed nicely—not in a suit this time, since Roscoe had encouraged him to expand his wardrobe and he had gone thrifting—gathered the stack of papers he meant to show Halley, and programmed Roscoe's address into his phone. He hadn't forgotten that she lived thirty feet vertically up from his room. He just wanted to be certain, absolutely certain, that her apartment hadn't grown legs and walked away since the last time he'd been there. Not that it would have. He was catastrophizing. His papers were damp from the sweat on his palms.

With one last desperate glance at his apparition in the mirror, he fled, letting his door slam behind him.

*In and out. In and out. Breathe. Everything's going to be fine. This can only go one of two ways, and either way is fine. Right? Wrong.*

He adjusted his tie, inhaled, and rang the bell.

"Coming!" shouted a muffled voice from inside. It didn't sound like Roscoe, and sure enough, it was Halley who opened the door. Her hair was wet, and she was wearing a bathrobe.

"I forgot you live downstairs," she said. "What are you doing here?"

"Is Roscoe home?" he asked, trying to peek inside. He thought he saw his roses in a vase on the kitchen table.

"She's at a job interview." Halley's lips were twitching. With a conspiratorial air, she leaned out the door. "It was *you* who sent the roses, wasn't it?"

Andy drooped. "Am I that easy to read?"

"Why shouldn't you be? They're pretty. You did great." She gave him a nod. "It's obvious that you're interested in Roscoe. It's probably obvious to everyone else too. Anyway, do you want to come inside? I just finished making coffee. Sorry I'm a mess. Sorry I'm talking so much. I don't drink coffee much, but Roscoe says it perks her up. I think it may have perked me up too much. Come on in, come in." Her fingers drummed against the door as she swung it open.

"Can I have whatever you're having?" He plopped down on the sofa, where he could admire his roses from afar without being too obvious about it.

"Sure." Halley set a cup of coffee on the table in front of Andy, with such impact that a few drops slopped over the edge. "Sorry about that."

"If you want to wait here, Roscoe should be back soon." She began digging through the stack of books on Roscoe's nightstand and handed him a copy of *I, Robot*.

"What's this?"

Halley's eyes had a mischievous twinkle. "What if I told you it's Roscoe's favorite? Would you read it?"

Andy opened the book.

"The science is dreadful," he said a few moments later. "This isn't how any of this works."

"Asimov was a chemist. It's probably just outdated."

"Hi! Hey, is that my book?"

The look on Roscoe's face was one of amusement. Andy barely

noticed that, though. He was more interested in the blazer and pencil skirt she was wearing. He'd never seen her dressed up before.

He hastily put the book down.

Roscoe set her briefcase on one of the kitchen chairs. "Halley, did you buy these roses? They're pretty."

"No." Somehow she kept a straight face. "I was just going—out to the porch," she said as she exited.

Roscoe yawned. "Usually she acts like a vampire this time of day. Says she's cold. I guess they had some kind of temperature regulation on the island to keep the electronics working, so Seattle winters are new to her."

"Yes." Sweat rolled down his spine.

"Can you believe I'm going back into video-game design?" She laughed bitterly. "I don't know what I'm thinking. I caused some kind of international crisis last time. I guess I never learn."

Andy set his papers down on the coffee table. "Well, I'm not much better than you. Radios almost got my friend killed, but I'm never going to stop working with them. I couldn't if I tried. They're the only thing that's interesting to me."

"That's my problem too." She crossed her arms on the table and laid her head down. Sighing, she added, "What were you doing here?"

"I was just stopping by."

"You could sit here for a while," Roscoe suggested. "Although I might just take a nap right here on the kitchen table. Would that be embarrassing? I feel like I should be more embarrassed than I am."

"I hope you don't get embarrassed in front of me," said Andy. He promptly blushed. "I mean, I hope you consider me a good . . . er, friend. Good enough that you don't worry about napping on the table when I'm around."

She gave him a thumbs-up and closed her eyes. A few moments later, before Andy had even decided on what he was going to say, she was sound asleep.

He looked at the roses one more time. Then he quietly left.

# 33

## HALLEY

**WHILE THE REST OF US WERE INTEGRATING** into society, finding jobs and visiting therapy and prison and cathedrals, Petra had been getting to know the local hospital staff.

It all came out when, at last, I mustered up the courage to call her. She gave me the short version of her backstory, but I dragged the details out of her. It turned out that she had stubbornly refused to see any doctor other than mine, and since he had no surgical tools and Roscoe objected to open-heart surgery with her kitchen knives, there wasn't much he could do besides beg her to go to the general hospital. At first, none of us could fathom the reason for her hesitation. But she knew something we didn't at the time: Hospitals are expensive. Expensive with a capital *E*, bright green dollar signs painted on the door. Back on the island, nobody paid for medical care. Here, it seemed, free medical care was as attainable as the moon—or less, since people had reportedly managed to get there.

One day, shortly after my conversation with Cal, Petra had collapsed while he was walking her home from a shift at the gas station. That explained why I hadn't seen him. He had barely left the hospital since Petra was admitted, except to work enough for a bare subsistence on cafeteria food.

There, in a corner room at the far end of the hospital, she stayed. Her heart problems required four sequential surgeries, but her condition was severe enough that they were all performed in one dangerous, twelve-hour operation. They said she should have had the work done when she was a baby, and they kept asking her why she didn't. She, of course, had no idea.

The first thing I did was apologize. The second was ask if I could visit. I could hear the smile in Petra's voice when she agreed, and that made me feel both guilty and relieved. Guilty that it had taken me so long, and that I hadn't been there for her. Relieved that she still accepted me.

It was a Monday morning, six weeks after our emigration. I had some chocolate for Petra because the hospital had decreed that she needed to fill out her gaunt frame before she could be discharged, and she was a long way from any description of a "healthy weight." I had brought my newly discovered favorite: chocolate-covered cherries in syrup. I had them wrapped in a red bow, and I was about to walk into her room. But her door was closed, and a frustrated voice sounded from within. Someone else had gotten there first.

I sat down in a nearby chair, placed the chocolates on my lap, and shamelessly eavesdropped.

"I broke a promise." Unmistakably Cal's voice, still as hoarse as I remembered. "I should have defended Halley myself, and I couldn't. The sergeant is dead because I couldn't get to her. The least I could do would be to honor his dying wish."

"You don't even know what it was."

"I do. The last thing I heard him say was supposed to be a country's name. It began with *I,* and there's a war going on in a country called Iceland. I'm sure that's what he meant to tell me. I have to go, Petra. If he hadn't died, he would have gone himself. But since he died doing what I should have done, it's my duty now."

"The sergeant was your enemy." Petra sounded irritated. "You don't owe him anything."

"Was he?"

"I think you have a different reason in mind."

I got up and stood on tiptoe in front of the glass window on the door. Cal sat at the foot of Petra's bed, and as I watched, he toppled back across Petra's legs with a tired sigh. She didn't look at him, fixing her gaze on the blank wall in front of her. But she put one pale hand on his hair and twirled it absently between her fingers.

"Iceland," Cal murmured. "It sounds miserable, doesn't it? Cold and snowy and bare. But I imagine green fields and mountains and waterfalls and lovely lights in the sky. I think there's a little town there where all the houses have colorful red roofs, and you can look down at them from a white hill made of pure, sparkling ice. There's never a night, sometimes. And sometimes it's the opposite, and there's never a day, but the stars shine all the time."

"Sounds like fairyland."

"I think I've been there before."

Now she looked at him. "You have memories from before the game?"

"I won't know for sure unless I go, but if I could find such a place, it would be . . . well, it would be perfect. That's part of the reason. The other part is what I said—that I owe the sergeant something for saving Halley. And . . ." He stopped.

"You don't owe him."

"I do."

"You don't."

"You weren't there."

Another pause.

"Can you imagine if the island had belonged to us?" Petra murmured.

"What's that?"

"If it was ours. If we liked it. If it was beautiful. Well, even if it wasn't beautiful, if it had just been ours. We would've wanted to fight for it."

"So?"

"So, maybe Iceland is yours."

He smiled. "I don't own it."

"But maybe it's your place. Where you belong. Your home, if any of us has one."

"My home?" He sat up abruptly. "You don't understand. If I did this, Petra, it wouldn't be enough to just do it for myself. Or for the sergeant. Maybe that would be noble, but it wouldn't be worthwhile. I'd do it for *you*. If my memories of this place are real, it's the place I want to take you. I want to have one of those houses with the red roofs, and I want to see you standing on the doorstep, and I want to put roses in your hands, and I want—"

"I never asked for any of those things."

"—the kind of peace that I'm imagining. I want to give that to you. In that place, there won't be any traffic noise. You won't have to live in a hospital. We'd be safe because I'd fight with everything I've got to make us safe."

Her fists were clenched around the hem of her blanket. "Why can't we just be happy with what we have?"

"You deserve better. Let me get it for you." He wrapped her hands in his, caressing her fingers. "Warsafe could never find us. Enlisting would give me a salary to pay your hospital bills and legal rights to stay there forever. You'd have your tiny house and your own room that you've always talked about. Unless . . ." His lips curled in a mischievous grin. "Unless you wanted to share it with me."

She turned her head away, but Cal placed his finger under her chin and drew her gaze back.

"You'd look lovely in a wedding dress, Petra," he suggested, his voice barely above a whisper. "What if we tried it? Would you wait for me if I fight for you to have a place that's home?"

Petra scanned Cal's face, doubtful, unbelieving, searching for the catch in his earnest brown eyes.

He waited. I think he would've waited forever. The only suggestion that he wasn't as patient as he seemed was the way his lips wouldn't quite stay shut, as though he had something he wanted to say.

"But," she said, her words catching in her throat, "can't there be an easier way? One that doesn't involve you leaving first?"

"If you tell me not to go, I won't."

"But if it's something you have to do?"

He didn't say anything, but his face said it for him.

Petra threw her arms around his neck. "I don't want you to go," she cried, hiding her face in his shoulder. "I just got you back. I thought we'd stay together from now on."

"Are you sure, Petra?" He caressed her hair, resting his chin on her head. "You don't have to agree. I know you still have some doubts. You once said we don't know each other. That I'm not who you thought I was. I never expected you to give a real answer until we spent more time—"

"I was an idiot. I'm sorry. I should have said it sooner." Her voice was muffled by his jacket. "Maybe it's true, but I don't care. The Cal you are now is the Cal I remember, and the Cal I remember is the one I want to wear that stupid dress for. We have three months of experience and three years of memories, and that's enough for me. Experience will catch up."

"You'd marry me?"

"I would. I will."

"Petra!" He kissed her, his hands tangled in her hair.

"Stop!" She pushed him away, ruffled, but a smile on her lips. "Don't you know someone's probably watching?"

"Do you care? I don't." But he didn't try to kiss her again. Instead, he hugged her, resting his chin on the top of her head. "I'll come back for you. That's a promise."

"I know," she scolded, shaking him off. "Go away so you can come back sooner."

He stood up and opened the door, and I stood there guiltily.

"H-hi, Petra." I waved, putting on a big, wide grin to hide my embarrassment. "I've been here for like, uh, thirty seconds, and . . . I brought chocolate!"

There was a long pause, and then Cal started laughing. Petra's lips trembled, and she joined in. With no idea what was so funny, I did, too, and we all laughed until our stomachs ached. And then we shared the chocolates, and then we laughed some more.

That was the last time I saw Cal before he left. They write to each other like all star-crossed lovers do, and Petra keeps all his letters in a drawer next to her bed in the hospital, and sometimes, when her hands are shaky from her medications, I help her write back, and I get to share a little of the lovely thing they have.

I'm jealous. A little. Maybe. But I'm happy for them too.

# 34

## HALLEY

**IT WAS SIX MONTHS BEFORE WE ALL—** well, most of us anyway—saw each other again. A few were conspicuously missing. Ponytail—that is, Sam, who had presumably been killed on the island. Three or four others who hadn't managed to get time off from their new jobs. One or two who hadn't responded to the group notice Roscoe sent out. Kazumi. And, of course, Cal, now a soldier.

Me?

The only entry on my résumé was *lemonade stand, manager and server, 13 years.* So I put my drink-making skills to work as a barista, softening the coffee's sourness with sweeteners that reminded me of my old saccharine lemonade.

Petra was fresh out of the hospital, dragging around a portable oxygen tank. She wore a thin gold band around her finger, and it didn't take a genius to figure out where that had come from.

Roscoe had a dress like a stick of pink cotton candy. More interesting, however, was the fact that Andy had a matching rose in his coat pocket, which he handed to her as she entered. She accepted it gracefully and tucked it into her pink hair. There it stayed for the rest of the night.

I had neither a fancy dress, nor a date, nor any prospects of one. Feeling a bit nostalgic, I was wearing the dreary old clothes I had worn when we left the island: a brown skirt, brown shirt, brown shawl, brown hair covering, brown you-name-it. Mother hadn't liked this idea, but I pointed out that I'd never have the opportunity to wear the clothes anywhere else, since they made me look like a cross between Gretel and an uncivilized wood fairy. She hated waste, so she reluctantly agreed.

I decided to take a survey and worked my way through the crowd, stopping everyone who would pay attention and asking them to explain what they had been doing since we left the island. I expected a wide variation of stories, but we had all been living nearly the same lives. Going by Andy's way of thinking, I organized my data by percentages. Roughly ten percent failed to respond to my survey questions or did not attend the party. Less than one percent (i.e., Petra) had spent the past six months in the hospital. Ten percent had purchased their own houses. Most of these had some marketable skill, such as construction, agriculture, or teaching. The remaining eighty percent—Andy pretentiously corrected this to seventy-nine—had been working miscellaneous jobs like the doctor and Mother had been, ranging from dishwashing to waiting tables to late-night gas station shifts. A few had enrolled in online colleges.

Everyone surveyed had learned what a dollar was, and ninety-nine percent knew about computers. The solitary exception to the latter group was the grandma who used to farm potatoes. She didn't know anything about computers, but because she was a bit deaf, she had a tidy allotment that allowed her to rent a ground-floor apartment with a garden.

It was Andy who had rented the venue. Seattle didn't have many places large enough for a two-hundred-person gathering, but he had discovered a farm that was usually reserved for weddings. There had been a last-minute cancelation, and Andy had jumped at the opportunity.

This astonished the rest of us, because we had been under the impression that Andy was jobless, incomeless, and well on his way to becoming a ward of the state.

"No offense, Andy," Roscoe had said, tentatively, "but I don't think the villagers will be able to cover travel costs and food costs. And if you ask them to chip in for the venue on top of that—"

"I can cover all the costs."

She was too delicate to ask the obvious question, but I had no such inhibitions.

"Well." Andy rubbed the back of his head, averting his eyes from our gaping mouths. "It was just a small invention—interesting, I admit, but very small—but the idea caught on."

Andy was afflicted with overwhelming modesty when it came to his science projects, but eventually Roscoe and I dragged the details out of him. Ever since Andy had used the automatic cooker gas line to explode the House, he had been thinking about why the concentration of gas had increased so quickly, and what about the cooker required so much energy. Over and over he had dissected his memories about its construction, and after some trial and error—he made it sound like this took a long time, but it must have been no more than a week or two—he produced a working automatic cooker. With Rilo's assistance, he had managed to acquire a pending patent on the product and sold the prototype to the local university for use in their cafeterias. Over the course of six months, he had become a scientific sensation and had amassed an alarming amount of money.

Thus I found myself eating bitter grape leaves off a silver tray, surrounded by everyone I had known on the island. Not a bad way to live. I hoped Andy had some more inventions lurking in that unpredictable brain of his.

"What do you think about this, Petra?" I asked. I had a glass of sparkling water with me, which I had taken off a waiter's tray, so I handed it to her. "Are you happy to be out of the hospital?"

She took a delicate sip and winced at the fizz. "Yes, it's nice. Although I feel like I have my own hospital with me." She gave her oxygen tank a disgusted shake. "I didn't need this while I was on the island, so why do I need it now? I was doing fine then."

"You were living off adrenaline," I objected. "Look at you now. Look at *us*. Drinking fancy water and eating steak, wearing floor-length dresses, some of us anyway, standing under a ceiling of fairy lights. Who'd have thought that you and I could talk to each other in front of the island's entire population, and nobody bats an eyelash? Prejudice melted the moment we all knew the truth. And they don't even know half of the story."

There was a pause. "I was thinking about designing jewelry."

I blinked. "What did you say?"

The lights on her prosthetic blinked rapidly, and she took another sip from the glass. "Jewelry is a luxury. Something you can only have if all your needs are met. I never had any on the island because I was so worried about staying alive, and what if someone choked me with my necklace chain or stabbed me with an earring? But now it's different." She held up her left hand, and the light glinted off her ring. "I like working with my hands. I can't do anything physically demanding, according to the doctors, and I don't have anything resembling what this country calls an education. So, why not?"

"Why not, indeed?" I was awed. "You'd be good at it too."

"I've been going to Cal's church," she explained, "because it reminds me of him, and because I was tired of not knowing where to direct my prayers. Or my requests, needs, questions—I don't know what to call them yet. But I met some ladies there who helped me know where to start. It's much more the Who than the where. It's all very new, but I'm learning. About everything, I think."

A loudspeaker squealed. Andy had started up the music before connecting the wires, creating a burst of electronic feedback and earning himself scattered boos from the crowd.

"What if they knew that wars will be fought in real life because we left the island, and we abandoned the *Warsafe* project?" Petra raised her voice to be heard over the noise. "Because we insisted that our lives matter? Would they still be so happy?"

"Maybe some of them will choose to fight. Or not. But it will be their choice either way, and that's the only thing that would make their sacrifice worthwhile."

She swung her oxygen tank over her shoulder and took my hands. I spun her to the loudspeaker's distant beat, admiring the way her dress flared around her ankles. It was so unnecessary, that dress—so unnecessary, and so beautiful.

We hadn't fixed the world. We hadn't stopped the war. With Kazumi's legal case ongoing, we hadn't even conquered Warsafe yet. But, by making our choice, we had shown that life is infinite. That two infinities are no more infinite than one, and that no price or number could be placed on the value of a freely loving, divinely loved soul.

"Are we allowed to live happy now?" I asked, lowering my arm and letting the music flow past me. "Can we really say we won, Petra, even if there's still so much to be done?"

She came to a stop with her hands on her knees, breathless with laughter.

"Yes," she said firmly. "Yes, I think we can."

# THE END

# ACKNOWLEDGMENTS

Roll credits!

This book would have languished forever as a .docx file without the Enclave Publishing team. Steve Laube took a chance on an econ-student-turned-writer who was drowning in coffee and final exams, for which I'll always be grateful. Eagle-eyed editors turned a draft into a manuscript. And so many others turned that manuscript into this book—marketing, typesetting, designing, and more. Working with Enclave has been a delight and a blessing.

Writing has its ups (pumpkin-spice lattes) and downs (recovering documents after a computer crash). My parents have been my steadfast counselors during both extremes and everything in between. Mom, Dad, thank you for your encouragement, advice, and prayer. The Mexican food. The beach writing sessions. The hugs. And simply for being my parents.

I still have my notes from the day I brought this story to the Hillsdale College Writing Club, where it was inspected, dissected, and vastly improved. You kept me motivated even during finals season . . . though maybe that's no surprise. Sometimes it's easier to write ninety-five thousand words than to push through a flashcard deck on nineteenth-century economic history.

To my incredibly talented friends, writers, artists, musicians, and generally beautiful people: Thank you for all your inspiration, and I can't wait to keep creating together!

Speaking of friends, someone at Hillsdale College had the wonderful idea to offer free printing services at the library. I believe my one-sided, double-spaced draft shrank the profit margin, but I'm grateful for this resource, among many others this school and its supporters have so generously provided.

My professors have pushed me to be a better writer, a better student, and a better person. Not only did you show me how to write, you also showed me what to write about and gave me my "why." Thank you for the classes, the office hours, the red ink, the tea and cookies, and the draft reviews.

I have a room in the dormitory, but I often joke that I live in the radio studio. From behind those microphones, I've had the opportunity to interview a wonderful cadre of writers, from Enclave and beyond. This book and its creation process are a relic of those collected stories and the tidbits of wisdom you shared.

Some of my prayers for this book came out in full sentences. Others were ungrammatical cries for help. Every prayer, no matter how chaotic, was fully answered. And so, to the Creator who gave me this story and told me to go write it, who heard my frustration and excitement and panic and enthusiasm and gently guided me though it all: May this story reflect You, and You only.

## ABOUT THE AUTHOR

Lauren Smyth wrote and published her first novel at the age of thirteen. Since then, she's been writing stories whenever and wherever she can—ideally, on a hiking trail or at the beach. Her nonfiction work has appeared in the *Wall Street Journal*, the Air Force Museum magazine, and the *Independent Review*. When she's not writing, you'll find her behind a microphone recording her podcast, *Grammar Minute*.

# IF YOU ENJOYED
# WARSAFE
## YOU MIGHT LIKE THESE OTHER NOVELS:

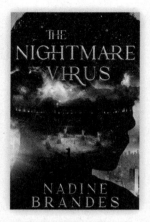

www.enclavepublishing.com